"I DON'T WANT TO HURT YOU, MEARA.

"I'll be leaving in less than two weeks, and this will be a long, painful war. It's quite possible I'll be killed."

"No," she said, as if voicing the denial made it fact.

"Yes, Meara," he insisted. His hand took hers as her chin jutted out obstinately. He had never wanted anything as much in his life as to take her someplace and make love to her, slowly and exquisitely. He could feel the passion in her, passion created by her lust for living, her obvious commitment to those she cared about, the sense of giving he always felt around her. He wanted her so much it was a physical pain, gut-wrenching agony.

"I don't know what's happening to me," she said, and the voice was so soft, so puzzled, he had to smile.

"Surely, you've kissed men before," he said tenderly.

"Never like that," she said with such awe that he had to smile.

ISLAND OF DREAMS

PATRICIA POTTER

HarperPaperbacks
A Division of HarperCollinsPublishers

This is a work of fiction. The characters, incidents, and dialogues are products of the author's imagination and are not to be construed as real. Any resemblance to actual events or persons, living or dead, is entirely coincidental.

HarperPaperbacks *A Division of* HarperCollins*Publishers*
10 East 53rd Street, New York, N.Y. 10022

Copyright © 1991 by Patricia Potter
All rights reserved. No part of this book may be used or reproduced in any manner whatsoever without written permission of the publisher, except in the case of brief quotations embodied in critical articles and reviews. For information address HarperCollins*Publishers*,
10 East 53rd Street, New York, N.Y. 10022.

Cover illustration by Maren

First printing: March 1991

Printed in the United States of America

HarperPaperbacks and colophon are trademarks of HarperCollins*Publishers*

10 9 8 7 6 5 4 3 2

To my nieces, Laura and Julie, and nephews, Bill and Stephen, who have all given me much joy.

Prologue

Summer, 1963

Meara O'Hara Evans wished the tears would flow. Perhaps they would loosen the vise around her heart.

She looked over toward her daughter. Lisa, now almost twenty-one, had never been able to hide her emotions, and tears were streaming down her face. How lucky she was. To be able to wash out even a portion of grief instead of locking it up inside until you wondered whether the wall within made you something less than human.

Meara's gloved hands knotted together as an honor guard carefully rolled up the flag on her husband's casket and, in almost jerky automaton movements, marched over to present it. She shook her head and nodded to Lisa. Lisa had the greater right to it. Her daughter had loved Sanders with no qualification, no reserve. Lisa had, quite simply, adored the man she believed was her natural father, the man who had been father in all the important ways.

The service was over, the sound of a lonely bagpipe stilled, but its echo lingered in the hot, heavy air. The bag-

1

pipe, a too familiar sound at funerals of law enforcement officers, had been included at the suggestion of John Malcomb, Sanders's partner. The pipes did, Meara thought, have a mournful sound.

Like the sound of her soul.

With the exception of her daughter, who knew nothing of the events of the spring of 1942, Sanders was Meara's last link with those two heart-wrenching weeks of her past, a past that now lived only in FBI files someplace and in the recesses of a heart that had never quite repaired itself.

Even that FBI file, however, was not complete. Sanders had been the only one who knew what really happened, who knew the truth about Lisa, about a man who called himself David Michael Fielding, about the love and hate and terrible violence which had marked Meara for life.

Which had dried her tears long ago.

There was movement now, and she felt Lisa's hand reach for hers and tighten. Obediently, as if she were daughter instead of mother, she stepped forward and carefully placed a rose on Sanders's casket. It was a rose Sanders himself had planted. He had loved his roses. It was a fine thing, he'd said, to produce something beautiful. He didn't say anything more. He didn't have to say that it represented peace in the violent, often evil, world he inhabited as a federal agent. Despite his profession, he had been a gentle man, a warm man.

Sanders had been her friend, her best friend, and her greatest sorrow was that she had been unable to give him more. He had loved her with a painful sweetness and yearning, and he'd had to live among the shadows of another man who had betrayed them both. Despite Sanders's every effort, he had never been able to block out those shadows, and he knew it. Worse, he had accepted the relationship gratefully, giving all and receiving little. But Meara could not give what was dead but never buried.

She looked at the great oak trees which shaded the cemetery, and the moss that draped from them like great gray shrouds. She had wondered whether it was really fair to bury him here rather than in Pennsylvania with his parents. But now she planned to live here, and she wanted him near. She couldn't force herself to leave this island, not even now. Jekyll Island, with its compelling beauty and obsessive memories, was to her like the apple in the Garden of Eden, a temptation that overrode every rational thought.

He was here. *He* had died here. She had watched the explosion that killed him. He had introduced her to love and then he had destroyed them both.

And she wasn't even sure of his true name.

A penetrating loneliness drove through her. Now she didn't have Sanders, the one person who knew and understood her. Her daughter's hand trembled in hers, but still Meara couldn't leave. She placed her free hand against the casket. One last touch, one last effort to tell Sanders how much he had meant to her, to say things she had never been able to say while he was alive. She grieved for him, for all she had not been able to give him, for all the pain they both had endured over the years, for the two weeks during which the sun had touched her life and then left it forever, leaving only a legacy of betrayal and sudden violent death.

Even J. Edgar Hoover dropped by the cottage later to pay his respects. The house was filled with FBI agents and other law enforcement officers who had worked with Sanders. He had been a popular man who had never lost his sense of justice, of compassion. Because of those qualities, or flaws as some of his superiors at the FBI saw them, he had never climbed the bureau ladder. He simply wasn't single-minded enough.

It was also the reason he had died, Meara had learned.

Sanders and three other agents had confronted a group
of suspected terrorists who had robbed a Wells Fargo truck
and killed the driver. One of the terrorists had been a
woman, and Sanders had hesitated before shooting. The
woman had not. Yet he had been good at his job because
people naturally trusted him. He could coax information
from both victims and suspects as easily as he had once
milked cows on his family's Pennsylvania farm. Meara had
experienced that skill firsthand.

She smiled slightly as still another man offered awkward
sympathies. The numbness was still there. The denial.
Thank God. In the meantime, she could smile blankly at
the stories being told, the affectionate remembrances.
Sanders. Lochinvar and Don Quixote. He had been both
to her. He had saved her life that summer of 1942 and had,
all the rest of it, tilted at windmills to repair her wounded
heart.

Meara looked over at Lisa, whose eyes, throughout the
day, had never lost the mist of tears. She saw Kellen Tabor
stand next to Lisa, his hand under her daughter's arm, and
she said a brief prayer of thanks for the tall young attorney
who lived in the cottage next to this one. He and Lisa had
played together for years, and now his eyes had changed
from teasing playfulness to something softer. Something
tender. Meara hoped that Lisa would soon share the feelings so evident in his eyes. But you couldn't direct love.
She knew that better than anyone.

"Meara?"

She turned and recognized John Malcomb, the agent
who had been Sanders's last partner.

His eyes were grim, a muscle flexing in his cheek. "I can't
tell you how sorry I am. If only . . ."

"If only . . ."

The two saddest words in the English language, Meara
thought. In any language. If only . . .

She held out her hands to him, taking one of his and clasping it tightly. "Don't, John. Don't torment yourself. There was nothing you could have done."

He hesitated. "Sanders was my best friend. He once asked me to look out for you if something happened to him. If there's anything I can do, anything at all, call me. Anytime."

Meara felt her heart slow, her hands tremble. Even now, Sanders was trying to protect her. She nodded, unable to force words between the growing lump in her throat. Sanders had never really realized that steel had formed within her, that strength and independence and finally confidence had replaced the naive young woman she once had been. He had wanted to protect. He still wanted to protect.

But she merely nodded. "Thank you, John."

They kept coming until she thought her face would break from the effort of keeping it composed. But she knew she must for Lisa, for Lisa was about to fall apart. Meara could tell from the trembling lips, the glaze over her daughter's eyes. Lisa had never really encountered death before, had never felt loss. Meara was proud of her, proud of the attempt Lisa was making. But that strength was nearly gone.

She nodded to John, who understood and gently, diplomatically started ushering guests out. Finally, there were only three visitors left: John, Kellen, and his mother, Evelyn.

Meara went over to Lisa and hugged her, feeling the slight withdrawal of her daughter. It deepened the grief in her, the sense of loss, but there had always been a certain reserve between them, a resentment on Lisa's part for something Meara had never entirely understood. Lisa had always been more her father's daughter, had always given Sanders her entire devotion, and although part of Meara ached from the quiet, barely obvious rejection, another part had been glad for Sanders. The two of them, father and daughter, had had a very special relationship, and Sanders had received the total, unqualified love that Meara had never been able to give.

"I'm going for a walk, love," she told Lisa, watching a flash of relief cross her daughter's face. It had only been those few moments at the cemetery when Lisa pressed her hand into her own that they had been united in sorrow. Now the chasm was back again, and Meara didn't know how to cross it.

She turned and walked out of the cottage door, across the dunes she loved to the wide gray beach alive with gulls and small skittering birds. The sun, a huge crimson ball, was streaming paths of gold against the gently churning water. Meara found the old log which she often used as a perch, and sat, wishing she could feel the renewal she sometimes felt here. But now there was only a lonely sadness, an isolation rising from the vastness of the ocean.

She needed to go away from this place. She knew it. She'd known it for years, but she could never stay away. Even now as she looked down the beach, even now when she was mourning Sanders, she thought she saw Michael far down the beach. She saw bits and pieces of him in others: the arrogant stance, the amused crinkling around the corners of his eyes, the impatient raking of sandy hair, the dark blue eyes which blazed with passion and deadly secrets. She saw bits and pieces but never the whole. The whole had been destroyed in flames, flames she still saw in her sleep.

As if on cue, the lone figure down on the beach lifted his hand, just as Michael had done so many times, and ran it through hair made gold by the sun. Meara's heart fluttered like that of a wounded seabird as the figure turned in the opposite direction and walked away. She even imagined he had the slightest of limps.

He's dead, she told herself. Just as Sanders is dead. Why today, of all days, can't you put him to rest too?

She had met Sanders two days after she'd met Michael. Even in her innocence, she had seen the difference between the two. One reflected calm assurance, the other raw magnetism and vitality and danger.

She had been too sheltered, too naive, to choose the right one.

She had been so young. . . .

Part One

Chapter One

Jekyll Island, Georgia
March 1942

ON THE DECK of the sleek cruiser, Meara watched the dark blue ribbon fly from her hair and skim across the water before disappearing under a wave. Her hair, a red-gold she would have changed in an instant if she'd had a choice, whipped around her face in the glorious ocean breeze.

She looked down at her two young charges who were competing to be the first to sight a dolphin, and her heart warmed with affection for them. Peter was eleven and Tara seven, and she had been looking after them during her summers since she was sixteen, five years ago.

This would be her last Easter here, on Jekyll Island, and she felt a bittersweet sadness, even while excitement swelled in her about her first real job this summer. *Life* magazine. She would be a staffer on the foremost magazine in America.

Of course, she would start as an assistant, a gofer, but

she hoped to change that rapidly. Armed with her journalism degree from Columbia and with Irish determination, she *knew* she would crash down the barriers of a predominantly male field, especially now in 1942 when the war with Germany and Japan was draining manpower from nonessential jobs.

But she had these two weeks to be part child, part nanny, part tutor. Meara enjoyed all three roles because the Connor children were bright and unspoiled despite their wealth. And she owed the Connor family much; they had paid her way through college. And they had given her mother, who had come to America as an immigrant and who had been almost immediately widowed, a lifelong job and a home.

A mist started falling, and she lifted her face to feel its cool March touch. She loved the ocean. She loved the island where they were to stay. She loved the elegant club cruiser carrying them all there. She loved life. An explosion of spontaneous, happy laughter burst from her lips, and it made the children start laughing too. Just like sillies, she thought, as other passengers looked on tolerantly.

"Look," Peter said, as a fish jumped high in the air.

"A dolphin?" Tara asked, her eyes full of wonder.

"I don't think so, love," Meara said. She hadn't wanted to spoil their game by pointing out that dolphins seldom ventured to this side of the island, separated from Brunswick by a river. Leaning down to whisper something in Tara's ear, she directed their attention to the marshes where tall grass blew in the wind.

When she straightened again, she caught the gaze of a tall man watching her intently, a smile on his lips. He was leaning negligently against the cabin of the cruiser, his body lean, even thin, and his face slightly pale as if he had been ill, but there was nothing at all weak about the blazing dark blue eyes that regarded her with such interest. Her eyes fell to his right hand which clasped the top of a cane, and she felt an immediate sympathy. She guessed he must be a soldier, a wounded soldier, and her heart went immediately out to him. America had been in the war four months now, ever since Pearl Harbor, and she was hearing more and more about the death tolls and huge numbers of wounded in the Pacific.

His smile suddenly widened as he noted her interest, and it deepened dimples indented in his cheeks. He was sinfully attractive, his features rugged and arrogant, and his eyes magnetic. She knew she had never seen him on the island before. She most definitely would have remembered. It was rude of her to stare. She started to turn her head back to the chattering children as she saw his rueful grin, and realized, much to her chagrin, that he knew exactly what she was thinking.

Meara's heart raced. In confusion, she stooped down to talk to Tara, and she saw her hands shake ever so slightly.

"When we get there," Tara said, "will you help build us a sand castle?"

"The best one ever," Meara promised, grateful for the distraction.

"And deep, deep moats?" Tara asked. She had just read a simplified and romanticized version of the King Arthur legend and had been full of questions about castles and knights and fair damsels.

"The deepest," Meara pledged.

"Oh, castles," Peter said scornfully. "We need to build bunkers against the Germans. My father says sometimes you can even see German submarines around here . . . He says that someone even saw Germans sunbathing on top of one."

Some of the smile left Meara's eyes. She had also heard the stories. The Connors, as well as other members of the exclusive Jekyll Island Club, had been warned about the proximity of German submarines along the eastern seaboard. Their obvious target, however, was shipping, both U.S. and British, and despite the warnings, the Connors, as well as the other financial and industrial leaders, had decided to return as usual this season to their private retreat on the Georgia coast, the Germans be damned.

This year, she had been told by the Connors, could well be the last season for the Jekyll Island Club in any event. Gas was in short supply. Transportation was more difficult. Labor was scarce. More and more of the members were thoroughly absorbed in the war effort and had neither the time nor inclination to spend leisurely days in the mild winter sun as they had during the past fifty years of the club's existence.

This Easter would have been the last time for Meara anyway, but she hated to see the great club, once called the most exclusive club in the world, close, its huge private cottages abandoned, and the elegant, comfortable clubhouse/hotel boarded. The club had claimed as members the Pulitzers, the Goulds, the Rockefellers, the Morgans, the Marshall Fields, the Vanderbilts, and the Auchinclosses among others. There had always been a magic "other world" feeling about both the club and the island it totally occupied.

Meara had been sixteen the first time she had seen Jekyll Island, and she had promptly called it an "island of dreams." Lush with moss-draped oak trees and rich in both wild and domestic flowers, it had always remained that for her, a place where dreams came true. Hers had. It was where the Connors had said they would finance her education, where she had spent so many happy hours during the day with Tara and Peter and pleasant sultry evenings with other employees, and even members, of America's great families. She had never been jealous of the wealthy members but had, instead, always felt privileged to experience a life-style that was rapidly disappearing.

She was so swept up in her reminiscences, she didn't hear the tap of the cane nearing her.

"Lovely, isn't it," a deep baritone voice said, and when she looked up, the tall, attractive stranger was looking straight at her, not at the island ahead, and she had the oddest impression that he meant her, and not the island at all.

For one of the few times in her life, Meara stared fascinated at a man. He was even more handsome up close. Or perhaps handsome wasn't the word. His features were too strong for mere handsomeness, too stark. His eyes were very dark blue, like midnight velvet cloth. They were framed by devilish angled eyebrows that made him look perpetually amused. His cheekbones were high and even gaunt at the moment, softened only by pronounced dimples when he smiled, as he was doing now. His mouth was wide, sensual, and curved beguilingly in an inquisitive smile. Yet despite all the outward signs of warmth, Meara sensed a reserve about him, a quiet isolation that lay hidden behind a charming surface.

He became more amused as she continued her survey, and Meara, filled with a certain discomfort, retaliated with her very practiced challenging look, one she had perfected over four years of competing with young men in a male-dominated field.

Meara had once been shy, even gawky, but her years as an "almost" member of the Connor family and her schooling at Columbia where she served as an editor of the university newspaper had built her confidence. She also had limitless curiosity, an essential quality, one of her professors once said, of a good reporter. Inherent shyness was usually overcome by her fierce compulsion to know everything about everyone she met.

But under the interested gaze of the stranger's intense blue eyes, she went spiraling back to those old days when she'd felt awkward and tongue-tied.

Peter saved the day. "Who are you?" he said with interest as he regarded the cane. "Were you wounded in the war?"

The man grinned down at him, a peculiarly boyish grin full of the confidence that Meara so wretchedly lacked at the moment.

"Yep," he said.

"How?"

"Peter!" Meara protested.

"It's all right, miss," he said easily. "I don't mind. Some shrapnel from an explosion." There was a barely perceptible accent in the deep resonant voice, one she couldn't quite place.

She tipped her head questioningly, and he smiled again with a charm which she suddenly felt was very, very practiced. But then warmth flashed in those incredible blue eyes of his, and she dismissed that instantaneous suspicion.

He bowed. "Lieutenant Commander David Michael Fielding at your service," he said and winked at Tara. "My friends call me Michael."

"Commander?" Meara queried. "The navy?"

"I'm Canadian," he explained. "I joined the British Navy when England declared war on Germany."

So that accounted for the slightly different accent.

It seemed suddenly very natural to talk with him. He was a wounded officer, obviously a gentleman and a very nice one, it seemed, by the way he talked to the children rather than above them.

Meara looked down at the leg he seemed to favor. "Is it coming along well?"

"Well enough. But I'm from a very cold part of Canada, and the doctors thought a bit of sunshine and exercise would help. One of them contacted a member of the Jekyll Island Club and wrangled an invitation."

"You'll be staying at the clubhouse?"

He nodded. "And you?"

Peter interrupted happily. "Mother and father have rented the DuBignon cottage."

"The DuBignon cottage?"

"There're several private cottages," Meara answered. "At least the members call them cottages. They're really more like mansions. One of them, the DuBignon cottage, can be rented by members of the club. It provides a little more privacy than the clubhouse."

Michael Fielding gifted her with a blinding smile. "You must be their sister."

Meara couldn't help but smile back. She didn't know when she had ever met such a compelling man, and now his easy manner was beginning to make her feel more comfortable. For some incredible reason, she wanted to reach out and touch him, almost as if to determine whether he was real. But instead, she straightened. "No," she explained, "I'm their . . ."

She tried to identify exactly what she was. Peter hated the word *nanny*, thinking it made him sound much younger than he felt he was. And she was not exactly a governess.

"She's our friend," Peter explained.

"Then I think you are very fortunate," the man replied conspiratorially to Peter, and Meara's heart flip-flopped in an uncommon way. She briefly, and secretly, examined that particular feeling, thinking flip-flop was not a very scientific, or literate, way of expressing exactly what was going on inside her, but then she'd never had much experience with this kind of internal confusion.

"Don't you think you should sit down?" she said, referring to his leg and seeking to distract attention from herself. She knew she was blushing, and she hoped that the windburn on her face disguised her reaction to him. But she knew it did not when she saw the amusement return to his eyes, to the almost gentle curve of his mouth.

"No." The answer was simple but it said a great deal more. He was making it very obvious that he wished to stay right where he was.

Once again, Peter raced undiplomatically to the rescue. "Have you killed many Germans?"

"What a bloodthirsty question," Michael Fielding observed with another grin, but there was a certain grimness behind it this time.

"But did you?" Peter persisted.

"When you're on a ship," Michael said, "you never quite know. They lob shells at you, and you at them, but you never actually see the enemy unless their ship blows up and you rescue some of them."

"I wouldn't rescue anyone shooting at me, especially not Germans," Peter grumbled.

"What if your ship sank and they refused to rescue you?"

Peter thought about it. "But if they did, I would be their prisoner."

"But you'd still be alive."

Peter shook his head. "My father says Germans don't take prisoners, that they kill survivors."

"Peter!" Meara didn't want Tara to hear any more. She hadn't thought Mr. Connor talked of such matters in front of the boy, although she knew he felt strongly about the war. An influential financier, he had already raised millions in war bonds and had even met with President Roosevelt on plans to expedite American war financing and production.

"I heard Father talking to another man about it," Peter insisted stubbornly, his lower lip beginning to inch out in rebellion.

"But talk of killing is nothing a gentleman discusses in front of two lovely ladies," the Canadian interceded, again with such charm that it took Meara a moment to realize how easily he had defused Peter. Peter's pout turned into a delighted smile at being called a gentleman, and Tara beamed at being classified with Meara as a lovely lady.

Meara couldn't help but smile with appreciation at the neat rebuke. His eyes were speculative and even admiring as they settled on her, and she felt ridiculously happy at his evident interest.

It was a feeling quite unlike any other she'd ever experienced before. Although she had gone through brief moonstruck stages as a teenager, she'd had little time for dating. From the time she was small, she had wanted to be a journalist, and she had worked hard to accomplish that in the same determined, compulsive way she did everything. It had not mattered that her mother was a maid and an immigrant with very little education, that Meara had never known her father. She had only known she wanted to write, that she must go to college. The Connors had made it easy for her, but she still had always worked, first as a maid for the Connors, then as a companion for the children. When she was at Columbia, she worked as a waitress as well as holding an important position with the university paper. She seldom dated, and when she did it was mostly to attend political events or concerts, and she had always made it very clear that she wished no deeper relationship, not now, not until she made her own mark on the world.

It was an attitude that puzzled and dismayed her mother, and was incomprehensible to many of her acquaintances. But once Meara made up her mind, nothing deterred her. And no member of the opposite sex had tempted her sufficiently even to consider deviating the slightest bit from the course she had chosen.

Until now.

Meara lowered her eyes before he could see what must be shining in them. She had never learned to hide her emotions. She laughed when she was happy and cried copiously in grief. She had an Irish temper, but usually it quickly wore itself out. She held a grudge only when someone purposely hurt a person she loved, and then she held that grudge forever. That unforgiving aspect of her personality, she realized, was not entirely admirable, but a saint she was not, and she had come to accept that un-Christian characteristic in herself.

Her unfortunate openness, Meara sometimes feared, was not an altogether good quality for a journalist. She also had a tendency to like most people, to always find something to admire or appreciate. Meara often worried about that too, afraid that perhaps she wasn't always the best judge of character because of that too-trusting acceptance. Yet she also knew she had a compensating ability to drive to the center of a problem, to focus on the one really important fact among hundreds thrown out.

She tried to find that piece of Michael Fielding now, the one really important quality that summed him up. Accumulation of wealth was her employer's. The drive for security her mother's. Her own? Ambition, she realized quickly. Ambition to be the very best at what she did.

And Michael Fielding? Usually she could guess immediately when she met someone. Usually she was right. But now nothing appeared obvious. She suddenly realized that despite his charm, his warmth toward the children, and the few comments he had made, she'd received no general impression of him, that it was well hidden somewhere deep inside and he was giving very little away.

"How long are you going to be on Jekyll?" she asked, her hand tightly clenching the ship's rail.

"Two weeks," he replied. That was the limit for guests at the club, Meara knew. Michael's face closed momentarily as if he were weighing his next words, and again Meara caught an impression of grimness before the smile came back. "Since I'm a stranger, I wonder if you and the children would help show me around."

Meara studied him.

"Oh, yes," Peter said, thoroughly taken with him.

"I think that's up to their parents," Meara corrected. The Connors were very wealthy, and since the Lindbergh baby kidnapping years earlier, they were also cautious with their children.

"And who might they be?" Michael asked softly.

Meara suddenly realized that while he had introduced himself, they had not. Peter had been too interested in the man's injury, and she'd been too mesmerized by his personality.

Peter remedied the problem of introductions quickly. "I am Peter Connor," he said proudly. "My father is Calvin Connor, and he's a friend of the president."

Michael Fielding looked suitably impressed, yet something else flickered in his eyes. Knowledge? Familiarity with the name? Amusement at Peter's pride? Meara couldn't quite identify it.

"And I'm Tara," Tara chimed in, forgetting shyness in her irritation at being left out of the introduction.

"Ah," Michael said, bestowing an approving smile on her. "The home of the Irish kings."

Tara looked puzzled.

"It is a very pretty name for a very pretty girl," he amended easily as his gaze returned to Meara. "And you?"

"She's Meara." Peter answered for her.

"Meara," he repeated slowly. "A rare and lovely name," he added, his eyes dancing at the confusion he found in her face. "Does Meara have another name?"

"O'Hara," Peter supplied accommodatingly.

"Meara O'Hara," he repeated, and warmth flooded

Meara as he said the name slowly and lingeringly. She had never thought her name particularly pretty before, but now the words sounded lovely on his lips, lovely and even magical as if he bestowed some special meaning to each syllable.

But then the spell was broken by approaching figures. Calvin Connor and his wife, Elizabeth, were suddenly with them, Calvin carefully scrutinized the tall man with them before looking questioningly at Meara.

"Mr. and Mrs. Connor," she said formally, "this is Commander Michael Fielding, a Canadian Navy officer who was recently wounded."

"Lieutenant Commander," Michael corrected, "although I'm grateful for the promotion."

Cal Connor's shrewd gaze ranged over the man, lowering to scan the cane, the way the man was standing. He seemed to recognize the military posture, even as Michael shifted slightly to favor his left leg.

Both men nodded slightly, eyes wary, as they shook hands and silently judged each other. It was an expression Meara had seen often in the circles of the wealthy. The barracuda look, she had always thought, an appraising gaze that passed between two strong men who wondered whether the other was adversary or possible ally.

"Where were you wounded?" Connor said.

"The Atlantic."

"Another ship?"

Fielding shook his head. "A sub."

A competitive gleam appeared in Connor's eyes. "Did you get it?"

"I don't know," the Canadian said. "Unfortunately, I was knocked out, apparently by shrapnel from an explosion. When I regained consciousness, I found myself floating in a life raft with a dead man. Some French fishermen found us, and eventually helped to get me back to England."

"Your ship?"

"Sunk, I found out later."

"Any other survivors?"

Michael nodded. "I'm afraid they wound up in German hands."

"What kind of ship were you on?"

"A destroyer," Fielding said shortly, the interrogation obviously becoming irritating.

Peter tugged at his father's hand. "Michael asked us to show him around the island. May we?"

Connor furrowed his brows. "Michael?"

The Canadian broke in the conversation. "I asked him to call me that. I'm a bit tired of military titles. I've been in military hospitals for several months."

"What are your plans now?"

"Another couple of weeks of recuperation. Then I hope to convince them to take me back."

"What about your leg?"

"You don't walk much in the navy." Michael grinned, and Meara could see some of her employer's natural suspicions fading. "And," Michael added in his precise accent, "England needs all the men it has."

Connor nodded at that. All the Allied countries did.

"Can we, Father?" Peter's voice interrupted again.

Cal Connor looked down at his son, his eyes softening.

"Can we show him the island?" Peter asked impatiently.

Connor looked up at the Canadian. "Why don't you join us for dinner tonight and we'll discuss it then?" It was obvious he was not going to allow Meara and his children to associate with anyone until he knew more of him. Yet Meara could see he was sympathetic to both the plea in his son's eyes and to a wounded ally.

Michael Fielding looked toward the woman who stood

at Connor's side. "Mrs. Connor? I wouldn't wish to intrude on your first night."

Elizabeth smiled. "I think we, at least my imps here, are the ones intruding on you. But we would very much like to have you."

Michael accepted easily with a smile and a nod. "Thank you, I would be delighted."

"Ask anyone for the location of the DuBignon cottage. Nine o'clock, then?" Connor said abruptly before turning toward the door of the cabin.

Meara understood the message in her employer's abrupt departure. She was not to allow the children to keep company with the tall Canadian until he had been thoroughly examined and accepted by Cal Connor.

"We have to go in," she said softly, reluctant to leave his strangely magnetic presence.

"Will you be dining with us tonight?"

"No, I eat earlier with the children."

"Perhaps I'll see you this afternoon, then, building sand castles."

So he had been listening earlier. "Perhaps," she said, knowing she should not say such a thing, especially after the silent warning from her employer. But nothing could happen on Jekyll Island. It was, she thought, the most peaceful, tranquil place on earth. All the guests at the club were gentlemen, either members or friends of members. The names of any guests had to be submitted and approved in advance.

His mouth moved into beguilingly boyish delight and approval. She would have promised anything at that moment, even her soul had the devil been available to take it.

He nodded and moved away, as if he too sought to break the sudden odd recognition that had flared between them and bound them together in some incomprehensible yet wildly reckless and intimate way.

Taking Tara's hand, Meara moved almost unseeingly to the door, feeling that some part of herself had just been torn away. It was replaced by a certain wonder, a distressingly strong anticipation, and for the briefest of moments, the feeling that her life had just changed forever.

Chapter Two

Mᴵᴄʜᴀᴇʟ Fɪᴇʟᴅɪɴɢ ᴋɴᴇᴡ he was in trouble. He had known it on the cruiser when he first saw the girl, her hair flying free and her eyes sparkling and her laugh floating in the wind like a spring song.

He had known it from the second his heart warmed. He'd never quite experienced that feeling before. And that uniqueness frightened him.

He justified his intrusion into the enchanting world of the girl and two children as part of his assignment, as a necessary step toward a goal he considered distasteful but necessary.

But now misgivings assaulted him as he looked around his room at the Jekyll Island Club. The taste was impeccable. Elegantly comfortable. Elegantly casual. Everything he had been led to expect. And more. There was something about this island. . . .

Or perhaps there was something about the girl.

He went over to one of the two suitcases he had brought with him. It was smaller than the other, but heavier. Checking once again to see that the case was still securely

26

locked, he placed it in back of the wardrobe and opened the other one, rummaging through the clothes, mostly new, mostly unfamiliar, that rested there. He had worn a uniform for years, more years than he wanted to remember, particularly during the past few years. He searched among the clothes until he found a lightweight white cotton shirt and a pair of casual tan slacks, the tailoring very American with its generous pleats.

Michael looked at his watch. Dinner was hours away, and he needed no lunch. The invitation to the Connors had been a real stroke of luck as well as a challenge. Connor was no fool. Michael had been briefed on each American financier and industrialist who visited the island. If he was accepted by the Connors, his task was half accomplished. Connor's acceptance would give him quick entree to the others, to the social events and habits of the other visitors to the island.

But although he knew he should keep his mind on the business at hand, he kept thinking of the girl. That realization surprised him, for he had never before given a woman much more thought than a night's pleasure. One reason had been his occupation. As a ship's officer, he was never any place longer than several days. There had never been time for attachments, even if he had wanted any. Then why, in a matter of minutes, had he been so completely charmed?

Michael limped to the window, which was now open to the soft sea breeze, and looked through the huge oaks draped with moss. He could just barely see patches of Jekyll Creek and the salt marshes beyond. The sea smell was familiar, still intoxicating as it had been from the first moment he sailed away from Germany on a tramp steamer. He wished he were back at sea, away from the plotting and machinations of ambitious men.

Ambitious men. His father had been one. He had died

one. His father had embraced National Socialism despite his aristocratic background, despite his wealth. But he had been a bully, and his temperament had suited the new bullies of this century.

Michael felt a puppet on a string now, strung and manipulated by men like his father.

A knock came at the door, and he moved toward it, opening it to the uniformed attendant. "Suh," the black man said softly, "tea will be served downstairs at three," and Michael nodded as the man backed away.

Michael was no stranger to blacks, having visited nearly every port in the world. But the grave soft courtesy of the servants and employees on this island was new. He looked out the window again and wondered whether time had come to a complete stop. It seemed that way here. He wished it had, wished it could.

Then he thrust aside the troublesome thoughts. He had been given few choices, and now he must do the best with what he had.

He had a few hours now, however. A few hours of his own. Michael ran a comb through his thick hair which had been tangled by the tangy sea mist. It was militarily short, but rebellious tendrils still had a tendency to curl and fall over his forehead. He would take a walk. A walk to clear his head, to investigate the island, to make plans. There were a dozen reasons, not to mention a certain young woman who might, at this moment, be building sand castles in the sun. As quickly as the limp and cane allowed, he moved to the door and down the corridor and the stately stairs.

When he inquired about the beach, he discovered it was more than a mile away. The club employee took a look at his cane and offered the use of what he called a "red bug." Michael soon discovered the red bug was a clever little motorized vehicle powered by gasoline. Consisting of little more than a frame, four wheels, two seats and a steering wheel, it was, the staff member said, remarkably adaptable to the crushed-shell roads, the beach, and the dirt trails. Everyone used them, the man explained, adults and children alike.

Feeling like the child he had never been, he soon discovered the vehicle perfect for exploring, and he drove past the elaborate cottages, down the roads lined with live oaks, their languid limbs laden with Spanish moss. Southern magnolias and palmetto abounded, as did blooming dogwood. The green carpet beneath them was dotted with fern and wood flowers, and the air was musky with the mingled sweet and tangy scents of wildflowers and the sea.

No one else was on the road, and aside from the *put-put* of his vehicle there was only the whisper of wind and the fetching song of a mockingbird.

He reached some old dune ridges, which were covered with a forest of wind-sculpted live oak tress, all their branches stretched out toward the interior in an odd, lopsided pattern. He parked and took up his cane, limping across the dunes to a wide beach.

Michael felt an inexplicable but fierce stab of disappointment that he saw no human figures, no woman and children, although there were hundreds of birds playing and hunting at the water's edge. The depth of his disappointment was really quite remarkable, and completely unlike anything he had previously experienced. He pondered briefly how those few moments on the cruiser could have made such an impact, and then dismissed the thought with the iron control he had so well developed.

Instead, he looked at the beach with a certain appreciation. It was low tide, and the sand appeared endless before it melted into the foam-licked gray water. He took a turn to the left, where huge oak trees, part of their knurled roots unearthed by wind and sand, clustered above the beach.

At high tide they would almost meet the water, challenging it to do its worst.

The sand was hard, not like the soft sand of many other beaches he had walked, and easy for his injured leg to maneuver. The leg was aching, for he had been on it all morning, but each day it grew stronger and he had extended his walks from half a mile to two miles. Usually by the time he finished, streaks of agony ran up and down the length of his calf, but he welcomed the pain. He had come so damned close to losing it.

Michael closed his eyes, remembering the moment when particles of metal had ripped into his flesh, tearing it open through the bone. He had been lucky. He'd had a fine surgeon who chose to try to repair it rather than amputate. He was then sent to one of the best doctors in Berlin. He didn't know why until later. And then he had wondered whether the price had been worth it.

But for today, he would forget the cost. Seabirds danced happily on the beach, and gulls swept gracefully down in the water. A cool breeze broke the unexpected heat of a late March day, and mild waves rushed in pleasant rhythm up the beach. The rich, unforgettable smell of water teaming with life filled his senses and melded there with the echoing wild, lonely call of a gull and the scolding heckling of smaller birds competing for a sea-discarded offering. After two months in a hospital and suffocating, claustrophobic days in a submarine, he greedily absorbed the sights and sounds and smells. He could almost forget why he was here. Almost.

He reached a curve in the beach, where it swung around to face the marshes, and he turned back, his limp becoming more pronounced as the leg rebelled. He wondered how far he had come. The sun was lowering now, its brightness fading slightly as the bright ball slid down the horizon. But still it favored the ocean with its rays, sending flecks of gold dust across its shimmering surface. Deceptively calm, deceptively peaceful.

Michael knew the ocean, knew the water in each of its moods. The sea had been his parents, his teacher, his security. He had run away to sea, at fourteen, lying about his age. He had run away from his father, from a mother who suffered repeated abuse and yet still adored the man who did it to her. Michael hadn't been able to understand, to accept, and he knew if he'd stayed he would one day kill his father. So he had left, and found the roughest, most exacting school there was. It was a world harder for him than most, for he carried a natural arrogance and charm which came from wealth and breeding, and those characteristics alienated the rough seamen. He'd had to fight his way to respect, to repeatedly prove himself by working harder, longer than anyone else. He'd had a natural aptitude and ear for languages and could easily slide in and out of the rough sea speech with its heavy emphasis on descriptive curses. His mother had been Canadian, and he spoke English as well as his native German, and during his travels picked up French and Spanish as well as a smattering of other languages. It was that talent, he knew, that had brought him to the attention of Admiral Canaris, the head of the Abwehr, German intelligence.

His gaze turned from the sea and found three figures on the beach ahead of him. His heart lurched with sudden pleasure and anticipation, and despite the pain in his leg his steps hurried as he moved toward them.

Meara's wind-tossed hair was even more glorious here as the sun seemed to center all its attention on catching each strand and painting it with a particularly splendid red-gold fire. Her profile was toward him, and as she had been on the yacht, she was smiling, her lips curved whimsically as she surveyed a crumbled tower. She wore a simple green dress which molded her slender body and which, he knew, deepened the emerald green of her eyes. She was barefoot, and long, slender legs bent comfortably behind her. Her lap was full of loose grains of sand, and her hands were caked with wet sand as she looked, her head cocked in mock dismay, at the fallen tower of a not very elegant sand castle. Absorbed in her task, she was oblivious to his presence. She was, he thought quickly, the most delightful sight he'd ever encountered.

"Enemy cannon?" Michael queried seriously and had the satisfaction of three faces looking quickly up, all of them flashing with welcome.

Meara shook her head wryly, but her eyes sparkled with warmth and mischief. "More like faulty construction techniques."

Michael smiled slowly as he looked at the three of them. Tara's blond hair, like Meara's, was damp with sea air and fell in tangled curls down her back as a seven-year-old face looked up at him with the open delight of a child confident that everyone was her friend.

Peter jumped to his feet politely. "Perhaps you could help us, sir." Despite the courtesy, there was an eagerness in his voice, even a touch of hero worship.

Leave! Every cautious, sensible part of him emphasized the command. Make an excuse and leave.

But nothing inside him obeyed. His gaze caught Meara's, a flow of energy and awareness passing between them with aching intensity, holding both of them motionless, neither able or willing to break the spell that enveloped them.

"Will you, sir?" Peter's insistent voice intruded.

"Willya?" chimed Tara.

"Will you, Commander?" Meara's request came softly, an irresistible plea dancing lightly in the air.

"I'm a sailor," he demurred with a disarming modesty. "I doubt my architectural abilities are any better than yours. Now if it were a ship . . ."

Meara looked down at another tower that was just now tumbling down. "They can't be any worse," she observed. Then she noticed the cane and the leg he had favored this morning, and she looked suddenly chastened. "Perhaps your leg . . ."

She sounded concerned and self-reproachful, and the warmth in him deepened. It had been a long time since anyone had cared, and he wasn't exactly sure how to react to it. He was a prisoner of that warmth, of hers and of his own. With a certain grace despite the obvious stiffness of the one leg, he lowered himself, feeling strangely out of place in so informal a position. He had never played in the sand before, had never really played at all. But all of a sudden, it seemed a very appealing pastime, especially when he saw the delighted approval in Meara's eyes. When her hand accidentally brushed his, the warmth became an ache that seeped throughout his body.

He had more skill than he thought, and his suggestions, based in part on the castles he had seen in Europe, produced under eager hands a very superior product, an elaborate European castle with towers and turrets and double walls.

Only rarely during the afternoon, as the sun began to dip, did he remember his real purpose here, and that he was only playing a role. He was doing as he had been told, ingratiating himself, making friends, beginning a betrayal that he already suspected would destroy him as well as the intended victims. Perhaps that was why, he thought, he was grabbing these moments for his own. Tomorrow, Hans would be here, and plans would begin in earnest. God, he detested the man he was being forced to work with.

"We're tiring you." Meara's voice interrupted his thought, and he knew he must be frowning, his eyes clouded.

"No, it's been a pleasure." His voice was softer than he'd intended, laced with a regret only he understood.

Peter began to move restlessly, and eagerly accepted Meara's suggestion that he and Tara play ball.

As they moved away, Michael turned to Meara. "How long have you been with the Connors?"

"Forever," she smiled. Fondness was in her voice as she continued. "My mother has been their maid for twenty years. I was too, for a while, and then I started taking care of Tara and Peter."

"Where is she now?"

"In New York."

"And your father?"

"He died just after I was born. An accident on the New York docks. He was a stevedore."

There was a challenge in the way she said the words, and he understood it only too well. By his very presence here, he had to be wealthy and of fine background. Michael sensed she had also felt the fierce attraction between them and was telling him, quite honestly, of her own history before another step was taken by either of them. She was, in her own soft way, asking him if it mattered. Sudden guilt, deep and bitter, battered at him like storm-swept waves. Honesty was the one thing he couldn't give. He was going to use her. He had no choice but to use her, but perhaps he could minimize the damage. He couldn't allow the magic between them to continue. Better she think him a snob. He had what he wanted, an introduction to the Connors and, through them, to the others on the island.

Any more was idiocy. But still he didn't leave. He damned himself, but still he didn't leave. For some reason, he didn't think Meara would be satisfied taking care of someone else's children all her life, though she obviously did it very well.

"And now? What are your plans now?"

She smiled, and he knew he had been right, and that she appreciated his seeing it.

"Writing."

He raised an eyebrow in question.

"I received my degree in journalism a month ago. I start with *Life* magazine this summer. Nothing very grand. An assistant to an assistant to an assistant," she added quickly.

"I think that's very grand, indeed," he said quite truthfully and with some surprise. His recent contacts with women had been few and temporary, and never with the apparently growing number of women choosing a career over marriage.

Meara's expression thanked him, and once more he felt a rare ripple of pleasure surge through him.

"And you?" she said.

"Back to war, I expect. If they will take me back now. The leg has healed better than they thought."

"Was it very bad then?"

He shrugged as if the wound was of little import. "It was . . . rugged, I suppose," he said, a little surprised at his own words. He had never expressed the extreme fear he'd once felt at the possibility of amputation. "At one time they thought . . ." The words died off, but Meara could imagine the rest.

"And after the war?" she said, wanting to drive the sudden desolation from his eyes.

"The sea, I suppose," he replied. "I'm a sailor by profession as well as by circumstance of war."

"With the navy?"

"Commercial shipping," he answered somewhat curtly, but his smile softened the words. "I would much rather talk about you." He was, he knew, slipping into dangerous territory. But then from Connor's attitude earlier, he knew he should be prepared for a much stronger interrogation this evening. One slip and he could well face a death penalty here as would his mother and younger brother in Germany. His hand unconsciously dug into the sand, and when he looked up again he saw a question in her eyes.

"A girl in every port?" she asked impishly, but with a hint of wistful seriousness in her voice.

"That's a slander," he replied lightly, some of the tension sliding from his body. "There's never enough time. I seldom left the ship when we docked."

"How did you come to my island?"

"Your island?"

Meara's grin flashed with humor and a little embarrassment. "I've always thought of it that way . . . my island of dreams."

Michael looked along the beach and toward the great trees hanging with moss. "I can understand why. It's very lovely. Anything seems possible here."

"At night, huge turtles come up and lay their eggs, and deer wander across the paths," she said. "And the moon paints the water with silver."

"Will you show me tonight? After dinner?" He hadn't intended to ask the question. He had what he wanted from her. He had what he must have. Anything else was reckless and dangerous and stupid. But his heart slowed as he waited anxiously for her reply, half hoping she would refuse.

"Yes," she said simply. He had never met a woman with so little guile, with so much openness.

And obviously one that could be so easily hurt, he told himself. He would, in some way, end this tomorrow. Tomorrow. But tonight, he would enjoy her company, relish the pleasure she created in him.

"I have one of those strange little cars. Would you like a ride back?"

Her eyes twinkled. "I don't think there's room for all of us," she said, "but I would like to see you in one."

"I feel like an overgrown child."

"Don't." She chuckled. "I have it on very good authority that the mightiest of the mighty have ridden them."

"Not the Goulds, or Joseph Pulitzer or the Rockefellers," he said in mock horror.

"Ah, you know our history then."

"Some. Not all. Perhaps you'll tell me more."

"Perhaps I will." She consented with a smile.

He stood reluctantly, awkwardly, with the help of his cane, his eyes never leaving hers, sketching in his mind that odd combination of intelligent curiosity, humor, and vulnerability. The latter was a strange quality for a journalist, but he suspected she could be very good. She had a way of drawing people out; she had done it very skillfully with him without ever appearing to do so.

Michael gave her a crooked half smile and waved to the children playing farther down the beach before turning toward the little red bug. His breath caught as he heard the children's laughter, and he tried to calm the sickness rising in him, even as he wondered at the new, even tender, feelings he was experiencing. He had shut himself off from them for a very long time, since the last violent argument with his father, and the blow that had sent him across the room while his mother had watched. He had run away and hired on the first ship he found, a Canadian freighter. The life of a common seaman was both hard and violent. He had become a violent and ruthless man in order to survive. He had thought nothing could ever really touch him again.

In the space of a few hours, he was discovering differently, that there was an opening, a vulnerable spot, in the protective shell he'd acquired long ago.

Duty, he reminded himself. Duty to country. Duty to the only family he had left, to a sick mother and a small brother whose lives he held in his hand.

Michael Fielding. Eric von Steimen. It was Eric von Stei-

men who had entered Admiral Canaris's office months
ago; Michael Fielding who left it.

He'd had a feeling of dread when he was singled out at
the military hospital and sent to specialists at an exclusive
Berlin hospital, and he knew even more disquiet when an
SS colonel and staff car picked him up when he was discharged. He'd immediately been suspicious of the fawning
pleasantries and concern, qualities he had rarely noticed
in that branch of the German military. He had disliked
the man. He had distrusted the attention. He had soon discovered his instincts had been disastrously correct.

"I'm a sailor, not a spy," he argued an hour later in Admiral Canaris's spacious office.

"You're much more than a sailor," Canaris had said.
"What is it . . . four, five languages you speak fluently?"

Eric had been silent, not wanting to confirm or deny
anything. He detested the current leadership of Germany,
yet it was his country and his duty to serve it. When war
had broken out between England and Germany, he'd returned to Germany, knowing he would be interned if he
stayed with the Canadian shipping line. His father was a
German staff officer. He knew he couldn't stand to be imprisoned in any way, and so, with mixed feelings and di-
vided loyalties, he had returned to the country of his birth.

He had joined the German Navy, hoping to avoid the
politics and fanaticism of some of the other services and
had been assigned as an officer on one of the destroyers.
The navy, more than any other service, allowed some limited independence of thought. He had steadily risen
through the ranks, drawing excellent reports from superior
officers, although he was suspiciously *quiet* in his *support*
of the Third Reich and the Führer. Still, he had a way of
instilling loyalty and bringing forth the very best in the
men he led, and fitness reports were invariably glowing.
Because captains did not want to lose him, they omitted

his often caustic references to the Nazi party and less than enthusiastic allegiance to Hitler.

"You have an opportunity to do a great service for your fatherland," Canaris said.

Eric forced his face to remain emotionless as the German admiral outlined his plan. Stifling his growing distaste and apprehension, Michael tried reason. Personal desires, he knew, would get him nowhere. "I've had no training in espionage," he demurred, "and my leg is still damned weak."

"We can give you all the training you need. Your injured leg is one of the qualifications for this particular job, that and your Canadian background. It's a perfect entrée onto the island . . . a wounded war hero."

"I know nothing of spying."

"All the reports on you emphasize quick thinking and ingenuity. Those are, my dear von Steimen, the two most essential ingredients of a spy. You also speak English flawlessly and have a knowledge of Canada. Your background and that of Michael Fielding match perfectly."

"Michael Fielding?" Eric queried.

"A prisoner we picked up from an English destroyer. He was from a well-to-do family in Canada, now all dead. Like you, he was with a Canadian shipping firm as an officer. Perhaps you've even met."

"Fielding?" Eric searched his memory. He knew the name, but he didn't ever remember meeting the man. "Where is he now."

"Dead of wounds."

"And his family is dead," Eric said wryly. "Convenient."

"Not really. We have been searching for the right prisoner and the right counterpart for months. Someone whose background could be checked thoroughly. No guest is allowed on Jekyll Island without investigation. This combination was particularly fortunate."

"I would prefer to return to the navy."

"*I* would prefer you would not." Canaris's voice was no longer pleasant. "Your father would have been most disappointed in your attitude, von Steimen."

Eric knew his face had tightened. "If you know so much about me, you would know that I never sought my father's approval."

Canaris turned keen ruthless eyes on him. "And your mother. She is Canadian, is she not?" The words held a slightly veiled threat.

"She is a German citizen. She chose to stay here with father when the war started."

"But your father is no longer alive, no longer able to protect her, and some might, well, question her loyalties."

The threat was no longer veiled, but open and ominous. Canaris looked at a file on his desk, and Eric knew it belonged to his family. "And your brother . . . how old is he now? Thirteen?"

Eric felt a cold chill run down his back. Heinrich had been conceived and born after he had left home, an unexpected arrival and never very strong. Eric had met him on visits to his mother, always when he knew his father was absent. The boy had been thin and sensitive, and Eric knew he probably went through the same hell he had as a boy. He had once warned his father about ever hurting Heinrich, and he had been strong enough and openly ruthless enough to be heeded. Dear God, he wished he had been able to get the two of them, his mother and brother, out of Germany, but his mother wouldn't leave her husband. When the older von Steimen was killed in France, Michael was at sea and it was too late.

"Your answer, Commander?"

Eric had nodded curtly. He'd had no choice.

It was Michael Fielding who left Germany weeks later in a submarine and landed in Canada.

A flock of birds flew up from the dunes in front of him, jerking him from his thoughts. He looked around toward the direction from which he had come. Meara O'Hara was watching him, her head tipped slightly as if she were analyzing something. Michael didn't smile this time as he moved on.

Dinner was every bit as exacting as Michael had thought it would be. He now fully understood the intensive training he had been required to take. He wondered, not for the first time, at the far reach of German intelligence. All his credentials could be verified: the shipping company with which the real Michael Fielding had been associated, the Chicago stockbroker who had been blackmailed into submitting Michael's name as a guest on the island, his distinguished family background. In addition, some secretary in British headquarters had changed the records of Michael Fielding to show a medical discharge rather than missing in action.

Michael had read dossiers on every member of the Jekyll Island Club and every likely guest who might be visiting during the Easter holidays, although their numbers had dwindled because of the war. There were other demands on their time.

Still, though many members had declined to spend the entire winter season here, some had decided to return for the few weeks around Easter. They knew this might be their last opportunity, since rumors abounded that the club would soon close for the duration of the war.

Connor, Michael knew, was among the shrewdest of the current membership of the Jekyll Island Club. Many were the sons and grandsons of the so-called robber barons, living off the fruits of their ancestors. But Connor was self-made, and had climbed elevated rungs of the economic and, eventually, social ladders despite his Irish ancestry. If Michael gained Connor's trust, he should pass muster with anyone else.

The inquisition started almost immediately over drinks and not very subtly.

"How does a Canadian come to our small island?"

Michael didn't have to fake amusement at the description. Jekyll Island might be small in terms of geographical size but certainly not in scope. He had seldom before seen such understated yet well-designed luxury in one location, and he had traveled the world.

The drinks were being served in the library with only Connor, his wife, Elizabeth, and himself present. Meara was no place to be seen, and again Michael felt a certain inexplicable loss.

He lifted his glass of very excellent Scotch. "To more small islands," he said wryly.

Cal Connor's expression relaxed slightly. "You like our little club, then?"

Michael chuckled. "Golf, skeet shooting, bowling, swimming, tennis, yachting, sailing. I don't think it's exactly what my doctor had in mind by restful."

"What doctor?"

"A surgeon at a military hospital in Canada where I was sent for some additional surgery. The hospitals in London were becoming too crowded."

"And your family? Did you not want to spend this time with them?"

Michael's eyes clouded. "There is no family. My mother and father died in an accident. There is no one else."

Probably nothing he could have said would have disarmed Cal Connor more, for Cal had grown up alone and now valued family above all else. But he wasn't quite ready to admit this stranger to his own family yet. He had seen Meara's face on the club cruiser as she had looked up at the Canadian, and Meara was dear to both him and Elizabeth, almost as dear as their own children.

"When do you expect to return to duty?"

"Another month, I hope."

The conversation was interrupted by a maid announcing dinner.

Connor lifted the remnants of his glass. "To a quick victory."

Michael followed suit. "To victory."

Catered by the clubhouse, the dinner was excellent. The menu included broiled oysters, fresh trout in an exquisite sauce, beef tenderloin, roasted potatoes, asparagus and tomatoes, and sherbet, each course accompanied by a different wine, and the meal followed by a superior port. Elizabeth had steered the conversation away from the war and had asked some questions of her own. She referred to Meara several times in very affectionate terms. Michael knew he was tactfully being put on notice.

He'd rehearsed all the answers. Many of them came easily. He'd visited Manitoba, the real Fielding's hometown, and he could speak of it without hesitation. He had roamed all over Canada one summer, trying to feel some kind of connection, a sense of belonging, but it had never come to him. He'd discovered in that unfulfilling journey that he was indeed German, that despite his father and the unhappy childhood memories he loved his own native land with a depth he had not expected.

So now he spoke easily of the multiple lakes and rivers and heavy forests of Manitoba with knowledge and even a touch of affection.

"It sounds beautiful." Elizabeth sighed.

"If you are part Eskimo," Michael said with a slight smile.

"It must be very different from this island."

"Yes. But they both have a wild beauty of their own."

"You must have seen many unusual places," Cal Connor interceded.

Michael grimaced. "I was first officer, which means I seldom left the ship. There are usually a hundred chores while in port. I'm afraid I did most of my sightseeing through books." He smiled a little self-consciously. Not only sightseeing but education, he thought privately. Unlike the real Michael Fielding, Eric von Steimen had finished his formal schooling at fourteen, although he'd had an excellent start in Latin and math and language at the private schools he'd attended before leaving home.

Elizabeth steered the conversation to activities on the island. "We usually eat dinner at the clubhouse," she said, "but Cal wasn't up to the formality tonight."

"Do you always come down for Easter?"

"The children and I usually come here before Thanksgiving and stay through Easter," she said, "and Cal would join us when he could. There's even a school here for the children. But Cal was so busy this fall, and then the Japanese bombed Pearl Harbor. I've been helping with war bonds and canteens for our soldiers. Very few of the other families have been here all season. It seems . . . somehow disloyal to enjoy ourselves when so many of our young men are dying." The words came wistfully, unexpectedly tugging painfully at Michael's conscience.

He had not expected to like those destined to become Germany's hostages. In all the briefings, he had been told these men, these members of the Jekyll Island Club, were ruthless, cold individuals who cared little about anything but making money and securing power. He had told himself they were not civilians but soldiers because of their participation in the war effort; they were even more dangerous to his fellow countrymen because they provided the guns and the airplanes and the ships. He had equated them, in his mind, with the memory of the powerful father he'd detested, making it easier for him to accept the role into which he'd been forced. But he liked Cal Connor with his blunt honesty and obvious affection for his family. He liked Elizabeth Connor with her soft manner and caring eyes. And Meara? At least she wouldn't be involved in his plans.

Or would she?

The strategy was to take only the men in a lightning swift attack launched from a submarine, to take them and hold them as prisoners of the Third Reich. The members of the Jekyll Island Club controlled nearly one-sixth of the world's wealth and were involved in nearly every aspect of the American war machine. The disappearance of even several of this group could cripple American production. The loss of these men, several of them advisers to President Roosevelt, would be incalculable. And the effect on American morale would be tremendous; the fact that Germany could stage a lightning raid on the coast would panic the entire east and west coasts of America.

"More wine?" Elizabeth asked, breaking into his thoughts, and he noticed the Connors were exchanging questioning looks.

"I'm sorry," he said, realizing that the smile had fled his face, and his inattention had been quite obvious.

"I'm the one who's sorry," Elizabeth Connor said. "I should never have mentioned . . ."

She faltered, and he realized that she felt she had erred in mentioning the dying, assuming perhaps that many of his friends had been lost. Once more, he felt pangs of conscience and regret streaking through him. God, how he hated this whole affair. He would give his soul, or what there was of one, to be back on a ship.

Connor broke in. "We're having a barbecue tomorrow. We'd be pleased if you could attend."

"A barbecue?"

Elizabeth laughed. "That was my reaction when I first started coming here. A distinctly southern tradition I think you'd enjoy. You can meet some of the other members and guests."

Michael knew he should feel a sense of triumph. But he didn't. Only a sickness in his gut. He'd been accepted. He'd accomplished in one night what Canaris and his people had expected would take him days, even weeks. He forced a smile. "Thank you, I would," he said, the sickness in him growing deeper.

The betrayal had begun.

Chapter Three

THE EVENING SKY glowed over the marshes. There was no other word for it. The moon had never seemed quite as large or as perfect, even when he was at sea. The stars had never appeared quite as profuse or bright.

The hour was late when Michael left the Connor cottage, and he did not expect Meara to be waiting. Reason hoped she was not.

Lost in thought, in a certain empty desolation, he didn't see her until he heard her soft voice call, "Michael." For a moment he stood still. Michael, not Eric. Remember that. She was calling someone who didn't exist.

But despite that warning voice, he felt pleasure and warmth run unexpectedly through him. He spun around, nearly dropping the cane, and saw her sitting in a swing under a tree, her face and body obscured by shadows.

As he approached, she looked young and infinitely vulnerable, and he wished he had never said anything earlier, had not asked her to meet him. She was lovely in the moonlight, just as she had been in sunlight. Her skin appeared translucent in the soft light filtering through the trees and flickering across her face as one foot nervously pushed the swing from side to side.

Michael wondered why he was so drawn to her. He had always chosen sophisticated women before, often jaded ones, who expected nothing more than a few hours of pampering and pleasure. Innocence had always troubled him, and he'd believed cynically that its presumed value had no relation to reality, especially for a man who had no intention of marrying. He preferred experience, not fumbling hesitancy and fear.

But as clear green eyes studied him with no little puzzlement of their own, he felt an uncertainty, an obsessive longing to be with her, to share in the obvious pleasure she took in everything, to know something of that exultant spirit that seemed to embrace everyone and everything.

He hadn't realized how lifeless his own existence had been until he'd seen her laughing with pure joy this morning. With just the joy of being alive.

Without will, without conscious thought, he held out his free hand, and she glided up from the swing and looped her fingers with his. The contact was jolting in its warmth. Jolting and yet oddly natural.

"You shouldn't be here with me," he said.

"I know," she replied.

"The Connors?"

"I'm full grown now," Meara said lightly, yet there was uncertainty in it too, as if she'd made a decision she wasn't quite sure was wise.

"Are you?" The question was wondering. "I feel an ancient with you."

She paused, holding him back as she looked up and studied his face. Her free hand went up and touched the barely visible lines around his eyes. "Methuselah," she said with gentle mockery.

"Perhaps not that bad," Michael responded, his mouth

turning upward at one side. "Not quite nine hundred and sixty-nine years."

She laughed. "Is that how old he was? I don't think I ever knew."

"Every bit," Michael confirmed solemnly.

"That's just a guess."

"No, I'm a receptacle for all sorts of strange and meaningless pieces of information like that," he said seriously, but with underlying self-mockery in his tone. "At one port, a man was selling an old set of encyclopedias for the price of a drink. There's a lot of empty hours at sea, and I went through each book, picking up the damnedest assortment of facts. Nothing useful, mind you, but I did discover how old Methuselah was."

They were walking again, down the road that led to the nearest beach. "And what else did you discover?"

"That lovely young ladies should not walk in the moonlight with strange men."

"Are you a strange man? I didn't think so when we met on the cruiser today. It was almost like . . . I had known you before, that I'd been—" She stopped, but he knew what she was about to say. The words hung in the air. *Like I'd been waiting for you.*

He knew the words, because he felt it too. From the moment he had seen her, he had felt it, that he had been waiting all his life for someone like her without quite knowing it. He was a fool for being here, for wallowing in something that was beyond his reach, that was bound to hurt her seriously if he let this . . . infatuation go any further. He didn't want that. God, he didn't want that. She was too full of joy, too completely alive, too untouched by the kind of violent life he'd lived.

His attention elsewhere, he stumbled slightly on a rock, and he felt the tightening of her fingers on his. He knew his limp was more pronounced, mainly because he had been on his leg so much today. She stopped suddenly. "Your leg—is it too far to the beach?"

Michael's hand tightened on hers. "Remember, I'm here for exercise."

"It's more than a mile," she protested.

"Ah, but nothing compared to watching huge turtles lay eggs, and the moon paint the water with silver," he said with an engaging chuckle as he repeated her words from the afternoon. They were said with a wistful amusement that seeped into Meara's being and settled cozily there. She had never felt so comfortable with anyone, so comfortable and yet so expectant.

When they reached the beach, however, there was a bonfire roaring ahead and the infectious sound of young voices. He saw a man stand and call Meara's name, but she shook her head and started to guide Michael away from the fire, but he hung back.

Michael looked at them and then at Meara. That's where she should be. Not with him. Dear God, not with him. What in the hell was he doing?

"Go to your friends," he said suddenly. "I'm more tired than I thought," he added, forcing his voice to a coolness he didn't feel. "I think I'll go back."

"I'll go with you," Meara said, wishing the bonfire would disappear.

"No," he said. "I don't want you to. It's early yet, and this is your first day here. See your friends." His hand withdrew from hers and he brought it up to touch her cheek, so smooth and perfect in the moonlight. "Please stay. For me. Or I'll feel that I've ruined your evening."

As his hand withdrew, Meara felt another kind of defection. The whimsy of several moments earlier was gone, and a stiff, cool stranger stood beside her.

"I shouldn't have brought you so far." There was self-accusation in her voice.

Her regret made him feel worse. "No need to worry. A little rest and I'll be as good as new. Why don't you join them over there?"

"But I don't—"

"Please," he said. It was almost an order the way he said it. He even recognized an odd hint of desperation in his own voice.

"All right," she replied, and he knew she wanted to please him. It was not knowledge he welcomed, and he knew his frown had deepened. He nodded.

But still she hesitated and for a second so did he, not wanting to leave her, reluctant to sever the rare bond that had so extraordinarily linked them since he first saw her.

"Good night," he said abruptly and turned around and left, his limp even more pronounced than it had been earlier.

It was a long walk back over the crushed-shell road, his footsteps and the strike of the cane resounding in the quiet night as the sound of the young people faded. He welcomed the pain in his leg, for it dulled the sensations that had been building in his body, deflected some of the terrible guilt he felt. He heard the muted sound of an animal rushing away from his approach, and he wished he could run, could escape. When he reached the clubhouse, sweat had beaded on his forehead from the pain in his leg and the bitter confusion in his mind.

He knew he had been a fool to press his endurance, but he had wanted those moments with Meara. He told himself that he'd believed the attraction would go away with familiarity, but it hadn't. Instead, her hand had fitted so well in his, and her piquant sense of humor delighted him. He had wanted to kiss her so badly, to fold her into his arms. Thank God for the bonfire.

Michael went directly upstairs. His room, which earlier had been so welcoming, seemed coldly empty. He opened the windows, feeling the clean ocean breeze, but he had never before felt quite as unclean. He tried to justify what he was doing as nothing more than an act of war, but it didn't work, not any more. In a matter of hours, everything had changed. He could not consider Meara, nor even Cal Connor, his enemy. He'd always hated duplicity and lies, and now he was wallowing in both, and tomorrow Hans Weimer would arrive.

He knew he could show no weakness to Weimer, nor the slightest interest in Meara, for the man would hesitate at nothing to accomplish their mission.

Michael poured himself a tumbler of the Scotch he had ordered earlier. From now on, he would keep his mind on his task, nothing more. Two weeks, and it would be over. Two weeks and he could return to sea duty. Two weeks, and he would change a number of lives.

He finished the whiskey. He placed the glass on the table, intending to pour himself another, but his abrupt, angry movement caused the glass to tip and fall, the glass shattering as it hit the floor. He swore softly to himself, then looked back out the window before pulling the curtain against the night and the moonlight and the thought of flickering flames down on the beach. He wondered whether Meara had a young man. And knew he was an even bigger fool for thinking about it.

Meara had watched him go with no little confusion. The warmth in his voice, in his presence, had left so abruptly it gave her a chill that had nothing to do with the night air.

She didn't understand anything about her reaction to him. She had never been so forward before, never so vulnerable to a man. But when she had taken the children back today, she was filled with an expectation and excitement that made rational thought impossible.

Perhaps it was only wartime, she told herself. She had seen the new, desperate urgency in the increasing number of quick marriages as men rushed off to enlist. Both weddings and love affairs had become more frequent as casualty lists mounted. There may not be a future, a tomorrow, so take what you can today, now. That was today's reality, today's new motto. Could her reaction be rooted in that fierce desire not to be cheated, not to miss anything?

Two weeks, and Michael Fielding would be gone, possibly forever, and it was excruciatingly important that she explore the feelings he excited in her, for they had never happened before. What if they never happened again?

Meara watched the flames shoot up in front of her, and her gaze measured those around the fire. This was the first night back on the island for many of them, a time to renew acquaintances and friendships. And they *were* friends. Among the young on the island, there were few class distinctions. The daughter of an Irish immigrant and maid, Meara had played tennis and picnicked with the sons and daughters of the wealthiest men in America. She had lunched with them and sneaked out late at night to hunt turtles. She had laughed and danced with them, but none had attracted her like the Canadian had. None had the exciting, dangerous reserve, none the fierce restlessness in eyes the color of the deep sea.

Brad, an assistant to one of the members who usually spent the season here, grinned happily at her. He'd been the one who called out to her. "I've missed you this season."

Meara smiled back. He often worked extremely long hours, yet he was always unflappable and pleasant. He had pursued her for two years, yet never obnoxiously so.

"I've missed the island," she said mischievously as his face fell slightly. "And you," she added.

"Tennis, tomorrow afternoon?"

"Mr. Connor is having a barbecue," she said, "and I have to look after the children."

"A walk then, tomorrow night?"

"I don't know, Brad," she said, wanting to avoid any commitment that might prevent her from seeing the Canadian again.

"I'll ask tomorrow, then," he said lightly, as the group burst into song. As they were about to break up, one of the young men, home from college, announced he was enlisting in the air force the next week, and that started discussion of the war. Three of their usual number had already enlisted in other services and would not be here.

"Dad says an FBI man is coming here," chimed in a younger boy, envious of the adventures ahead for his older companions.

Brad frowned. "Why?"

The boy shrugged. "Dad says there've been a number of U-boat sightings around here. He says the Nazis have spies every place."

"But here?" asked the future air force recruit dubiously. The island had always been a world unto its own. Peaceful. Safe. Secure.

"I think everyone's seeing spies in their bed," said another carelessly. "They've already rounded up every Japanese they could find."

There was a silence as the group watched the remnants of the fire die. The talk of war had destroyed the peace of the evening, the dreamlike atmosphere of the island. In twos and threes they drifted down the road to the cottages or the clubhouse. Meara and Brad were the last.

"Can I walk you back?"

She shook her head. "I just want to stay out here a few more minutes."

"Alone?"

She nodded, and he smiled in the moonlight. "I like it

too, sometimes," he acknowledged with quick understanding. "It's really peaceful at night. I'll see you tomorrow." His hands buried in pockets, he trudged back through the sand, and she thought again how nice he was, and yet she felt nothing but a mild affection. No fierce beating of the heart, no quivering of her legs, no bubbling excitement at his nearness. She had, until today, always believed those feelings only myth, alive in books alone.

Meara sat down in the sand and hugged her arms around her legs, gathering them against her body as she looked out over the moon-swept sea. It was so incredibly lovely and peaceful when thousands of miles away men were dying. Or maybe even a few miles away; she was only too aware of the wolf-pack U-boat attacks on American shipping along the whole eastern coast.

She wondered how it would feel to be fired on, to kill or be killed, how it would feel to have hot metal rip through her body. The long recovery must have been just as painful as the actual injury for Michael Fielding, whose leanly muscular body spoke of an active life, and whose restless impatience with his own current limitations was evident.

Meara touched the hand that so briefly had been held in his, and she imagined she could still feel its warmth. The warmth of a stranger. She smiled into the darkness. If a mere touch of his hand did this to her, what would be the impact of his lips? Heat curled around inside as she thought of it, and she wondered at these new sensations. A virgin, she had never gone beyond exploratory kisses, which always failed to live up to expectations. Somehow she knew his would.

Meara noticed a couple down the beach, their silhouettes coming together in the moonlight as one head lowered to meet the other. And she envied them. Envied them with all her heart.

*   *   *

Hans Weimer kept his face empty of expression as he sat on the boat carrying him to the island from the port city of Brunswick. He would return again tonight. Most of the day workers on the island lived in Brunswick, and he had engaged a small room in a boardinghouse.

He ignored the others on board. His pale blue eyes wandered listlessly with a certain blankness. Supposedly he was suffering from a form of battle fatigue acquired in the Pacific. It was a good cover, since he had merely to look blank at any difficult questions.

He had easily obtained a job as a gardener for the Jekyll Island Club because of the severe shortage of manpower. He had shown his medical discharge papers, a letter from his doctor, and references reputably from a prior position as gardener before the war. Nothing further had been required.

Fools, he thought. Gullible fools. There was a certain innocence about Americans that both repelled and fascinated him.

His hand moved convulsively over his lap as he had been instructed by a doctor in Berlin. The movement was a nervous reaction, he had been told, that would strengthen his role. He doubted whether it was necessary, but neither he nor his instructors believed in leaving anything to chance.

Von Steimen should already be in place. Von Steimen, Hans thought contemptuously. He didn't trust his partner for many reasons, and neither, he suspected, did his own superiors. Hans had sensed almost immediately he had been sent as much to watch von Steimen as to assist him. But von Steimen, it had been explained, was essential to the plan. Although Hans spoke English fluently and even with a midwest accent, he did not have von Steimen's aristocratic bearing, the ability to fit in easily among the powerful and wealthy, nor did he have—what was it Canaris had said—charm. But Hans hadn't minded overly much; he knew he had something much better. Power.

Hans bitterly resented what he considered von Steimen's privileged past, a background that had no place in today's Germany, and he had hated von Steimen for being part of it. The aristocracy had brought Germany to its knees twenty years earlier; its cowardice had produced defeat. Such a humiliation would never happen again. Hans, and people like him, had the power now. And they wouldn't relinquish a bit of that control to thin-blooded weaklings.

Hans knew the von Steimen name well enough. A wealthy Berlin family. Even though von Steimen's father had been a Nazi and a "hero" of the Third Reich, Hans still harbored deep dislike and suspicion for anyone of that class.

Just as vitriolically, he distrusted Eric von Steimen as he distrusted many of the military establishment. They had no loyalty to the führer, to the man who had brought glory back to Germany. The dossier on von Steimen was revealing in many ways. The naval officer had never joined the Nazi party and was known to make less than favorable remarks about the führer. Hans had been opposed to his selection for this mission, but he had been overruled by Canaris, who had known von Steimen's father and believed in the son's loyalty. They had gone over the files of thousands of men, Canaris had said, and none fit the peculiar requirements as well as von Steimen.

But to Hans, a member of the SS who had been borrowed for this mission because of his American background, von Steimen was one of the supercilious, disloyal military officers whom he detested. When they had been brought together in Canaris's office, Hans had seen the brief, contemptuous look von Steimen had given his black

SS uniform. In succeeding meetings, von Steimen had been both arrogant and condescending. Condescending!

A long time had passed since anyone had been condescending to him, not since he'd joined the SS and started his rise in the elite organization. His black uniform usually produced fear, not contempt, and his pale, icy eyes did nothing to alleviate that fear. But they'd had no impact on von Steimen, who sometimes looked at him with amusement, as if he were a small boy strutting in his father's clothes. The barely hidden derision had brought back memories of his childhood, when he had been sent to an aunt and uncle in America, relatives who hadn't wanted him and who had made his life a misery. He had returned to Germany at eighteen and joined the Brown Shirts because it was an outlet for his rage and ambition. When war broke out, Hans had joined the SS, reveling in the power he accumulated. He had a basic raw intelligence and ruthlessness that attracted attention, and he was made an officer, a position which brought him more accolades, particularly in ferreting out and punishing traitors and secret Jews. But when America joined the war, he was sent to Berlin because of his background; he spoke English like an American, a very valuable commodity in certain secret activities.

He had savored the opportunity, both because he hated Americans and because success would mean further advancement and, hopefully, the notice of the führer. He had proudly told his son, a member of Hitler Youth, that he had been hand-picked for one of the most important missions of the war, and he had taken deep satisfaction in his son's pride.

Only the selection of von Steimen as his partner had colored his enthusiasm. It would be good to teach the Americans a lesson. He looked forward to seeing the fear on their faces, the same kind of terror he had aroused in others who dared to challenge the Third Reich.

The sound of American voices on the boat brought back the taunts he had suffered as a boy. His father had died in the First World War, and his mother had starved to death. A neighbor had written his mother's sister in America, and he had been grudgingly taken in.

But while his aunt was German, his uncle was American and had fought in the war. Hatred for Germany ran high in America; many veterans were still suffering from the effects of poison gas, and in the intolerant, working-class neighborhood of Chicago, Hans had been called every name possible, the most mild being kraut, and he was beaten frequently by other children as well as by his uncle. He wore second-hand clothes and worked long hours in his uncle's small store. When he was seventeen, he started stealing money from his uncle, who had never paid him the first nickel in wages, and at eighteen, he had accumulated enough to return to Germany. He left one night, robbing the cash register of everything and taking whatever else he could convert into cash. Germany was his country, not America, and now he would enjoy being part of America's defeat. A very important part.

Hans would enjoy killing von Steimen if his . . . accomplice made one wrong move. Hans should have been given leadership of this mission, not von Steimen, who was technically in charge because of his military rank. But Hans took secret pleasure in knowing something the naval officer didn't know, hadn't been told. Canaris had warned Hans not to give the final orders to von Steimen until the night of the planned raid.

Hans wanted to grin as he thought of von Steimen's reaction. But he kept his face blank to the other workers, who somehow knew to stay away from the new gardener.

Instead, they chatted quietly among themselves as the boat approached the dock of the Jekyll Island Club.

Upon arriving on the island and finding his new employer, Hans listened carefully to instructions, nodding and answering in monosyllables. When this mission had been planned months ago, he had been given intensive instruction in gardening, especially those plants and flowers found in the southern United States.

"Yes," he mumbled when asked whether he could prune the thousands of Cherokee roses that graced the club property, along with the colorful jasmine and wisteria. When the supervisor left, Hans studied the clubhouse and cottages with contempt. Such waste. Such extravagance. His eyes found and gauged each of the residents: the nattily dressed men who seemed not to have a care in the world, and the pampered women whose gazes flickered over him carelessly as if he were beneath notice.

He would show them exactly how they misjudged him.

He hid a secret smile as he thought how completely their lives would change. Soon. Very, very soon.

Chapter Four

MICHAEL DIDN'T SLEEP at all that night. It was a problem he'd seldom had before.

At sea, he never knew how much sleep he might get, so he'd learned quickly to take what he could, to snatch a nap here, a few hours there.

But nothing worked now. He was so damned torn, as if he were in the middle of a tug of war, his heart pulled one way, his mind another. He had always followed his own instincts, but now they had deserted him. There was no guide here. None at all.

He'd always felt an obligation to his mother, a need to make up for some of the suffering she'd suffered at the hands of his father, and a responsibility to protect his younger brother. He had deserted them once, although he knew it had been necessary, for he'd no longer been able to contain his own rage. He would only have made things worse if he had stayed. Yet there was a guilt that wouldn't die, and he knew he couldn't desert them again.

There was also an ingrained loyalty to Germany, his homeland. *My country, right or wrong.* Where had he heard

61

that? But it was true. God, it was true. No matter how hard he tried to run from it.

Sleep continued to elude him. At dawn, he finally rose and walked to the window. The sun was coming up over Jekyll Creek, a rosy sheen backdropping the huge oak trees. Michael shaved and dressed in casual gray slacks, white shirt, and dark blue sweater. He wanted to explore the island before he met with Hans, locate a site for the radio, and determine the most feasible route for the submarine to approach. He had already arranged for a bicycle, a less conspicuous form of transportation on the island's winding paths and wide beaches than the red bug. It would also be good exercise for his leg.

Michael saw only a servant as he went down the steps. He could hear the kitchen staff preparing breakfast, but he saw no other guests up at this hour. He found the bicycle he had engaged, and tried it gingerly. It was the first time he had used one in years. Riding was precarious with his stiff leg, but after a few tries he was able to compensate for the injury.

The morning was beautiful. Moss hung in great silver shawls from giant oak trees, and the lavender of wisteria mixed with the wild white dogwoods glistening with morning dew. As he reached the beach, large graceful gulls were swooping over the water in search of their first meal of the day, and sandpipers were making fresh tracks on pristine sand.

Michael thought of the bombing in Berlin, the litter of death throughout much of Europe, and wondered if he were in a time warp. If so, he never wanted to leave it.

Unbidden and unwanted were thoughts of Meara. She would be rising now, perhaps even looking out over the salt marshes as he had earlier. He knew he had puzzled her last night, but it was better that way. Better to hurt a little now than a great deal later. Yet he kept seeing her as she was on the boat, her hair flying and her eyes dancing and her laugh dominating the wind. It had been so natural, so carefree, as if everything in the world was good and happy and just.

Much of the island was heavily wooded. The Jekyll Island Club had initially been mostly a hunting club for gentlemen until it became more family oriented with lawn bowling, tennis, golf and swimming. The wilderness hid bountiful wildlife, and the forest was very dense in some areas, its edges reaching almost to the water at high tide. Knurled roots of great oaks lay revealed in the sand; small palm plants obscured the ground. With the heavy undergrowth, it was a perfect place for an invasion, and he wondered at the lack of security of the island. There were only a few guards, all of whom looked as if they had never encountered anything more troublesome than a momentarily lost child.

God, how he hated what he had to do. The more he saw of the island the more he wished it could remain undisturbed, away from the harshness of war. He wondered at his own thoughts, for he couldn't remember when he had been sentimental or soft or undisciplined.

Michael followed the curve of the beach, grateful for the hard-packed sand which easily supported the bicycle. The beach, and the woods above it, was utterly undisturbed. Jekyll could have been a deserted, exotic island except where the club was located. He laid down the bicycle at the point where the beach swung around again toward the marshes, and he walked into the woods. The undergrowth was heavy and he could hear the frightened scattering of animals. He worked his way into a deep clump of trees and studied the area carefully. There were no visible paths, no sign of recent human intrusion.

He was to make radio contact with a sub at midnight the next evening, late enough that the sub could surface safely for a brief time. He would ask for a picnic basket tomorrow and bring the radio here in the basket, then return back to this spot late in the evening.

That decision reached, he made his way back out of the woods, picked up his bike and pedaled slowly back to the clubhouse. And Hans.

It was midmorning when he arrived back at the clubhouse grounds. He quickly found Hans leaning over a rose bush. Nothing, he thought, could be more incongruous as Hans and roses.

He had disliked the man when he met him, and nothing since had changed his opinion. Hans Weimer was everything Michael detested about the "new" Germany. Fanatical. Cruel. Strutting in his feared black uniform as if he were God. Michael had seen similar antipathy in Weimer's eyes. They had trained together for two months in wary silence. Unlike others in the American program, they had never shared a beer during their rare time off.

Michael had been forced into this mission, and he guessed that Hans was very aware of this fact, while Hans was obviously an enthusiastic and committed volunteer. Michael had killed, but it had been as one soldier in battle with another. He suspected Weimer killed for the pleasure of it.

But he had to admit, as he watched, that Hans looked nothing like the arrogant SS man Michael knew him to be. The man slumped slightly even when he straightened up from his chore, and his eyes were mild and blank. There was something of a glazed expression on his face, and his hands moved nervously. He was, Michael thought, a superb actor.

"Those are lovely roses," he stopped to say.

Hans shrugged, his eyes carefully wandering over Michael's expensive clothes.

"You'll have to tell me your secrets, someday."

Again, Hans shrugged.

"No trouble?" Michael said, his voice lowering.

"*Nein,*" Hans said, his voice only a harsh whisper. "And you?"

"None. I've been invited to a party this afternoon. Most of the members who are here for this season should be there."

"How many?" Hans asked tensely.

"As far as I can tell, fourteen who are on the list."

Hans grunted in disappointment. The list given them by German intelligence had included a hopeful twenty-five names.

"There's a war on," Michael said sardonically, and his reward was a baleful look.

"The radio?" Hans queried.

"In my room. I found a location for it this morning."

"I want to be with you when you transmit."

"Impossible," Michael said shortly.

"I'll work late and miss the boat."

"A new man? You want to provoke suspicions?"

"It's natural enough. Making a good impression."

"No," Michael said. "I won't take a chance of being seen with you at night. This meeting is dangerous enough."

Hans glared at him but quieted, and Michael read his every thought. The man could not argue now with Michael's decision. But Hans obviously didn't like it one bit. He lowered his head and stooped over again, his hand tightening on the sharp shears.

Michael smiled to himself. One minor victory. As if he had all the time in the world, he lazily remounted his bike and completed the ride to the clubhouse, his eyes ranging over the grounds. But he didn't see a slender woman with two active children. It was just as well.

He rested for several hours. The damnable leg. The bicycle had placed unfamiliar demands on it, and the damned thing hurt like hell. But he couldn't stop the restlessness of his mind. He had picked up several magazines, including a *Life*, downstairs, but he couldn't concentrate, not even on the war news.

Fourteen. Fourteen of the wealthiest and most influential industrialists, financiers, and businessmen in America were gathering here.

There were many more people on the island. Guests and members who were not on the list, their employees, and employees of the club itself. Michael's job was to arrange to have those targeted assembled in one location on the night of the raid. It meant he had to befriend as many of those people as possible and hold a small party on that night.

Cal Connor would be of immense help. Michael had believed acceptance, particularly in view of his fictitious though partially true background story, would be much more difficult than it was proving to be. But each guest had to undergo review before being admitted to the club premises, and apparently his credentials had more than passed approval; otherwise he would never be here tonight. Once accepted by the club leadership, a "stranger," as he was called on the guest register, was apparently accepted by everyone else as well.

Michael was quickly discovering that the Jekyll Island Club had a relaxed social air. Because of the decline in membership since the Great Depression, the club had been actively soliciting associate members. Possible future members were welcomed cordially, if not effusively.

Michael knew he had been chosen, in large part, because he could easily associate with this group in a manner Hans never could. His wound was another factor. Canaris had believed the injury would attract sympathy from Americans who had watched war from afar and who had only recently been plunged into the thick of things. Patriotism was running strong in the country.

Canaris, Michael admitted grudgingly, had been right in all his suppositions, but the realization did not improve his dark mood or the foreboding of disaster that permeated the air around him.

Reluctantly, he dressed for the Connors' party, choosing a pair of blue trousers, white shirt, and tie. He joined a stream of others who looked at him curiously as they walked to the DuBignon Cottage.

The grounds of the cottage were full of people and wonderful smells. Against the background of polite voices, a small orchestra played a combination of light classics and popular songs.

Cal Connor greeted him with an enthusiasm that surprised Michael, and he was quickly introduced to members as a wounded ally. He was readily accepted and peppered with questions about the war in Africa, and British losses to German U-boats.

Most of those present, Michael suspected, probably knew more about U-boat victories than he did. The U-boats were Germany's one great weapon at the moment now that Goering's air force had been decimated in the Battle of Britain. The toll on Allied shipping had been incalculable, although the total losses were kept from the American public. The subs were able to go anywhere with impunity, a fact which made possible Canaris's plan for Jekyll Island.

"And the Pacific?" Michael asked in return. "Is there any more news in the Pacific?"

One man shook his head regretfully. American and Filipino troops were currently stranded on the Bataan Peninsula, and the United States, along with Britain, Holland, and Australia, had just recently lost fourteen ships in the disastrous Battle of the Java Sea. Nothing had improved since then.

"MacArthur will get them out of Bataan, though," one man commented. "The Japanese will pay for Pearl Harbor, and soon."

The talk turned to Africa and the seesawing battle between Rommel and British troops. "When will the Americans send troops?" asked Michael.

Cal, who had joined them, shrugged. "The Pacific is the greatest concern now, that and getting ships through to England."

As if to remind them of the U-boat menace, a woman standing across the lawn with several other women, spoke loud enough for everyone to hear as she pointed upward. A blimp was laboriously plowing through the clear azure sky.

At Michael's inquisitive expression, Cal grinned. "Looking for subs," he explained.

"Are those things really useful?"

Cal's grin faded. "I don't know," and Michael knew it must be classified information. He watched as the blimp moved easterly, like a fat sea cow lazily sunning itself. The theory, he knew, was that the slowness and height of the blimp allowed searchers to see shadows lurking beneath the ocean surface. He wondered how far offshore was the German sub he was to contact tonight.

He was still distracted when Peter approached, a wide, happy grin on his face. Michael couldn't help but respond in kind.

Michael looked around for Meara and saw her in the swing where she'd been waiting for him last night, her gaze on Tara who was playing with several other children. As he looked, her face turned toward his, and he saw the vivid green that seemed to sparkle out to him with an impish, challenging invitation.

"The commander," Peter confided proudly to the men standing around, "helped us make the best sand castle ever."

One of the men, a stockbroker from New York who was not on Michael's list, chuckled. "A man of many talents, Commander?"

Michael smiled back. "And, as they say, master of none. Sand castles are a nice change from war."

"I don't doubt that," the man replied as a shrewd gaze raked Michael's lean body and easy confidence but hesitated slightly on the cane. "I imagine you're tired of war talk, especially from men who have never seen action."

Michael was not. He was picking up more information than he'd ever expected. One man had talked about the increased production of his steel company, another about a new navigational device his firm had developed. His mind quickly absorbed these pieces of information, part of him amazed at how quickly America was able to energize its war machinery, another knowing, as part of him always had, that once again Germany had taken on more than it could handle. He also realized how very important this mission was, regardless of how little he liked it.

The disappearance of these men could throw war production into chaos for months, if not years. There would be battles for control, holds on loans, and confusion.

He answered questions automatically, aware that Cal Connor had urged his son to go play and that Cal himself had moved away and was speaking to two other men who had just arrived. One did not seem to fit the common denominator of wealth and power. The newcomer was tall and compactly built and wore a less than tailored suit. But there was also an alertness about him as he appeared to study each guest, resting a moment on Michael, and it was an inspection that gave Michael pause. It was a policeman's gaze, one he had learned to recognize the world over.

He debated with himself whether to approach the men, finally surrendering to curiosity. Better to know a threat. He made excuses to his companions and moved toward Cal, pausing briefly to take a glass of champagne from the tray of a circulating waiter. The smell of cooking pork permeated the air, and laughter and talk were growing louder.

"Commander," Cal Connor called, and Michael tensed briefly before willing a smile to his face.

Michael nodded and threaded his way to Connor's side. "Two more guests I would like you to meet. John Graves and Sanders Evans. They're also staying in the clubhouse. Gentlemen, this is Commander Michael Fielding, British Navy."

"You're a long way from home, Commander," the taller man observed, his brown eyes inquisitive. There was a quiet air of friendliness, even gentleness, as the man glanced at Michael's favored leg. The unexpected softness jolted Michael far more than instant suspicion would. That friendliness, he sensed, was deceptive, a tool used easily and naturally but a tool, nonetheless.

"I'm Canadian," he answered with an equally friendly, equally deceptive smile.

"You're still a long way from home."

"A lot of people are now," Michael said dryly. "The warmth of your island is a strong lure after the Atlantic in winter."

"You were stationed in the Atlantic then?"

"Sub hunting," Michael confirmed.

"Any luck?"

"Two, before we became the hare."

"Going back?"

"I hope. I received a medical discharge, but I hope to convince them I'm well enough to sail again."

"I would like to hear about it."

Michael hesitated. There was something about Sanders

Evans that rang any number of bells, all of which warned him to stay away from the man.

"Not much to tell. A lot of waiting, searching, a lot of lonely hours, a lot of fear. Like any other soldier or sailor, I think." He decided to turn the tables. "And you, Mr. Evans?"

"I'm with the government," Evans said uninformatively. "John is with the Defense Department. We're just here for a few days of vacation."

Michael nodded, not believing a word of it. His eyes went to Graves. Not a policeman. Graves was older, a bit pudgy. His eyes were intelligent but not wary, not like Evans's vigilant ones.

"Perhaps we can have a drink later," Evans persisted.

Michael nodded. "Perhaps, but I think right now I have a previous engagement with young Mr. Connor." Michael's gaze went to Peter, who was beaming up at him.

Evans surrendered temporarily. "Until later, then," he said.

"Later," Michael agreed and, after several moments of conversation with Peter and a pledge to teach him how to shoot on the range later, he made his way over to Meara. Her eyes brightened even more, and despite the disquiet that had just filled him, he knew a certain exultant pleasure just to be near her, to be recipient of both the smile on her lips and the one in her eyes. She moved over in the swing, inviting him to join her, and he did, folding his lean body in the swing with a sigh that hovered between an odd excitement of being next to her and relief at having a reason to leave Sanders Evans, of dropping, if only for a moment, from the tightrope he was walking.

He leaned his back against the corner of the swing which seated two and looked at her with an obvious enjoyment that brought a flush to her cheek. She was wearing a rose-checked sundress, one that hugged her gentle curves. The color complemented the green eyes and barely tamed red hair tied back in a green ribbon.

Meara O'Hara, Michael thought, was not beautiful in the traditional sense. Her features were too determined, the chin jutting proudly out, the high cheekbones emphasizing startlingly intelligent and vivid emerald eyes, and a mouth too wide for true beauty. Yet when she smiled, there was a magic about her, a warmth that reached out and enfolded everyone in its path, an uninhibited appreciation of life that was new to him, new and incredibly appealing.

Too appealing.

Particularly appealing when she demanded nothing of him now, no words, only his presence. He thought it odd that he could feel so comforted, so suddenly right, in silence. He lifted his hand to rake his hair in a persistent habit he couldn't break, and his hand touched her shoulder. There was an instantaneous reaction, and it obviously affected her as well as him. He felt heat start at the point where his skin touched hers and then flood through the rest of his body. The quick, involuntary shudder of her body said more eloquently than words that she felt it too, felt it and was startled, perhaps even frightened, by it.

He was discovering emotions he had never felt before. Desire, certainly, but something much stronger, much deeper. A need to touch, to hold, to share. Overwhelming needs that were painful in their intensity. He tried to shake them and looked up and around, and found Evans's gaze on him, or was it on Meara? For the first time in his life, jealousy struck him, and he was amazed at the virulence of the reaction.

"Can you go for a walk?"

Meara, as if lost in her own emotions, simply nodded. "I have to tell Mrs. Connor first."

Michael nodded and watched as she rose gracefully and sought out Elizabeth Connor, speaking briefly as Elizabeth flashed a knowing smile and nodded. He rose slowly, grabbing his cane as much out of tension as for support.

Meara rejoined him, her own hands clenched behind her, and her eyes nakedly open and happy. God, what did he think he was doing?

They walked silently down to Jekyll Creek, which ran in front of the clubhouse, and along its banks. Across the deep creek were miles of salt marshes, peaceful and serene. The path was deserted since most of the current residents at Jekyll were attending the Connor party. Meara and Michael could still hear the small string band playing popular tunes, including "Don't Sit under the Apple Tree (with Anyone Else but Me)," and Glenn Miller's "Little Brown Jug." The softly poignant sounds mixed with that of the gentle laughter of waves as they chased each other up against the creek bank, each curling around in its special way and lazily returning to where they belonged.

When they reached a place on the bank where trees shielded them from other eyes, Meara stopped and ordered him to turn away from her. A little confused, he did so, and when she spoke again he turned back. She was holding shoes and stockings in her hand, and her feet were once more bare and burrowing happily in the grass.

Feeling a little like a boy on his first picnic, he promptly sat down on a log and took off his own shoes and socks as she stood above him, smiling approvingly. She leaned down, offering a hand, and it looked terribly inviting. He took it but was careful not to give any weight to her. Instead he balanced himself on his good leg, reaching down with his left hand for the cane. He suddenly lost balance and she went down with him, her body falling alongside his in unanticipated and unplanned intimacy.

Electricity ran between them, sparking and sizzling in ways that baffled and confounded both of them. There was only action and reaction, a hardening on his part, a softening on hers that melded together in complete compatibility.

His arms went around her waist and hers around his neck, her hands playing with the thick gold hair, and her body arching uncontrollably against his as their lips touched, first in surprised exploration, then a wondering gentleness that sent them both tumbling into a world without limits or restrictions or barriers. It was theirs for the moment, only theirs, and neither had the will to question it.

Michael found himself doing something he had never done before with a woman, moving his lips lightly across her face, wanting to taste the essence of her, the sweetness that was both nurturing and stimulating. He felt her body tremble and knew it was not from experience but instinct, for there was a shyness there too, a kind of awakening.

Then he felt her lips, doing exactly what his had, touching lightly along his face, and he felt a tenderness he didn't know he had. A tenderness and a fierce desire to protect.

To protect!

He forced himself to move back, his hand entwining in hair that felt like silk, copper-colored silk that had come free of its ribbon and fell over the side of her face in lovely profusion. Her eyes were misty green but not with tears. They were like stars, glinting like flecks of sun caught in an emerald sea.

"Christ," he uttered. It was the mildest oath he could summon at the moment. Her dress was covered with grass particles and fragrant pine needles, her hair curling in the humid air, her lips swollen with the taste of his, and her face flushed with emotion. He moved even farther back, forcing his hand from her hair.

"Do you have any idea of how altogether irresistible you look?" he asked, his voice hoarse.

Her face clearly reflected confusion, a certain wonderment, but then she looked at her grass-stained clothes and bare feet. "You're teasing me now," she said, a note of pain creeping into her voice as she wondered why he was once more distancing himself from her. Although neither his voice nor words showed it, his eyes did. The warm intimacy was gone.

"No," he said solemnly. "I think you're quite the loveliest girl I've ever seen, and you don't know how difficult it is not to kiss you over and over again."

"Then why—?"

"I don't want to hurt you, Meara. I'll be leaving in less than two weeks, and this will be a long, painful war. It's quite possible I'll be killed."

"No," she said, as if voicing the denial made it fact.

"Yes, Meara," he insisted. His hand took hers as her chin jutted out obstinately, and his heart hurt. He had never wanted anything as much in his life as to take her someplace, someplace private, and make love to her, slowly and exquisitely. He could feel the passion in her, passion created by those other qualities in her: her lust for living, her obvious commitment to those she cared about, the sense of giving he always felt around her. He wanted her so much it caused physical pain, gut-wrenching agony.

"I don't know what's happening to me," she said, and the voice was so soft, so puzzled, he had to smile.

"Surely you've kissed men before," he said, his voice tenderly amused.

"Never like that," she said with such awe that he had to smile. His hand helped her straighten up until they were both sitting quite respectably although their hands touched.

"I'm honored," he said formally with a teasing note.

"Don't," she said, sensing that he was about to draw back again.

"Don't what?"

"Go away like you did last night." She hesitated a moment before slowly continuing. "I don't mean when you actually, physically left, but moments earlier when you retreated somewhere inside yourself, someplace you closed to me."

She was incredibly instinctive, Michael thought. Even more than he had thought. She was such a mixture of naïveté and wisdom. It was a miracle she hadn't seen more, but then over the years he had become a chameleon, uniquely able to fit into any situation or any place, be it the roughest Hong Kong bar or a millionaire's club. It was a questionable ability at best, and it had dragged him into this goddamned situation.

"I won't," he said, "but neither do I wish to ruin your reputation or your place with the Connors. He warned me very diplomatically last night that you're very important to them."

"They're very important to me," she said, confused at his change of subject yet unwilling to do anything that might make him leave. She wanted very much to know more about Michael Fielding, more about the way he made her feel, more about the happiness that danced inside her heart merely because she was with him.

"Why?" he said.

"They paid for my education," she explained, and she smiled at his obvious surprise. "They hired my mother just after my father died. They've really been foster parents in a way, and when I did well in high school they offered to send me to Columbia. Sometimes I feel I'm almost a sister to Peter and Tara."

"And a friend," he said softly, remembering Peter's introduction.

"Oh, yes, that too. The Connors have been bringing me here since I was sixteen to look after Tara and Peter. They know I love it as much as they do." There was wistfulness in her voice. "Every time I come it's like a renewal, a re-birth, of something . . . elemental inside me."

"And in a few weeks you will return to New York and become a journalist. . . ."

"But I'll come back here. Always."

His hand curled around hers at the emphasis of the last word. She would too. He had little doubt that she would do anything she set her heart on. And hopefully she would forget him, forget what would, must, happen in twelve more days.

It was almost as if she read his thoughts. "We're so far from the war here . . . every trouble seems washed away by the rhythm of the water, as if—"

"As if what?" he prompted gently.

"As if evil can never touch here."

Evil has a way of reaching everywhere, he wanted to warn her. And what was evil? They were enemies, he and she, by mere accident of birth, and that was the way of most wars. The people who fought them rarely had anything to do with their inception, and they seldom fought for ideals or principles but for loyalty to the place of their birth. There was evil in his country; he had seen it, but most of the fighting was waged by people like him, people caught in events, in a certain place and time, and there was no escaping it.

"You're doing it again," Meara accused.

"I'm sorry," he said with a small twist of his lips.

"What were you thinking about?"

"How lovely both you and this island are. You fit together."

"And you? Where do you fit?"

His eyes suddenly clouded. "Nowhere, Meara. I don't think I really fit anywhere." With that enigmatic reply, he stood carefully and, using the cane for support, offered his hand to her.

"Everybody fits someplace."

"Ah, perhaps I just haven't found it."

But even as he said the words, he had the terrible, empty feeling that now he would never find it. Not now. He released her hand and buried that fist in his pocket.

Meara, fearing she had said something wrong, that she had made him remember something he did not wish to recall, tied her hair back again with the ribbon and brushed the sand from her dress. But she couldn't brush the feel of his lips from her mind. She stopped at the same log he had used to take off his shoes, and she replaced her stockings and shoes while he again looked away across the salt marshes in that distant way he had.

She wanted to touch him. More than anything in the world she wanted that, but his whole bearing warned her away. When she was through and moved next to him, his face was carefully controlled. When he looked at her, there was no hint of the softness he had shown earlier. He was again the warrior from across a continent. A stranger who seemed intent on remaining that way.

Meara determined in that moment to pull down those barriers. And she would. He just didn't know it yet.

Chapter Five

Meara was in agony for the next two days. Her stomach was queasy, her mind muddled. Everything she had come to expect from herself—common sense, reliability, practicality—had suddenly cracked apart, and all she could think about was the tall Canadian whose smile made her heart melt and whose reserve made it break.

How could anyone, any man, affect her after so few days, so few hours together? But any such reminder of the foolishness of her feelings did nothing to improve an appetite that had failed or give strength to the trembling occasioned merely by the sight of him.

For she did see him. And frequently, although she sensed he was going out of his way to avoid seeing her alone despite a heated intensity that flared in his eyes when they rested on her. She watched him talk to numerous members of the club, to their wives, to the club employees. He seemed to have an insatiable curiosity about everything and a charisma, a reserved charm, that attracted people to him.

Peter was completely captivated, especially after Michael

gave him a lesson in skeet shooting, and the Canadian was the main topic of conversation among all the marriageable girls, both staff and members' daughters alike, on the island. Yet he seemed to pay them no attention other than grave courtesy.

Meara had several free hours every afternoon, time set aside for the Connors to spend with their children, usually at the pool or on horseback, which the children adored.

Michael Fielding had made no further attempt to see her, much less be alone with her. She finally accepted a tennis game with Brad, who also sometimes had the afternoons off. Perhaps, she hoped, the activity would take her mind off Michael.

The club had both inside and outside courts, but the day was lovely and Brad's employer had reserved one of the outside ones. When she arrived, there was another couple waiting: Kay, the daughter of Brad's employer, and a man she had seen at the Connors' barbecue but whom she had not met.

Introductions were quickly made, and Meara instantly liked the newcomer, Sanders Evans. He had quiet, watchful eyes but also an endearing, even shy smile. It seemed out of place on an otherwise rough-hewn face that indicated strength and determination, and even a hint of tragedy. He was not a handsome man, not like Michael. Yet he had a very nice face. He was, Meara perceived immediately, the kind of person you would seek if ever in trouble.

"I saw you the other day at the Connors," he said with a smile.

She nodded. "How do you like the island?"

"Very much," he said.

"Vacationing?"

"Partly."

"And the other part?"

But they were interrupted by Kay. "If you don't mind, Meara, we thought it might be nice to play doubles."

"I'm not very good," Sanders said apologetically.

"Good," Meara said. "Neither am I, but these two are very good. You should balance us well."

He did. Sanders played with Kay, and Meara with Brad. Although Meara was quick and had good instincts, she'd never had much time to play and she often lobbed her balls outside the lines. Sanders often committed the same error, and both of them laughed at their own mistakes while Kay and Brad dueled together. The score went back and forth until finally Meara aced her serve, and she and Brad triumphantly called themselves winners.

Afterward, they ordered drinks and sat outside and talked about the game. Or Kay and Brad talked about the game. Sanders Evans, half listening, looked at Meara with interest. But Meara couldn't concentrate on him or the conversation. She gazed constantly around the grounds of the clubhouse for a tall blond-haired man with a limp.

Kay was talking. "Meara's going to work for *Life* magazine in a few weeks, and I hope to get a job in Washington when I finish school this summer."

Sanders looked over at Meara. "You're a journalist, then?"

"A very beginning one," she said lightly, a bit embarrassed. She was proud of her job, but it was only an assistant's position.

"Still," he said with admiration in his eyes, "they take only the best."

"The war made it possible," she said. "Otherwise, I'd probably never have had a chance."

They all knew what she meant. Jobs mostly reserved for males were now opening to women with so many of the country's young men enlisting or being netted by the draft. The war was already changing the society in which they lived. Meara knew it would change even more in the future. There was already a freedom today that never would have been possible a year ago. Quickie romances. Quickie marriages. There was a desperation in the air now, particularly around those men being sent to the Pacific, and those in the navy who braved the now deadly Atlantic and Pacific waters. Even she was caught in it.

The four of them were quiet, each locked in thoughts of their own. Meara knew Kay had recently lost a close friend, a pilot on an aircraft carrier in the Pacific. Brad was debating whether to join one of the services, even though his current job was considered critical to the war effort and he was exempt from the draft.

Meara glanced over at the newcomer, Sanders Evans. His eyes were dark brown and expressive, his hair a dark pecan shade and cut neatly. His clothes were suitable but did not have the elegance of the usual guests at the club. He was tall and looked remarkably fit, his body solid without any trace of excess weight.

He smiled under her examination. "You're wondering what I do?" he said.

"A little," she said, half embarrassed by her open scrutiny but more than a little curious.

"I coordinate certain activities in the government," he answered with an appealing smile that was more than a little self-effacing. He was saying nothing, less than nothing, but he did it with such aplomb that she had to smile. Someone at the bonfire the other night had said an FBI agent was coming. She was suddenly sure it was Sanders Evans. He didn't really fit any other picture.

But he didn't fit that one either, she thought. She had always thought of FBI agents with stern faces and hard eyes, and he had neither of those. Her thoughts went immediately to Michael, who radiated danger and even a certain recklessness. Somehow, she could envision Michael with a gun much more readily than she could Sanders Evans.

As if her very thoughts had summoned Michael Fielding, she saw him approach. He was wearing blue again, a color that made his eyes even bluer than usual, and his blond hair richer against skin which was rapidly tanning. Meara knew her body was stiffening against the onslaught of the wildly turbulent emotions he always created in her. He stopped at the chair where Brad was sitting and nodded to her.

"Have you met everyone?" she asked, inwardly scolding herself for the breathless quality she knew was in her voice.

"I think so," he said. "Kay, isn't it?" he said, turning first to the girl, and Meara felt her heart contract slightly at the immediate flush on Kay's face as she nodded. Michael then turned to the two men. "I've played billiards with Brad, and . . . Mr. Evans and I met two days ago."

"It's Sanders," Evans broke in.

"Sanders," Michael agreed.

"Won't you join us, Commander," Sanders said, and Meara wondered at the slight edge to his voice. There was a similar tone in Michael's. She wondered why.

But the thought didn't stay long in her mind, not when Michael turned his eyes on hers, and the blue seemed to swallow her up in them.

"Did you win?" he queried, eying the tennis rackets and her tennis dress that showed, even as she sat, long shapely legs.

"Barely, thanks to Brad."

"Do you play?" Kay asked tactlessly, forgetting about his leg and the cane he had leaned casually against the table.

"When I was a boy, long ago," he replied diplomatically.

"You said you were Canadian. What part?" Sanders asked.

"Manitoba," Michael said easily.

"A bit cold for tennis."

"Not at all," Michael said. "Especially in the summers. It can be quite pleasant. Where are you from?"

"Washington now. I grew up in Pennsylvania."

"Washington's a busy town now, I hear."

"Not quite as busy as London. Have you been there much?"

"Only hospitals, I'm afraid. My ship was based in Portsmouth."

"It must be terrible to have strangers firing at you," Kay observed tightly, and Meara knew she was thinking of the friend who had died.

Michael looked at her carefully, and his voice was sympathetic when he said simply, "Yes, but like anything else you get used to it."

"I don't think I ever could," Kay responded, her hands trembling slightly on the glass she held.

Michael's voice softened. "Have you lost someone?"

"In the Pacific," Kay replied softly.

"I'm sorry."

Meara heard the regret in Michael's voice, and she liked him even more than she had before. Kay's question had been invasive, something he had seemed to shy away from earlier. Yet his reply had been kind. Liked? Dear Lord, it was more than that. She wanted to lean over and touch the strong hand that rested on the table. She wanted his eyes to possess her as they had two days ago on the swing. She wanted the touch of his lips again, and this time she knew she didn't want to stop there. She took a quick swallow of lemonade, her hands clutching the glass in something akin to desperation. She didn't want him to notice, to see the need she knew must be shining in her eyes. She looked down at her watch.

She rose and forced the words. "I have to go."

The three men all rose with her. "I'll walk you over," Brad offered.

She smiled her thanks but shook her head. "You stay here and finish your drinks. And thanks for the tennis."

"Tomorrow?"

She looked quickly at Michael, whose face was inscrutable although his lips tightened. He didn't want her to. She knew it. Yet he said nothing.

"Yes," she agreed.

Brad turned to Sanders and Kay. "Will you play again tomorrow?"

Kay nodded eagerly, although Sanders hesitated, his gaze moving from Michael to Meara with curiosity. "I don't know," he said. "Can I let you know tomorrow?"

"Please do," Meara said suddenly, and immediately questioned her motives. She had never played flirting games before, but an aching part of her wanted to show Michael Fielding that she didn't care that he had virtually ignored her for the past few days.

"It's an invitation hard to refuse," Sanders said.

"Then don't."

"I'll do my best."

Meara, suddenly, inexplicably formal, turned to Michael. "Good afternoon, Commander."

He nodded, his dark blue eyes even more enigmatic than usual. "Miss O'Hara," he said in the same formal tone, but their gazes held, both challenging, and the electricity darted between them with such force that it was obvious to everyone at the table.

He made no move to accompany her, and filled with both confusion and bitter disappointment, Meara made herself move away from the table without looking back. It was almost time for the children's dinner, and then they would listen to "The Shadow" on the radio. It was Peter's favorite program, and because he liked it, Tara also clamored to listen although Meara didn't think the youngest Connor entirely understood the show. Tara's interests ran more to dolls and princes.

The Connors ordered dinner for Meara and the children, and then went to the clubhouse for the evening. Once Tara and Peter were settled in front of the radio in the study, Meara found a book and curled up on a sofa. But her glances kept darting back toward the windows, toward the path to the clubhouse and the moon she couldn't see except in her mind, and there it loomed brighter than ever, inviting and seductive.

Uncustomarily restless, she read Tara a story while Peter read a book of his own, and then she tucked them in bed and went out on the porch. She was alone. There was only one servant who had accompanied them, a maid, and she had already retired to the servants' quarters on the top floor. Meara's room was next to the children's; a spacious, comfortable room, it seemed more like a jail cell tonight. Meara wandered out to the swing and watched the sky. A few wispy clouds skittered across a partial moon, sending shadows darting along the ground in their own game of hide and seek. She heard the distant hoot of an owl, and the sound of other night creatures—the croaking of frogs and hum of nocturnal insects. An occasional firefly added its brief glow to the lamps that lit the clubhouse and cottages.

For the first time in years, she felt lonely, unsure of what she wanted. She had been so positive about her life since the year she was eight and wrote her first story. She had wanted to be a writer. She had wanted to be independent. But now the excitement of a career, while still strong and bright, was suddenly not enough.

Through the trees, she saw the lights of the clubhouse and listened to the faint strains of band music. She wondered if Michael Fielding was there with Kay or some other woman, or why, after that kiss on the beach, he had virtually ignored her. Was the caress that disappointing? Was she so inexperienced that he sought excitement someplace else?

Meara had never thought herself pretty. Her hair was too bright, too, well, wild, and her chin too determined. Her eyes were her best feature, but they didn't make up for the rest, not like Kay with her soft blond beauty. She had never really cared so very much before. She liked being a friend to the boys she met. She liked competing with them with her pen and brain. She liked doing what they did, playing baseball and tennis and running. She had never liked dolls as other girls did, nor had she wanted to play house. She wanted to play cowboys and gangsters.

Until now.

She heard the sound of footfalls, and she looked up to see the Connors, hand in hand, walking toward her. They were unlike many of the other couples who came here, who rarely spoke to each other. They genuinely cared about each other, so much so that Elizabeth had given up the regular November-to-Easter season because Cal was so busy and couldn't come as often as he did in past years. Instead, she had involved herself in charitable activities on Long Island and in Washington where Cal now spent so much time.

"Meara." Elizabeth's voice sounded light and happy. "Why don't you go over and join the young people?"

"I might go for a walk," Meara replied.

"Good," Elizabeth said. "We'll see you in the morning then."

Meara stood. She wished she knew what she wanted to do. She didn't want to go by the clubhouse. She did not want Michael to believe she was pursuing him. But she didn't want to go to bed either, and she didn't want to read.

Holy Mother, but the world had turned upside down.

Halfheartedly, she swung for a while longer while debating what to do. She finally shook her lethargy and took the road down to the beach. Perhaps a long walk would help her sleep tonight.

Michael had spent a miserable evening. Every self-appointed matchmaker at the club had introduced him to a woman. Sanders Evans kept his eyes on him with a curious intensity. Christ, but he wanted to be with Meara.

He was quietly pleased he had an excuse not to dance. He had been spied alone at a table by the Connors and invited to join them. The Connors' table was frequently visited by other members of the club who swapped news of friends and of the war, and speculated who else might arrive for the Easter holidays.

As the hour grew later, his interest waned. He had to leave by eleven. The sub was expecting his transmission at midnight. He had already carefully plotted the coordinates for the U-boat's arrival at Jekyll. His carefully phrased questions had revealed that the only possible approach was through Jekyll Sound, and even that was dangerous given the tides and shallow waters in this area.

Michael hated each step of the deception. He hated what he was doing. He hated it more each day as he met, and usually liked, most of his anticipated targets, particularly Cal Connor. He had to think of them as targets, objectives, not people or victims. He comforted himself with the fact that they would only be interned, probably in fairly comfortable surroundings. If all went well, there should be no casualties, not according to the elaborately drawn plans.

But deep in his gut, he knew Hans did not have similar scruples. He also knew that the best laid plans often went awry.

When the Connors finally left for their cottage, Michael

went up to his room, anxious to rid himself of the tuxedo which was required dress. He very quickly replaced the formal clothes with a pair of slacks and a sweater, and made his way down the hall to the stairs, taking a quick look to find them empty before descending. He cursed his limp briefly. It slowed him, and he still hadn't quite adjusted to the slower pace. The doctors said it was a matter of time, but he often chafed at the slowness. The leg did seem much better than it had been a month or two ago, and he actually needed the cane less and less, usually when he had overly strained it.

The bicycle was where he left it, and once more he looked around before mounting it. The clubhouse fairly blazed with lights, and he was grateful that there was a chill in the air this evening. It had kept most people inside.

He didn't see anyone as he pedaled down the road to the beach. The dark water of the creek and the darker shades of the marshes beyond reflected silver from the moon. There was just enough light to see the white crushed-shell path he was taking, and he moved steadily down to the crossroad that ran along the water. He finally veered off onto the beach itself, stopped and left the bicycle. The high tide was in, rushing over the hard packed sand that usually supported wheeled vehicles. He moved along the sand dunes, stopping occasionally to glance out at the water, and then turning his head back, scanning every part of the beach and dunes for any movement.

Satisfied, he continued on, glancing occasionally at his illuminated watch. The moon slipped entirely behind the clouds. He was close now to where he had hidden the radio.

Michael had secreted the wireless yesterday, carrying it from the clubhouse in a wicker picnic basket he had ordered and then emptied in his room, replacing the food with the radio. He had once more driven the little red bug, finally locating a lonely, protected site along the south beach where he had covered the radio with loose dirt and leaves. He had not wanted to risk transmitting from the clubhouse.

Michael had spent the remainder of yesterday doing what he had been told to do: charm. He had played bowls with one group, billiards with several men who were there without wives. He also went swimming in the pool, working on endurance, on strength until he could barely move. The water was cold, but then he was used to the cold waters of Europe and Canada. He went an entire day fighting his attraction to Meara, denying the need to see her. He'd felt lonely but triumphant until this afternoon when he returned from skeet shooting just in time to see Meara and the others playing on the tennis court.

He'd stood there and watched. She'd been fast and graceful, and he secretly applauded her final volley. He remembered it now, seeing her stand victorious in the short white dress. She'd hugged Brad with enthusiasm, and Michael felt that increasingly familiar spasm of jealousy that was so surprising. But that brief jolt had been nothing compared to the swift anger that flooded him when he saw Sanders Evans at the table with her, his gaze seldom moving from Meara's face.

Michael cursed himself for thinking of the woman when he should be thinking only of the radio transmission. He hoped to hell that there were no tracking stations to pick it up. It still amazed him, this lack of security on the Americans' part, the confidence that their shores wouldn't, couldn't, be invaded. Yet if some ship in the vicinity happened to find this particular frequency, he could be in very deep water himself.

He had no illusions about his fate if discovered. Spies were executed. He wasn't quite sure whether America hung or shot spies, but neither prospect appealed to him.

The fact that kidnapping was involved would do nothing to mitigate his fate. He cursed again, this time including Canaris and everyone else connected with his selection for this particular mission. When he returned to Germany, he would find some way to get his mother and brother out of the country and Canaris would lose his hold. Hold? Goddamnit! His weapon.

Finally reaching the hiding place in the woods, he extracted the small flashlight he carried in a pocket and quickly uncovered the radio, his hands working quickly and mechanically.

He glanced at his watch. Five minutes before the scheduled transmission.

Michael sat, listening carefully for any sounds other than those normal for the forest and surf, but there were none; only his own harsh breathing sounded alien. Exactly at midnight, his fingers moved rapidly over the keys. Receiving immediate response, he sent the coordinates for the submarine to approach the island and confirmed through code words that all was going according to plan. Within three minutes he was through, and in another two had camouflaged the radio to his satisfaction.

Michael looked at his watch. He had enough time to return before the evening was over at the clubhouse. It was Friday night, and he'd been told dancing extended into the morning.

Michael emerged from the woods onto the beach and walked toward where he'd hidden the bicycle.

Meara had started down the beach. She didn't know how long she'd been walking, but she could no longer hear the music from the open windows of the clubhouse, the often bittersweet romantic songs that had now assumed new significance.

The beach hid secrets tonight, she thought, as lace

clouds continued to turn the moonlight on and off like some faulty light switch. Light gray foam rode atop waves washing up on the beach, leaving a jagged trail of silver in their wake. The air was cool, but she wore a sweater and she enjoyed the crisp feel of the breeze sweeping off the sea. It made her feel alive, alive and tingly and again curiously full of anticipation. As if something was going to happen. She knew she should go back; it was getting late, but there was no fear on this island. Everyone here had been well-screened. Violence was something that never happened. Still, she knew she couldn't sleep this night. So she trudged on, as if guided by some invisible force.

Suddenly, the form appeared, seemingly out of nowhere, appearing as one of the clouds released the moon. Meara immediately knew who it was by the determined set of the shoulders and the limp Michael Fielding never allowed to hold him back. She saw the cane, but he was using it sparingly, determined, she assumed, to strengthen the leg as much as possible. She had seen pain etched in his face several times toward the end of a day.

She stood there, silent, still. She'd had no way of knowing he was here, and yet somewhere deep inside she realized she had, in some way, expected him. Wish fulfillment, perhaps. Had she really wished so hard that he'd materialized out of air?

But no, he was quite solid as he approached, his head cocked to a certain inquisitive angle as he saw her. The moonlight, now mischievously quite bright, shone down on his dark blue eyes, on the hair silver-gold in its glow. His lips were not welcoming, nor were they hostile. More perplexed, as if he too were mystified by this coincidence. Or was it fate? More and more, Mear was becoming to believe in fate. Perhaps that was why she couldn't drive him from her mind. Perhaps that was why she felt such a strong sense of belonging with him.

His height seemed to dwarf her as she looked up, finding wary eyes that didn't appear entirely welcoming. The reserve was back, the barrier that he had occasionally placed between them.

Meara felt some of the anticipation, some of that immediate joy which had bubbled so quickly within her, fade. "I . . . didn't know anyone was out here," she said, hating herself for the slight quiver in her voice. But it matched the trembling along the length of her spine.

His eyes suddenly softened as a wry smile creased his lips, and his hand reached out, touching her elbow with sudden gentleness. "You never remain still, do you?"

"Neither, it seems, do you." Meara flinched at the hesitancy, the wanting, in her voice.

"I needed to be alone for a while."

"Me, too." It was a ridiculous reply, but honest. She couldn't tell him just why she had wanted to be alone, that she had wanted to think about him.

The silence stretched tautly between them. Meara wanted to ask so much. But he didn't make anything easy, even with the confused, slightly more accessible look on his face. He was tense, and she didn't know why. But she saw it in the stiffness of his body, felt it in the tightening of his fingers around her elbow. "Meara," he whispered raggedly.

Then she didn't have to say anything because his lips descended upon hers with a violence she hadn't expected. There was desperation in the kiss, desperation and a kind of seeking that corresponded with her own confusion.

Her lips answered, and then her body as he drew her close, and they embraced on the lonely beach with the sound of running surf their background music, more haunting, more compelling than any man could pen. His kiss deepened, his tongue probing into her mouth with a recklessness that kindled her own.

Nothing else mattered except the need they were creating in themselves and each another, feeding on each other, tasting, exploring, reacting, each touch sending them further and further away from reality and into a spiral that seemed to have no end.

Somehow they sunk down to their knees, the sand cushioning them as they melded together, and the exploration continued, his lips trailing kisses over her face and her neck. Meara returned each one, following his lead, knowing from her body's reactions what was happening to his. She felt bold and shy, reckless and cautious, sure and uncertain. So many things. So many confusing things. She had never thought herself passionate except in pursuit of goals she now recognized as passionless, yet now every part of her tingled unmercifully. Her heart hurt and her body ached, and a storm, a hurricane, was building inside, feeding on every touch, his and hers, until suddenly she was doing things she had never considered doing before.

Moving closer to him, she relished the heat of his body even through their clothes. Her hands twisted though his thick, crisp hair and her tongue tasted the exotic flavor of him, an intoxicating essence all his own, a mixture of sea spray and soap and a musky cologne. She laughed with the pure delight of all the new sensations, wonderful, delicious, unbelieveable sensations that made the rest of her life, a life she previously believed fulfilling and exciting, colorless and empty in comparison.

They rolled over in the sand like two wrestling children, and she felt the dry, cool grains against her face and legs, and there was a sensuousness to the sensation just as there was to the sight of the moon and stars above, and the sound of waves playing against the beach. Sight and sound and feel were magnified, each sensation growing upon the last until the slightest touch sent pulsating, heated ripples racing through the core of her.

She closed her eyes, then opened them to see the blue of his own. His eyes, usually so unfathomable, were intense and scorching as they searched her face with a possessiveness she thoroughly enjoyed. A smile, part incredulous, part accusatory, played on his lips.

"Sea witch," he whispered into her ear.

"You're a bit of a magician, yourself," she said fancifully. "Like a male genie rising from the ocean."

His hand felt her hair. Like silk. And her face was incredibly wistful and enchanting in the moonlight, her trembling lips stretched into a shy tentative smile that reached into his heart and squeezed it so hard that he could barely breathe. Magic, sorcery, fate. Whatever it was, he cursed silently. Fate. He had almost decided it was fate. But how could fate be so capricious, so cruel. To give and then take away. He leaned down, his lips touching hers gently.

"You taste like the ocean," he said as he nibbled on her.

"And you like a sea breeze." She nuzzled his ear.

His arm tightened around her. "This is not wise."

"I know." But it was said with such satisfaction that he had to smile despite himself.

"I'll wager you've never done this before."

"No," she agreed. She didn't have to ask what. She thought she knew what he meant: this peculiar intimacy, this unique sharing of a place, a moment. More than that. The awareness of exquisitely painful feelings they aroused in each other, the unspoken anticipation of what would surely come.

"You know nothing about me."

"Yes, I do," she disagreed softly. "You like children, and walking at night, and you build a spectacular sand castle."

"And sand-castle construction is vital to your approval?"

"Oh, yes, quite definitely."

"Anything else?"

There was a momentary silence. There was one other vital piece of information, but she couldn't bring herself to ask it.

His hand released her, and he sat, looking out at the ocean.

Meara felt the closeness seeping away again, just as it had before. Her hand reached for his and clutched it as a drowning person might. She didn't care whether she seemed forward, she only wanted him to come back to her, not lost out there in the emptiness of a black sea. There was a sudden melancholy between them, a sorrow that emanated from him and that encompassed her.

"Are you sure," she said, trying to discover the reason for his silence and also compelled to discover another important fact, "that sailors don't have a girl in every port?" She tried to keep the question light, but there was a certain earnestness in her voice that she couldn't hide.

"No," he said with a bit of dry amusement. "There are far too many sailors and not nearly enough girls."

"And you. Do you have someone . . . special . . . waiting in Canada or England?" She meant much more, and she knew he knew it. The words were unspoken. *Do you have a wife? a fiancée? a lover?*

"No," he said gently. "It wouldn't be fair. Not now."

The pain started in the core of her. He was warning her. He was telling her there was no future beyond this night, this week, this spring.

"I've never felt like this before," she blurted out honestly, partly chagrined for saying aloud what she had admitted secretly.

He pulled her back against his chest until they were both looking out over the water, and his hands caressed her arms, rubbing up and down in both comfort and barely restrained passion. Meara felt the almost invisible trembling of his fingers.

She felt his lips against her hair. "I know," he said.

She leaned against him, knowing a wild esctatic joy as she felt his strength against her, his hands touching her tenderly, his breath whispering against her hair. In all her life, she had never known, had never realized, she had emotions quite so wild, so deep, so needy. All her vaunted independence lay in ruins, like the sand castle she had built. She had constructed a world she believed strong and sure, and now it had crumbled into individual grains of sand next to the pull and strength of this man.

Yet he was promising nothing. As the waves had erased the sand castle, time would take him away. To violence she couldn't really comprehend. She took his hand in hers and brought it to her mouth, nuzzling the back of it, the almost invisible gold hairs on the back of his now tanned hands. They were strong hands, the fingers lean and tapered but the palms hard and powerful, callused from years of hard physical work. He was such a contradiction. She had seen and met many wealthy people, some of whom were born to money and others, like Mr. Connor, who had made it. Michael wore the easy grace of one born to it, yet there was also a hardness, a wariness that didn't fit.

"Do you have any family?" she asked, wanting so badly to pull something from him, to try to extract some small piece of him for herself.

She felt his body stiffen, but she held onto his hand for dear life. She wasn't going to let him escape this time.

"No," he finally answered, and the sudden chill of his voice warned her from probing further.

But she persisted. She couldn't help it. "There are no ties then, anyplace? No home?"

"No." Again, the reply was short, curt, unresponsive.

"And you don't . . . want one?"

He sighed, a whisper of breath on her cheek, but his answer was curiously flat and unemotional. "I . . . expect very little, Meara," he said. His hand moved restlessly along her neck. "You're a planner, aren't you, Miss O'Hara?" he asked unexpectedly.

"I'm afraid so," she admitted self-consciously. "I decided when I was eight I wanted to be a writer, and everything has been a straight line since."

Until now. The words hung between them.

"I've never planned anything," Michael said slowly.

"Why?"

"Why?" He repeated the question musingly. "I suspect you like everything tidy, bundled up neatly with ribbons and bows," he said, his voice gently mocking. "Perhaps I've been at sea too long and learned to anticipate the unexpected. A typhoon, a hurricane, even a sudden squall can waylay the best of crews, the sturdiest of ships."

"Properly warned, you can take precautions," she inserted, not entirely liking the direction his thoughts were taking. Or the way they made her feel, the way they crawled into her soul.

"But sometimes you're not 'properly warned,' " he said. There was something in his voice that was almost accusatory. As if she were the unexpected storm. Flickers of heat ran through her, flickers of intense desire.

"And then what?" she asked unsteadily. "What do you do then?"

"You batten down the hatches," he replied, dry amusement again in his voice, and Meara thought how attractive it was, how . . . intriguing. As if he were mocking himself.

"And then?"

"Ride it out."

"And when you're safe in harbor again?"

"You repair the damage and hope it's not fatal."

"And you go back to sea again," Meara said.

"Yes." The one word had a finality about it that sunk like a stone in Meara's stomach. He had been saying much more to her than the surface meaning of the words, but she didn't exactly understand what. She did know it was a warning.

"To risk another storm?"

He chuckled, a sound coming from deep in his chest, and she felt it echoing in her own head which was leaning against his heart. It was a nice sound, warm and amused, and she sought to hold it in her mind, in her memory.

"Always to risk another storm," he confirmed.

"You don't think I would? Risk a storm, I mean."

"I don't know." The laughter was suddenly gone and his voice was somber. "The first storm, yes, but the second? Planners are wiser than that."

"And you're not wise?"

"Not now, not this minute, not since I've met you," he answered slowly.

"Is that so bad?"

There was a long silence. Then his hand turned her head so he could see her face in the moonlight. "How old are you, Meara?"

"Twenty-two."

Meara saw a sudden bleakness in his eyes. "You're so damned young."

"How old are you, Methuselah?" she countered, trying to lighten his sudden dark mood.

He hesitated. "Thirty-one."

"Hardly dottering," Meara observed.

"At times, I wonder," he said slowly. His hand touched her cheek. "Don't ever lose that joy of living, Meara. Don't ever let a storm overwhelm you."

Meara wanted to say more, but he was rising and bringing her up with him. "It's time to go back." He leaned over and kissed her, his lips tender but they didn't linger, not as she wanted them to.

She stood on tiptoe and her fingers touched his mouth. Meara knew somehow that if he left now, it would be the end of whatever there was between them, whatever could be. Her body ached with internal tension, with fierce wanting, but even more than that was her mind, crying out to experience totally what she instinctively knew was a once-in-a-lifetime moment. He was the man. She knew it with all her heart. He was the one she would love. The only man. Already loved with an intensity all the stronger for its brevity, and the knowledge there might never be more time. She didn't understand at all. She didn't understand how quickly it all happened. She only knew she couldn't let him go, not now, not without more, and if there was one thing Meara was, it was stubborn and determined when she wanted something. She knew it was both a weakness and a strength, this single mindedness. It had seen her succeed in a field everyone said was closed to women. It had made her second in her class and had helped her obtain a job all her classmates envied. Because she never quit, never gave up. Full speed ahead and damn the consequences.

"Don't go," she said, and there was both a plea and a promise in her voice.

Meara saw his lips tighten, his eyes blaze with passion, and felt his hand touch her neck softly, a finger making stroking movements. Then his mouth quirked up at one side in a gesture of surrender, and once more he bent his head so his lips met hers with restrained yearning that soon became something else. Storm met storm, fused and exploded. Tumult and brilliant electricity, intoxication and desperation, flowing from both, enveloping both in instantaneous ignition.

His hands pulled her to him, and once more they were on the sand as the water serenaded them and the moon caressed their bodies with its light fanciful touch.

Chapter Six

MICHAEL KNEW IN that moment he could have her. He wanted her more than he'd ever wanted anything in his life.

But as he looked at her face, shy and afraid but stubbornly determined, he knew he could not.

He saw the fear, the reservations, even if she wouldn't acknowledge either.

Michael had no experience with virgins, and that she was one he had no doubt. He didn't have to know more to realize that one weak act on his part could destroy her. He couldn't allow that to happen.

His body ached for her, ached for the relief she could give him, but something even more basic reached out and stopped him. The storm, the fire storm, still raged, but his lips softened on hers, his tongue withdrew slowly, reluctantly, from the welcoming mouth. He drew back slightly, not enough to be rejection, and he still held her closely to him with a tenderness she couldn't mistake.

"Michael?" she whispered.

He kissed her cheek, and his hand ran along her neck, reluctant, reluctant to let go.

"Don't look at me like that," he almost groaned.

"Why . . . ?"

He moved slightly away from her. "Because it's too soon, lovely lady. Because the moon is bright, and the water silver, and the waves are singing a primitive love song, and I'm but a genie who will disappear. We're both in a different world tonight, a magic world that will end when dawn breaks. I don't want you to wake up and be sorry."

"I won't," she said, and her voice almost broke.

"I won't take that chance," he said. "I've never cared enough about anyone before to . . . hurt this damned much. Allow me to be noble this one time," he said with that wry self-mockery that so fascinated her.

Meara swallowed as she looked up at him, at eyes that were vividly deep and unfathomable. She wondered what he was thinking, but she knew from the way he touched her, like priceless crystal, that he cared. Part of her, the good Catholic conscience part of her, was grateful; the wild, wanton self that she was just discovering was aching for something that went beyond a kiss, beyond his touch.

His arms were still around her, although not so tightly, and he was searching her face as if he was looking inside her soul. And it was his for the asking. She didn't know at this moment whether she was grateful or resentful that he was being so careful with it.

The puzzlement must have appeared on her face because he grinned suddenly, his hands tightening around her. "You don't know how difficult you make nobility," he said with a slight chuckle as his lips touched her forehead.

"Do I?" she said hopefully.

"Ah, yes," he replied, a groan in his throat.

She was silent for several moments, her hand on his leg as he held her. There was an intimacy about their closeness, and Meara thought how perfect these moments were, how completely rare they must be. She felt infinitely precious to him, and her heart hurt from feeling so much emotion. She could feel the tension in him, in the careful way he held her, the emotion that played between the two of them.

"I'll . . . miss you," she finally said, hesitantly. He would probably never know how much she would miss him.

"You, pretty lady, will be far too busy to miss anyone. I'll be looking for your byline."

Meara turned and stared at him. "I thought that would be the most important thing in the world."

"It still will be."

"I don't know," she said hesitantly, unsure of her goals for the first time in years.

He tipped her chin up until she was facing him. "Yes, you do," he said. "You told me you've worked all your life for this."

Meara turned her face away from his. "I . . . wanted to be independent."

His voice softened. "Why?"

"My father . . . died before I was born, and my mother . . . she had a very bad time until she found a place with the Connors. She doesn't know how to read or write. Her whole life had been her husband, and when he died her heart broke. I don't think she ever really got over him. I . . . don't think she ever really lived again. She breathes, but she doesn't feel."

"And you were lonely?"

"Not really. I had books. They were my friends. Books and people. I've always liked people. But I never felt . . . like I really belonged. Then I found I could go places through writing. That I could make my own place."

"And that's important to you."

"Yes." But some of the surety was gone. She wondered

at this moment if she wouldn't exchange it all for days, weeks, months with David Michael Fielding. Or whether he was part of a dream himself.

She felt his arms tighten around her, as if he felt some of that insecurity she had felt as a child. She had told herself she no longer felt that way, that her life was full with her mother and the Connors and her career. But now she knew she had never quite left that seed of insecurity behind. She had hidden it well, but it was still there. Except in his arms.

"Now," he said lightly as if to disperse the thickness of emotion between them, "you will become a famous journalist."

"A good one would do as well," she retorted wryly.

"You will be, Meara O'Hara," he said, no doubt at all in his voice. "And I think I had better walk you back before . . ."

The word hung between them, just as their explosive reactions to each other did. The night was simply too overpowering, the sky too jeweled, the lullaby of the water too irresistible.

With a groan, he released her and felt her suddenly shiver with the cool wind blowing in from the ocean. Their bodies had kept each other warm until now.

They were both covered with sand, but it was dry sand, easily brushed off, and he did so, his hands moving over her tenderly and lovingly, lingering even after all the grains had disappeared. Her slender form was lovely in the moonlight, proud and straight, her skin an ivory tint, and her hair, now loose, like a golden red halo. He didn't want to leave, to sever the magic between them, to destroy the momentary illusion that they were the Adam and Eve of this world, alone and still free of fear and violence and hate. His lips touched hers because they could not stop from doing so, and he could feel them both trembling as their mouths met, and he was filled with an anguished melancholy, the knowledge that the war had made everything fleeting, made every moment infinitely precious and something to be savored and hoarded, for it may have to last a lifetime.

His hands traced her slender form, touching lightly, almost worshipingly, and he marveled at the wells of tenderness that gave his hands a gentleness he had never known they had. He felt consumed by a glow of light, of a warmth that filled him so completely that he suddenly realized exactly how lonely he had been, how completely bereft of love and affection. Now that he did know, he wondered if he could live without it again.

Michael only knew he must. His mother and brother's lives were at stake, and even if they weren't, he knew Meara would despise him for what he was, even now. For the deception, for the lies.

He forced his hands away from her with one last whisper-light touch of her cheek. He tried to smile, but he knew it was crookedly unsure at best. It had been a long time since he had been unsure of anything, but now he was flooded with uncertainty and self-doubt.

Michael thought his restraint would cool their passion. But he was discovering that it had only deepened his need and made more electric the air between them, the bond between them even tighter as she looked up at him as if he were God. God, for christsake. She wanted, needed, more from him, and he wanted to give more. Then realization hit him as hard and with as much shock as a pailful of ice water on a sweltering day. He loved her. For the first time in his life, he loved. He felt gutted, his insides twisting with a sick agony. Christ, what was he doing to both of them?

His hold on her tightened. "No matter what happens, I want you to be happy. Always know that—" He stopped, the words stuck in his throat. He saw her face, demanding that he continue.

One of his hands moved to her chin, lifting it until she looked directly into his eyes, while the other held her tightly against him. His eyes willed her to understand, to remember, even as he saw her confusion at the fierce, almost angry, intensity of his voice.

She nodded, although there was now fear in her expression as though she realized he knew something she didn't, something beyond the expected dangers of war.

He dropped his arms and turned away from her, toward the ocean, watching as the moon seemed to gild the crest of waves. The infinity, the power of the ocean made him feel helpless. He was nothing but a pawn. They both were. Being moved around by a giant hand that cared nothing for the pain and destruction that followed. But then he knew that was too easy. He'd made his choices, and now he had to live with them. He had returned voluntarily to Germany although he'd known what it had become. He'd returned partly because it was his home, his country, but he'd also done it to escape internment. He had almost made love to Meara tonight although he understood fully the final bitter outcome.

But, Christ, he wanted these moments to continue, to go on forever, to feel so electrically alive and filled with so many emotions, both tender and savage. Since he was a boy, he had kept everything, every feeling, contained in a box within him, and now they were exploding outward with a force and impact that superseded everything else, every ounce of his restraint and good sense and iron self-discipline.

Michael felt Meara's hand on his arm. It burned him down to his core. It seemed so fragile at the moment, so fragile and trusting and innocent. "You're a million miles away again," she said. "Did I chase you that far?"

Despite the attempted lightness of her words, her face was hurt and puzzled. "The problem, sea witch," he said, "is you bring me too close."

"And you're afraid of closeness?"

"Yes," Michael answered simply, surprised at his own admission.

"I'll have to try to ease that fear."

He stared at her. Sand was caught like flecks of silver in that glorious copper hair, and her face was smudged with a streak of dirt, or sand. Her eyes were wide and wistful, and her mouth kiss-swollen. He knew he would always remember her this way, this way and also the way she was that day on the cruiser when he first met her, when he saw the carefree tilt of her head and heard the entrancing laughter. Two Mearas. Equally as lovely. Equally as enchanting. Equally as vulnerable. "I think it's time to return."

She had already tied her hair back, and she nodded reluctantly. He gave her one last look, finally tearing his gaze from her and forcing himself to remember where he was and who he was and what must be done.

They were on the beach, just below where he had left his bicycle. "The bicycle," he said wryly, and disappeared for a few moments. Thank God she liked the beach and ocean well enough not to think it odd he would ride down here so late at night. He placed the cane in the basket and started to lead it, grateful that his hands were doing something. Otherwise, he knew, he would touch her again. But still the walk would prolong the minutes with Meara, and he wanted those, needed those.

Later, he knew, he would welcome the pain that always came after too much exercise. Perhaps it would overcome the other pain in him.

He felt her hand touch his on the bicycle, and he realized she needed the reassurance, the contact. "Hell with this," he said, and guided the bicycle to a dune out of the sea's reach, laying it there. "I'll send someone for it tomorrow," he added as one of his hands took the cane and the other hand clasped hers tightly, sensing, rather than seeing, her body relax slightly beside him. He was confounded she hadn't asked for anything, not promises or declarations. His company, it seemed, was sufficient. The realization did nothing to relieve his self-loathing. Nothing, he knew, could ever do that.

They were silent on the way back, Michael lost in his own thoughts, his own emotions, knowing instinctively that Meara was probably the same. The touching of their hands, for the moment, was enough.

As they arrived at the path leading to the clubhouse and the Connors' cottage, Michael saw the barely visible outline of a man, standing against an old oak tree. He knew instantly who it was. Sanders Evans.

The man's face was turned toward them, and Michael knew he had been following their progress. He wondered how long Evans had been there. It must be nearly two in the morning or later. Had Evans also been there at midnight when Michael had bicycled toward the beach?

Michael knew that he had been fortunate in more ways than one to meet Meara this evening. A moonlight walk with a woman as lovely as Meara was anything but suspicious. He looked down at Meara to see whether she had noticed the watcher, but she said nothing and he thought she had not. When he glanced up, Evans was gone.

"We'd better part here," he said, looking toward the still well-lighted clubhouse.

Meara hesitated, her face turned upward as if she wanted to say something. Her hand stretched out and touched his arm in unspoken supplication. He leaned down and his lips touched hers, briefly but very tenderly.

It was enough. She smiled tenuously, a wistful smile that

ravaged his soul. With obvious effort, she took the path to the Connors' cottage, turning back only once and only very briefly to look at him.

There was still a lot of activity in the public rooms of the clubhouse despite the late hour. As Michael walked in the side entrance, he passed the card room where two couples were evidently deeply involved in a game of gin. He heard the sound of voices in the billiard room and was about to mount the steps when he heard Sanders Evans's voice. "Care for a nightcap?"

Michael turned slowly. Evans was standing in a space just off the stairs, a private nook of the lobby. He held a glass in his hands.

Michael shrugged. "Why not?" He didn't want to go to his room alone. He didn't want to be alone. He didn't think he could tolerate himself.

He followed Evans to a table and watched as the man signaled a waiter.

"Scotch," Michael told him. "A little water. No ice."

"European style?" Evans asked the question easily, but Michael felt himself tense inside.

"Sailor style. There's seldom a surplus of ice either on a ship or in some of the ports where she docks."

"You must have seen much of the world."

"Some of the least attractive parts. A lot I'd rather not have seen." Michael sat down, stretching his injured leg in front of him. God, it ached. He leaned over and massaged the calf down to his ankle. The leg of his slacks came up, and he knew Evans could see part of the vivid scar that ran up his leg.

"Still giving you a lot of trouble?"

"Some," Michael replied carelessly. "I've been trying to give up the cane, just for a few hours a day, but I'm afraid I overdid it tonight."

"I can understand why. It's quite beautiful out there."

"I thought I saw you."

Evans nodded. "I didn't mean to intrude. I just wanted some air before going to bed."

"Have you been here before?"

"No, it's a little rich for my blood. I wouldn't be here now if it weren't for John."

"Where is he?"

"Retired early."

"You've been friends for a long time?"

"No," Evans said. "But war seems conducive to making friends quickly." It was a facile answer that revealed little. Michael wondered for the briefest of seconds if his companion meant Meara.

Michael merely nodded. He thought about prying more, but he had been reckless enough tonight.

The Scotch came, and he sipped it slowly, using the time to study the man opposite him. He believed his cover was well protected, as well as it could be. There were holes in any story, but he hoped there wasn't enough time for anyone to find them.

"When did that happen?" Evans finally asked him, flicking his eyes toward Michael's injured leg.

"Five months ago."

"What do the doctors say?"

"It will never be as strong as it was, but it should do well enough. They had to do a bone graft, and the muscles are damnably weak from disuse." He shrugged. "It's just such a bloody nuisance."

"Cal Connor says you plan to return to duty."

"I hope so. I was medically discharged, but I'm trying to pull some strings. As soon as my doctor approves. He suggested coming here, thought it might help regain my strength. Limited exercise, he said. But I'm afraid I have a tendency to want to do everything too quickly."

Sanders Evans smiled slowly, a warm, disarming smile. "I know. I was injured once. It gets damned frustrating."

"Should I ask how?" Michael watched Evans carefully. It was a leading question at best, obviously conveying the impression that he suspected Evans was not what he seemed.

"Nothing as dramatic as a war wound," Evans said easily. "A case of not ducking when I should."

"Interesting defense job," Michael observed dryly.

"At times. At other times, infernally dull."

Michael finished his Scotch. Sanders Evans was maintaining no more pretense. The agent was smart enough to know his own cover was weak at best. Michael hoped like hell his was much better.

"I think it's time I join your friend in retiring for the night."

Sanders half rose, lifting his empty glass in salute. "I enjoyed our conversation."

Strangely enough, Michael thought as he painfully climbed the steps, so had he.

Sanders remained in the parlor, nursing his brandy. He liked Michael Fielding. It was difficult not to. Yet something about him seemed wrong. And Sanders's instincts were usually right.

He wondered briefly if it could be jealousy. From the moment he had seen Meara O'Hara, he'd been attracted to her, more than he had to any other woman since his wife, along with his child, died three years ago in an accident. The two women had the same quick smile, the same easy personality that made a stranger feel welcome almost immediately. He'd watched her with the Connor children, observed the open affection between them, and he'd felt the first stirring of interest in a very long time.

But then he'd noticed very quickly how she looked at

Michael Fielding and the way the two of them walked to the river together from the Connor picnic, and he'd warned himself to back off. But earlier today there had been a certain chill between the girl and the Canadian. He sighed philosophically. Obviously any problem had been settled.

He took another sip of brandy, wondering again about Fielding. He'd seen the Canadian descend the stairs earlier and slip outside. When Fielding hadn't returned, Sanders had become interested. It was that damned instinct again. But now it seemed there was no more to it than a pretty girl.

Still, something nagged at him, and he didn't know why. Everything about Fielding fit. He was obviously wounded. No one could fake those scars nor the obvious difficulty with which he moved. Sanders had also recognized the Canadian accent in the man's speech.

Damn. What, then, bothered him? The ready acceptance, perhaps. Fielding had almost immediately won the affection and respect of everyone here, especially of Cal Connor and his children. Fielding had been here no more than five days and had already met and befriended everyone. Resentment? Resentment was unfamiliar to Sanders. He had been content with his life until his wife and child died, and since then he'd buried himself in work. He finally shrugged. Perhaps he was just tired, seeing shadows where there were none.

It wouldn't hurt to run a check, however, although Sanders had personally felt, from the very beginning, that this whole trip had been unnecessary. However, Director Hoover did not, not after he learned the names of some of the guests staying at the Jekyll Island Club over the Easter weekend. The director had already suggested that the club be closed because of its accessibility to German subs and vulnerability to attack. After his arrival, Sanders had learned that the club would indeed be closed, that this was the last season, not because of any threat but simply because of sheer economics: gas rationing, decline in man-power, and the members' lack of time to use the facilities. War had made time a very precious commodity.

The visit to the island had been presented as a holiday for Sanders. He had just completed a grueling three-month case involving German spies in New York, and he'd been tense and tired and long overdue for some vacation and rest. Hoover had summoned him into his office, smiled tightly in a way Sanders had learned to suspect, and an-nounced Sanders would be rewarded with this trip to the coast. Just keep his eyes open. The arrangements had been made with John Graves, a member of the Jekyll Island Club and a political ally of the director.

But it was not the kind of vacation Sanders enjoyed. He did not like fancy places. He did not like formal dress. He did not care for many of the activities offered.

It was not that he was a snob. He simply felt uncomfort-able. He would much prefer a simple steak rather than the heavily sauced dishes that were snatched by waiters every time he blinked. He preferred beer to wine, and he de-tested champagne, which seemed to be the standard drink here. And he had little in common with the other guests. Moreover, he did not like being on guard every moment. He'd had enough of that in the past year.

Meara O'Hara had almost changed his mind about his so-called vacation. He had thoroughly enjoyed the tennis game, even though he was no longer good at the game. He was highly competitive and he liked sports, but working his way through college, then law school before joining the FBI, hadn't left him much time for play. There was even less time after his marriage; if he had one regret in his life it was that he hadn't had enough time for Judy or his daughter.

He sat back and studied the rich, thick rugs and elegant furnishings. From the moment he had set foot on the club cruiser he felt he'd entered another time. Perhaps that was why Meara O'Hara had made such an impact on him. She seemed the only real thing here, the only flesh and blood person. Could that be why his hackles rose at seeing her with Fielding?

Still he would check on Fielding. He would call his office tomorrow and ask for a background check.

He looked at his watch. Three o'clock. He drained the last of the golden red liquid in his glass, thinking briefly how the color resembled Meara's hair. Sanders shook his head at his own folly and followed Fielding up the stairs.

Meara slipped in the door and floated upstairs. The door was never locked here on Jekyll Island. Nor were there any questions about her whereabouts. She was of age and, on past visits to Jekyll, she often attended dances or bonfires or went turtle hunting and didn't return until late.

But she was glad no one appeared to be awake. She knew she must be a total mess. Grains of sand were still in her hair, inside and outside her clothes, on her face.

Meara had never until this past week anticipated making love outside marriage. The idea, in fact, had never even particularly appealed to her. Like any young girl, she had, during her teens, been in love with the idea of being in love. Yet no kiss, no brief caress, had ever tempted her beyond those mostly unsatisfactory and even distasteful experiences.

But from the moment she had met Michael Fielding, her body had changed and she was filled with a need and yearning she couldn't believe was wrong. She had thought she had been ready tonight, but . . . perhaps he had known her even better than she knew herself. Tonight, at least.

Tomorrow? She didn't know about tomorrow.

She went to the window and opened it, looking out at the sky above. *I love him.* She wanted to sing it, to yell it. But instead she whispered the words over and over again. Those words, and his name. His name. Michael. She rolled it around in her mouth, tasting it, loving it.

Meara had been afraid to say the words tonight, to say even his name, because she knew she would be saying the first in saying the second. But she could say it here.

First love. Last love. Only love.

Michael.

Chapter Seven

Saturday dawned bright and sunny, and after a leisurely breakfast Meara took Tara and Peter to the beach. The day was a perfect island day. Warm but not too warm. A breeze but not too much breeze. Sun but not too much sun. Pleasant but not burning.

Perfect. Meara thought life was perfect. She had been unable to sleep all night but she felt awake and alive and wonderful.

She had gone over the events of the previous night a hundred times, and she had, nine times out of ten, reached the same conclusion. Michael might disapprove of a wartime romance but she believed he cared very much for her. Otherwise how could he have been so gentle, so concerned.

She was sure he would find her sometime today, and her heart sang at the thought. All of her hummed and tingled and anticipated. It was wonderful being in love. How could she have ever thought it would not be?

The three of them wandered down the beach, hunting turtle tracks and pink-and-silver shells. The water was a silver blue in the sun, and they all sampled the temperature with their feet, running back as the cold water wrapped around their ankles. Then Meara sat while Peter and Tara chased birds, laughing and giggling and tripping over themselves. The children dug frantically for crabs, which burrowed much too quickly in the sand for small hands, but disappointment was quickly abated when they found a perfect sand dollar.

Meara watched them, wondering for the first time what it would be like to have children of her own. Children with deep blue eyes and golden hair. She tried to think of her ambitions, of her upcoming job, but now it seemed far away. It was that which was illusory now. Her only reality was Michael Fielding.

She was firmly convinced he would seek her out, that they would make plans for the evening. She'd already committed to tennis today, and Michael was well aware of that. She had mixed feelings about the obligation. She liked both Brad and Sanders Evans, and any other time she would have looked forward to the spirited competition. But now all she wanted was to spend every moment she could with Michael. She wouldn't even allow herself to think of eight days hence, when he would return to war and she to New York.

She closed her eyes and let the sun bless her. Peter and Tara were well trained around water. They were, Meara thought gratefully, both really good kids. Like hers would be. Funny she had never thought that way before.

It was strange how her priorities had changed in such a short period of time, priorities and needs. She knew she had been lucky in many ways, although she realized she had also made some of her own luck. She could easily have slipped into domestic service as her mother had. It had been what her mother, who had never had high aspirations, had expected. When Meara had expressed hope for more, her mother had thought she should go into teaching or nursing, never a man's occupation. A man didn't want to marry a woman who competed with him, she said, and to her mother, marriage was the ultimate and only choice.

But the world was changing, and Meara had wanted to be a part of that change. Why shouldn't she have the same chances, the same opportunities as men? But she had to fight for each one, from her advisers who told her she should teach to professors who took delight in baiting her.

Although Meara wished there wasn't a war, she was fully aware of the opportunities and freedom it provided. She had been ready to grab both. But now the realities of the fighting were too close. Death and injury no longer touched only people in the newspaper. They happened to real people, to Michael, and to those like him.

To the best of all the young men. Meara's fingers dug into the sand as waves of sadness passed through her. She thought of last night and how much she had wanted to be a part of Michael, to know what it was truly like to love and be loved. Perhaps she would never know, or having once known, she would be like her mother, never able to love again. She didn't know. She didn't know anything anymore, only that she needed Michael Fielding, needed him in a way she had never thought she would need anyone. And if she didn't explore that need, she was bitterly afraid she would spend her life wondering. Wondering and regretting.

"It's mine."

"I saw it first."

"But I picked it up first."

Meara opened her eyes. The really good kids were standing boxerlike, eye to eye, the pitch of their voices increasing with every word. "Come show me what it is," she intervened.

Peter, with the item clutched in his hand, ran over to

her. It was a piece of metal, so light it had not sunk in the sea which had carried it here. Meara took it in her hands and fingered the smooth edges on one side, ridges on the other. Part of a photo frame, she imagined. Her fingers ran over ridges that probably had held a cherished photo now long gone. Meara could only imagine where it had come from, who once had owned it, or what loved one had graced it. Jekyll Island was not far from the shipping lanes to England, and there had been any number of allied ships sunk along the coast. Her natural curiosity reached out and wondered, and she felt an infinite sadness. Someone was probably missing, and someone else was waiting. Holding the piece of gold-colored metal, she could almost feel the emotion of those involved, and again she personally and profoundly felt the hideousness of this war. She thought of waiting helplessly, awaiting word of Michael, not knowing whether he was alive or dead, not knowing if he was injured and hurting, or alone somewhere in a life raft waiting desperately for rescue.

She suddenly hated the Germans, hated the U-boats that preyed and destroyed and killed wantonly.

"What is it?" Peter asked impatiently.

Too young. He was much too young to understand. And he shouldn't. "Just an old piece of metal, love," she said. "Why don't you and Tara go up to the dunes and bury it so the edges won't hurt anyone."

"But I want to keep it," Peter wailed.

"Why?" Meara asked practically.

"Because . . . well . . . maybe it's part of a bomb or something," he said hopefully.

"You *are* bloodthirsty," Meara smiled. "But I think it's more like a frame of a stove." Nothing, she knew, could be duller to Peter.

His young face fell, then brightened again. "Maybe it came from a German sub."

"Perhaps," she said agreeably, "but we will never know and it has some very sharp edges, so why don't you give it a nice burial."

Peter made a face, but he sensed that Meara's mind was made up. He'd learned long ago what that meant. "All right," he sighed, "but I get to tell mother and father."

"Me, too," chimed in Tara, who didn't understand why there was such a fuss. Her sharp eyes had found it, but the only reason she'd then wanted the object was that Peter did. Now her interest completely waned as she spied a small lizard darting across the sand, and she went speeding after it.

The sun was high, signaling noon, when they left the beach after a proper and respectful burial of the sea's offering. As they started toward the path, she saw Michael, leaning against a great oak tree, watching them. Peter saw him at the same time and went scrambling over, winning an engaging grin in response.

Meara felt the thumping of her heart accelerate, her blood grow warmer, and her throat catch. He was incredibly handsome, leaning lazily against the tree, the tawny hair mussed by the breeze. He was wearing white slacks and a blue shirt, its sleeves rolled up to the elbows, showing the tanned muscled strength of his arms. His eyes, a deeper, richer blue than the ocean, were unreadable as they studied her until they reached her feet. As usual, she was barefoot, a pair of sandals in her hand. His eyes crinkled at the edges as he regarded them with interest, and she felt suddenly awkward. It seemed he always appeared at her most windblown and disreputable.

He bent his head gravely as he listened to Peter's rapid excited chatter, and Meara knew the boy was speaking of his discovery, the piece of metal. The pleasant expression on Michael's face stiffened, and he looked at her again before he said a few words to Peter and then walked toward her. He was using the cane again, and his leg seemed stiffer than usual, probably from all the exercise last night. Her face flamed as she remembered the nature of some of the exercise.

His hand came out and touched a lock of hair. "You still look like a sea witch," he said, but there was a hesitancy in his voice, a rare note of uncertainty.

Tara looked up with interest. "A witch?"

"A good one," he amended quickly with a wry twist of his mouth, "but none the less powerful."

"Like the Wizard of Oz?" she asked.

He looked up at Meara. "Wizard of Oz?"

"Where have you been?"

"Obviously not where I should have been," he observed.

"That's all right," Peter said. "He knows better stuff, like how to shoot."

Michael lowered himself awkwardly to one knee. "That's not better 'stuff' at all," he said. "Sea witches and wizards are much more important."

Peter looked at him with betrayed disbelief.

"But that's for girls."

Michael laughed. "Not always. I like witches quite a bit."

"You do?"

"Certainly."

Tara tugged at Michael's shirt, tired of being left out of this male conversation. "Will you help us with another sand castle?"

"Not today," he said, "but perhaps tomorrow."

She gave him a beatific smile, satisfied for the moment with the answer.

Michael stood and looked at Meara, his smile gone. "I would like to talk to you later."

She nodded, struck by the sudden grimness of his voice. "Mr. and Mrs. Connor always spend most of Saturday with the children. After lunch, I'm free, except for tennis at two."

A muscle tightened in his cheek. "I've accepted an invitation to go along on a cruise among the islands this afternoon. I understand we won't be back until late. Tomorrow. A picnic, perhaps. I can ask the clubhouse to prepare something." It wasn't exactly a question, more of a statement.

A ripping pain tore through her. She had wanted so much to see him today, to talk with him, to be with him, to know him better. She tried not to let it show. After that brief whimsy with the children, he was now at his unapproachable best. Meara had never seen anyone do that quite as aptly: to be charming and easy and warm one moment, and a million miles away the next. It frightened and intrigued her, the very illusionary aspect of him exciting and challenging.

Meara nodded. She was off all day Sunday, but his own guarded expression made hers equally so.

"I'll pick you up at noon?"

"I attend church with the Connors."

"One, then."

"All right," she said, carefully withholding any disappointment.

He studied her for a moment, his expression serious and unsmiling, and she started to feel the beginning of fear. And uncertainty. "Michael?"

He'd started to turn away but now he faced her again, his eyebrows furrowed, the laugh lines gone.

Meara wanted to say something, but his face was hard, and it was as if he'd never teased the children. It was almost as if someone else were standing there. She shook her head. "Nothing. I'll see you tomorrow," but this time she couldn't quite conceal the baffled hurt.

He gave her a half smile that said nothing, that seemed

to be something he used on occasion to avoid commitment, on those occasions when some part of him left her, although his body remained. She shivered suddenly. She really didn't know much about him. She had thought she did, but when he retreated her like this she wondered.

Imagination, she scolded herself as he limped toward the road, and she was flooded with a warm possessiveness. Nothing had changed since last night. He was lightning swift in his moods, probably, she thought, because of the war and the things he had done and experienced. But he had been wonderful, as usual, with the children, charming them so completely that they never even argued in front of him, never questioned as they did nearly everyone else.

Tomorrow. She would find out more about him tomorrow. She had always been very good at that, discovering little pieces about people, probing so gently they didn't realize what she was doing. It was her interest, interest that was real and honest, that always seem to make people confide in her. With a little time alone with Michael Fielding, perhaps he would do the same. Yet doubt nagged at her. She'd never met anyone like him. He was obviously a very private person although when he wished, he could converse with anyone. He was obviously a loner, the way he sometimes sought solitude, apparently needing no company other than his own. Perhaps the sea did that to one. There was an element of that in herself, the need to be alone at times, so she could well understand a similar need in someone else.

"Meara." A hand impatiently pulled at hers. "I'm hungry."

She shook her head. There was no reason for disappointment, no reason he should drop all his plans for her. She would be alone with him tomorrow. She would feel his arms again, and everything would be all right.

Meara smiled brightly at Tara. "So am I, love. So am I."

Fool. The more he tried to extricate himself, the deeper he was pulled into the quicksand of caring.

Michael truly enjoyed the Connor children. They were bright and outgoing and appealing. Whenever he was around them, he retreated into a warm cozy world that had no ugliness in it.

They so thoroughly drew him into their small intimate circle he felt as if he were an honored and beloved guest. For moments at a time he could forget why he was here. He could believe himself an honest part of a charmed, protected world.

But there were no protected worlds any more.

He had to force himself to think of his mother, his brother. His duty. The bloody duty. Every time he thought of the sub approaching this island, he was filled with crushing sickness.

Michael had avoided Hans all morning. Unable to sleep, he'd left his room before dawn and found the bicycle. Instead of returning, he had sat on the beach, watching the sun rise, weighing his options and finding none.

He had absolutely no illusions about Canaris. He didn't doubt that the admiral would carry out every threat, whether he had been a friend of Michael's father or not.

Nor did he have any illusion about Hans Weimer. Michael knew he would have to be very careful around Meara and the children, or Weimer might try to use them in some way against him. If his "partner" had the least suspicion that Michael was beginning to care for them, there was no telling what Hans might attempt.

It was for that reason he'd proposed the picnic for Sunday, when Hans would not be on the island. And he'd planned his meeting with Meara carefully today. Far away from the clubhouse grounds. An accidental meeting on the beach. Nothing more.

In the meantime, he had important successes to report to Hans: the contact with the sub, the growing relationships he was developing with the targeted members of the Jekyll Island Club. The cruise this afternoon would involve several of them.

He would not let himself think ahead, to the moment those who had offered open friendship would fully comprehend who he was, and what he had manipulated.

It's war, he told himself. War. He would be saving German lives, perhaps thousands of them.

But, Christ, at what price?

Meara's tennis game, never really outstanding, was a disaster. She couldn't keep her attention on the ball. She kept looking toward the clubhouse, at every person who ascended or descended the steps.

They had tossed coins for partners, and she and Sanders Evans exchanged wry looks when they were paired, each sympathizing with the other.

Sanders, however, was unexpectedly good and saved them, if not from defeat, from abject humiliation. Meara kept apologizing for misses while his face registered surprise every time he returned a particularly difficult shot.

They were laughing when it ended, Meara and Sanders winning only one of the games and howling triumphantly as they did. As they had the day before, they had drinks together, Meara and Kay a gin and tonic, Sanders a beer, and Brad a whiskey.

Meara enjoyed the companionship, yet part of her kept watching, even though she knew Michael was probably now far beyond her sight. She tried to concentrate instead on Sanders, who was talking of Washington.

"There's not a hotel room in the city," he said. "It's frantic."

"Do you live in Washington?"

"Now I do. A small apartment," he replied.

"Now?" Meara's question was soft. She'd seen a trace of sadness in Sanders's eyes.

"My wife . . . didn't like Washington. We had a house in Virginia." Pain was in the words, but he didn't say any more, and Meara didn't want to probe wounds. She had one of her own at the moment.

Kay diplomatically changed the subject. "And before that? I can't quite place your accent."

"Pennsylvania. My father owns a farm."

"But you like cities?"

"I didn't care about farming, which was fortunate. I have two older brothers who did, and the farm wasn't large enough to support us all."

"Do you miss it?" Meara asked.

"Perhaps the peace sometimes. But other than that, no. It's a solitary life, and dependent on so many things you can't control."

"You like what you do now?"

He shrugged self-consciously, not altogether at ease with the attention. "I don't know if I really like it. But I think it's necessary."

Meara noticed his discomfort and liked him even more for it. There was an obvious strength and integrity about Sanders Evans that attracted her, although not in the way Michael Fielding did. There was no rush of the blood or mad thumping of the heart or tingling of nerve ends. But there was an instinctive liking and trust.

By common consent, the talk turned lighter, to the music of Glenn Miller and Tommy Dorsey, and the latest films, particularly "Mrs. Miniver," which was all the rage at the moment. Apt, Meara thought privately, but she said little, letting Kay and Brad do most of the talking. Sanders did the same, although Meara often found his gaze on her. He was older than they, although Brad was in his mid-twenties. Sanders was probably of an age with Michael Fielding, she guessed. There were other similarities between the two men. Both, she knew, were used to responsibility; she could see it in their eyes, in the way they held themselves.

The rest of the afternoon passed pleasantly as the four of them sat and sipped cool drinks while the sun dipped low. Finally, Brad and Kay left, leaving Sanders and Meara alone.

Meara knew she should leave too, but she needed some companionship at the moment, even the hint of admiration in Sanders's eyes.

For a moment, an awkward silence stretched between them. Meara took a sip of the drink, which was now mostly melted ice. For want of a better question, she blurted out the one which had been in her mind since he'd mentioned a wife. "Do you have children?"

He hesitated a moment before saying in a low, controlled voice, "I did. A daughter. She and my wife were killed in a car accident three years ago."

Meara closed her eyes. "I'm sorry."

"It's getting easier to talk about. For a while, I couldn't even say the words, as if they weren't true unless I spoke them."

"And now?"

"The good memories are taking over. Little by little, the pain dulls. It's always there, but it becomes easier to live with."

Meara pushed the glass around the table in front of her. "I don't know if I could ever cope with that kind of loss."

He smiled slightly. "I didn't think I could either for a time. But you do. Now I can look at Tara Connor without flinching and think how pretty she is. At one time I couldn't have done that."

Meara looked away. She had avoided thinking about the possibility of Michael's death. She didn't think she could bear it, yet she had known him only a few days. What must it be like to lose a wife and child? Someone you loved as much as Sanders had apparently loved his family?

Sanders must have seen something in her face.

"You're afraid for someone?"

Meara nodded.

"Michael Fielding?"

Her eyes widened.

"It's none of my business, Meara, but I've seen you together several times."

"It's that obvious?"

"Perhaps not to everyone. But I'm accustomed to putting two and two together."

"And you do that often?"

"Yes." The answer was so short yet so confident Meara had to smile, and that brought a smile of his own, as if they shared a secret.

"I'll remember that," she said.

"But don't tell anyone else," he warned with some humor.

"I think everyone already suspects it."

He raised an eyebrow.

"There's a rumor floating around that an FBI agent is here. You seem the only possible suspect."

"So much for stealth," he admitted wryly. "But I really am here on vacation."

"There's nothing very ominous about this island."

"Except the tennis players," he said dryly.

"You did very well for yourself. But me . . ." Meara shook her head with disgust.

"You were preoccupied."

"You noticed?"

He nodded. "Where *is* Commander Fielding?"

"On a cruise along the islands."

"A very unimaginative man, the commander," Sanders said. "I could think of much better things to do." She flushed, knowing he meant being with her.

As if he knew he'd made her uncomfortable, he quickly retreated from the subject. "What about tennis tomorrow, just you and me. I think we need some practice if we continue playing with those two."

"I'm sorry, I can't. Not tomorrow." She saw a brief flicker of disappointment in his eyes. And a loneliness she now understood.

"Perhaps Monday?"

Meara hesitated. She wanted to spend every moment she could with Michael, but she liked Sanders. She liked him very much. "I think so."

"Good." He rose slowly. "I'll reserve the court for three o'clock."

She stood and held out her hand, noticing how very gently he took it. "Thank you for the game," she said. "And the company."

"My pleasure," he said.

As she walked away, she felt his gaze on her. She knew if it hadn't been for the mention of Michael, he would have asked her to dinner. His interest hadn't been disguised, but neither had he pressed her in any way.

Meara looked toward the docks. One of the boats was readying to take the day workers back to Brunswick. A club yacht, used for pleasure trips along the islands, was gone. She wondered who was along, particularly which marriageable young daughters.

The uncertainty returned. The uncertainty and the doubt and the hurt that she had pushed from her mind this afternoon. They all flooded back now with a vengeance. She thought of Michael's grim face when she last saw him, the dark blue eyes that gave so many conflicting signals.

She made herself a sandwich but couldn't eat it. She found a book but couldn't read. She was tired but couldn't sleep. She kept remembering the feel of him. The fresh salty taste. The way her body had responded to him. The gentleness. The sweetness and then the swift wild passion. Her body tensed with the newfound feelings, with the remembrance of profound discovery.

Meara finally willed herself to bed, to a restless sleep disturbed by persistent feelings of unease.

Michael massaged his leg in his room. It was getting stronger. He was able to go for longer periods of time without the cane, and ordinarily he would have been elated at the long-awaited progress. But he felt no elation, only quiet hurting desperation.

He couldn't have asked for a more successful afternoon and evening, and yet all he felt was cold, hopeless desolation. The yacht had skirted around the entire island and visited two neighboring islands, Sea Island and Saint Simons. He had mentally catalogued every detail about each of them: the shore lines, the distances between the islands and the coastal city of Brunswick, the strength of the current. He wasn't exactly sure why; he shouldn't need any of that information, yet it accumulated in his brain, almost as if by plan.

A veritable feast had been served aboard the ship, along with the usual abundance of champagne and good wines, and conversation. There had been eight people, including two families, one with a son in college and the other with two daughters, each of whom eyed him speculatively. Both were attractive enough, but neither had Meara's lively sense of humor or passion for life, two of the qualities which had most attracted him. They seemed totally lifeless in comparison. Michael was polite, more than polite, and by the end of the cruise had received an offer of a job after the war.

When he had trained in Germany for the mission, he had never realized how difficult this job would be. He hadn't liked the idea of spying, but he'd never expected the depth of guilt he would know, or suspected he would like and admire the people he meant to betray, certainly not that he would love one of them.

Hans, he knew, had no such scruples. His eyes had shown only satisfaction when Michael had reported successful contact with the sub. Satisfaction and a certain malicious gleam. He had wanted to know everything, every move Michael had made, every conversation he had had.

At least Hans would be off the island tomorrow when he met Meara. It would be, he knew, the most difficult meeting in his life. He had to convince her that whatever there was between them was over. He wondered exactly how he could do that when everything in him longed to touch her, to hold her again. Only she, he knew, could warm the icy chill within him.

He rose and went to the wardrobe where his suitcase was stored. It was exactly where he had placed it, two inches from the back wall of the handsome oak furniture. He took a key from his pocket and leaned down, studying the lock and the strand of hair that was stretched undisturbed across it.

Michael unlocked and opened it. The army Colt pistol was where he had left it, wrapped securely in a pair of slacks. He felt the lining where tiny vials were hidden, small containers of sedatives and even one of poison. There was no sign of disturbance. Even if there had been, he doubted whether even the most diligent of searchers would find the hidden lining, and the gun was innocuous enough. He was, after all, a soldier.

Michael closed the bag, running the strand of hair over the lock once more, and replacing the suitcase back in the exact location. He didn't know why he had checked, perhaps to remind him why he was here. Perhaps because the presence of Sanders Evans disturbed him more than a little.

But it would be over soon. A few more days and it would be over.

Chapter Eight

Michael picked up Meara in the red bug, for the picnic.

She was sitting in the swing, her hair in a braid, and dressed in a white cotton blouse and full skirt that moved gracefully as she stood and walked toward him, a welcoming, expectant smile on her face.

Open and happy, it was a smile that stabbed.

He stepped out and took her hand, helping her settle down on the seat, which was more like a perch than anything else. Her hand was warm, but it clasped his firmly, and he felt the now familiar darts of searing heat invade him.

Michael couldn't help but look at her. Her eyes were such a vivid green, loving and searching in such a way that everything in him responded. His hand went up and brushed a wayward curl from her face, his mouth bending in a slight smile.

"God, but you're lovely."

Her smile was blinding. So much, he thought, for distancing himself.

He took his hand from hers and started the little car,

134

watching not the path but the wisps of red-gold hair that escaped from the braid and the effervescence in her eyes. Her hands knitted together, long tapered fingers moving nervously, belying the calmness of her face.

"How was tennis yesterday?"

"Terrible." Her tone was so full of disgust he had to smile.

"What happened to you and Brad?"

"Brad played with Kay."

There was a brief silence. "You played with Evans?"

"Yes."

"He seems pleasant enough." Michael's tone was non-committal.

"He's very nice. And lonely, I think."

Michael looked over at her questioningly. "Why lonely?"

There was a slight pause. "His wife and daughter were killed in an accident."

Michael raked a hand through his hair as he considered the information. Evans and Meara obviously had a long conversation yesterday. Had he been mentioned? Had there been questions asked? Aside from those concerns, he felt a certain jealousy again. It was like a disease, the way it gnawed at him, and he didn't like the flash of sympathy he felt toward the federal agent. He was feeling entirely too many things already.

He didn't say anything more as the car followed a path lined with oaks and palms toward the other side of the island and a deserted beach there.

A silence stretched out between them, long and painful, although the air was pregnant with questions Meara feared to ask, and painful warnings Michael couldn't give. Tension radiated between them, tension mixed with desire that was increasingly potent with each silent second until Meara could bear it no longer. She sought the most innocuous statement possible, just to break the quiet duel between them.

"Peter asked me whether you would give him another skeet shooting lesson."

"What did you tell him?" Michael's voice was slow, deliberate, yet there was a tense edge to it.

"That this is your vacation, that you needed rest."

He stopped the car and looked at her without replying, his gaze consuming her. Michael ignored her words as waves of silent heat radiated between them, just as pressure grows in the air preceding a violent storm until the very air is ripe for explosion.

This is crazy, he thought. This was the very thing he had sought to prevent. He had meant to say good-bye, to end this . . . infatuation in the kindest way possible. He should have known that being alone with her was not the way to accomplish it. He struggled to recapture some sanity, some discipline. He forced his hands to relax, his mouth to bend into what he knew must be a caricature of a smile.

Slowly, he tore his gaze from hers and glanced around. They were in an isolated place of the forest. Without the *put-put* of the cart, the air was infinitely still until a woodpecker broke the silence with a steady, rhythmic drilling. Just beyond a stand of trees, they could see the gray of the sea, pounding against an empty beach.

"Is this all right?" he said in a forced voice, not looking at her, barely hearing her soft, uncertain acquiescence. He took the blanket and basket in one hand and looked at his cane in distaste before picking it up. Otherwise, he knew, he would be tempted to put his arm around her. He swore quietly to himself as they walked down an overgrown path to the ocean where he spread out the blanket. He waited for her to sit, and then he folded himself into a sitting position, one knee raised to rest his arm. The basket was ignored as she watched him steadily, warily, as if she knew what was coming.

"I haven't had any rest since I met you," he said, finishing the thought that had started in the little red bug.

"I know," she said. "Me either. I didn't plan on you."

"You said the other night you always plan everything."

"Very carefully," she admitted.

He put a finger to her chin and played with it a moment. "They're good plans . . . a good future. A chance to make your own future."

He saw her eyes cloud at his words, and he knew she didn't want him to continue. He didn't want to. Her cheeks were flushed, and her mouth trembled at his touch. Those wonderful green eyes were caressing him in a way far more sensual than any human touch he'd ever felt.

His hand traced a path along the line of her chin and then her cheek to where it caught a curl between his fingers. "I brought you here to apologize for the other night." There was a catch in his throat.

"But you've done nothing—"

His voice was suddenly harsh when he spoke. "I didn't want you to think, to believe—"

"Don't," Meara replied softly, afraid of what he was trying to say. "I'm not asking for anything," she said, but her voice trembled despite her best intentions. It couldn't end like this. It couldn't.

"It's wrong, Meara. The timing's wrong. Everything's wrong. The island makes it seem right, as if we were the only two people in the world. But it's not right. Not for you. I don't want to hurt you."

Her chin went up stubbornly. "I know you're . . . going back, and I realize you're worried about that. You don't have to worry about me."

"It's more than that, Meara. I'm not the kind of man who settles down. I'm a wanderer. I'll always be a wanderer." He saw the hurt well in her eyes, and he would have given his life right then if he could change things. But giving his life wouldn't change anything at the moment. He realized with sudden clarity that he *had* been a wanderer, but that wandering no longer held any attraction for him. Meara did. Only Meara. But it was too late. It had always been too late.

"I know," Meara said in a strained voice, but somehow her fingers had crawled into his, and the conversation wasn't going at all as he had anticipated. He'd thought to anger her, but there was so much understanding in her eyes, so much awareness and yet love, that he was silenced.

"I've never felt this way before," she continued slowly, hesitantly. "I never thought I could. It's a gift, a wonderful gift that I'll always remember." Her fingers played nervously with the golden hairs on the back of his hand and moved, as if she didn't want to relinquish touch, up and down his arm made bare by rolled up sleeves. The slightest movement of her fingers created sparks that traveled rapidly, igniting a hot blaze deep inside him. He felt his loins tighten, responding to her every exploratory touch.

He reached out and drew her against him, his body disobeying his mind. He had already bitten from the forbidden fruit and now it was irresistible. Irresistible and within reach. That was the terrible part. He ached from wanting her, ached to touch her, to fullfil the promise hinted at the other night. He had never known moments like those before, the blazing passion that roared between them. How could he need someone so badly? He who had never needed anyone?

If only he didn't care so damnably much!

He forced his hands still and spoke in slow, measured tones. It was a speech he had rehearsed. He just hadn't realized how difficult it would be to deliver. "You have the whole world in front of you. Don't let me get in its way."

He stopped, then continued determinedly, but raggedly. "But know I care about you, that I will always care about you. No matter what happens, never doubt that."

Meara looked around to face him, her expression puzzled at the intensity of his words.

"Sometimes," he said slowly, "there are obligations. Obligations that must be met. No matter how distasteful they may be."

Meara's puzzlement was obvious, and he knew he was speaking in riddles, dangerous riddles. He struggled to lighten his tone. "I don't know about you, but I'm hungry." He realized she wanted to say something, to ask questions, but she didn't. It was apparent in her face, and he thought even more of her for stifling the curiosity he knew he had aroused.

She leaned over the picnic basket, taking out the items wordlessly. Yet there were questions in the air, as loud as if they had been screamed outright.

They ate silently, listening to the gulls above them as the birds circled greedily, convinced of ultimate edible reward. The food was probably really quite good, Michael thought, but now it tasted like chalk and he had to force himself to eat it. Meara's enthusiasm was no greater, he noticed.

And, damn, the wine was flat. Or seemed that way. Everything was bitter. Bitter and flavorless.

He looked up and saw the blimp browsing slowly over the sea, watching, searching.

Meara saw his glance. "I hope they find something. We found a part of a picture frame yesterday. It must have come from a ship."

"I know."

"I hate them," she said, her voice even more fierce as she thought of him returning to sea, thought of the danger to him.

"All of them?"

"Yes," she said fiercely.

"I don't expect they're all bad," he said carefully. "Many don't have a choice. Germany's their country."

"They sink unarmed ships and kill sailors in the water. They've invaded and killed throughout Europe. Loyalty to evil. What kind of loyalty or allegiance is that?"

Michael closed his eyes briefly, blocking out the sun, trying to block out the words. When he opened them again, he was surprised that the sun was still there because he only felt a cold, hard darkness.

"You're a journalist, Meara. There're always two sides."

"Not this time," she said stubbornly.

"Perhaps not." He surrendered, knowing he had already said far too much.

"Are you anxious to go back?" Her voice was tight.

He raised an eyebrow. "Part of me, maybe. It's what I do best, sailing. The sea. Another part would like to stay here, like this, forever. How about you? I would think you'd be anxious to start your job."

"Part of me." She mocked gently. "And part of me would like to stay here, like this, forever." Her voice grew wistful. "I'll always think of you here."

He didn't want her to think of him at all. He recalled the hatred in her voice when she spoke of Germans. Any hope of understanding, of forgiveness, had been quashed at that moment. Not that there ever was any. The hatred was natural enough, given the war between their two countries, but it was also very, very painful. Meara, with her joyous laughter and open heart, did not come easily to hate. But when she did, given that passionate nature of hers, it would be strong and unrelenting.

He poured them both a fresh glass of wine, truly needing it for the first time in his life. Every part of him ached to take her in his arms, every part but the logical, working region of his mind which even now could envision the disgust and fury soon to be in her eyes.

As if she sensed the battle within him, she was silent. The easy companionship between them was gone, but the electricity was still there, raw and vital and pulling, sizzling like an exposed, snaking wire ready to burst into flames.

His hand tightened around the glass and it broke in his hand, fine crystal falling in his lap and glimmering in the sand, light gold wine darkening the sun-kissed grains.

With a short apology, he spun upward, ignoring the sudden pain in his leg and Meara's surprised exclamation. He pushed his hands in his trouser pockets and stalked across the sand, alone and angry and confused in a way he'd never been before.

Meara watched him go, his shoulders squared and his legs stiff, the limp less noticeable, she guessed, through sheer will. She wanted to go after him, but something told her not to.

The tension in him had been palpable since he had picked her up. She could taste it, feel it. It had frightened her, for it took him away to a place she didn't understand.

There was a quality about him, never more so than now, that gave her pause. She had noticed it before, but he appeared so easy, so adaptable with people that she hadn't been able to identify that allusive impression until now.

But now she saw an aloneness about him. Not loneliness, not like that she had seen in Sanders Evans. Loneliness came from needing people and not having them. But this was something different altogether.

Meara remembered the moments of reserve, the times he had escaped into some inner place. She had watched him with people, winning them easily to him, yet there was always something distant, a part of him standing back and watching.

Her fingers carefully gathered the pieces of crystal which

had exploded into the sand and blanket, her mind grateful that there was something to do. A piece of glass cut her finger and she sucked at it, trying to stem the blood as well as the flood of emotions. Love. Grief. Confusion. Need.

Michael had been trying to tell her something, but she hadn't understood what. Only that it was some kind of farewell, and the thought pierced her like a dagger as she looked at his form moving along the beach, his blond hair ruffling in the cool, fragrant, giving breeze which always blew at this time of the year. He looked so solitary, but he also looked as if solitude fit him, was a part of him.

She loved him. How very, very much she loved him. And she knew little more about him than his name and that he was a Canadian. She didn't know how to contact him, or where he was from, or whether he had friends or family. When he left, he would be gone completely. Except for memories of a halcyon time when love came and the sun shone with uncommon brightness, and the night succored with gentle graciousness.

Meara had always thought love was something that came slowly, that you planted and nurtured and harvested. She had never expected it to bloom full blossomed without reason or sense, nor that it could fill the mind and soul and senses so completely and to the absolute exclusion of all else. Consumed. That was one word, but even that didn't describe the strength of a pounding, swelling heart, or the vividness with which it made every facet of life. The sun was brighter, the sea bluer, the air fresher, the songs sweeter. Her skin tingled with the blaze of the spring sun, or was it the remembrance of his touch. The world was somehow newer and brighter, and every second was precious. And the internal ache more painful than any she'd felt before.

Michael had disappeared around the curve of the beach, and she wondered whether she should go after him. As he had walked away, everything about him said stay away. Yet she needed him with a fierceness that made no more sense than anything else. She felt he needed her too, despite his veiled warnings of minutes earlier.

She carefully wrapped the broken glass in a cloth napkin and placed it in the picnic hamper. She stood stiffly, her legs cramped from the stillness with which she had sat, and, wisely or unwisely, she followed the footsteps in the sand.

She found him sitting down, almost completely out of sight, near a sand dune. He was staring out at the sea, his form motionless, like a statue. He didn't turn when she approached, but she knew from the sudden stiffening of his body that he knew she was there. Meara sank down next to him, her hand touching his arm slightly. She heard a sigh, like the rustle of wind against the sea oats growing in profusion along the dunes, and his arms went around her and pulled her close to him.

She looked up and his eyes were dark and depthless, the muscles in his jaw working furiously. "I need you," she said simply, and she saw something like agony flash across his face before his lips met hers in angry, urgent yearning. Now there was no stopping. She knew it as she looked up at the almost hopeless anguish in his face.

The sun played over them as they loved. Quietly and intensely. Because of her inexperience, he'd moved slowly, slow and tender and gentle, his hands guiding and soothing and resassuring. He saw the flicker of fear in her eyes, but almost immediately it disappeared in her growing passion as her body arched against his own with a need to give. He felt her moment of pain as if it were his, and he hesitated before continuing, urged on by her legs which had instinctively wrapped around him, seeking to bring him even further into her despite the hurt.

He felt sensations new and poignant and aching and glorious as he moved, teaching pleasure, learning giving, and he knew he had never really made, or given, love before. He was seized by elation and a wondering happiness. But it faded quickly as he looked into her eyes, trusting and rhapsodic, and knew where this would end.

But still he held her against him, not wanting to let her go. Her body was soft and yielding against his, and he wondered how they'd divested themselves of clothes. He didn't even remember now. He was only aware of the reality of her closeness, of the pleasure it gave him, of the feeling of well-being that he knew was temporary.

In less than a week now, she would know him for what he was. A spy. A seducer. She would think he'd made love to her in furtherance of his own aims. To help him destory her country. She would never believe it was for herself. But he had to make her believe that. He had to leave her that.

So little time. The fragility of the moment made every sensation more prolonged, more precious. Raw physical need was still there, on both their parts, yet he had a fierce desire to give rather than receive, and the moments stretched into blissful infinity as he savored the sound of her heartbeat, the taste of her, the feel of their bodies together, the gentle friction of skin against skin. Feelings were exquisitely intense as they built, one upon another, until the world was a spinning top full of swirling colors and uncontrolled motion.

When they finally parted, the sun was setting and they sat silently, watching it, their hands entwined. Splashes of crimson spread across the sky, blending into incredibly soft shades of pink and gold. The sea was swept by the last glimmering golden glaze of a lazily descending sun, and the first star was already visible overhead as a partial moon emerged in the fading daylight. Meara thought the earth resembled a velvet-lined box of jewels, some bright, some muted, but each beloved for its own special qualities.

Her own body felt like a jewel, cherished and polished and glowing. Her face flamed where his mouth had trailed kisses, and her core still trembled and throbbed with the warmth of him. His hand held hers tightly although the lines of his face were stiff. With what, she didn't know. She hoped it wasn't regret, for she could regret nothing.

He finally turned to her, an odd bafflement in his face. "I'm sorry, Meara. This should never have happened."

Her eyes, deep and green, searched his. "I'm not."

He smiled slightly as his gaze met hers directly. "You're the most honest woman I've ever known. And the most special." She wanted something else, and he knew it. She wanted words of love, but he couldn't give them. He couldn't compound his crime that much.

When they arrived at the Connor cottage, dusk had turned into darkness and he accompanied her to the door silently. His hand touched her face, and then he leaned down and kissed her lightly. "I didn't mean for this to happen."

"You were trying to be noble again. I'm glad you didn't succeed."

That enchanting honesty again. Enchanting and damning.

"God, you *are* a witch!"

She looked up at him, a quick mischievous smile on her lips. "I'm beginning to find all sorts of benefits in being one."

He couldn't help but smile back. "You're incorrigible."

"I know," she replied with satisfaction, her eyes laughing at her own daring.

The smile disappeared from his face. "I care about you, Meara. Never doubt that."

He had said the same words before, and now she felt the same sudden apprehension as she had then, the peculiar knowledge that he was trying to tell her something,

something she should know. A momentary fear ran through her.

"Tomorrow?" she asked hesitantly. She had never before asked a man that question, but she had to know. She had to.

"Perhaps," he said shortly. Then, watching her stricken face and knowing he couldn't leave things that way, not now, he amended the one cruel word. "I'll see you on the beach tomorrow. I promise."

Her hand touched his briefly. She opened the door, and she heard the Connors listening to the war news on the radio in the parlor. She heard snatches as she stood there, reluctant to move. She heard something about bombs and Berlin, and she saw his face tighten.

"Good night," he said abruptly, and then he was gone, only the clean spicy scent of him remaining. She heard Peter's voice and the rush of footsteps and she closed the door. Slowly and reluctantly.

Offshore in U-275, Klaus Hasser looked through the periscope at a convoy of American ships. Perfect targets. Three tankers and four additional merchant ships guarded by only two escorts. He could destroy one of the tankers, and the escorts could do nothing. They wouldn't dare leave the other ships to chase him.

But his orders were clear. He was to take no chances, none at all. He was to avoid all contact with enemy ships.

Frustration filled him. This trip had been anything but pleasant. The already crowded U-boat was filled to capacity, past capacity, with twenty German marines on board. He understood they were also to take on additional men, women, and children in a few days, and he had spent hours trying to work out the logistics. Already bunks were used by turns, and it was difficult to move from one area to another.

He had been assured that he would not have the un-wanted passengers long. Another submarine was on its way, scheduled to meet with him Easter Sunday to take aboard the human cargo. But still, he didn't like it. He didn't like anything about this mission. The waterway to the planned landing was extremely difficult, shallow with unpredictable currents. And his submarine had never been intended as a passenger ship.

It was dangerous, and he was damned if he liked being commandeered by German Intelligence. A destroyed ship was tangible proof of success. It was his reason for being, not this cloak-and-dagger stuff.

Still, he had no choice, so he ordered periscope down and swore. He hated this waiting. The crew was already quarrelsome and would be more so, given the inactivity and crowding.

Six more days. He shook his head as he saw, in his mind, the convoy disappearing out of range.

Chapter Nine

It was almost as if he were two different people, one of whom he didn't recognize.

Michael hesitated on the beach. He had started out before sunrise, watching the pale glow wash and color the water and earth with silvery brilliance. He had needed this time alone, a time when no one else was around. He'd needed the time to think.

The plan had been proceeding far more successfully than even the greatest expectations. He had played whist, poker, and billiards with members of the club. He was welcomed at every table, in every room. He was listened to respectfully and included in invitations. He had been asked to play golf but had demurred regretfully because of his leg.

He had already mentioned hosting a party before he left, a thank-you, he said, that had been impossible for the club members to decline. It was to be, he said, a revival of an old custom at the club, a men's after-dinner get-together. He had been regaled with tales of the club, and how private meetings and discussions there had had profound effects on the country, how in 1910 members secretly drafted a plan for sweeping bank reforms, how the first continental phone call originated from Jekyll Island by member Thomas Vail, who was president of AT&T, how Joseph Pulitzer discussed events of the day with other members.

The enthusiasm with which his invitation was met did not fill Michael with triumph. Instead, he was being consumed alive by a steadily growing despair, a despair he had to hide. The lives of his family depended on his acting ability, on his skill in pulling off what could be the espionage coup of the war.

Christ, he wished he could run away. Now. Run from the conflicting needs that were ripping him apart. And that wasn't all. He wanted desperately to take Meara with him, to be young and carefree and happy with her. He wanted, God help him, to protect and preserve those short idyllic periods of time when he had closed out the rest of the world.

Michael had never really been young. Or carefree. Or open. Growing up in a home racked with violence, he had created a distance between himself and others, becoming an observer rather than a participant in and of life. It had been the only way he could survive.

That ability to distance himself had served him well when he went to sea. He could divorce himself from the stifling, cramped curse-filled quarters, from the exhaustion of a boy's doing a man's work, of laboring around the clock at times, of tolerating the violent roughhousing and often malicious teasing. None of it had been easy for a boy raised in physical, if not emotional, luxury.

But survive he had, and the protective covering had grown more insular over the years. He knew he had been a damned good officer because he never allowed emotions to interfere in a decision. Although he cultivated an easy manner on the surface, a facile charm he had known and despised in his father, he'd never had any close friends of his own, had always steered clear of any emotional attachments.

Michael had feared he might have inherited his father's violence, the twisted strain that had ruined his childhood and reduced his mother to a weak, totally dependent woman. He had been conscious, all his life, of restraining his own temper, particularly after the one instance as a boy when he knew he was capable of killing his own father. That had frightened him more than any thought of retribution from the man who had sired him.

He'd had to fight. A freighter in the twenties and thirties was a hard school. Michael had learned early to protect himself. But he only did so when absolutely necessary and then with restraint. He perfected a discipline that ruled every facet of his life.

But something had happened to that discipline here. It lay in tattered rags around him. Hunger, raw hurting hunger, had chewed through every defense he had. He had tasted youth and laughter and hope, and he wanted more. He wanted to hear Meara's voice, to feel the spontaneous joy swelling up inside, to realize again the sense of belonging and warmth and pleasure of joining his body with hers. Not using it, as he had used women's bodies in the past, but becoming one with her. To give as he had never given before. He'd never felt that kind of desire until now, and he knew it was because he had never been truly alive until he came to this island.

Michael stared out the window of his room. Three more days until the submarine came, before Hans would lead a group of German marines to the clubhouse where, according to plan, most of the intended targets would be gathered at a party hosted by him. Only Sanders Evans was a threat; there were no armed guards as such on the island, only two watchmen who had probably never fired a gun in their lives.

Evans would have to be taken care of in some way, and prior to the submarine's arrival. A harmless but potent drug, perhaps. Michael didn't want to kill him, but if Hans suspected the man's identity, there would be no question of Evans's fate. For some reason he didn't understand, Michael did not intend for that to happen. Evans was an enemy, but there was something about the FBI agent that Michael liked and admired. And envied.

Perhaps he would invite Evans to his room for a drink the evening of the raid. Evans would come, he knew. Michael fully realized that Sanders Evans was, at the very least, more than a little curious about him.

His reluctance to kill Evans was quixotic, he knew. He had, without emotion or guilt, directed gunfire that had surely killed dozens if not hundreds of men. Now he wondered if his suddenly strong aversion to killing—no, murder—derived from the fact that he actually knew Evans or because he now had a new appreciation of life.

An appreciation, he knew, that had a very short time to exist. Minutes. Hours.

Two days had passed since the picnic, two confusing days of sliding from one persona to another, from a man finding love for the first time to a soldier whose duty was abhorrent but essential.

Sometimes he thought he was going mad.

Despite his best intentions, he had not been able to keep away from Meara and the Connor children, although he made sure such meetings were always on the beach, far away from Hans's probing eyes. He knew her routine now, knew where she would be at nearly every hour. If he were within sight of Hans, he would pass them by, if not, he would stop and take forbidden pleasure in a few stolen moments.

Part of him hoped that Meara would never discover his role. That the plan would proceed so smoothly that he would simply be part of a group which disappeared. But he knew that scenario was too much to hope for. There could easily be resistance, even bitter fighting, death, violence on this island that was so special to Meara. Her island of dreams could become her island of nightmares.

The thought was excruciating, and yet he still could not break away from her. He realized he was like a lemming swimming to its doom or a moth slowly burning to death. Yet he was as helpless to save himself as they. The compulsion was simply too overpowering.

He was only too aware, much of the time, of two sets of eyes on him: Sanders Evans's and Hans Weimer's. He was not amused by the dichotomy of the situation. Neither side trusted him.

To make everything complete, he no longer trusted himself.

From the edge of the pool in front of the clubhouse, Meara watched Peter and Tara race across the pool. Oblivious to the chill of the water, they swam like little fishes, almost as much at home in the water as they were on land.

There was also a lifeguard on duty, and Meara allowed her thoughts to wander, gazing expectantly toward the front of the clubhouse, hoping to catch a glimpse of Michael.

In the several days since the picnic, he'd seemed to avoid her although they had met and talked twice on the beach. She would have been devastated by his desertion had she not seen the pain in his eyes each time she saw him and the way his hand reached out to touch her when they stood together. There was no disguising the awareness that always ran between them. It reverberated in the air like distant thunder. She felt it. She knew he felt it.

She sensed he was trying to avoid hurting her. He would be leaving in several days, perhaps not to return, and he was trying to minimize the impact. Yet there was no way to minimize her feelings now, and she was determined to tell him that, to tell him she would take every moment she could now, and never regret the ones they may not have in the future.

Meara told herself that the very fact he was trying "to do the right thing" said he cared about her, perhaps even loved her, she hoped wistfully. If it were otherwise, wouldn't he readily take what was offered?

She looked down at her bathing suit, pleased that she had spent precious money in buying this new one. It was a two-piece suit, a trifle daring for her usual conservative taste. The color, a rich forest green that she knew complemented her eyes, had prompted the unusual purchase. This was the first time the weather had been truly warm enough to wear it, and she was both nervous and expectant at Michael seeing her in it. Her figure, she knew, was slim and pleasant enough, but nothing spectacular. She had few of the curves some of the other girls here had.

"Meara." She turned around and watched Sanders approach, and she smiled in return. He was in a swimming suit and a loosely fitting shirt, and he looked fit and attractive. She liked him more each day, and any other time she would welcome his company. But now all she wanted was a few moments alone with Michael. A few moments which, she hoped, would lead to more.

But immediately she was ashamed as she saw the flash of pleasure in Sanders's eyes.

"May I join you?"

"Of course," she replied. "You've been down to the beach?"

He nodded.

"Many people down there?"

His eyes were knowing. Kind and knowing. "A few. I saw your Canadian friend return from one of his long walks."

Meara tried to appear indifferent but she could feel a blush crawl up her face. The question came quickly to her lips, splashing out before she could prevent it. "Is he still down there?"

Sanders nodded, and Meara felt his sharp gaze penetrate right through her. There were questions in the look, questions that she couldn't answer. Questions and a hint of sympathy.

She was surprised when he quietly voiced one of those questions. "Has he said much about himself, about his family?"

"Only that he doesn't have any. Why?"

Sanders didn't answer for a moment. "I don't know," he finally said slowly. "It's just that . . . I don't think I've ever seen a man who seems quite so alone."

Meara stared at him. So he had seen it too. It was curious because Michael mingled so easily, and with so much warm charm, with others. She didn't realize anyone else had noticed the brief seconds, sometimes only a quick flash, of emptiness, of complete isolation, that she had glimpsed in him.

Sanders watched her closely, realizing that she had seen the same thing he had, and he was surprised. He was a trained observer. Meara was not. Still, it probably meant nothing. He had checked with FBI headquarters and his superiors had found nothing odd about Michael Fielding. Sanders still, however, felt a vague disquiet that was pure instinct and had asked for a more thorough investigation.

"He nearly died. Perhaps, that's why," Meara answered slowly. "I would think that would give anyone a sense . . . of needing time alone."

"Could be," Sanders observed neutrally. "His leg seems

to be getting better. But then I don't think I've ever seen anyone work so hard at making it that way."

She hesitated, not quite sure of the reasons for Sanders's interest. "So he can go back and get shot at again," Meara finally replied, resignation in her voice. "Why do men like war so much?"

"I don't think it's a case of liking," Sanders said. "At least not for most men. It's more of a case of necessity, duty if you wish. Or honor."

"But he doesn't have to go back, not with that leg."

"Perhaps he does . . . for himself," Sanders said.

"And you?" It was an unfair question, she knew, especially when he stiffened slightly. But his questions worried her in a way she didn't understand.

"I have my own job," he finally said cautiously.

"Catching spies?" she said, her curiosity over his occupation surfacing.

He shrugged. "I do a lot of things."

"Can you tell me about them?"

"It's not that interesting. Mostly waiting. Or pouring over books and figures until you think you're going blind."

"What kind of books?"

Sanders grinned, his body relaxing. "Now I see the journalist in you."

"You're avoiding the subject."

"I'm on vacation."

"But you're not really enjoying it."

His glance was sharp, once more surprised at her intuition. "No, I don't guess I am. Except for you. I'm not used to this kind of luxury. I don't really enjoy it."

"Then why did you come?"

"It was . . . suggested to me."

"And you always take suggestions?"

His mouth twitched at the corners at her pert persistence. "Depends on who they come from."

"You haven't found any spies here?"

"Nary a one." He grinned.

"Good," Meara said, leaning back with her two hands based firmly behind her on the cement near the edge of the pool. "Now you can relax, or do you ever really relax?"

Sanders looked at her intently. She continued to surprise him with her perceptiveness. "Whenever there's a very pretty woman around."

"I don't think I believe you," she replied with a slight smile. "I doubt if anything really distracts you."

"You should tell my boss that," he replied with a slow, lazy smile. "But I don't think he'll believe you." He glanced out at Tara and Peter, who were conducting a water fight in the pool. "I think Tara needs some assistance," he said. He took off his shirt and slipped into the water, giving a short yelp at its cold temperature.

Meara watched as he swam easily over to the youngsters and bent his head over to speak to Tara. It must be difficult for him, she thought as she remembered the pain with which he spoke of his own wife and child. She dived into the pool and swam to them, joining Peter's cause while Sanders became Tara's champion. In seconds, they were splashing and laughing together.

He was an easy man to be with, despite what must be an often violent occupation. There was something nurturing about him, even with those eyes that looked as if they saw everything. He would make a good friend, she knew, a very loyal one. She had seen the admiration in his eyes and knew he had been on the brink several times of asking her out. Yet he showed today that he realized her interest lay elsewhere, and offered companionship instead.

Unlike many women, Meara had always had men friends, friends in the nonromantic way. Many of her ambitions and interests were comparable to theirs, and because she had her own goals she seldom thought of men as possible conquests or marriage partners. She didn't indulge in many of the usual games between men and women, and had shunned relationships that might affect her career.

But since she had met Michael, she was beginning to feel more and more like a woman. She now understood, only too well, the illogical pull between two people, the obsession that had always escaped her until now. Obsession. Was that another word for love?

She finally pleaded a chill, and lifted herself easily back to the edge of the pool, watching as Sanders continued to play with the children. The sun was at its most pleasant, warm and caressing as it often was in late March on the island, and her skin dried quickly. She closed her eyes, enjoying the light warmth, the sense of well-being it stirred in her.

"Meara." Peter's demanding voice broke into her thoughts. She looked to the pool where he stood on Sanders's shoulders, ready to dive into the water. She smiled at him before looking away, looking toward the road to the beach.

He was there, walking slowly and deliberately, and she remembered what Sanders had said, and now, more than ever, she felt it—a stark, lonely quality. But when he saw her, his shoulders straightened almost rakishly, and he flashed a crooked, even abashed, grin at her.

The change came so quickly she thought she only imagined her first impression. But nothing mattered, nothing but the electrification of the air as he approached, his gaze running swiftly and approvingly over her bathing costume, devouring her, possessing her.

He sat on the edge of a chair to rest. He wasn't using the cane again today, and she heard the slight sigh of relief as he sat. She could only wonder at the determination that made him exercise his leg so thoroughly when there obviously was much pain. She wanted to massage the deep scars she had seen on his leg, to run a hand along the ridge of his firmly set jaw, to erase the lines around his eyes. She wanted to touch. She wanted to touch and be touched.

Instead, she rose as gracefully as possible from where she sat on the cement, and walked to the chair next to his. Heat radiated between them. Heat and excitement and uncertainty. She watched his body tense ever so slightly as she neared. His gaze rested on her for one intimately intense moment before moving to the pool where Sanders now relaxed against the side before swinging up and joining them.

"Commander," Sanders acknowledged.

Michael's gaze shifted from Meara to Sanders. "Michael," he insisted.

"Another early walk on the beach?"

Meara wondered if all Sanders's conversations were on the inquisitive side, but Michael appeared to take no offense. "It's the best time of day. You should try it."

"Maybe I will," Sanders replied lightly.

Meara looked from one man to another. There was a challenge and wariness between the two men she really didn't understand.

Yet there was something else too, something similar between them. An elusive similarity. Strength, maybe. Determination?

She knew Michael well enough by now to detect the slight tension in his body as he ordered coffee from a waiter making a circuit of the tables.

"How long are you staying?" Michael asked the other man.

"Through Easter. And you?"

"The same."

"And then?"

"To London."

"How is London these days?"

"Grim," Michael replied. "Bombed-out buildings, shortages of everything."

"I hear the morale is still good though, especially now that British bombers are giving Germany a taste of its own medicine."

Michael's stomach tightened. His mother and brother were in Berlin, and the British night bombing had been a continuous source of fear for him. But he kept his face impassive.

"The British," he said, "are survivors."

Sanders's eyes clouded slightly. "My wife and I went to London years ago. It seemed so peaceful. It's difficult to think of it today."

As he had difficulty thinking of Berlin. Michael looked at Meara. Fire and destruction. Mindless, impersonal, violent death raining from the sky. He looked upward, watching some clouds drift across the peaceful sky. They were innocuous looking now, puffs of lace against a rich blue background.

"War seems a long way off here," he said, more to himself than to the others.

"I know what you mean," Sanders replied dryly. "But a ship was blown up not far from here a few days ago. Those damned U-Boats seem to have free range of the sea."

Michael grimaced. "I think the return to England might be as dangerous as actual duty."

"How will you be going?"

"A Canadian transport."

"You've already made arrangements then?"

Michael nodded.

Sanders picked up the watch he had taken off before entering the pool, and looked at it. "I have some telephone calls to make," he said apologetically. "I'll see you both later."

As Sanders walked toward the clubhouse, Michael's gaze returned to Meara. Her face was turned toward the pool where she could keep an eye on Peter and Tara. But he saw her chin lift slightly, and he knew that she was fully aware that his attention was on her.

He felt that curious split within himself again. Part of him wanting to stay, the other part warning him to leave.

"More coffee?"

The waiter was back, and Michael hadn't even noticed him approaching. God, what was happening to him? He looked around for Hans, but thankfully he didn't see him.

He nodded, and the waiter refilled his cup. Michael's hand reached for it, his fingers accidentally brushing Meara's. Or was it accidental?

Michael realized as skin burned skin that he no longer knew, that he no longer had complete control of himself. His eyes met hers, and once again he was lost in the swirling emerald brightness, in the soft plea that reached wordlessly out to him.

The tightness in his middle became a vise, and he felt life squeezing out of him, a life that could be restored only by touching her. But he dared not, not with the possibility of Hans lurking around, spying.

He could almost laugh at the thought. Almost laugh with pain, with the horribly poor and ironic joke. He exhaled deeply, trying to retain some sanity, some balance. Michael felt Meara's hand move over his, as if she discerned the turmoil in him, the deep, biting hurt, the confusion.

"I have to talk to you," she said softly. "Later, perhaps. Alone?"

Her voice was full of uncertainty, with an obvious fear of being rebuffed, and he understood what he had been doing to her these last several days. He had avoided her because he thought it best in the long run, but was it? Was there some way he could try to make her understand?

"You're free this afternoon?"

She nodded, her eyes flaring with hope, and again he felt torn between what was right, and what was easy. Except nothing was easy. Nothing. Nothing was painless. Nothing would be painless.

There was no best thing. No right thing. Yet he felt a sudden buoyant hope that had no basis in common sense. It was just there, a sense of elation that he would again spend time with her, feel for a few more hours what it was to be loved and wanted. What it was to love in return. To feel the bright blast of sunshine in what had been a dark shadowy place.

Damning himself for every kind of fool, he nonetheless continued in his folly. "I'll arrange for the motorboat this afternoon. We'll go over to Saint Simon's Island."

Away from prying eyes. Hans's eyes. Sanders's eyes. Away from the island.

"Commander!"

He turned around to see a dripping Peter standing in front of him. He forced a smile at the expectant face. "Hullo," he greeted the boy.

"I swam across the pool twenty times," Peter said proudly.

"I noticed. A regular little shark."

Peter puffed with pride. "Yes, sir. I was hoping you would race me."

Michael considered the request gravely. He liked Peter very much. If he ever had a son . . .

"I think you might destroy my ego," he finally said, quite seriously.

Peter flashed his wide grin. "I hope so, Commander."

"That's a challenge I can't resist," Michael said, pushing

the chair from the table and rising. "I have to change. In ten minutes?"

"Me, too," chimed Tara.

Meara laughed. "Why don't you race me?"

"All right," Tara said.

"The last one in is a dead duck," Meara said as she glanced gleefully at Michael. The world was suddenly a wonderful place again. She would have this afternoon with Michael. Her heart pounded fiercely as she took several steps to the side of the pool and gracefully dived in, aware that he was watching.

But when she came up, his back was to her, and he was moving toward the clubhouse.

She heard Tara scream with delight as the girl paddled out to the middle of the pool, and she told herself it didn't matter that Michael had left. He would soon be back. And there was this afternoon.

This afternoon. Her hands squeezed the water, throwing up handfuls in pure delight. This afternoon.

Hans stooped over a hedge and watched the girl in the pool. She was too thin for his taste, her hair too red, but she was striking. There was no question about that.

Something about her bothered him, and he wasn't quite sure what. Perhaps it was the way von Steimen seemed to tense when she was around. Hans had asked his partner about her and received a curt answer. But then all of von Steimen's answers were curt.

Hans would be glad when this business was finished. He hated his subservient pose, and he despised the people he met. The servants were groveling, the guests condescending, looking at him as if he were less than a man. And he worried about von Steimen. He had never trusted the man or his commitment to this job, and his uneasiness had grown during his few conversations with him. The man was deliberately keeping him in ignorance, answering his questions with short impatience and contempt.

But there had been nothing concrete he could pinpoint. He had his own radio in his room in Brunswick, a radio that von Steimen knew nothing about. Hans had, so far, resisted the temptation to use it, to double-check von Steimen. The U-boat was to surface every other night at midnight, but he had no proof that anything was wrong. Only a vague feeling. And that, he knew, might well be a product of his deep dislike of von Steimen. He did not want to look like a fool.

But he had watched von Steimen very, very carefully. The man seemed to be doing exactly as he was told, mixing with the other members. Von Steimen had already told him his party was set on the night of the raid, and that everything was going according to plan. There was no real reason to doubt him.

Until today, when he had seen the girl touch von Steimen's hand and the way von Steimen had responded, the way his eyes had lingered on the girl.

His hands moved as he considered the incident at the pool and minutes later when von Steimen returned. He watched the man race the boy across the pool while the woman watched. Hans didn't like the sound of laughter, not at all. Not from the woman, not from the boy. Particularly not from von Steimen.

His apprehension increased.

Yet, he told himself, he had been watching von Steimen carefully, and there had been no previous indication of interest in the girl, nothing more than what seemed accidental meetings. It probably meant nothing. Saturday, it would all be over. He would be on a submarine back to Germany, and probably to a Knight's Cross and promotion. He could already see the pride in his son's eyes.

Hans turned back to the roses he was trimming. He

would keep an even closer eye on von Steimen all the same. Perhaps he would even arrange to stay on the island tonight without von Steimen's knowledge.

Help was scarce on the island now, and an offer to work late and stay in the employees' dormitory would probably be met with gratitude.

He looked back at the pool. Von Steimen had left. The girl and the two children were drying themselves, preparing to leave. Perhaps he was being overly concerned.

Perhaps.

Chapter Ten

T HE BOAT BOUNCED up and down the swells, splashing cold water on its two occupants as it darted through the pewter-colored water.

The day was cooling, the sun shadowed by increasingly ponderous-looking clouds. The water was frothing more than usual, its usual blue color gray with snowy caps.

But nothing could take the fine edge from the day for Meara. It could have been the most splendid, glorious day in all history. Her every nerve tingled with the nearness of Michael.

She leaned back in the seat and watched him with pleasure. He handled the boat with such easy competency, even through the choppy waves, that she could readily see him at the helm of a mammoth ship, guiding it into port.

She could, in fact, imagine him at the wheel of a two-hundred-year old sailing ship, his gold hair catching the sun as he pirated his way across the seas. There was something in that proud tilt of his chin, the icy blue eyes, and the lean strength of his body that summoned images of adventure and danger.

Meara silently scolded herself for such romantic fancy. She had never indulged in such nonsense before although she had read hundreds of historical novels, just as she read everything she could find.

Perhaps it was the giddy, joyous feeling his presence created in her. Perhaps the way he looked at her with tenderness. Perhaps the graceful movements of his body as he turned toward her and reached out a hand in reassurance after they bounced over a particularly contentious wave.

He hadn't needed to take her hand. She felt very safe with him. She had felt safe with him from the beginning. Physically safe if not emotionally secure. But now she felt that too, because each time he looked at her he couldn't disguise the sudden softening of his expression although she could tell he tried.

She had been bitterly afraid earlier in the day that he had changed his mind about the trip to Saint Simons Island. A servant from the clubhouse had presented himself at the Connor cottage with a note, and for a moment Meara feared that he had decided against their outing.

But no. The note merely asked her to meet him at the dock. He had an errand to run near there, he'd said. She hadn't questioned the request but only felt a surge of delight that she would be with him. She'd known he was fighting something within himself, and that whatever it was concerned her. But she thought that if she had enough time she could convince him that she was indeed grown up and knew what she was doing, knew the risks, and was willing to take them without regret.

Michael had been at the dock when she'd arrived, and he wasted no time in handing her into the boat and shoving off. They had been there no more than two or three minutes. She hopefully attributed his efficiency to his desire to be with her, as she desired so much to be alone with him.

There was little conversation. The wind blew strong, and the waves were rough. Michael focused all his concentration on keeping the boat on course and as steady as possible. Meara didn't need words; it was enough to be with him, to look at him, to share the warm pleasure that was always a part of his presence.

It gave her time to wonder about him. After Sanders's interest, she had become even more curious, more intrigued. It continued to bother her that she knew remarkably little about him, although he had not appeared to avoid her questions. He was, she had realized, a master at deflecting them.

But she had today, and the cloudy day was magnificent, the sea spray invigorating, the wind intoxicating. There was only the sky and earth as boundaries. Her hand crept out to his, which rested on the wheel. His fingers entwined around her hand, clasping it tightly until another wave bounced them. His gaze returned to the sea in front of him, and then he released her.

Still, there was an intimacy between them, as if their thoughts were touching, if not their bodies. A quiet intimacy that needed no words, only each another's presence.

Because he went slower in the rough water than the boat's regular speed, the trip to Saint Simons took more than an hour. When they arrived, a car was waiting for them, and Michael directed the driver to the Cloister Hotel, which was located nearby on adjoining Sea Island.

Michael smiled when he saw her surprised look. "They told me about this place at the clubhouse and I phoned ahead for reservations for tea."

Meara had heard of the Cloister, but had never been there. It was a public hotel, unlike the Jekyll Island facility, yet it had attracted some of the outstanding celebrities of the time, including actress Sarah Churchill, Eugene

O'Neill, Sherwood Anderson, Lillian Gish, Bennett Cerf, and even Charles Lindbergh.

Meara looked down at her clothes, a casual sundress and sandals.

"You look lovely," he said, interpreting her glance and taking her elbow. He helped her into a car waiting there to carry them the short distance to the hotel.

The next hours were pure fairy-tale magic. In some ways, the hotel was similar to the Jekyll Island clubhouse: elegantly comfortable, without pretension. A man played the piano while Meara sipped tea and Michael a brandy, and delicious sandwiches and pastries were served. Michael was, by far, the most striking man there, and his attention was completely on her, his dark blue eyes fastened intently on her face as if memorizing every detail.

Nothing was real. Everything was real, particularly the racing of her heart and the quickening of her blood, the elation she felt at being with him. All the questions she was going to ask fled her mind. She wanted nothing to shadow the raw desire in his eyes.

Then a twisted smile curved his mouth as if he realized his face was saying too much.

"I'll miss you, Meara," he said softly. "More than you'll ever know."

"Will you write?"

His eyes were bleak as he seemed to consider her request. "I'm not very good at that."

"But I am," she said impishly. "I can make up for both of us."

"I'm afraid the mail's very unreliable," Michael replied grimly. "I don't want you to wait and worry."

"I won't," she promised.

"I'll keep up with you through *Life.*" A teasing note was back in his voice but, it sounded forced.

"Give me at least five months to make a name for myself," Meara answered, her voice gently mocking herself.

He reached out a hand to her cheek, indifferent to the sympathetic stares around them. "One month," he said, "and no more for someone as determined as you."

"You will write, won't you?" she persisted, part of her aching and frustrated over his refusal to commit, another part reacting to the ever-so-tender touch.

"It may be impossible."

"Do you want *me* to write?"

She watched him as a nerve moved in his cheek. "It'll be a very long war. I don't want you to wait for me. There will be others—"

"No," she replied with absolute certainty, and she saw his jaw tighten again.

"It's the island," he tried again. "If we'd met someplace else . . ."

"The same thing would have happened," she finished for him. "At least for me." There was a note of pain in her voice.

His face closed, and she could no longer tell what he was thinking. Instead, he signaled for a waiter, quickly paid the bill, and rose, his hand taking her elbow protectively. She measured her step to his limp, although she was learning that even that uneven gait was fast when he was so minded.

When they arrived back at the dock, Michael excused himself and disappeared in a boat store for several moments. When he emerged, he took her hand and helped her back into the boat, his clasp firm but casual.

The water was still choppy, the clouds even fuller than before, almost as if they wanted to drop from the sky. The earlier pleasant wind was cool, almost stinging, as it swept in from the open sea.

Meara looked at his profile. It was harsh and withdrawn,

and she knew achingly that nothing had been settled, that she was just as uncertain as ever about his real feelings.

"Where are we going now?"

"Back."

Meara hesitated. Tomorrow was Good Friday. She would spend much of the day watching the children, and she planned to attend special services at Faith Chapel in the afternoon. Although she and the Connors were Catholic, they attended Faith Chapel, the only church on the island, during the season.

And Michael was leaving Sunday.

"Can we stop at the beach on the way back?" The question was open and blatant and one she had never dreamed she would make. But then nothing was as it had been. She would never again be as she was two weeks ago.

Michael looked down at her, his eyes that unfathomable blue, protective and uncommunicative, and she started to wilt before the unblinking gaze. But then, miraculously, his face relaxed although his expression was wry as he finally nodded. His hand was warm and reassuring as he helped her into the boat which was moving jerkily in the waves.

When the boat was underway, he held his arm out and she moved over, inside it, feeling the warmth of his light embrace. She snuggled up against his chest, knowing that her question had been right, that this was right.

The wind caressed her face, the drops from the sea washing her with a salty mist. Despite the uncomfortable and unsatisfying discussion at the Cloister, she felt reborn, exultant, hopeful. He could no more stay away from her than she could him. She knew it now. No matter how much he tried, something in him wouldn't, couldn't let go.

She looked up at him, and just then a gust of wind shook the ribbon from her hair and it streamed out, wild and free. He looked down at her, and she saw raw naked longing in it. His lips touched her face, his tongue licking the mist away, while one hand continued to steer the boat through the cresting waves. A hard, jolting thump threw them against each other, and he eased the speed until they were at a bare crawl, just enough to keep the motor running. He took his belt from his slacks and tied the wheel to an arm rest, aiming the boat toward the now gray island that was Jekyll.

Mist was all around them, the sky was as gray as the sea, all different shades of gray—from pearl to pewter. The boat strained at its tether but kept going, slowly, very slowly, toward the island as Michael pulled her completely into his arms, his mouth hungrily tracing the lines of her cheeks and then her neck before seeking her mouth.

She heard thunder but knew it was not from the sky. She felt the searing heat of lightning and knew it was not from nature. Piercing streaks of need thundered and burned inside her, and her arms went around Michael with the urgency of impending loss. She felt the same desperate desire in him as his arms possessed her as completely as his lips. He was trembling. So was she, but she had never expected it of a man, especially one as sure and strong as Michael. Her heart slammed against her ribcage and she opened her eyes to look at his face. The corners of his eyes were wet, and she wondered for the briefest of seconds whether it could possibly be tears. But no, it must be sea mist, the tiny drops of water carried by the wind. His tongue felt salty as it explored her mouth greedily, seeking every little hollow to tease and inflame.

Just as their bodies blended together across the seat, the boat leapt upward, falling straight down, and a huge wave washed into the boat. Michael grabbed the wheel, a part chuckle, part curse exploding from deep in his throat as he sought to bring the boat back under control.

"That was damned stupid," he said with such sheer self-disgust, she had to laugh at him despite being soaked from head to foot.

"I think it was wonderful." She giggled, unable to help herself. She felt free, freer than she'd ever felt before in her life. Free and wild and at one with the elements, part of the rushing wind and the churning sea and the sheer perversity of both.

He shook his head at her exclamation, but a smile replaced the frown.

"Let's not go back yet," she yelled through the wind.

"You'll freeze to death."

"Not if we build a fire."

Michael looked toward the horizon. Although the light mist appeared to encompass everything now, it wasn't heavy enough to soak potential firewood. The time must be around six in the evening. The boat carrying Hans back to Brunswick would leave around six-thirty. It would be far better if he and Meara did not return before the man left, particularly looking this way.

Meara's hair was wild, and her face flushed from the wind and his kiss. Their clothes were soaked. He felt inside his jacket pocket for matches and brought them out. They were, through some miracle, still dry.

He didn't want to leave her. God help him. He couldn't leave her. Not now. Not when she looked so enchanting with that hopeful smile and passion-glazed eyes and hair dancing like flames in the wind.

As they neared the island, he looked for a small cove where the water wasn't too shallow and the sand wouldn't choke the motor. He finally found what he was seeking, the entrance to a small creek, and he cut the motor, letting the boat drift to the shore until the propeller hit sand. He rolled up the legs of his slacks and went over the side, shivering slightly as the cold water hit his skin. He kept his hand on the rope attached to the back of the boat and he held his arms out to Meara.

"Your leg." She demurred. "I can walk myself."

"No," he said with such emphasis and sureness that she didn't question his silent order further. She felt his arms go around her, felt their confidence and strength as they held her firmly.

His gait was surprisingly graceful, and she sensed it was through sheer determination. In seconds he lowered her to the beach, his grin smugly satisfied.

She shook her head sadly. "Masculine ego."

He grinned back, more carefree than she had seen him in several days, almost as if he, as she had, felt more in tune with the wild private world they were sharing than the calm civilized one they usually inhabited.

"I feel like Robinson Crusoe," she said.

"As long as Friday doesn't come along," he qualified, and Meara loved the light, laughing sensuality in his voice.

"My sentiments exactly."

"But then we have to build our own fire," he warned.

"Small price."

His hands went around her waist and he pulled her to him. Her clothes were drenched and clung to her body like a second skin. He felt her shiver and reluctantly released her. "I'll secure the boat and get some wood."

"I'll help," she said, not willing to let him out of her sight.

He pulled the boat in as far as he could, then secured the long rope to a heavy log on the beach. He held out his hand and she took it, their fingers entwining in both an intimate and companionable way.

The underbrush was heavy, and it didn't take them long to gather enough twigs and thick branches to start a fire. In minutes, Michael had one blazing, and they sat in front of it, savoring the warmth of the flames and of each other.

He held her in front of him, her back to his chest, his arms around her waist as they watched the curling, flickering streaks of orange-and-crimson flame reach for the sky.

A cinnamon glow colored the horizon as the cloud-shrouded sun set, and even the sea took on the shade, glints of gold flashing on pewter. Gulls hopefully swept the sea for one last meal of the day, their mournful cries echoing in the quiet, muted dusk.

Meara felt tears at the back of her eyes. Her fingers played along the blond hairs of his wrists, and she looked up at him, knowing that he, at the same instant, had lowered his lips to kiss her. Lazily at first, they kissed, lips touching lips with featherlike gentleness, each prolonging every exquisite magical moment.

The kiss deepened, slowly, each step relished and treasured before proceeding to the next one, as if they both had decided separately that the majesty of the mountain was that much greater when climbed slowly, when each plateau was reward in itself. To touch and be touched was enough at first. Meara's hands lost themselves in his thick hair which curled with the sea air, locks wrapping themselves around her fingers as if they longed to be there.

Meara lifted her eyes and saw the flames of the fire reflected in his dark blue ones. Then she felt his hands moving toward the back of her dress, opening it and unhooking the brassiere under it. His fingers cradled her breasts for a moment, then pulled the dress off, his gaze running over her body with a fierce possessiveness. Slowly his hands touched everywhere, sending increasingly urgent sensations cascading through her body. His lips followed them as one of his hands unbuttoned his shirt and then his slacks. Without actually taking them off, he pulled her body close to his, and the combined friction of cloth and skin against her own naked body did things to her that she could not quite comprehend. She had thought she had reached the summit of feelings the other day, but they seemed pale compared to those she now experienced.

Her skin was alive with feeling, with wanting, and the core of her was a mass of writhing nerve ends, the pain sweet and exquisite in anticipation. She felt him shudder and knew his own body was reacting in similar fashion, hardening and trembling with a need that went beyond lust or passion.

Their bodies came together, and he entered, deep and throbbing but carefully, tenderly, as if each touch was to be savored and collected and remembered. But as he went deeper, the urgency became greater and Meara felt him love her inside, felt him reaching for more and more of her, and she joined him in his movements, her legs going around his, helping him to reach the core of her, to become completely one with her. Without consciousness, she gave him every part of her, every piece of her body and heart and soul. "My love," she whispered.

She felt his response, not in words, but in his body, the way his hands moved and the way he moved inside her, like a dance of love with sensual, prolonged movements, each designed to prolong pleasure, to incite each hidden feeling and exploit it until the dance turned wild and uncontrollable, reaching beyond familiar feelings, rocketing to places unknown in flashes of white hot splendor. . . .

Meara lay silently, Michael still fused to her, his hands moving gently over her body as if he didn't really believe she was here. The urgency was gone, but a honeyed sweetness remained, a quiet contented joy. Completion.

She had never realized anything was missing from her life before, but she knew now the peace of being as one with another, the joining of heart and soul. She knew the ultimate in pleasure, the ultimate in happiness, the ultimate in loving. She sighed with the new knowledge, a low purr that hummed in the still night air.

Michael heard the sound with his ears and his heart, and
he felt pain arcing through him. For a few moments he had
felt whole and alive and vibrant, but now reality slowly
crept in, flooding him with guilt. But still his hands would
not leave her.

He withdrew slowly, gently from her body, but he cradled her in his arms, not wanting to let her go. She moved
in them so trustingly, so completely giving of herself, that
his pain deepened. This would be the last time he would
see her like this, and he wanted the memories, not only
his but hers, to be soft and gentle. He wanted her to know,
in the days ahead, that he had truly cared for her, had
loved her. Did love her. Would always love her. He knew
that now. He knew it as he held her, as his lips touched
the damp softness of her hair.

But he could not have her. Not at the price of his mother's and brother's lives.

Michael moved back imperceptively, his hand resting on
her breast. Its shape fit perfectly into his hand and responded once more to his touch. He swallowed with need.
The need to hold onto her, to this brief but intense discovery of life, real life, of giving and taking and loving. Of feeling weak, of feeling strong, of just feeling. Only now did
he fully realize how little he had really felt anything in the
past.

His hand moved down to hers, and he felt her tremble.

"Cold?" he said softly.

"Not next to you."

He touched her cheek, exploring his face. "I've no
right. . . ."

"You've had every right."

"I don't want you to hate me." There was an aching regret in his voice that reached into every corner of her.

"I won't. I couldn't."

"I didn't want this to happen."

Now her fingers inched toward his. "I don't think either of us could avoid it."

"I should have."

Meara shook her head. "No."

His eyes clouded in the firelight. "You've given me something I didn't know existed. Don't ever think otherwise."

The lump in Meara's throat grew larger. He was speaking as if he would never return, as if he were certain of his own death, once again as if he knew something she didn't.

"I love you," she whispered, no longer able to keep the words within her.

Michael winced at the words, as if they were body blows. Abruptly he rose. "We'd better return. The water is getting rough."

Meara hesitated, then nodded. The night clouds were looking thunderous, the waves cresting higher. She felt some of the joy seep from her at the sudden rough, harsh tone of his voice. She had the sick feeling that this would be the last time they would be together. "Will I see you again before you leave?" She couldn't keep the waver from her voice, but she was determined to be strong. For herself. For him. She wanted his memories of her to be like that.

He went completely still. Would they see each other again? Not if he could help it. Certainly not like this. But he hadn't been able to help anything up to now. He had succumbed to her as easily as a small boy to a plateful of forbidden cookies. The problem was she would pay the higher price. Perhaps. Because now he knew his own price would be lifelong hell. He had started something that would haunt him the rest of his life.

"I don't know," he finally said.

"Will you be going to New York before leaving?"

"No."

Meara winced at the harsh finality of the word, and she leaned down for her clothes, wondering if she had misled herself to think that he'd really cared, that she had wanted it so badly that she had fooled herself.

Then she felt his hand on her again, and the soft deep sound of his voice. "I'm sorry, Meara. It seems I'm always saying that. It's just . . ."

"Just what?"

"God, I don't know." The answer was almost an expletive. Violent. Confused.

But they had no more time to explore the raw open feelings. Rain came. Sudden and heavy. Dousing the fire and making everything black except for the white caps of the water.

Michael quickly helped her into her clothes, pulling on his own impatiently before racing toward the boat, Michael's stiff leg unexpectedly fast. He grabbed the rope holding the boat, and his arms strained with the force of its movements. He helped Meara in before pushing the boat into deeper water and, with one hand, twisted his body easily up into the driver's seat. He used an oar to get them a little farther out, fighting against the tide that sought to bring them back. Finally he started the boat, and, rocking and smashing into heavy waves, they slowly made progress toward Jekyll Creek and the dock at the Jekyll Island Club.

Michael, grateful that the force of the sea was taking every ounce of his concentration, did not have the opportunity to say any more to Meara. An anxious club employee awaited him at the dock. When he delivered Meara at the cottage, both Connors were also hovering with anxiety. Storm warnings were out.

He apologized for the worry he had caused, saying they had heard nothing and had gotten caught in the rough seas on their way back and had to maneuver very slowly. Being caught in the storm was, thankfully, excuse enough for the calamitous condition of their clothing.

Michael was invited in for a brandy, but he excused himself, saying he needed to get into dry clothes. He turned and stopped by a bedraggled Meara, who nonetheless looked quite beguiling to him. "Thank you," he said quietly.

Her eyes had never looked greener, never deeper, as they searched his face, looking for answers he carefully kept concealed.

"I'll never forget it," she whispered.

"Neither will I. Never." Before he could say anything else, something he might later bitterly regret, he turned and left.

Michael woke to the almost imperceptible sound of a knob turning and the door opening. Although his head was foggy, he knew he had locked the door earlier.

It had been a bad evening. He had returned to his room, ignoring several invitations from those at the clubhouse, and buried himself in a bottle of Scotch. It had done nothing to solve his problem or his emptiness or his overwhelming sense of guilt. Why was he so powerless around Meara? His best intentions were little stronger than a feather in a hurricane whenever he looked into those great green eyes, not to mention what happened to his body.

He had indulged his own needs again, ignoring the consequences. He had meant to explain a little today, to try to do something to mitigate the pain when it came. Instead, he had made it even worse. He had, God forgive him, even whispered love words to her. He had lost himself in the sense of well-being she always aroused in him, in the sense of rightness about their union.

But nothing in the world could excuse it. Nothing.

So it had been very late when the liquor finally dulled his brain and his thoughts, and he fell into a listless sleep. But the noises, the stealthy, secretive sounds, brought him to sudden awareness. He twisted around to see who was entering the room, the alcoholic fog dissipating in the flash of danger that raced through him. His gun was in the wardrobe. His knife also.

The door closed again, and the brief illumination, provided by the light in the hall, was cut off. But not before Michael saw Hans's tall, bulky form enter. Michael leaned over and turned on the light next to him, sitting up abruptly in the bed.

"Du bist wohl von allen guten Geistern verlassen." The German words burst from Michael's lips before he could recall them, but Hans's sudden presence had thoroughly disconcerted him.

"Have I lost my senses? I think it's you who have done so. What else have you lost?" The words were threatening.

"I don't know what you mean."

"I watched you come back with the girl tonight. I've watched you with her. What exactly does she mean to you?"

"Nothing," Michael spit out, his stomach hurting. "It's my job, damn you. To make friends with these people."

"She's nothing but a servant."

"She was my introduction to Connor. They think of her as a daughter."

"Don't you think you're carrying this 'introduction' a little far?" Hans's voice was sneering.

"You know nothing about my job. You were passed over for this particular phase. Remember?" Michael said with contempt, knowing his words were a mistake but unable to withhold the stark rage at being spied upon. Rage, and fear for Meara. "There was a damned good reason for it," Michael added harshly. "You know nothing about these people."

"And you do, pretty boy?" An equal amount of venom was in Hans's voice.

"Enough to carry out my part, if you haven't ruined it by this stupid visit tonight."

"No one saw me."

"No? It was an idiotic thing to do."

"I just wanted to remind you of your duty."

"I need no one to remind me of duty. Particularly you."

"No? I wonder," Hans said silkily.

Michael held his tongue, but curses vibrated in his throat, just barely held in check.

"You're a fool, criminally so," Michael said, finally restoring an edge of cool disdain to his voice. "Taking a risk like this."

"Ich lasse mich von ihnen doch night fur dumm verkaufen."

Michael smiled coldly. "If you don't want me to take you for an idiot, then don't act one. Everything is under control, at least it was until now."

"Remember what happens if it isn't. Your mother. Your brother."

Michael's lips tightened. "Don't threaten me, Hans. Not now. Not ever."

Hans's eyes were pale and cold. "Just so you understand."

"I don't need you to explain my duty, or responsibilities. Now get out."

"I'll meet you Saturday at noon. We will go over the final details."

Michael merely stared at him coldly. "Get out. Now."

Hans nodded. He opened the door slightly and looked in the hallway, then slipped outside. "Saturday," he said just before he closed it again.

The word echoed ominously in the room after he left.

Meara finally gave up trying to sleep at midnight when a clap of thunder seemed to shake the room.

She rose and went to the window. She could see only

darkness now, but she could hear the roar of the wind through the open window.

She knew she had been fooling herself. She had told him, she had told herself, over and over again, that she would be satisfied with these brief days, but she knew now she was not. And never would be.

Some part of her had believed in fairy tales, that once a prince awakened his princess he would stay with her forever. Part of her, although she had not admitted it to herself, had truly believed that Michael would finally sweep her up in his arms and ride away with her.

Meara realized in the past few hours how foolish a thought that had been.

He had tried to tell her. Over and over again, he had tried to tell her there was no future. He had tried in so many ways. No matter how much she had probed today, she still knew less than nothing about him, not how to write him, not how to reach him, not anything. At first it had added intrigue and mystery, even that odd sense of vulnerability that sometimes showed in him, that aura of loneliness that reached so deeply inside her.

But now she realized how little he was leaving her. How much and how very little.

Michael was like the fog settling on the island, gray and mysterious. He would be gone with the sunlight. But, oh, how magnificent it had been for one timeless moment.

Yet she wondered how she could go through life with that particular haunting legacy, and whether the sun would ever again be quite so bright.

Or even if it would shine at all.

Chapter Eleven

GOOD FRIDAY WAS the worst day Michael had ever known.

He had been a greater fool than he had earlier thought. He had underestimated Hans. His judgment, the one thing in which he had always trusted, had been lacking since the first day he had come to Jekyll Island.

Not only had he knowingly started a relationship destined to end in disaster, but he knew now he'd also placed Meara in grave danger.

Michael had a very bad feeling about Hans. He had never liked the man, but he knew Hans was capable. Capable and very, very dangerous. No matter what Michael had said last night, he knew German Intelligence did not use fools, borrowed or not. The SS man was sly and clever and dedicated.

Now Hans knew about Meara, had even surmised that Meara was a weak link in Michael's armor.

Perhaps even worse were Michael's own traitorous thoughts. He was already looking for options, telling himself it was only wise in the event something went wrong.

After Hans left last night, Michael had started planning. In his exploration of the island, he had noticed several small, very unseaworthy-looking boats, probably belonging to some of the year-round employees who lived on the island. But none of them had motors, only oars that were adequate near shore but not for a longer trip and not through the strong tides to the mainland. Today he would go back to Saint Simons and purchase a small motor, just in case he might have to leave the island quickly and quietly. His mind had also, almost subconsciously, started listing alternative plans. He had a great deal of cash with him, and a list of places where he could get more. In his particular role, it had been important that he seem well-heeled; guest or not, the cost of staying at the Jekyll Island Club was prohibitive.

He smiled dryly, a smile that didn't reach his eyes. No matter what happened tomorrow, the bill was one thing he needn't worry about. But if anything did go wrong, and he somehow survived the next few days, he would need money, and he would need to keep it dry and safe. Just in case.

Michael looked in the mirror. His eyes were bloodshot, his face drawn, his mouth set in a grim smile. A stranger looked back at him. A stranger who no longer knew what and who he was. Christ, he ached to be with Meara, to fill the emptiness that clawed at him with the talons of a vulture.

In lieu of something to do, he checked his suitcase again. The lock was still untouched, the money safe, the gun in its place. He wouldn't put anything past Hans, including rifling through his belongings. But everything seemed to be exactly as he had left them.

Michael paced the room, feeling like a trapped tiger. Wherever he looked, he saw Meara's face. It was imprinted indelibly in his brain no matter how hard he tried to erase it.

It clouded his judgment, his efficiency. Hell, it affected everything. So did the need to protect her.

Just as he needed to protect his mother and brother.

Goddamn Canaris and his schemes.

Goddamn his own weakness.

He dressed and went downstairs to breakfast and to make arrangements to rent the motorboat again. After descending the steps, he paused at the door, looking out. It was gray and dismal, drizzling a little, but while the water would be choppy, he thought it would be navigable.

Meara would be caught inside the cottage with Peter and Tara, and again his mind splintered between what he wanted and what had to happen. He closed his eyes against the overwhelming need to see her, and opened them to reality. The dining room was full, full of the people who, if everything went according to plan, would soon be on their way to Germany tomorrow night.

If everything went according to plan!

He moved from table to table, speaking to the various members, reminding them of the party Saturday night. He had already ascertained who would not attend, and where their rooms were. They would be taken by separate squads of German marines. He hoped like hell that Cal Connor would be at his party as indicated. He didn't like the idea of his fellow countrymen storming the Connor cottage. He was only too aware now of Meara's stubborn determination. If he didn't know anything else at this moment, he knew he wouldn't let anything happen to Meara, not if he had to yield his life to prevent it. But if he was forced to intervene for some reason, he knew he had to do it in such a way that his family in Germany wouldn't be affected.

He had reached the conclusion that if anything were to go wrong, he would have to arrange his own and Hans's

death. In the name of the Fatherland, he thought ironi-
cally. There could be no question of Michael's loyalty or
dedication, or his family would pay.

Sanders Evans was in the dining room, and Michael
stopped briefly to greet him. Anything else would be suspect. But every moment was growing more and more difficult. He liked Sanders as much as he disliked Hans, and
what did that say for a mission to which he was committed?

Sanders was as outwardly affable as ever, seemingly open
while Michael knew that his job required that he be otherwise. Michael had wondered more than once what was behind the good-natured likability of the man. He was jealous
of Sanders, the way he and Meara appeared so easy with
each other, ridiculously so, he knew, but then everything
going on inside him these days was intense. As someone
who had tried to avoid feelings most of his life, he now
didn't know how to cope with what was happening. He
felt like a machine whose internal workings had gone awry.

"I heard you went over to St. Simons," Sanders said.

Were there no secrets on the island? Michael cursed silently to himself. He should have known, but then he
should have known a lot of things.

"I'd heard about St. Simons, and the Cloister, but I
should have paid more attention to the weather reports,"
Michael replied wryly. "We were almost swamped several
times."

"So I heard," Sanders replied. "Being a sailor must have
helped."

"Sometimes nothing helps," Michael replied slowly. "It
wasn't a wise thing to do, especially with Meara along."

Michael noticed that Sanders's eyes, at least, agreed.

"I heard you talking about going over again. Mind a passenger? I would like to see St. Simons myself."

The question was innocent enough, and Michael didn't
see a way of refusing. And he understood. There was noth-

ing on Jekyll Island other than the club: no store, no other restaurant, no people other than the members and employees. If it had not been for Meara, Michael would probably be climbing the walls. "It will be rough," he warned.

Sanders shrugged. "I'm a pretty fair sailor myself. My wife's family had a boat. And I'm getting damned restless."

Michael hesitated. "All right," he said finally, trying to keep his voice matter of fact. "I have a few things I'd like to get. I'll drop you at the wharf and meet you for lunch at the King and Prince Hotel."

"Sounds good."

"I'll make arrangements for lunch. We'll leave in an hour."

"I won't be interrupting anything?"

Michael looked up, surprised.

"Meara," Sanders explained a bit awkwardly.

"No, she's going to Good Friday services with the Connors."

"Easter," Sanders said. "It's a little difficult to think of it this year."

"Because of the war?"

Sanders nodded. "It's going to be a long one. And mean."

"All wars are mean. By definition."

Sanders shook his head. "Germany and Japan are different kinds of enemies. The bombing of London showed that."

What about the bombing of Berlin, Michael wanted to ask. But his eyes merely darkened. He didn't want to think about that, didn't want to think about his mother and brother trapped in the city.

"I'll meet you in an hour. I'm going to take a walk before we go," Michael said abruptly.

"In this weather?"

"Exercise," Michael said. "Besides I like the rain. Always have."

"There's something lonely about rain," Sanders said, a trace of sadness in his voice.

"Maybe that's why I like it," Michael said, surprised at his response. He hadn't meant to encourage Sanders's conversation, but something in him responded. Could it possibly be a need to explain, a need to be understood when it was all over? He dismissed the idea instantly. He had never felt the need to explain anything in his life.

Sanders's suddenly sharp gaze caught his eyes, but it moved away quickly, leaving Michael with the impression of intimate communication. It was the last thing he wanted. The very last thing. Or was it?

Despite himself, Michael enjoyed the other man's company on the bumpy ride over to the other island. They had pulled the canopy over the front seats, and the sound of soft rain hitting the canvas seemed to create a rare companionship. When they arrived at the St. Simons wharf, they separated. Michael waited until Sanders had disappeared into a store before he approached the wharf attendant and described his needs. The man nodded, said he had a small used motor he would sell. Michael entered a small shack and examined the motor thoroughly. He purchased it in cash, along with an empty gas container, a hose, and a canvas cover, and he asked that they be wrapped. Michael returned to the boat, storing the package in the back where it was unlikely to be seen. He then found another shop where he purchased a money belt said to be waterproof. He also bought a short length of rope.

He had two more stops to make: a clothing store where he purchased a lightweight jacket, a drugstore where he found several magazines. The latter two were only excuses, reasons for a shopping expedition. When he was through, it was twelve, time to meet Sanders, a chore he didn't relish. He liked Sanders too much for his own good. For the good of either of them. In little more than thirty hours he would have to disable Sanders. Michael realized his face was probably as grim as he felt, and he saw Sanders's puzzled expression. With considerable effort, Michael summoned up a smile.

"I envy you," Sanders said finally as they were seated in the dining room of the King and Prince Hotel.

"Envy me?" For a moment Michael thought the man meant Meara, but the next words indicated he was wrong.

"Going back to sea. Where everything is clear. There's the enemy and you."

Apprehension ran through Michael. Was this another tact of Sanders? "And your war?" he said carefully. "Isn't that clear too?"

"Sometimes. Sometimes not."

It was one of Sanders's classic nonstatements, and it did nothing to lessen the tightening of Michael's stomach. But then he saw Sanders's wry smile and realized with both discomfort and relief that Sanders was probably lonely.

He had sensed that these two weeks had not been the most pleasant for the other man. While Sanders was obviously comfortable with himself, the agent was, nonetheless, out of his element among people who had made an art of moneyed pleasure.

From the very beginning, from the first time they met, there had been a commonalty between them. Michael had not understood it then. He still didn't. But it was there.

"You could always quit. And enlist."

"I've thought about it, but . . ." Sanders shrugged, leaving the question unanswered.

"Where will you be going from here," Michael asked. "Or was this really a vacation?"

Sanders looked nonplused. "It's called that, but it's not one I would have chosen."

"What would you have chosen?"

Sanders's face went blank. Three years ago, he would have said taking his wife and child to a beach. Now he didn't want to see a beach again, had avoided the beaches on the island for that very reason. He didn't think he could bear the ghosts.

Michael saw the flicker of pain in the other man's eyes. He *was* lonely.

"I don't know," Sanders said finally, and Michael knew it was not an admission readily made.

The meal came, and the two men were silent, using the food to cover the sudden awkwardness. There was no more suspicion in Sanders Evans's eyes. Conversely Michael wished there was.

The boat trip back to Jekyll was, thank the gods, rough enough that conversation was almost impossible. Michael dropped Sanders off at the dock, accepted his thanks with a nod that was a dismissal. He watched as Sanders left the dock, heading back to the clubhouse, before asking the attendant to fill the tank with more gasoline.

Michael restarted the boat, steering it slowly down Jekyll Creek. It was low tide now, and the mud along the banks readily visible. At high tide, the submarine could approach partially submerged, but the timing would be essential; the prisoners would have to be captured and on board within a short time frame. Any trouble at all could ruin the complete effort. Michael wasn't at all sure that that wasn't exactly what he wanted to happen.

He steered the motorboat slowly in the quiet but deep waters of the creek. He rounded the corner of the island into the sound, tracing the approach he had given the submarine. He would have to contact the sub again tonight, and Hans would make the final call tomorrow night. Michael would tell Hans the location of the radio tomorrow, but not before. It gave him a measure of control, and he was only too aware that he needed all the control he could get with the other man.

Michael finally found the landmark he was seeking. He had spied the small fishing boat days ago when he had explored the island in the little red bug. Some part of his mind had also filed away the certain configuration that guided him to the location from the water. The boat should be right above the bank.

He steered his own craft to the bank and killed the motor. He took off his shoes and socks, rolling his trouser legs high before climbing to the back of the boat and unwrapping the recently purchased motor. He siphoned some gas from the club boat into the gas container he had purchased and climbed out of the boat, taking the anchor rope with him and tying it to a tree. He then returned to the boat and took both the motor and gasoline into the woods. The fishing boat he had spied earlier was still there, old and rickety but, he judged, usable.

The bank was covered with palm fronds, and he made a small nest for his cache of motor and gas, and covered them with the thick green leaves, his hand lingering on top for a moment. He hoped he wouldn't have to use them. But it was an escape route, and the sense of survival he apparently had been born with was insistent.

He shivered a little with the damp chill of the day. Or it could have been something else. He looked at his watch. Four in the afternoon. Tea would be served at the clubhouse. Perhaps Meara was there now.

But despite his discomfort, he knew he couldn't return yet. Too much gas had been siphoned off. He would have to wait until the length of his ride justified the loss. Gas was systematically checked when anyone left or arrived, so no one would run out. He could hardly return within a half hour with nearly half a tank gone.

He leaned against a tree. His leg was beginning to ache

again. His whole being seemed to ache. The closer the job came to fruition, the colder and emptier he felt. He had never known he had so many hidden chasms inside, places that Meara had filled with her laughter and her hope. He had not realized he'd had little or no hope himself, that he had been an onlooker of life but never a participant. Bitterly, Michael considered that he had been little more than a drone; even now part of him moved practically and mechanically on, while other parts, namely his heart and what honor he had, felt crushed. He had been arrogant before in feeling, no, knowing, he didn't need anyone. It had come as a distinct shock to him that he did, and exactly how much he did.

But try as he might, he could think of few ways out. It was possible, of course, that the plan could work perfectly. If it did, no one would die, and no one left on the island would know of his involvement. Canaris had wanted to keep him "virgin," in the event he could be of use again. The admiral did not want a file on a blond, blue-eyed German who spoke English perfectly and who would always have a limp. But Michael swore to himself he would never do it again. He would find some way to get his family out of Germany, and then he could defy Canaris. He cared little now about what happened to himself.

"Bloody damn." It was no longer amusing that he even cursed as the Canadians and English often did. And he had the worst kind of feeling that nothing would go well tomorrow night. Nothing. But still his brain functioned, practically and even chillingly efficient, as if programmed to do so.

He had thought of ways to sabotage the plan, but short of going to the authorities, which would mean betraying his country, going to prison and almost certainly being responsible for the deaths of his mother and brother, he saw no reasonable way out.

He could only hope the mission would be completed with as few complications as possible, as little violence. It would be to Germany's advantage, he knew, to keep the prisoners, or hostages, well. But the initial attack by German marines could be bloody.

He turned his mind off. It was too painful. He could only follow the path already proscribed for him. Follow it and play it out to the end. To the bitter end.

Meara didn't stop searching. The dining room was full of members and their families who had just gone to the Good Friday services.

The Connors had asked her to join them at the club-house for tea. The children were with them, both unusually quiet after the church service. They were all still in their best clothes, Tara and Peter looking extremely handsome and grown-up. Ordinarily Meara would enjoy this ritual, but she was filled with disquiet and an unusual apprehension. It was, she told herself, because Michael would be leaving shortly, and there had been no resolution to anything. A final good-bye would be preferable to this agony of hoping and waiting and expecting.

At the moment she would sell her soul, which she valued highly, if Michael Fielding appeared in the dining room and made his way over to their table.

Meara sensed a shadow behind her, and her heart started to thump more vigorously as she turned. But it was Sanders Evans, not the tall Canadian.

She forced a smile, and from the wry expression on his face she knew he had seen her sudden disappointment, and understood it.

Cal Connor half rose, and asked Sanders to join them. "Miserable weather," he observed as Sanders sat down.

Sanders nodded. "Commander Fielding took me over to Saint Simons."

Cal's eyes brightened with interest. "Our Canadian guest can't seem to stay away from boats."

Sanders nodded. "The sailor, in him, I suppose. I was ready for dry land, and he took off again."

"I think he's probably restless after months of recuperating," Cal offered with a shrug.

Meara was silent. So he had gone back to St. Simons. And now? Was he avoiding her? Or was what Mr. Connor said correct? He was restless. Restless and ready to return to war. To leave her. How could she bear losing him now, knowing for the first time how completely obsessive love could be? To her. Obviously not to Michael Fielding.

Meara took a sip of tea, willing her emotions to behave.

"What about tennis?" Evans asked suddenly as he watched her hands tighten convulsively around her tea-cup.

"Why not," her employer said, as Meara looked in his direction for approval.

Meara nodded. Anything to keep her mind from Michael.

"I'll check to see if the inside courts are available," Sanders said as he rose. He raised an eyebrow. "An hour?"

Meara nodded, half hoping they would be. Half hoping they would not. Michael might not find her there. If he was looking for her.

But they were, and Meara excused herself to return to the cottage and change clothes. Elizabeth Connor and the children decided to go with her, leaving Sanders with Cal Connor.

"How did you like your stay with us?" Cal asked.

"Interesting."

"Tactful if uninformative," Cal observed.

Sanders smiled. "I'm afraid I'm not used to this kind of life."

"Neither was I, but it's amazing how quickly you adapt," Cal said ruefully.

Sanders knew about Connor, that he had been poor, that he had worked his way through college and through sheer brilliance had broken through both class and economic barriers.

"I don't think I ever could," Sanders said honestly.

"Because you really don't want to."

"Perhaps."

Cal shrugged. "It's the end of this kind of life, anyway," he said. "This will be the last year of the club. It's already been announced. They say it will reopen after the war, but I doubt it. Membership, particularly since the depression, has fallen off. It was useful to me in the beginning, still is in business ways. Elizabeth and the children love the island, but its time has passed. Do you know that people used to move from one resort to another, all year round? No one has the time to do that anymore. If the war hadn't killed this club, time would have." Sanders nodded in understanding. He had received a thorough briefing before he came. He knew that the Jekyll Island Club had originally been formed as a private hunting club and had later evolved into a family social resort. The deaths of original members and the effect of the depression had sliced the membership of what was once called the most exclusive club in the world. Membership had originally been limited to one hundred and had once been almost unobtainable; now the club was soliciting members,

"The end of an era," Sanders observed.

"I'm afraid so."

Cal looked out over the dining room: the rich paneling and the elaborate mantels over the fireplaces, the elegant furnishings that even he had never quite been comfortable with. He had married Elizabeth Newton, and she had been his entry into this kind of life. He had enjoyed it at first, still did at times, and the contacts had been good for business. But now the ever increasing costs outweighed the business and social values, even the satisfaction of a poor boy grown rich and accepted.

This would have been his last season, war or not, and even this season, which usually lasted four months or so, had been condensed into two weeks. The trip had been more for Elizabeth and the children than himself. And Meara. It had been a kind of graduation present for her. He had always known she loved it more than anyone. Her dreaming island, she had once told him.

Perhaps it was exactly that for her. Cal had not missed the looks that passed between Meara and the Canadian, whom he had instantly liked. He also liked the plainspoken man across from him. He wanted the best for Meara who, like him, had overcome strong odds to get ahead. He had helped in every way he could, including the job at *Life*, although she would not have received it were she not qualified or if the editor hadn't agreed with his recommendation. Cal had thought the career was what she wanted, although he had wondered at her lack of serious boyfriends and the common desire, as he understood it, for women to get married. He had been surprised at Meara's sudden and apparently intense attraction for the Navy officer. He had watched with interest.

"This has been sort of a useless trip for you, hasn't it?" Cal observed.

Sanders shrugged. "It often is."

"Not very pleasurable?"

"No," Sanders said frankly.

"An honest man."

"Who has to go get ready for tennis." Sanders grinned. "The redeeming factor."

"And Meara?"

Sanders paused a moment. "Another redeeming factor, if she didn't have her eyes fastened someplace else."

"You've noticed?"

"I would have to be blind not to."

"Hummm. I like Fielding, but I wonder what will happen after Easter, and he returns to England."

"Love is never convenient," Sanders observed, rising as he said the words.

"No, I don't guess it is. But I worry about her. She's like another daughter to Elizabeth and me."

"She's lucky."

"We've been lucky. She's wonderful with the children. We'll miss her."

Sanders nodded. "I have a couple of calls to make before tennis."

"Anytime you need anything . . ."

"Thank you," Sanders said with a nod of acknowledgment. He left the table and found a private room with a telephone in it. He called Washington and reached his superior. "Any more news on Fielding?"

"No. Everything seems to check out so far. Want us to continue checking?"

Sanders hesitated. He'd had his suspicions about Fielding until today. But there had been a deeply troubled look in the Canadian's eyes lately, not usually a typical reaction of miscreants. "No. Most of the members are leaving Monday. Fielding's leaving Sunday. I think he's who he says he is. There's no reason to think otherwise."

"What about that famous instinct?"

"Wrong this time, I think."

"All right. I'll pull the dogs off. Have a nice Easter."

"I'll try."

"And, Sanders, thanks."

"You owe me one," Sanders retorted to his superior. Sanders slowly put down the telephone. He hoped to hell he was right. He went up to his room to change clothes.

Michael arrived back at the dock and went directly to his room in the clubhouse. His clothes were wet but not more than they should be after a ride in a motorboat. He quickly pulled on a pair of clean trousers and a sweater and went in search of Hans.

He passed by the window of the indoor tennis courts, and a fleeting glance showed Meara and Sanders Evans playing tennis. Jealousy ripped through him like a whip. She was so light, so fast, so graceful as she moved. He heard her laugh, and his heart skipped.

One hand clawed at his side. It was better this way. He knew it was better.

He thought of the moments and hours they'd had together. So brief and yet they had filled his life for the first time. He loved her. He would always love her. But he could give her nothing but pain and misery. He hesitated, but then moved on. He didn't want Hans to see him staring like a love-starved fool.

Michael squared his shoulders and started walking again.

Chapter Twelve

Hᴀɴs ʟᴏᴏᴋᴇᴅ ᴀᴛ the woods, anger welling up in him and turning to an ice-cold hatred.

He had followed Eric von Steimen, running at a distance, following the tracks of the bicycle in the sand. It had not been easy, for the moon was hidden behind clouds, and only by extreme concentration could he follow the almost indecipherable tracks. At least the drizzle had stopped.

There was something about the ease with which von Steimen associated with the hated Americans that disturbed him. More than disturbed him. He knew, of course, that von Steimen was supposed to do exactly that. Yet, von Steimen seemed to go beyond what was necessary.

Hans had seen him with the woman, and then later with the man that he couldn't quite figure. He wasn't like the others. There was something a bit awkward and uncomfortable about him, as if he were out of place. Hans knew that feeling. He knew it and he hated it.

All his life he had been out of place. But no more. Now he held an honored position, as did his son, in the new order. Kurt would never know the wounds, the taunts, the derision, that he had known. After the successful conclusion of this mission, the Weimer family would be respected and hailed throughout Germany.

Hans had kept vigil on von Steimen since last night. He had seen him leave in the boat today with the tall American, return, and leave again, alone. It all appeared very suspicious to him, especially later when he watched von Steimen pause outside the tennis court and saw the unguarded expression of pure longing on his face as he had looked inside.

Hans had decided, then and there, that von Steimen was unreliable.

Hans volunteered again to stay Friday night. Extra hands were needed to prepare the festivities for Easter, to cut the needed flowers and to prepare for the Easter egg hunt for the children. He had smiled agreeably and pleasantly, and the fools had jumped at the offer.

He knew that von Steimen was to make contact with the sub tonight. He planned to follow and make sure that von Steimen was fulfilling all his job, not just the pleasant part of being waited on hand and foot and enjoying the decadence of this place. He planned on listening to every word. And he wanted to know the location of the radio.

But now he had lost his quarry. The man had simply disappeared into the woods, and there was no trail to follow, not even with his sharp eyes.

Hans knew it would be useless to go any farther. He would only get lost. No. He would wait here, in the shadows, near von Steimen's bicycle until the man reappeared. Then he would try to retrace the footsteps.

He didn't know how long he waited. He wore only a cheap watch, a watch a gardener would wear, and he couldn't see the hands in the darkness. But he guessed it was an hour or more before von Steimen emerged from the woods.

Instead of going to the bicycle, von Steimen walked to the edge of the water and stood there, almost blending into the sea with his dark clothes.

The arrogance was there in his stance. Arrogance and independence and something else. Hans couldn't figure it, and he didn't like things he didn't understand.

Hans remained silent, moving farther into the dunes and the grass that shielded him, and looked again. Von Steimen's profile was to him, but the darkness covered the man's expression. Hans recognized indecision, and his distrust grew. Nothing, and no one, was going to rob him of his triumph. Nothing. Particularly this supercilious aristocrat.

Von Steimen, after what seemed hours, finally turned and limped toward the bicycle. Hans dug deeper into the side of the dune. He would take no chances with the bastard. He knew a way to ensure the man's loyalty. Loyalty which he had always questioned.

Hans had watched von Steimen's gaze follow the girl, had seen him play with the Connor brats. Hans had leverage. He knew he had leverage. And he knew he would enjoy using it.

He would show von Steimen who was the leader here.

Ignoring the chill of the day, Michael swam his usual hundred laps across the pool. He was used to cooler temperatures and had often swum in even colder waters.

He needed to dissipate the tension building within, to block out his thoughts, to concentrate only on the next lap.

Michael had taken only coffee and toast for breakfast, and even that had made his stomach turn with unfamiliar anxiety. He wished the day would go away, that he didn't have to think about tonight, or German Intelligence, or Hans, or the submarine hovering off the coast.

He stretched out his arm, feeling the satisfying pull of muscles as his injured leg followed suit. In the two weeks here with his strict regimen of bicycling, walking, and swimming, the leg had improved immensely. The doctors in Berlin said he would always have a slight limp, but he could feel the strengthening of muscles, the compensation being made by some muscles for the injury sustained by others. The splintered bone was also strengthening. He could feel it.

It should have made him feel better. But nothing, he knew, would ever make him feel better again.

He reached out again, pushing himself, seeking the edge of exhaustion, of blankness, for a few moments.

When he finished the hundred laps, he swam to the edge of the pool. He was alone; the gray overcast day was not inviting. He was grateful for that, at least.

With one graceful movement, he was out of the pool. He wiped himself quickly with a towel and slipped his arms into a shirt, shaking his head to rid it of excess water.

He looked out toward Jekyll Creek and the dock. A yacht, three launches, and the motorboat were tied up there. There was no movement around them. Michael picked up his watch from the table where he had left it. Ten in the morning. Ten more hours before the submarine was committed, nine before he and Hans made the final transmission.

Hans. Michael looked around and finally found the stopped figure leaning over a garden of jonquils, the delicate yellow flowers that colored the grounds in early spring. He saw Hans return his look. The blank expression was on the gardener's face, and only a second's recognition passed between them.

As if he had all the time in the world, Michael strolled over to where the gardener worked.

"Everything set?" Hans's words were almost indistinguishable.

"Yes," Michael concurred.

"How many at the party?"

"Ten of the sixteen."

"The others?"

Michael extracted a package of cigarettes from the pocket of his shirt, and held it out to Hans. With a subservient but grateful lowering of his head, Hans's hand reached for the package, his fingers taking the only cigarette left in it. But he didn't light it, merely stuck it carefully in his uniform pocket. He knew it held a map and directions to each room and cottage where their targets should be.

"The final transmission is scheduled for seven," Hans reminded Michael unnecessarily.

Michael nodded. Dinner was at eight. His party was planned for ten. The submarine should arrive at the wharf around ten-thirty, and the attack was scheduled to commence at eleven.

"For the Führer," Hans said with an empty smile on his lips.

Michael felt the other man's animosity radiating from him. He was being baited. He knew it. "For Germany," he corrected tonelessly.

"Meet me at the power plant at six-thirty," Hans said. "All the other employees will be through by then."

"I'll have to get the radio."

Hans's face showed a flash of triumph. "No need. I have one with me."

Michael stared at him. He hadn't even been aware that Hans had one. He should have known. The Abwehr was very, very thorough. Another misjudgment on his part.

But he didn't allow his thoughts to show. "In your quarters? Isn't that a bit reckless?"

Hans shrugged. "I know what I'm doing, Oberleutnant," he said curtly. "I naturally needed a suitcase since I was so . . . accommodating in helping out."

"It was still a risk."

"Not nearly as great a one as going to the other side of the island for your radio."

Michael's face stiffened. He had been followed. He should have known, damn it. But he had been preoccupied.

"Six-thirty," Hans repeated in a whisper. This time it sounded like an order. "I'll take care of the telephone lines just before then."

Michael's eyes met Hans's briefly, and challenge sparked between them. Challenge and dislike. And distrust. The emotions were so strong, they seemed to disturb the very air around them.

"Six-thirty," Hans said again.

"I may be a few moments late. I don't want to be missed," Michael contended, his eyes unfathomable. He turned and walked away without giving Hans a chance to argue.

He went to his room and changed clothes, taking a rare cigarette for himself. Meara would probably be in the dining room for lunch. He sat on the bed, his elbows on his knees and his chin resting on clasped hands. Nothing in his life would be as difficult as seeing her today, knowing as he did what would happen later.

He had, until now, been partially able to compartmentalize his mind, to separate her from what he must do. But no longer. Part of him realized how much she would hate him when she discovered what had happened.

Now she would. There was no way to avoid it because he had decided to neutralize Sanders in such a way the agent would not die. He had weighed various alternatives and found only one feasible one, and that meant revealing his true identity. The option of disappearing, as if he were one of the kidnapped, was no longer viable for him. But after tonight, he would have enough to pay for, without adding Sanders's murder to the list.

Sanders Evans would be there to comfort Meara when his role was known. There was both solace and agony in the thought.

Michael rose and went to the suitcase. He unlocked it and, using a pocketknife, cut a small opening in the lining, retrieving several small vials. He selected one and placed it in his pocket, returning the others to the hiding place.

He could delay no longer. He had to find Evans and confirm a drink later this afternoon. Michael put on a tie, knotting it easily, added an English-style tweed jacket, and left the room.

He stopped briefly and spoke to the clubhouse manager about his party that night. He had already ordered champagne and port and the best cigars available, and he was assured that he would find everything to his liking.

The dining room was still full at one o'clock. He immediately spied Cal Connor's table. The children were there, and so was Meara. It was Peter who frantically waved to Michael as he started in another direction.

He could not ignore the boy, not with Cal and Elizabeth Connor looking at him. He changed direction and went over to the table. He did not want to look at Meara, but he couldn't escape it.

Meara graced him with that lovely smile of hers, and he felt his heart constrict. It was so spontaneous, so filled with love, that he couldn't help but respond, but he knew it to be only a shadow of his usual smile.

"Will you join us?" Cal said.

Michael looked down at the table. The Connors were finishing their lunch, and he started to demur.

"Please," Cal said, and Michael had no logical reason to refuse, although he heartily wished he had. To be with her was sheer torture. Nor did he feel comfortable with Cal's easy friendliness. Because of him, Cal Connor's life would be turned inside out in a matter of hours. God only knew how he and the others would be treated. He didn't want to think about it. That wasn't his responsibility.

Or was it?

"What time will you be leaving tomorrow?" Connor asked, his eyes darting from Meara to Michael.

"The noon launch," he said.

"You won't be attending Easter services then? Peter and Tara were hoping you could go with us."

Michael's throat tightened even more as he looked down at the two children. There would be no services tomorrow, no father to take them. Their faces were so damned trusting.

"I thank Peter and Mistress Tara," he replied gravely, "but I have a train to catch in Brunswick."

Peter's face fell, and once more Michael felt guilt shuddering through him like an erupting volcano.

Elizabeth smiled at him. "If you ever come to New York, please come and visit us."

Michael's fist clenched under the white linen tablecloth. How much more could he take?

"Thank you," he said slowly. "You've both been very kind, you and your family." He included Meara in his look, and saw her lips tremble.

"Nothing is too good for a neighbor and an ally," Cal said in booming good humor.

Michael's fist tightened even more.

Peter grinned. "I'll remember everything you showed me

about shooting. I sure hope the war isn't over by the time I'm old enough to fight."

"I hope it will be over long before then," Michael said softly.

"I want to kill some Germans," Peter objected plaintively.

"Don't ever wish for that," Michael said, and he knew his voice was hollow. "Don't ever wish for death." He hoped the despair didn't show. "Anyone's," he added quietly.

He saw Elizabeth's approving smile. Kind. Gentle. Then the smile turned toward Cal, and Michael saw the love in it. He knew that feeling now, knew how powerful it was. How weakening.

As if on signal, Cal started to rise. "Let's go, Elizabeth, children." He had quite deliberately ignored Meara in his summons, and looked benevolently at Meara and Michael as he stood, silently ordering them to stay as they were, and ignoring Peter's protest.

"I'll take you riding," he promised his son, and protests were immediately halted. In seconds, the four of them were gone, leaving Meara and Michael alone. It had all been very neatly done.

The waiter came and took Michael's order, and he asked if Meara would like some dessert. She shook her head.

"I'm sorry," she said. "They didn't give you any choice."

"Choice?"

"You've been avoiding me. I didn't mean for them to corral you."

"Perhaps I wanted to be . . . corraled."

"Did you?"

Michael was silent. The challenge was there again. The brave challenge. She didn't beg, but neither was she ready to surrender.

"I don't know," he said honestly.

"I won't ask for any promises."

"You deserve them."

"What would you do? Run?"

He couldn't help but smile at her expression. Impish, like an Irish leprechaun, yet there was also a wistful expression, a silent longing. One that matched his own.

"How did you get so wise?"

"Why are you afraid?"

"Because you should have tomorrow, and I can't give you that."

"No one knows what will happen tomorrow. Can't you just accept today?"

His hand reached out for hers. He was mindful of the other people in the dining room, but at the moment they didn't matter. "It shouldn't be enough for you, Meara. Not ever enough. I'm a sailor, a wanderer. Even if I survive the war, I'll always be that."

Her eyes looked through him, to the shadow behind his eyes, to, he thought, his soul.

"There's something else," she ventured carefully.

"Isn't that enough?"

"No."

God, he loved her. Tenacious. Bright. Intuitive. How lucky he would be in other circumstances. How damnably lucky.

His food came, and he released her hand. He stared at the meal with indifference, but it gave him a reason to look away from her.

"Michael."

He glanced up. Her eyes were compelling, so green and deep that he could get lost in them.

"Thank you."

"For what?" He could barely get the words out.

"For these days, this week."

He laid his knife down. Christ, he couldn't take any more. He felt the tense muscles in his jaw work, and he could find nothing to say. Nothing.

Her thick dark lashes lowered over her eyes at his silence, and he knew she thought she had chased him away, had asked for more than he could give, even in this small way.

And she had. But he couldn't bear the look in her eyes. His hand once more touched hers. Silently he tried to convey words he couldn't say, and he saw that she understood. Tears glistened at the edges of her eyes and he knew she realized he was saying good-bye.

"I won't see you again?" Her voice was unsteady.

"I don't think so."

She hesitated. "You can always reach me at *Life* magazine."

He nodded.

"I love you," she whispered, unable to keep the words back although he knew she had tried.

His mouth worked. The stark agony of this moment would never go away. Never.

"Be happy," he finally said as he pushed back his chair and left.

Meara would never know how she spent the rest of the afternoon. She wandered aimlessly about the grounds. She thought about going to the beach, but she couldn't stand the thought of the loneliness. Not now. Not this afternoon. Instead she moved under the moss-covered oaks and stared into the salt marshes beyond Jekyll Creek.

It was over. She had never stopped hoping for a reprieve, never stopped believing in one. But now she'd stopped believing. He was going. And he had made it clear he wouldn't be back.

She finally went back to the house. Cal and Elizabeth

were dressing. The couple had been invited for cocktails at one of the cottages.

Elizabeth took one look at Meara's face and asked whether she and the children would like to eat at the cottage. They would order food from the clubhouse. Meara nodded indifferently. She didn't think she could ever eat again.

Elizabeth whispered something to Peter and Tara before she and Cal Connor left. The children went to the study where they turned on the radio, and Meara was mercifully alone. Images, bright and shining, haunted her, as did Michael's face, sad and troubled, as he had said, so finally, his farewell.

She heard a knock on the door and slowly went over to it, opening it to see a man in coveralls. She had noticed him before, a new gardener, one she hadn't seen before this latest trip to Jekyll.

His face look frightened. "A man fell . . . I think he might be hurt," he mumbled. "He told me to come here."

Seized by fear, Meara didn't think to ask why he had come here and not the clubhouse. "Michael!" she exclaimed.

"I don't know his name. He just told me where to find you."

"I'll send the children for help."

He shook his head. "He said he didn't want to bother the others . . . something about a war injury."

Meara didn't hesitate any longer. He wanted her. Only her. She went in the study. The children would be all right for a few minutes. She told Peter she'd be gone only a short while.

The man quickly led the way. The door into the power plant was open, and the man stood aside. "I helped him in there," he said.

Meara went first and was just inside, looking frantically

around when a dirt-encrusted hand covered her mouth with a handkerchief. She smelled ether and she struggled against its sickening odor. Everything started to go black. She could feel herself falling. Michael, she tried to call. Michael. It was the last thought she had.

Chapter Thirteen

HANS LOWERED THE woman and looked at her with satisfaction before tying her hands and feet. Although unconscious, she was breathing easily. He had purposely kept the dosage small.

Now for the children.

But first the telephones. He had earlier located the cables which went over to the mainland. After one last look toward the woman, he moved silently to cut the island's contact with the outside world, slicing the cords with his gardener's shears. He wasn't worried about reaction at the clubhouse. The phones were frequently out, particularly in bad weather.

After severing the connection, he quickly returned to the DuBignon cottage, and he rapped sharply on the door. When answered by a boy of ten or so, he said haltingly. "Miss O'Hara said for you two to come with me."

"But why?"

Hans shrugged dumbly.

Peter hesitated. He had been warned repeatedly about

strangers, but this was Jekyll Island, and nothing happened on Jekyll Island.

"She said to hurry."

The last sentence convinced Peter. He called for Tara, who was always ready for an adventure.

"Come with me," the man said, and Peter was glad that the man didn't try to touch him. There was something about the gardener he didn't like, but if Meara wanted them, or needed them. . . .

Peter puffed up with importance as he shut the door and hurried alongside the man. They were moving toward the power house. Peter looked toward the large clubhouse. "Shouldn't we . . .," he started.

But the man only walked faster. The door to the power house was closed but unlocked, and the man opened it, waiting for Tara and Peter to go inside.

"Meara," Peter called out apprehensively. He didn't like the darkness, didn't like the man who had brought them. He started to back up, but the man caught him, and a foul-smelling rag was pushed against his nose and mouth. Peter attempted to jerk away, trying to get loose, trying to give Tara time to run. But he couldn't call out because of the cloth in his mouth, and everything was getting fuzzy.

The boy went limp in Hans's arms, and the little girl was screaming. Hans shut the door with his foot, effectively cutting off the noise. He dropped the boy to the floor, then used the rag on the girl. In seconds, she was still.

Hans turned on the switch inside the room. The woman and two children lay on the floor. The woman should wake soon; the children would take longer.

Hans took the rope he had stolen earlier from one of the storerooms and quickly tied the two children, just as he had tied the woman. He gagged the woman, but not the children. He didn't want them to choke to death, not yet, not before von Steimen arrived. Then he didn't care what happened to them.

He sat down, carefully taking the gun from the trousers he wore under the club coveralls. Like Michael's, it was an American military pistol which, if it had been found, he could explain away as a souvenir of a former soldier.

He looked at his watch. One hour before von Steimen was to meet him. By then the girl should be awake. He could barely wait to see von Steimen's face. Or hers when she found out who her hero really was.

Michael spent the afternoon visiting with various members of the club. He saw Sanders Evans and invited the man to his room for a drink at six.

Sanders readily agreed.

At six exactly, there was a knock at Michael's door. He had changed into his evening clothes, and he had completed all his preparations. He had taken the small vial he'd extracted earlier from the suitcase and poured a portion of the liquid into the bottom of a glass on a table near the window and slid it into the shadows behind the bottle of Scotch.

He glanced quickly around the room. A servant had started a fire in his fireplace since the evening was chilly. The room looked warm and inviting.

Sanders was also dressed in evening clothes, the cloth and style not as elegant as Michael's, but they fit Sanders's muscular body well.

"What will you have?" Michael said. "Scotch, brandy, port, even gin."

"I'll take brandy," Sanders said. "Gin is for you British."

"Canadian," Michael corrected easily. "I prefer Scotch."

He went over to the table where the bottles and glasses

were, the one with the drug slightly behind the bottles, and he quickly poured brandy into it, swirling it gently. He then poured himself some Scotch.

Michael handed the drink to Sanders and sat in an elegant armchair across from the one Sanders had selected. He sipped at his Scotch.

Sanders crossed his legs comfortably. "When does your ship leave for England?"

"Two weeks, if there are no complications."

"From New York?"

Michael shook his head. "Canada. I'm taking the train from Brunswick tomorrow, then another from New York up to Quebec."

Sanders grinned. "I'm probably on the same one. At least to Washington."

"We'll have company then." Michael's gut tightened. Sanders would be neck deep in trouble Sunday. He took a sip of his Scotch, watching as Sanders did the same.

Michael looked down at his watch. "I'm afraid I have to meet someone at seven. I hadn't expected it."

Sanders took the hint and another sip of the brandy, a longer one. "Dinner?"

"With the Lees."

"High-powered company."

Michael grimaced slightly. "They're friends of the man who sponsored me here."

"It seems to have been beneficial," Sanders observed, his eyes moving down to Michael's leg.

Michael looked at the cane in the corner. He hadn't used it now for days, not even in the late afternoon or evening. "Yes."

Sanders took another sip of the drink, and his free hand suddenly gripped the arm of the chair. He shook his head. "What . . ." He tried to focus on Michael. "The drink . . ."

The glass slipped out of his other hand. He tried to rise, but he fell back. "The drink . . . drugged . . . ?"

Michael watched emotionless, but his own hand clutched his glass tightly as he saw the accusation, the sudden awareness in Sanders's eyes.

"Who . . . are you?" It was all Sanders could manage.

Michael said nothing, only watched as Sanders tried again to struggle to his feet, a groan escaping his lips as he fought so hard to move but failed.

"Poison . . . ?"

"No," Michael said, not knowing whether Sanders understood or not as the agent's eyes closed and his body slumped in the chair.

Michael looked at his watch. Fifteen more minutes before he was to meet Hans. He rose and went to the window, waiting until he was sure the drug had completely taken effect. He looked down at the glass that had dropped from Sanders's fingers. A pool of liquid was spreading over the rug. He was slightly surprised at how fast the drug had worked, at how little was needed. It was more potent than he'd been told.

When he was certain Evans was soundly under, he went over to the chair and picked the agent up, staggering under the weight. He carried the man to the bed, laying him down carefully and checking his pulse. Evans was breathing easily. Thank God for that, at least.

Michael took several of his ties from his suitcase and quickly tied each of the agent's hands to a bedpost, doing the same to his feet, until the man was spread-eagled. Still another tie, his next to last, was used to gag Sanders. The latter was probably not necessary; Evans should stay asleep for hours. But Michael couldn't take any chances.

He wiped his hands and went out the door, locking it behind him. Michael limped toward the stairs.

He saw a number of the club members and their families

collecting in the elegant lobby, around the great fireplace with its carved wood mantel and a wild boar's head hung over it.

He could almost see the animal's knowing, malevolent eyes directed straight at him.

He murmured some greetings and stepped outside into the cool air. Rain had been falling periodically during the day, and now it was evening. The sky was not the rich blue it had been the first days of his visit, but a violent, frothing, angry gray. There was no light, not the first twinkling of a star. But gas lamps lit the grounds, and he stepped off the porch as if getting some fresh air. He moved silently into the shadows of giant live oak trees, and then his pace quickened, despite his leg. He was learning to adjust.

The submarine would be close now, waiting for the tide to allow it entrance. Waiting for the tide and the final transmission. It would not enter Jekyll Creek until the contact was made and the final code word given.

The foul, threatening weather had completely cleared the grounds. Those going to dinner from the cottages had already made the short trip to the clubhouse. The power plant was toward the back of the grounds, behind and slightly right of the stables. The door was closed.

Michael looked at his watch. Five minutes late. As he reached the small building, he heard the beginning of a scream inside and pushed open the door.

Meara woke slowly, her stomach turning over and her head aching. She tried to move but she couldn't, and she didn't understand why. Then she felt the harsh burning of ropes on her wrists as she struggled to open her eyes. Heavy and sluggish, they didn't want to open. Through sheer force of will, she finally forced them and they slowly, painfully, focused through a dark, hazy cloud.

They found a man dressed in a gardener's uniform, his

hands fondly caressing a pistol, his eyes paler and colder than any she had ever seen. Slowly, she remembered her last conscious moments. The gardener. But he didn't have that cold, vulture look then. He had looked simple, helpful. He had said something about . . . Michael.

Michael.

She tried to speak, but a cloth filled her mouth, and she suddenly gagged, choking on the foreign substance. Meara felt raw panic. Panic and fear as she sought desperately to breathe, only to pull the cloth deeper in her throat. She thought she was suffocating and fought the bonds around her wrists until they tore into her, ripping her skin.

The man walked slowly, lazily, toward her and leaned down, taking the gag from her mouth, but there was no pity in his eyes, only a fanatical fire.

"Fräulein," he said mockingly.

Meara's eyes widened at the odd title. "What . . . ?" Her mouth was so dry she could barely get the question out.

"I thought I would invite you on a little journey."

Meara tried frantically to arrange her thoughts, to understand something of what was going on. But her mind was still fuzzy from the drug. "The . . . children . . . ?"

"Oh, they're going too. Along with some rather interesting gentlemen and their families."

"Where?"

"Germany." The answer was triumphant.

Terror and disbelief started to build within Meara. "You're insane."

"No, fräulein. In a very few hours, you will be a . . . guest of the Third Reich." He smiled menacingly, and Meara realized he was very serious. She struggled to clear her head. What was happening?

"Just think," the man said. "Think of the turmoil America will be in when we spirit away its top industrial and business leaders. Of course, there will be a little discomfort, but von Steimen will see to their . . . needs. And yours. He's very good at that." The tone was conversational, mocking, taunting her to ask more.

"Von Steimen?"

"Oh, I forgot. You know him as Fielding. Michael Fielding. He played his role very well, don't you think?"

The horror that Meara had felt minutes earlier was nothing compared to that which rolled over her now. Horror and loathing and disbelief. And sickness. A terrible, stabbing agony that twisted her insides until she doubled up with pain.

Waves and waves of pain. They assaulted her mind, her body, her every thought. Michael. Michael with the tender touch and the soft words. Michael with the eyes that reached inside her and stole her soul. Michael to whom she'd so easily given her heart. Everything in her denied her captor's words.

She tried not to believe. Dear Mother in Heaven, no! A lie. Nothing but a lie. Meara struggled to understand, to reason, but there was no reason in her. The man was lying. But why? Why would he lie? Toward what end if he was who he said he was? But still she fought against the growing fear, the convincing evidence. "You lie!"

She heard his low malevolent chuckle. "Oh, he is very, very good. The Abwehr trained him well. Of course, as a German aristocrat, he naturally is an arrogant bastard, like all the others here." Hans smiled coldly. "Of course, you weren't much of a challenge. We even laughed together about you. A fine diversion, he said, as well as a Judas goat."

If she hadn't believed him before, doubt now started creeping into her mind, slowly, insidiously like a slithering snake. He was enjoying her pain, and she only briefly wondered why. She closed her eyes and tried to picture Michael as she had last seen him at lunch. The strong face, the dark blue eyes which had seemed to love her, his easy, friendly way with the children, with the Connors.

Lies. All lies. The smiles. The touches. The lovemaking. Why?

To reach the Connors. Judas goat, the man had said. The cramps, the sickness she'd felt before, paled compared to the shooting agony that racked her now. Not only had he betrayed her, but he had made her betray her own country, her family, her friends, her young charges.

Don't think of it, she told herself, fighting down billows of panic and revulsion. Don't think of him, or you'll lose control. Don't think. You have to do something. You must. Her hands balled into fists and her wrists fought against the ropes that bound them.

"It will do you no good, fräulein, and your lover should be here shortly. To make the last arrangements for your journey, and that of the others."

Focus on something, Meara told herself. Focus on anything but Michael. The children! She saw them lying still in a corner.

"What did you do to Peter and Tara?" Concentrate, she reminded herself over and over again. You have to concentrate for the children. *Michael*, she screamed silently in her mind.

"Ether. Like you. But a heavier dose. They're alive, hostage to their father's reasonable behavior."

"And me? What good am I to you?"

"I haven't really decided," the German said. "A gift for von Steimen perhaps."

A lie. Meara saw it in his eyes. She was a governess, worth nothing. She didn't even know why she was alive now except that it must have something to do with Michael.

Von Steimen.

Bile stuck in her throat as she remembered his whispered endearments, yet part of her couldn't quite believe it was all a lie. Perhaps it was some trick, a terrible joke. She looked at her captor, at the man's pale blue eyes lit with malice, and she knew this was no joke, no mistake, no dream.

"What are you going to do with Mr. Connor?"

"Oh, he'll be a guest of our government."

"In a concentration camp?" Meara asked flatly.

The man shrugged.

"And the children?"

He shrugged again.

Meara opened her mouth to scream, though she knew no one could probably hear her, not through the door and across the grounds. But she had to do something.

It was partially out of her mouth when the door opened, and Meara saw Michael's tall, lean body fill the doorway.

Sanders fought the effects of the drug. He had faked part of his reaction to it when he first realized what was happening to him.

He didn't have to fake much. His reflexes had slowed, his eyelids had grown heavy. But he had sipped his drink very slowly, and when the drug, whatever it was, started to work, he realized immediately what Fielding had done.

His mind had immediately reacted, knowing there was probably little time. The first question was why.

Flashes of images hurtled through his brain. Director Hoover's fears, his own first suspicions of Fielding, the systematic courting by Fielding of members of the club. God, he had been a fool.

He stuttered out a few words, then allowed his eyes to close as they had wished to do. He felt Fielding's hands move him to his bed and, from a growing mental distance, felt his hands and ankles being tied.

But a portion of his brain still functioned. As Fielding

had tied his hands, Sanders had managed to twist one fractionally, leaving, he hoped, enough room in the cloth to work it free.

He felt the gag being stuffed in his mouth, and it was all he could do not to react. Fielding's hands had hesitated an instant, and Sanders sensed a reluctance in his adversary, but then the gag was tied firmly in place.

Sanders waited until he heard the door open and close, and the key turn in the lock. He then tried his bonds. He was so sleepy, so damned sleepy that his efforts were weak at best.

He rested for a moment, fighting the drug with all the will he had. Dear God, what was happening? He thought of the members here, of what was at stake, and he tried again. And again. And again.

Sanders tried to yell, to moan, to attract attention, but the gag was too tight, and the rooms were well built and well insulated. He could expect no help.

He wanted to sleep. How he wanted to sleep. But he couldn't. He wouldn't allow himself that luxury.

Don't hurry, he told himself. Don't hurry or you'll just make the knots tighter. He tried to relax his arm, his fingers feeling for the knots, for the little bit of room he needed.

Give, damn it. He felt the tight knot with his fingers, yet he had a little wriggling room. Just a little.

What was going on? Who was Fielding?

Just a little more effort. Just a little more. Damn this sluggishness. Damn Fielding.

His eyes closed, and he willed them to open. Perhaps a moment of rest. Only a moment. He felt drowsiness shroud his senses, and again he fought the overwhelming temptation to sleep, to surrender to the fog that had now nearly encompassed him.

No! He started fighting the bonds again.

Chapter Fourteen

MICHAEL'S FACE HARDENED as he surveyed the room in front of him, his usual enigmatic eyes turning frigid.

His glance flickered from Hans to Meara to the children and back, briefly, to Meara. The fear and repugnance on her pale face; the bloodless lips sliced through him like a knife, but he allowed nothing to show in his face as he turned to Hans.

"Michael," she said, her voice quivering slightly with a pain and uncertainty that twisted the knife inward. "What . . . ?"

He wanted to rush over to her, to comfort her, to protect, but he knew he couldn't. He would be signing both their death warrants, and possibly those of the children. Instead, he kept his eyes curtained as he turned to Hans and spoke in German. "What's the meaning of this?"

Hans smiled mirthlessly as he straightened. The girl's scream had ended the second she had seen von Steimen. His hand remained on his pistol, and he moved several feet away.

"I have some orders you haven't seen, von Steimen."

Michael's lips tightened as he realized Hans's use of his name and English was *purposeful*. He looked at the pistol in Hans's hand and knew the deliberately careless pose was anything but that. Hans was ready to use the pistol, and he was keeping it more or less aimed at Meara.

"What orders?" he answered roughly.

"We're to take the children with us, as additional hostages."

Michael looked at him unflinchingly. "All of them?"

"Five exactly, including these two. The other three also belong to our soon-to-be guests."

"I had no such orders." Michael kept his voice hard and cold as he fought to keep his gaze from Meara.

Hans shrugged.

"And the girl?"

"It was the only way to get the children. I also thought she would be a gift for you." Hans's voice was coldly amused. "I doubt if anyone cares what happens to her."

"What if someone misses her? You could ruin everything."

"I don't think so," Hans said. "By the time she's missed, the submarine will be here."

"Why wasn't I told about this?"

"Perhaps you weren't completely trusted," Hans replied softly.

Michael looked at Hans with contempt, then stepped over to where the children lay, and felt the pulse in their neck. Both were alive, their breathing regular. He looked over at Meara, at the green eyes which were now filling with even more confusion, confusion and something more virulent. Something like hate. A part of him died that moment, pieces of a heart already so brittle that, like a mirror, it shattered in sharp-edged pieces, slicing a swath of destruction through his soul.

But at least she hadn't been hurt. Not physically. Not yet.

In those few seconds, Michael made his decision. It was one he knew now he had been considering for the past few days, but had not admitted it to himself. That was why he had bought the motor, why he had bought the rope which he had left in the motorboat, why he'd had a duplicate key made for it.

In the past week, everything in him had rebelled against his assignment. There were things he would do for his country and his family, but this was not one of them. Michael had never known he had a sense of honor before, but now he found he did, and he also knew he couldn't betray those who had befriended him and·the one person who had loved him. He couldn't allow the kidnapping of children, of innocents.

At the same time, he knew the consequences of capture. He could perhaps escape execution if he confessed, if he provided information about German Intelligence. But if he did that, then his mother and brother would be killed.

Both of his identities, Michael Fielding and Eric von Steimen, would have to die. Michael looked at Meara. Smudges of dirt and what could be tears ravaged her lovely face, but her eyes were clear. Not challenging but full of loathing. That was important. When he "died," hate would make her forget easier than love.

He looked down at his watch. "Seven o'clock."

Hans didn't move. "The radio is over there in the corner. You start the transmission."

Michael nodded and went over to the suitcase on the floor, opening it quickly. He started twisting the dials, moving his body between the radio and Hans, and hunching down. One hand found a battery and quickly removed it, rolling it behind a piece of machinery. He tinkered with the radio a few more moments while his other hand found the knife which was strapped to his ankle underneath a sock. He slipped the weapon into a pocket of his jacket.

"It's not working," he said. "What in the hell did you do to it?" For Meara's sake, he had to make her believe that he distrusted Hans's loyalty to Germany as much as Hans obviously distrusted his own. A falling out between thieves.

Michael heard Hans's German oath and then the hammer of Hans's pistol being drawn back, but he knew the man couldn't risk a shot.

"Get away from there," Hans said, suspicion heavy in his voice. "Over next to the girl," he further directed as he leveled the barrel of the gun toward Michael's stomach.

Michael did as he was told, moving slowly, keeping his eyes on Hans. When he reached the wall where Meara sat, he relaxed against it casually, as Hans turned his head toward the radio and tried to work it himself. When nothing happened, Hans started to check the batteries.

Michael knew the minute Hans saw the battery was gone, he would realize what had happened. But the moment's realization had given Michael the few seconds he needed. As he lunged for Hans, Michael's hand slipped in his pocket and withdrew the knife, letting it slip down near Meara as if by accident. He didn't have time to see whether or not she saw it, for the gun in Hans's hand was turning toward him once more. Michael's movement propelled him into Hans, his hand deflecting Hans's fist, and he saw the gun bounce out of the SS man's fingers before they were both on the floor.

Hans was quicker than Michael in getting to his knees, but then Hans was a street fighter and wasn't impeded by an injured leg. His fist went into Michael's stomach as Michael tried to rise, but one of Michael's hands caught Hans around the neck, and they fell back on the floor together. The two men rolled over on the floor, each pummeling the other with one fist while seeking to keep the other man from reaching the gun which lay on the floor.

Michael felt the blows rain down on him, tasted blood as it spurted from his nose and a split lip. Yet filled with rage and frustration, he was doing an equal share of damage. Blood was also pouring from several places on Hans's body, and his opponent's breath was coming in heavy gasps.

Despite his long hospitalization, Michael knew he was in better shape than Hans. His daily swims and walks, the bicycling, had increased his stamina, and he'd always been quick, while Hans was heavier and slower. He permitted himself a quick glance over at Meara. She had indeed found the knife, and he saw that she had freed her hands and was now working on the ropes around her ankles. In seconds she would be free and possibly out the door. He couldn't let that happen. Not yet.

His momentary distraction was treacherous. He felt a heavy blow to his face and, stunned, he released Hans. Hans dived for the pistol. Through the corner of a bloodied eye, Michael saw that Meara had reached the weapon first and had it in her hand. As Hans grabbed for it, the pistol went off, and Michael heard Hans grunt, then fall to the floor.

As Michael painfully rose to his knees, the gun was once more pointed at him, but Meara held it now. He wondered whether the shot had been heard. He doubted it. The air was cold, and the wind was blowing. Windows were closed. And they were far from the clubhouse. But still, it was possible.

Cautiously eying the gun in Meara's hand, Michael got to his feet and leaned painfully against a wall. "Are you going to shoot me?" he said finally, his voice neutral, almost as if he were asking about the weather.

Her hand shook, but it didn't waver. She started to open

her mouth, but clamped it shut. Michael very slowly and carefully leaned down and touched his fingers to the pulse in Hans's throat. Feeling nothing, he straightened up again.

"Is he . . . ?" Meara's voice was trembling, her face white with shock.

"Yes," he said simply, wishing desperately he could take back these hours, these days. He wanted to move over to her, to take her in his arms, to wipe the horror and shock from her face. And he could do none of those things. He could only make her hate him.

Everything about her was frozen. Her hands, her eyes, her posture. Michael was afraid to move, afraid that she might suddenly shatter and the gun would fire.

"What are you going to do?" he said finally, keeping his voice calm and cold.

"Who were you trying to radio?"

"One of our submarines."

She swallowed. "You really are . . ."

"German. Yes."

"Everything was—?"

He didn't answer. He couldn't. She took it for an admission of guilt.

"A spy? A German spy." Her voice was disbelieving still, but it was getting stronger. "My God. You can't . . ."

Michael was silent.

"Dear God, you used me," she cried again, and this time her voice was only an agonized whisper, a sound more devastating to Michael than hatred. Her hands tightened on the trigger. "It was easy, he told me. He said it was so easy." Her voice broke, and her body shook as if she were freezing. Michael's throat constricted until he couldn't breathe. His heart shattered as he saw the bitter betrayal register in her face, watched the brilliant eyes dim with understanding. He screamed silently inside, wanting to die himself, but he still had others to protect. God help him, dying would have been easy now.

As he stood there silently, watching realization take full hold of her, he knew that living would never get easier, that he would live with this moment the rest of his life. It was worse than anything he had ever imagined, or could imagine. He died slowly inside, much slower than Hans had.

And yet he stood. A living dead man.

He watched her, the lips which were quivering ever so slightly, the eyes filled with hurt and disillusionment and remnants of horror every time she looked at him and down at the body of Hans Weimer.

Yet neither of them moved.

It was as if, he thought, they were both caught in a photograph, each frozen forever with emotions and passions so strong that they were incapable of movement or decision or even words.

Michael knew every moment he remained was dangerous. The shot might have been heard. If not, he would soon be sought when he didn't appear at his dinner engagement. Someone might check his room and find Evans. Yet he couldn't take his eyes from her, from the dawning understanding of all that had happened these past two weeks, what she thought she understood.

"You bastard," she said in a cold, brittle voice that belied the calmness.

He took a step toward her.

"Don't," she said with a strained voice, and he stopped. "Are there any more of you?" she asked.

Any more of you. He and Hans. Spies. Enemies. He hadn't known the pain could get worse, but it did. "No," he said quietly.

"And the sub."

"Without the radio transmission, it won't come in."

"Why should I believe you?"

He had to make her hate him, to believe he was no better than Hans, who would steal children. Perhaps he wasn't. He moved closer to her and saw her hand waver. He took another step.

"No," she said.

"You won't shoot me," he said in an emotionless voice.

"Yes."

But then he was directly in front of her, and his hand whipped out, knocking the gun from her hand. "I'm sorry," he said, his voice suddenly soft. He tried to keep gentleness from it, but he couldn't. It was there, but he realized she didn't hear it. She only heard what she wanted to hear now.

"It's over now," he continued. "You've won. I've lost." He hadn't meant to, but he bent his head and his lips touched hers, his mouth violent with need against her un-yielding one. When he finished and released her, her hand went back and she slapped him as hard as she could, the impact echoing in the small room.

He smiled crookedly, as he had that first day on the club cruiser, and then he whirled out the door. She followed, staring as he moved quicker than she'd thought possible toward the dock. She knew she should run for the club-house and alert them, but her legs wouldn't move.

Frozen. She was frozen with incomprehension. A play. It must be only a play. A play of blood and death and be-trayal. German. My God. Judas goat. Whispered words, tender touches. Judas goat. My God. Dear God in heaven.

She couldn't breathe, she couldn't move. She couldn't feel. Anything. She didn't think she would ever feel any-thing again.

The gun. She looked around for the gun, but her eyes, dazed from shock and swimming with tears, couldn't find it at first, but still she tried. She finally caught sight of it under some pipes. She would have to step over the dead man. The man she killed. Killed. Dear God.

Somehow she forced herself to do it, to lean over and pick up the gun, and she turned back to the opened door. She could still see his shape moving toward the dock. She aimed toward the moving figure, but her hands stilled on the trigger; she couldn't pull it. Damn it, she couldn't.

He was a spy. A German spy. If he were captured he would be executed. He had used her to betray her country. Why should she care? Why?

She ran out the door, but she could no longer see him. And then she saw Sanders Evans rushing from the clubhouse. She screamed at him, and he turned in her direction.

"The dock," she said. He had a gun in his hand and he started loping toward the dock, Meara behind him. It was raining heavily now, but she didn't feel the pelting drops. She didn't feel anything, only a numbness.

Just as Sanders reached the dock, they heard the start of a motor. Sanders continued running, across the wooden boards now, his shoes echoing in the night. Meara watched him kneel, pointing his gun toward the sound. There were no running lights, no lights at all, even the club lights were out. Meara heard several shots and then the river and the sky seemed to explode into an inferno. She reached Sanders, and they both looked out to where the last sound of the boat had been heard. There was nothing, only drifting pieces of fire falling from the sky. Meara's legs suddenly collapsed under her.

"Michael," she screamed as she started to fall, and she felt Sanders catch her and hold her close as sobs racked her body.

The commander of the U-boat, Klaus Hasser, had been standing tensely beside his radio for the past thirty minutes. They were three miles from the entrance into Jekyll Creek, and the sub had surfaced for the transmission. Hasser had blessed the weather. The night was inky, and rain came down in torrents, making it impossible to see more than several feet. He tapped his foot impatiently, willing the transmission to come through. He was not to enter Jekyll Sound without it.

By eight, he knew something was wrong, but still he hesitated. The mission was vitally important. Then he heard an explosion and saw a brief fireball in the distant darkness.

Others would have heard it too. He could no longer afford to wait. He gave the orders to submerge and set course for open sea.

Part Two

Chapter Fifteen

CHRIS CHANDLER'S HANDS tightened compulsively over the spilled contents of the envelope as his gaze moved unseeing across the rich paneling of his office to the bank of windows overlooking the bay.

His office had once been his sanctuary. He had designed it that way. A tranquil place to keep memories at bay.

But no more. Not even pretense could make it so. Fear grasped at him, just as it had twenty-odd years ago. Twenty-one years, in fact. Twenty one years and two months. He could even calculate the days and hours.

He did not fear for himself. God knew he had lived with worse things. Guilt. Regret. Loneliness. Always the loneliness. And phantoms. Phantoms which followed him everywhere, from a glimpse of red hair on the street to nightmare-plagued nights.

Chandler leaned back in the swivel chair, his gaze returning to the newspaper article he had torn from the paper that morning, and the sheaf of papers still clutched in his fingers.

Some part of him, he realized, had been waiting for this.

Waiting all these years. An excuse to go back, to recover something that had been lost, something he had always felt was meant to be his: Meara, and the feelings he had never known prior to those weeks, nor since. He had tried to bury those memories. Knowing with terrible certainty that he had, deliberately and consciously, destroyed any possibility of recovering her, he had tried, instead, to create a new life. He knew now he had simply marked time, had existed for this moment. The years wrapped up in this room had not been life but penance. Empty years. Solitary years.

He had once believed he'd had no choice in what had happened. But now he realized a man always had choices. And he had made poor ones. Except for the last, the most painful of all.

Chris ran fingers through his crisp sandy hair as he always did when thinking or worried. With his other hand, he straightened out the newspaper clipping. It was coincidence that he had found it just minutes after reviewing the thick packet that had arrived from Europe. He usually scanned the paper after opening the mail, but the contents of the envelope had so disturbed him that he had almost failed to pick up the morning paper.

He'd glanced restlessly over the headlines. Most of them involved the civil rights demonstrations in the South, the the conflict in Vietnam, and President Kennedy's upcoming trip to Europe. June 15, 1963. Nothing very unusual. He started to lay it down again but habit was strong, and after he'd made a mental note to try anonymously to contact Sanders Evans and tell him of the contents of the European package, he'd picked the paper back up again, scanning it rapidly, only to find Evans's name staring up at him from one of the pages.

Now he read the article for the third time, although his mind had already memorized the contents.

The story briefly told of the death of FBI Agent Sanders Evans in a shootout with extremists who had robbed a Wells Fargo armored car and killed two guards. The robbery apparently was intended to provide funds to bomb public buildings in protest of the growing conflict in Southeast Asia. Violence to stop violence. Nothing really surprised Chris anymore. He had been a part of the greatest idiocy and criminality of all history.

Agent Evans had left a wife, Meara, and a daughter, Lisa. There were no photos, of course. It was the violent death that was news, not the personal tragedy left in its wake. There was nothing of the grief of a wife and daughter, or one of those intrusive photos of personal pain newspapers seemed to like so much.

Chris wondered about them now. Meara and her daughter. Did Meara's eyes still sparkle like the sun hitting the ocean waves? Did Lisa have the same glow, the same wonderful sense of adventure, the same honest courage, as her mother?

He had no right to find out. And every right.

He placed the clipping on his desk and picked up the thick sheaf of papers, thumbing through them once more. A report from the German detective agency he employed. There was a copy of a recent visa application for Kurt Weimer, and a long report of Weimer's suspected Odessa connections and secret neo-Nazi sympathies. Suspicions, that was all, the report said, and even those were apparently kept private by the people who held them. Kurt Weimer was an influential and wealthy figure in West Germany, an economist of international reputation.

And Weimer was coming to the United States for a high-level economic conference on Sea Island, off the coast of Georgia. His expected arrival was in four weeks.

Chris's hands shook as he considered the ramifications of the two seemingly separate, yet linked, pieces of information. Weimer's visit to Sea Island could not be a coincidence. It was not accidental, he knew, that Meara and Lisa Evans now lived on neighboring Jekyll Island.

Not when Weimer had spent the last few years making inquiries about the Evans family.

Something cold and deadly settled in the pit of Chris's stomach. He knew Kurt Weimer was plotting revenge, that something terrible was planned for the only two people in the world for whom Chris gave a damn. And Sanders Evans was no longer alive to protect them.

He thought of Meara, of the first time he had seen her with her red hair flying free in the wind, and her laughter floating over the water as she leaned down and whispered conspiratorially to two children. Her green eyes had been so vividly alive that they'd nearly blinded him. He had never met, nor had he since seen, anyone so free, so lovely, so full of love and life. He still remembered that quick "isn't life wonderful" smile that had made it wonderful indeed. He had lost his heart then, and had never regained it.

Even as he had accepted that each hour was stolen, that they would both pay an enormous price for the theft, he had never guessed exactly how great a price it would be.

He had not known until years later when he had hired a detective agency to find her and discovered she had given birth to a daughter, Lisa, nearly nine months to the day after they had made love.

Chris's hand crumpled the typewritten pages concerning Kurt Weimer. They were in danger now, Meara and Lisa. His love. His daughter. They were in danger because of what he had been twenty-one years ago, because of so many betrayals. His betrayals. And he was the only one who could help them, because he was the only one who knew the whole story. The only one still alive.

He buzzed his secretary.

"Make a reservation for me on a flight to Atlanta on—" he looked at his calendar—"July nineteenth. Also arrange for a private plane there for me."

There was a short silence. "What return date?"

"Leave it open."

"The meeting with Bill Hatch is July twenty-sixth," the secretary reminded him. "He's in Europe and won't be back in Seattle until June thirtieth."

Chris swore to himself. For a moment, he had forgotten the meeting. Bill Hatch was a competitor whose company Chris had been eying for a long time. Hatch had just let it be known that his company was for sale and Chris was but one of several potential buyers. Profitable and privately owned, it was a perfect adjunct to his own company, Northwest Lumber. He wanted nothing to do with public companies; he couldn't afford the exposure and publicity they inevitably produced. Yet some competitive part of his nature wanted to keep his firm growing. Work blotted out so many other things.

"Allen can handle it," he said, referring to his vice president of finance.

There was another silence. Chris Chandler seldom allowed anyone to substitute for him, especially in a meeting as important as Sally knew this one to be. But there had been an unfamiliar edge in his voice, a tension that warned her not to say anything.

"Yes, sir," she said quickly, although her unasked question buzzed through the wire.

"Confirm everything as early as possible," Chris stressed.

Less than four minutes later, Sally told him he had the reservations. Chris rose and walked over to the wall of windows overlooking Puget Sound. He had chosen Seattle as his headquarters because of the water, though Portland was nearer his base of operations. The Pacific coast was different, wilder, than the usually calm Atlantic around Jekyll Island, but the salt air, the unmistakable perfume of the sea, seemed to bind him to Meara, to her and to the one place he had been happy if only for the briefest of times.

Evans would be gone a month by the time he arrived. She would have said good-bye to one dead man.

What would she say, do, when confronted with another one?

He remembered the last time he saw her, her eyes full of disbelief and loathing and horror. She would hate him. Most certainly distrust him. She could also ruin him, send him to prison with one word. Spy.

But that didn't matter now. Nothing mattered but her safety. That and his daughter's. *His* daughter.

A muscle throbbed convulsively in his throat as he returned to his desk and forced himself to concentrate on a contract. Suddenly, nothing here meant anything. Only Meara. Only his daughter.

Dear God, keep them safe.

But if He couldn't, then Chris would. Any way he could. No matter the price!

Four weeks later, he leaned back in his first-class seat on the flight to Atlanta and shut his eyes. Damn, but the memories kept flooding back.

Eric von Steimen. Michael Fielding.

Was there anything left of the two men in him?

He was Chandler now. Successful American businessman. Von Steimen disappeared years ago, the name completely buried in his mind when he learned his mother and brother had died in an American bombing raid of Berlin. There were no more von Steimens.

And Michael Fielding? Chris Chandler had also tried to bury him, but that had been far more difficult. Michael

Fielding was the one of the three who had really lived, who had felt, who had laughed and loved. As much as Chris had tried in the past years, he had not been able to force those two weeks from his mind. They were as real to him today as they had been twenty-one years ago.

Grateful that he did not have a seat companion in the small compartment, he took out the fuzzy photo the detective had sent him years ago.

Chris remembered the beach where the picture had been taken. Meara was sitting on a blanket, a ten-year-old child next to her. It was a black-and-white photo, wrinkled and worn from being handled so often, and he could tell nothing about the child's eyes although the hair looked blond. The detective said the girl's eyes were blue. Deep blue. Like his own. There were other pictures of his daughter, but this one with Meara was his favorite.

Lisa was nearly twenty-one now, and a new graduate of the University of Virginia.

A stewardess interrupted his thoughts. He declined the offer of a meal, but decided on a Scotch and water. God, he needed something.

If Meara had hated him the night of the explosion, she must doubly so now. He had ruined every dream she'd ever had. The job at *Life* magazine, her career as a journalist, had all been sacrificed when she found herself with child. With *his* child. How she must have despised him.

At least, he thought, she'd had Sanders. Throughout the years he vacillated between gratitude and jealousy every time he thought of them, every time he realized Sanders had taken far better care of Meara than he ever had. Gratitude usually won, especially in the latter years. But in the beginning, it had been pure hell.

He would never forget those first desperate, miserable, pain-racked weeks after his escape from the island. He'd reached Savannah where he'd bought some clothes and an old car. Then he'd headed west.

Every place he went, he searched the newspapers. In Savannah, there was a news report about an attempted kidnapping of two children on Jekyll Island. The attempt, according to the story, had been foiled by the governess who had shot the kidnapper in self-defense. She was declared a heroine by the mother and father. A photo of Meara accompanied the report, but it didn't look like her. There was nothing of joy in the picture. There had also been a murky photo of the kidnapper, taken apparently from his false identity papers.

There was no reference to Germans or submarines. The kidnapper was a gardener, a former soldier who was apparently mentally deranged as a result of combat.

But then, of course, there would have been no mention of German involvement. If word had leaked out of the planned raid, panic would have spread across the entire eastern coast. He later found another item, a short report of a Canadian who had been lost in a boating accident. For the benefit, he thought, of members of the Jekyll Island Club. He wondered now, twenty-one years later, if they had ever learned how close they came to disaster that Easter weekend.

He had reached Chicago four days later, and there he put his extensive training to use in trying to bury Michael Fielding. He found a cemetery and wandered through it, happening upon a small marker for a three-month-old baby who had died in 1909. Christopher Chandler. He wrote down the name and drove to the northwest corner of the United States, a place in which he thought he could get lost.

When he reached Portland, he headed toward a small isolated logging camp. He had no difficulty finding a job:

the draft and enlistments had drained the logging industry of men while the need for lumber grew.

His limp explained why he wasn't in the service, and he worked hard at learning the logger's trade. Hard physical work made it possible for him to sleep at night, to forget Meara's laughter, to forget the loathing in her eyes, to forget that last anguished cry despite all she had felt about him.

In a year, he had made foreman. Despite his reticence, his natural leadership always emerged, and he gained the company's attention when he risked his life to save another logger and then rudely swept away all attempts to reward him. Instead of allowing him to retreat back into anonymity, his perceived modesty had had the opposite effect. Chris was named superintendent, and when the owner's only son was killed in the Philippines he had seized on Chris as a substitute. Six years later, the owner had died of a heart attack and left half the firm to Chris, half to his sister. Chris bought her out three years later.

Using work as a substitute for feeling, Chris had built the company into one of the most successful private firms in Oregon, swallowing up smaller unsuccessful firms and making them profitable. Although he anonymously gave money to various charities, one of which was a journalism scholarship at the University of Oregon, he declined all invitations to be on boards. He wanted no attention.

He had lived with the possibility of being discovered every day of his life. Part of him, perhaps, even wished for it, although he knew what would happen. Only several months after his own escape, he'd read a story in the newspapers involving German spies—saboteurs—who were set ashore on Jacksonville Beach in Florida. One of them was George Dasch, who had lived in America for several years and then found himself caught in Germany when the war started. Unlike Chris, Dasch had surrendered himself when he'd reached American shores and reported the landing. Despite that, he had been tried and found guilty of espionage and given a prison sentence. His companions received the death penalty.

That episode had quelled all Chris's illusions about his future if his true identity were discovered. Even now he could be arrested and imprisoned, he supposed. Certainly deported.

And Meara? What would she do when she discovered he was still alive? Alive and living in the United States.

She hadn't been able to shoot him that night, but then everything had happened so fast, and she'd been stunned and confused. She'd had twenty-one years to hate now.

Dear God, he whispered to himself. He closed his eyes as he realized the shock she'd have in seeing him again. Yet he had to warn her. Had to protect her.

"Are you all right?" The stewardess bent over him, her face concerned, and he forced a smile and nodded.

"You looked like you were in pain."

"I was just thinking of a business problem," he said.

"It must be a big one," she said. "Another drink?"

He nodded. He seldom had more than one drink. Like so many other things, it was dangerous. But this once . . .

When the drink came, he stared at the golden color, remembering a similar shade shimmering across the sand the afternoon he'd made love to Meara. He wondered if Meara's body was still slim, yet curved so enticingly in the right places. He felt himself tensing inside at the forbidden thought. It had been so long.

He had not made love to a woman since Meara. He had thought about it; he was no monk, but something always stopped him. Part of the reason was penance, his own painful penance for the agony he had caused someone he loved. But there had been other reasons. He hadn't had time or opportunity during the first years; he'd simply worked himself into a stupor each day. When he'd reached a position of some wealth, he was wary. Women were curious, and he couldn't afford curiosity, he couldn't afford involvement. After Meara, he'd had no wish for the kind of liaisons he'd had as a ship's officer: mindless, physical acts with little or no feeling. The idea repelled him.

Chris hadn't needed sex; he'd needed warmth to combat the cold, icy feeling inside since that night so long ago. Sex, he knew, would just make it colder. Emptier.

But now he grew warm with need. With the kind of longing she'd created in him so long ago and which had haunted him for years.

His hand tightened around the glass, and he allowed himself a large desperate gulp.

The hovering attendant approached him again. "We'll be in Atlanta in one hour. Is there anything I can get you?"

There was an invitation in her eyes, one he'd seen many times before. He shook his head and leaned back in the seat, letting her take the now empty glass.

Hours now. Only hours.

The single-engine plane his secretary had ordered was waiting for him. Chris arranged for payment, presented his license, and filed a flight plan, carefully going over the route. He'd always been a cautious pilot, ever since he won his license five years earlier. He liked the freedom of flying, just as he had once enjoyed the sea. But now it held little joy.

He landed at the Brunswick airport near dusk and rented a car. He'd spend tonight in Brunswick and find a realty company tomorrow.

The window of his hotel room looked out over the marshes to St. Simons Island. He couldn't see Jekyll Island, or the new causeway that led to it. The smell of the marshes and the sea was just as he remembered, and he felt eager anticipation even though he knew he was a fool to do so. Meara's husband was recently dead. Even if Sanders was still alive, Chris knew he could expect little but scorn and possible exposure from her. Yet he couldn't rid himself of the anticipation that ran through his mind and body.

Chris called a real estate firm and made an appointment for the morning. He told the agent he understood homes were available for rental on Jekyll Island, and he was interested in a furnished cottage.

For how long?

Chris hesitated.

"Most owners require at least a two-week minimum," the agent added helpfully.

Chris agreed and asked that a list be ready when he arrived. He sat down and studied the telephone book. He found a Sanders Evans on Beachview.

He knew something about Jekyll Island through the detective agency he had hired to track Meara. The club had closed after that Easter of 1942 and never reopened, the clubhouse and cottages abandoned. The island had been sold to the State of Georgia in 1947 and it had been transformed into a state park with motels, camping grounds, public beaches, and some private residences that were often rented. Meara had owned one in her own name for the last five years.

Chris wondered if the island had been ruined, or if it still retained the almost mystical beauty of years ago. Or had it been mystical only because of Meara?

As dusk developed into evening and evening into night, Chris remembered every moment of those two weeks. Every glorious, painful moment.

He wondered whether Kurt Weimer had arrived yet on Sea Island. And what the man was after.

*   *   *

Meara wandered restlessly through the house. Sanders had been buried more than a month now, but she still missed him. Dear Mother, but she missed him.

They had often spent time apart. After being transferred from one city to another, he had returned to Washington, and they'd bought a small house in Virginia. He was still often away on assignment, gone for months at a time. But she'd always known he would be back, that his warm brown eyes would see her with affection and understanding. She would miss that most of all. She wondered what she should do about the house in Virginia. Lisa would be going to law school in Washington, so perhaps she should keep the house for Lisa's use. They had enough money with Sanders's insurance and her own income from freelance writing to support both residences. At least for a while.

The cottage, one of the first built after the state bought the island, was hers, free and clear, except for the taxes. It had been a surprise bequest from Cal Connor when he'd died six years ago. She'd almost refused it, but Elizabeth Connor had convinced her to keep it, that it was something Cal had very much wanted. Meara had always refused any payment or reward for protecting the Connors' children, and Cal had known how much she'd loved Jekyll. It was his way of finally paying what he considered a debt.

Meara had felt, then and now, like a fraud. She had felt that way twenty-one years ago when she unwillingly became a heroine. No one on the island, other than Sanders and her, knew exactly what had happened that night. After the explosion, when people came running out of the clubhouse, Sanders had taken complete charge. He had calmed everyone down, saying only that there apparently had been a kidnapping which had been foiled by Meara. The explosion? He didn't know yet.

He and Meara, who had been silent with shock, had

taken Cal and Elizabeth Connor to the power plant where
Tara and Peter were unconscious and bound . . . but alive.
The Connors were embarrassingly grateful to Meara, who
felt everything was her fault. When she tried to tell them,
Sanders steered her away and said she needed rest. She
was sedated, and the next day, between bouts of tears and
self-accusation and grief, she was made to understand national security concerns. The island had been vacated immediately, and Meara, accompanied by Sanders, was taken
to Washington, presumably for medical care but in reality
for endless questioning.

It was Sanders who stayed with her, who probed gently,
who made her understand that no outsider must know
what happened that night. Not the American public. Not
the Germans who had so easily breached American defenses.

When Meara had finally repeated everything to him,
every word that was said that night, a strange expression
passed over Sanders's face as he'd asked, over and over
again, every movement Michael Fielding had made.

"He was trying to call the submarine?"

Meara nodded, her eyes blind with tears.

"And he accused the other man, the gardener, of losing
a battery?"

"Yes, and he . . . they were going to take the children."

"Did Fielding say so?"

"He didn't disagree."

"But why the fight?"

Meara looked at him with a lost expression on her face.
"I don't know. Everything happened so fast."

"I wonder . . .," Sanders said after they had gone over
it several more times, but he never finished his sentence
as another agent entered the room.

He never did say what he wondered, but she had asked

him what had happened to him that evening, how he knew to come after them with the gun.

"Fielding tried to drug me," he said.

"Tried . . . ?"

"The dosage was light, which was . . . odd," Sanders said. "He could easily have killed me. That would have been the smart thing."

Meara looked up, wanting to believe, wanting so desperately to believe that there had been more to Michael Fielding, or von Steimen or whoever he was, than a deadly spy.

Sanders took one of her hands in hers. "We'll never know a lot of things," he said.

"There's no chance—?"

"That he survived the explosion? No," Sanders said. "I saw him pull away in the boat, and the explosion was just seconds later." He hesitated a moment, then added. "For what it's worth, I think he really cared about you. I saw the way he looked at you."

Meara shook her head. "He merely used me. How can you use someone you care about?"

And how can you love someone who betrayed you so completely?

She'd never been able to answer that question. She'd thought the love would die, quick and violently, as he had died, but it hadn't. She never had an opportunity to forget, to try to forget; six weeks later, two weeks after she went to work at *Life*, she discovered she was pregnant.

Sanders had kept an eye on her, calling her frequently. He had called the day she had discovered she was pregnant, and he heard the raw, painful desperation in her voice.

"What's happened?" he asked with concern, his voice soft with sympathy.

She couldn't tell him. She stuttered a denial that anything was wrong. The next day, he was at the door of her apartment and he wouldn't leave until she blurted out the news.

He took her in his arms, holding her as one would hold a child. "Will you marry me?" he said unexpectedly.

She stilled, her eyes meeting his in disbelief. She hadn't known what to do. She was Catholic and wouldn't even consider an abortion. Yet what would she do with a baby? How would she support it? How could she taint a child with the label of bastard? The bastard of an enemy. A spy.

Sanders's offer was an answer, yet she couldn't do that to him. She didn't love him. It wouldn't be fair. She told him so in a shaking voice.

"I know you don't love me," he said. "But I think you like me, and that's a good beginning. Meara, I'm lonely. I have been since my wife and baby died. I'll love the child. I'll take care of you. And I'll be getting the best of the bargain."

Lost and miserable and lonely, she'd finally agreed. But she'd always known he didn't get the best of the bargain. She'd given him a home and child, but she'd never been able to give him her whole heart, and she'd realized very quickly that that was what he wanted.

She stopped her pacing to glance at her typewriter. She had been in the middle of an article about Georgia's barrier islands for a travel magazine when she'd been notified of Sanders's death. It was due next week, but she had no heart for it now. Not now. She wondered if she ever would.

"Mother."

She started as Lisa came in. Her daughter's eyes were sad, solemn, as they had been for the past month. Meara wanted to take her in her arms, to comfort her, but she was afraid she might be rebuffed, and she didn't think she could bear that now.

"Darling?" she said, looking at her golden-haired daughter with eyes the color of the deepest ocean. Her coloring was so much like Michael's. A familiar lump clogged her throat.

"Why . . . don't we go back to Washington for the summer."

"But I thought you were going to stay here this summer, work for Kellen's firm."

"I'm not sure I . . . want to stay here."

Meara reached out a hand and was grateful that Lisa didn't move away.

"Why, honey?"

Lisa looked at her stubbornly. "I don't think Daddy ever liked it here."

Since she'd been left the house, Meara and Lisa had come here each summer when Lisa wasn't in school. Sanders would usually make it for the weekends, but Meara had never noticed Sanders's reluctance. He had been proud that Meara had defeated her demons, had even urged her to come back in the beginning. "You can't hide," he had said.

"I don't know what you mean."

"Oh, he never said anything, but sometimes he got such a sad look on his face when he didn't think you were noticing."

Meara felt broken inside. "What?" she said in a ragged whisper.

"It doesn't matter," Lisa said in a flat voice.

"But it does," Meara said. "It does to you."

"I don't know. I don't know how I feel any more. I just miss him so much."

"I thought you liked it here."

Lisa's eyes clouded. "Maybe I did, once."

"I'll go back with you."

"No," Lisa said. "I'm almost twenty-one. I'll be in law school next year. I'm old enough to be on my own."

Meara didn't know she could hurt this much, not any more. Lisa had never said before that she hadn't wanted to stay at home while she finished school. Because of Sanders. She knew that now.

"Lisa . . . don't go. Not now."

Lisa hesitated at the raw pain in her mother's voice, then her face stiffened. "I'm going to the cemetery."

Meara nodded. "I'll go with you."

"No," Lisa said. "I want to go alone."

Meara surrendered. "All right. Will you be home for dinner?"

"I don't know."

"What's wrong, Lisa?"

Lisa wanted to tell her. She wanted to tell her mother she wished she could be as strong as she. She had always wanted to be that strong, that perfect, that . . . controlled. But she couldn't. Her own tears came so easily. She couldn't understand why her mother's didn't. Even when her mother touched her, there was a kind of remoteness about it, a remoteness that protected but didn't always comfort. "Why don't you ever cry?" Lisa said finally, almost hopelessly.

Meara closed her eyes. How could she explain that she used up her tears long ago. Tears didn't help. Tears didn't bring people back, or recall events.

"I loved him," she whispered.

"I know," Lisa said, ashamed of what was almost an accusation. Her mother had always been there for her, for her father. Strong and sure. But right now Lisa needed something more than that. She swung around, almost running out the door, slamming it behind her.

Meara heard the noise, and opened her eyes.

Once more, she thought bitterly, she had failed as she looked around the spotless, empty, lonely room. For the second time her life seemed to lie in tattered threads. And there was no Sanders to pull them together again.

Chapter Sixteen

THE MORNING DAWNED bright and sunny.

Chris was used to little sleep. He had not slept well in years, and three or four hours was sufficient.

He shaved quickly, looking carefully in the mirror. How much had he changed in twenty-one years.

He was fifty-two. His blond hair was still thick and held only the slightest, almost undetectable, hint of gray. His body was as taut and lean as it had been twenty years ago. He worked hard, and he cared little about food; it was fuel, little more, and he used it as such. Eating could be a lonely business, especially if you never invited anyone to share it, so he subsisted on coffee and a piece of toast in the morning, usually a quick sandwich or salad at lunch, and often skipped dinner altogether.

His face had aged. Even he could see that. Lines stretched from his eyes, and his skin was dark from being outside so much; he was never happy delegating complete authority, and he often visited the various logging sites.

How much had he changed? He didn't know. No one was a good judge of his own appearance, but he was aware

253

that the angles of his face had hardened, that lines had etched deeper around his eyes although he seldom laughed. The furrows came from the sun and work and time.

To hell with it, he thought. He wasn't here for courting. He was here for one purpose, to protect Meara. He wished like hell Sanders were still alive. Chris knew he could have gotten word to Sanders Evans, could have talked to him. Part of him had always known that. His first thought when he'd been told of Kurt Weimer's trip was to call Sanders and put the problem in his lap. But Sanders was dead, and there was no one he could trust, no one who knew exactly what had happened that night, no one who would believe him. He would only risk jail, leaving Meara alone and unprotected.

It was July, and blistering hot. He checked his suitcase for suitable clothing. There was little. The temperatures in the northwest were cooler, more comfortable, and most of his clothing consisted of either business suits or the rough logging shirts and trousers he wore on site.

He finally chose a pair of dark blue slacks and a light blue cotton long-sleeved shirt, rolling up its sleeves past his elbows and leaving the neck open. He looked at the gun he had purchased before leaving Washington. It was steel gray and deadly looking. He had bought the pistol immediately after deciding on the trip to Jekyll, and he'd been to the practice range several times to replenish old skills. He had been surprised at how naturally the weapon fit into his hands and how quickly his aim had returned. It was a surprisingly uncomfortable feeling. He had wanted to put that behind him.

The broker at the real estate office was more than prepared for him.

"Stan Cable," he said as he introduced himself. "I think I have a few listings you might like. Are you sure you want

Jekyll? There's a greater choice on Sea Island and Saint Simons."

"Jekyll," Chris said.

"I have one on the beach, but it's quite expensive, and we'll need references."

"Where on the beach?" Chris asked curtly.

The realtor showed him a map.

"Where's Beachview," Chris asked.

The realtor showed him the main street that ran along the beach for a distance, then veered slightly away. Small streets split away from Beachview, most of them ending in small cul de sacs.

Chris nodded. He had a good idea from the map where Meara's house was. The available rental was two blocks down, overlooking the water. It was perfect.

He wrote down three names and telephone numbers. "Your secretary can check the references while we sign the papers and I check out of my hotel."

"But you haven't seen it," the man protested.

Chris gave him his most charming smile. "I trust your judgment," he said.

The realtor grinned. "Yes, sir."

Two hours later, Chris signed the papers and handed Stan Cable a check.

Chris stopped at a store to get some groceries. Coffee and bread and some cold cuts. He didn't know what was on the island now, and he didn't want to run into Meara by accident. He needed to control the situation. If, he amended silently, control was even a possibility.

He doubted whether anything or anyone could control what was coming. But he had to try. God knew it would be difficult enough without an audience. He had to meet her alone. But then, he thought wryly, she might not even recognize him. Twenty years was a long time.

Chris drove slowly over the causeway, remembering the

agonizing, bitter trip in the small motorboat years ago. The water was calm now, like gray velvet. He passed over a short drawbridge that spanned the intracoastal waterway, and then he was on the island again.

The great moss-draped oaks were as he remembered, but so much else had changed. The crushed-shell roads and dirt trails had been replaced by pavement. As he reached the main road, he saw several low-slung motels and a small shopping center. Care had evidently been taken to preserve much of the natural beauty, and the landscaping was still exquisite. But now there were cars and people where once there had been serenity and solitude. The sense of majestic isolation was gone, stolen forever.

He turned down the road which led to the Jekyll Island Clubhouse. It stood empty and deteriorating and abandoned, as were the magnificent cottages that ringed it. They were like discarded toys, lifeless and without magic because there was no longer anyone to love them. He felt a deep sense of loss as he looked at the empty, cracked pool, the rotting boards around the tennis courts, the general air of neglect over something once so grand.

He remembered the orchestra music that had drifted softly from the dining room when he and Meara had walked the lush grounds, the light, bubbling sound of cultivated voices, the well-dressed men and women at an afternoon picnic, the game of bowls in the afternoons.

Something of history and a remarkable period had been swept away by time and events. He hated to think that he might have been partly responsible, or had the closing simply been the natural end to one of the last storybook eras, its time already gone when he had entered it?

He left his car and walked out to what was left of the abandoned wharf. The club launches were gone, of course. And the yacht. The marshes looked so peaceful, so peaceful today in the sunlight, so different from when an explosion had lit them with fiery red light.

"Michael!"

He could still hear her agonized cry ringing out over the river. It had haunted his nights for years, and now it seemed to echo over the calm, even water. He shivered in the heat, his insides as cold as ice, as that night returned in its entirety, every terrible second.

How did he believe he could come back?

He turned abruptly and strode to his car, yanking the door open with a force that shook its entire frame. He started the engine and turned down the narrow paved drive to the main road and to the house he had rented.

Kurt Weimer had arrived that afternoon but was not to be disturbed, the operator at the Cloister Hotel on Sea Island informed Chris when he called from his rented house. Was there a message?

Chris answered with a negative, saying he would call back, and thanked her. He hung up, but he didn't move from his rigid pose.

He'd hoped against hope that something might happen at the last moment, that Weimer wouldn't arrive. The more he'd seen of the island, the more he had realized how difficult meeting Meara would be. Perhaps, he wondered, he was anticipating trouble where there was none. Perhaps Weimer's visit here was exactly what it was purported to be.

His sixth sense told him something else altogether. His gut coiled in a tight knot as he thought of the rumors surrounding Weimer.

He replaced his good shoes with a pair of comfortable loafers and ventured down to the water where he turned left. Meara's home was, he knew, two blocks to the right. He hadn't seen anyone even remotely resembling his mental picture of her, and he felt relatively safe from encountering her.

Chris found himself moving toward the place of the picnic so long ago. It was now a state camping ground, he knew from the map, but that made no difference. The pull on him was incredibly strong, as were so many of the sights and smells since he first arrived on the island. There were so many memories of the one time he had felt so spectacularly alive.

He found the spot, at least he thought he had. Everything about it had been ingrained in his memory. He looked at his watch; the hour was late afternoon, and the tide was coming in, reaching its fingers farther and farther up the beach toward the dunes and the wind-sculpted oak trees that stood so tenaciously against the sea and wind.

Chris wondered if Meara ever came here, if she ever remembered as he did. Why else would she continue to come here year after year?

He had wondered about that. He had seized upon those few sentences in the detective's quarterly reports. Starting in 1950, she had returned to the island at least once a year and then more often after she had received the cottage.

Chris knew about that too. Thank God she'd had friends that night, and the weeks and months that followed. Thank God she'd had Sanders Evans. And thank God she had apparently never come to hate the place she called the "island of dreams."

Paralyzed by an odd enervation, he stayed on the beach, watching people come and go with a strange detachment. Tomorrow morning he would park down the street from Meara's house and see who came and went. If Weimer made no move toward Meara, then neither would he. Meara deserved some peace in her life.

*　　　*　　　*

Kurt Weimer had engaged one of the beach cottages at the Cloister for his two-week stay. An assistant was staying at the main hotel, but Kurt wanted privacy.

He had waited a very long time for this. The conference was a minor one, one he usually would have refused until he learned its location.

The coast of Georgia. The place where his father had died.

Kurt had been eleven when he learned of his father's death. He had been a leader in Hitler Youth and was immensely proud of his father's position in the elite SS.

Kurt cared little about his mother, a weak, ineffectual woman, but he deeply admired his father in his handsome black uniform and aura of authority. The other boys took notice and were respectful, although they might talk mockingly behind his back. Once he had heard two boys ridiculing his father, and he had informed on them. The next day, they were gone from school.

His father took him for long walks, and Kurt had sensed the fear from those they passed. He felt it and he enjoyed it. He felt important, somebody. His father told him how Hitler had given pride back to Germany, to the German people. He must never forget that pride, his father said. The Third Reich would last a thousand years and he, Hans's son, must be prepared to assume his rightful leadership in its future.

The Third Reich. The future of Germany.

Before his father left the last time, he had told Kurt that he had been especially selected for a glorious mission for the Fatherland, one that could help win the war. The Weimers would be honored, he'd said. The German Knight's Cross would be his father's award, presented by the Führer himself.

Kurt had told all the other boys in Hitler Youth, and

had waited. And waited. Four months later, two men came to visit his mother, and he'd heard her sob.

Hans Weimer was dead in the service of his country. But neither he nor his mother were told why. Kurt was left with a letter from his father, a letter telling him always to be loyal to the Führer, to the new and strong Germany, to the Third Reich. It became young Kurt's most treasured possession, especially as the war worsened. There were those who did not believe, who betrayed the man and the party who had brought Germany from chaos, but Kurt believed. His faith never wavered. Not even during the last dark days of 1944 and the first months of 1945 when Berlin was bombed day and night, and the allies and Russians closed in on the doomed city.

At fourteen, he led what was left of his Hitler's Youth comrades, some boys twelve and younger, to defend the beleaguered city. He fought until he was wounded, and still he fought. His small band annihilated, he was finally pulled away by a German officer who had seen enough and tried to surrender. Kurt shot him.

Another officer had watched everything and approached Hans carefully. "Ah, a fine little fighter. We'll need you in the days ahead," he said, and identified himself as a member of the SS.

They escaped Berlin together, the officer and the boy, disguised as forced laborers. Kurt hadn't liked the idea, but his companion promised there was honor ahead. The first priority, he'd said, was to help as many loyal Germans as possible to escape the Allied net. All the members of SS were marked for persecution. But if they escaped, they could work secretly in other countries and someday restore the glory of the Third Reich. The name of the organization was Odessa.

The officer was Stefan Kranz, and he became another father to Kurt. He had money, a lot of money, though Kurt never knew where it came from. He bought a new identity for himself and offered to adopt Kurt. But Kurt was proud of his father, and he decided to keep his own name. But he did stay with Stefan.

Kurt soon discovered that Stefan's wife and twin baby sons had been killed in the fire bombing at Dresden. They had been sent away from Berlin for safety. Two days later they had died in the raging inferno which had once been among Germany's most beautiful cities.

Stefan, Kurt knew, had one great goal in life: to restore the Third Reich to its proper place, to finish the job Hitler had started. Dozens of former SS officers and concentration camp personnel passed through their home to America, to Brazil, to Argentina. Kurt kept scrupulous records in code as to their number and destination. They would be asked to repay some day.

Kurt had an excellent teacher in Stefan Kranz, who was both charming and witty and yet possessed a cold, calculating intelligence. Stefan had come from a good family who only reluctantly followed Hitler, but Stefan had quickly recognized the opportunities to become powerful and rich under the regime, and he grabbed at both. He was a master at thievery, and had emerged from the war a very wealthy man, mostly from confiscation of property, both of Jews and dissidents. But he had lost his power and he wanted it back, and he saw a way of doing it through young Kurt.

He taught Kurt good manners, how to converse, how to charm, how to dress. Stefan, impressed by Kurt's abilities and loyalty, sent the boy to the university. He guided Kurt's academic career, telling him that if one knew how to manipulate money, one could manipulate countries. Odessa had huge financial backing, the result of stolen art and property and money; someone would be needed to guide its investments, to use its funds to buy foreign government leaders who would assist members of Odessa, and to weaken those who refused to cooperate.

When he graduated from the university with the highest of grades, Kurt was employed by the West German Finance Ministry where he rose rapidly. He made a name for himself in economics, all the while guiding enormously successful investments for Odessa. He knew many of the organization's secrets, the location of its members. He knew how to subtly blackmail them into providing more and more funds.

At thirty-two, he was considered one of the leading lights of the West German government, an impeccable liberal, an anti-Nazi. If a rumor ever surfaced, its carrier was quickly and efficiently eliminated. Odessa had a very long and influential reach.

But through each step of his success, Kurt Weimer had never forgotten his father, had never stopped wondering exactly what had happened to him in the spring of 1942. In 1957, he finally found several pieces to the puzzle, although all files concerning his father had evidently been destroyed. By accident, he encountered a former intelligence officer who had recognized his name and told him what he knew of the landing on an island off Georgia. The mission had been aborted suddenly when the German agents, including his father, had failed to transmit the final code. Subsequent attempts to locate either of the agents failed, although there had been two articles in the paper which were noted by Nazi agents. One described the heroic shooting by a young woman of a man attempting to kidnap two children. Another was a brief account of a drowning. Both were reported because they involved deaths at the same approximate time.

Kurt had sent someone to check both articles. The story of the kidnapping included a photo of the supposed kidnapper, and Kurt recognized his father. He had been killed by a woman named Meara O'Hara, now Evans. As Stefan hated Americans who he blamed for the deaths of his wife and son, now Kurt felt the same rage toward the woman who had killed his father. He had learned charm from Stefan. Now he learned revenge.

He would take from Meara O'Hara Evans what she had taken from him: the person closest to her.

I've got to get my life in order.

Meara knew it had gone awry long ago, and she'd never quite managed to put it back together again.

It was her dreams, she thought. Once they were gone, she hadn't known where to go.

She'd tried. She tried to be a good wife, a good mother. She's even, belatedly, tried to be a journalist. But the big dreams were gone, and the ones taking their places never quite fit the big jigsaw puzzle she'd designed as a child.

You've been lucky, she told herself. You had Sanders for twenty years. You have Lisa.

But she was so empty, lost, alone.

So much was her fault. She'd stood at a distance for such a long time, and she had tried to protect Lisa in all the wrong ways, becoming too much of a strict disciplinarian, secretly afraid that Lisa might some day succumb as she had. Lisa reminded her so much of herself: emotional, stubborn, determined.

Meara had strengthened herself against emotion, and she tried to make Lisa the same way. While she still enjoyed the sun trailing over water or a splendid sunset or feeling Sanders's arm around her during a walk, there was something inside that held back, which watched, afraid to participate. She couldn't forget the one mistake, the one that ended in murder and betrayal, the one that almost caused the death or capture of her adopted family, the children she loved. How could she ever trust her judgment again?

Lisa had felt it and had turned to Sanders, and his un-qualified and open devotion.

But Sanders had always understood, and that was why his loss had been so devastating. He had been a buffer, teasing her until she allowed Lisa to do whatever it was that she wanted so badly. But now the barrier had no gates, and Meara didn't know quite how to tear it down. Or even whether she could. Her mask of confidence, of tranquility, was such a complete fraud.

Meara looked out over the ocean. Maybe it was time to leave the island behind. Forever. Return to Virginia. But what did she have there now? She had always expected eventually to live here full-time. It was why she'd had Sanders buried here. Now she wondered whether it had been wise.

Sanders had been the one to bring her here years ago, saying she had to face the island, the ghosts, that he would help her. And he had. The island had reclaimed its magic, its peace and rhythm overwhelming the bad memories.

She thought of Lisa's words. *He got such a sad look on his face when he didn't think you were noticing.* Was it true? Had he only pretended these years to like the island? For her sake. Or was it Lisa's imagination? He had often seemed as pleased to come as she, saying the island was a tranquil change from his often unpleasant job. Had she really fooled herself that much? Had he thought she saw Michael Fielding here? She had, probably too often, but she had also enjoyed the time with Sanders—their long walks, the soft sunsets and even gentler sunrises, even the violent storms that lit the sky with pyrotechnics which would put the best fireworks to shame.

Meara shook her head. Jekyll held altogether too many reminders of the two men who had so influenced her life: one with such bitter results, the other with soothing ones.

She called Raggedy Andy, their dog. He'd been curled

up under a table during the short argument with Lisa. Andy, Meara knew, did not like dissension and usually hid when any was in the air, a leftover, Meara often thought, from his earlier days of likely mistreatment.

Now he emerged, his tail wagging tentatively, his whiskered face poking anxiously at her leg. She leaned over and reassured him, thinking she needed it as much as he did. As if he understood, Andy pushed his body next to her leg, trying to get as close as possible. It was, she knew, his way of trying to comfort.

"It's all right, Andy," she said, and his tail wagged with a little more enthusiasm.

"Want to go for a walk?" she asked, wanting to make someone or something happy. Andy responded with delight.

"All right." She would finish her article tonight and get it in the mail tomorrow afternoon after polishing it. She would send out queries to other magazines. She had done well in the past few years as a free-lance writer for regional magazines and had sold several short stories to *Redbook*.

And she would think seriously about selling the cottage.

She had to break the hold of the island. She was only forty-three; there was time to explore new worlds, to do more writing, perhaps even a novel.

But not, she knew, as long as she stayed here, locked to the past.

Next week, she would call a realtor. Next week, she promised herself.

Chapter Seventeen

Lisa knelt by the grave, and placed a fresh rose there. Other flowers, laid there only last week, were now brown, their color gone, the stems brittle. The sight magnified the hollowness inside her.

She missed him. So much. He had always been there for her, even when he was out of town on assignment. He called nightly, always listening to her litany of real and supposed disasters with patience and sympathy. He was warm arms, loving smile, and comfort.

It was difficult to believe him gone now. Whenever he came into a room, he filled it with uninhibited affection. She had been his girl. She still expected him to appear any minute, his eyes crinkling with a smile as he saw her.

She'd wanted to be like him. She would go to law school in the fall, having finished college in three years by doubling up on courses. She'd wanted to join the FBI; it didn't yet admit women, but the time was coming. He'd said it was. And she would be ready. She knew it required either a degree in accounting or law, and she'd never been good with numbers.

In the meantime, her father had urged her to consider practicing law, and she had worked with Kellen's firm for the last several years during the summers. She'd always been in a rush for everything, like her mother, Daddy said. But she wasn't like her mother at all. Her mother was too cautious about everything, cautious and often overly protective, always urging her to slow down, to discipline her emotions and enthusiasms. Lisa didn't want to discipline them.

"Daddy," she whispered.

But there was no answering voice.

She stood there for several more minutes. She felt rather than heard the man behind her. A hand rested on her shoulder, and she knew it was Kellen.

"I went by your house to ask you to dinner tonight," he said. "Your mother said you might be here."

Lisa merely nodded, her body tensing slightly.

"She's hurting too, you know," Kellen said.

"I know," Lisa said. But we can't seem to talk, she wanted to continue, but couldn't. It was too private. And she didn't understand it herself. There had always been an invisible shield between herself and her mother. Oh, her mother did all the right things, but there had never been the closeness, the spontaneous touching and hugging that her father had considered such an essential part of life.

Kellen reached down his hand to hers and pulled her up.

"Let me take you to dinner tonight."

"It's too soon," she said.

"It's been more than a month, and it's Saturday night," Kellen said. "I don't think your father would have wanted you to become a hermit."

Tears filled Lisa's eyes again. "Oh, Kelly, I miss him so."

"I know," he said. No one could miss the closeness between the father and daughter. It had been one of the first things he had noticed when the Evans family started spending the summers at the house next to his, that and the startling blue of Lisa's eyes. She'd been a charming, precocious imp who, over succeeding years, had grown even more lovely, with eyes like the midnight sky and hair the color of gold. She'd always asked the damnedest questions. And each summer she seemed to grow prettier. When she was eighteen, he'd decided that he would marry her some day.

But she was not ready for that yet, he knew, and so he'd held his words and waited until the time was right. She had grown up in the shadow of her father's work and thought it adventurous and fascinating. She was determined to have a career of her own, unlike her mother, she said, who lived such an uneventful life. She, Lisa, was going to do more with her life.

So he merely teased and lightly courted her, listening to her innermost thoughts and dreams. They both dated others, but often depended on each other for escort to island oyster roasts and other events. He'd kept his kisses light, except for one evening when a kiss had gotten away from him, deepened far more than he'd ever intended, and she had responded with far more fervor than he'd expected. He'd been careful since then, taking everything a step at a time. He cared about her too much to risk forcing her into a marriage she didn't yet want. The exercise in self-restraint, however, was often torture, a test of willpower that was straining against the limits he had set.

Time. Time was all he needed. As an attorney with offices in Brunswick, his practice was varied and interesting, and he was convinced that he could eventually dissuade her from her current goal of law enforcement and into the firm if he didn't rush or push. She had worked for him as a receptionist/secretary for the past summer and was remarkably quick and able.

His hand tightened on her shoulder, and she leaned back against him.

"Go to dinner with me," he repeated.

Lisa relaxed, feeling at home there. In some ways, he was like her father, uncomplicated and warmhearted and dependable. And so nice. As long as she could remember, he had always been there for her. She had told him her dreams, her hopes. He was, and always had been, her very best friend.

"All right," she said.

"The Cloister?"

Lisa didn't care. She only knew she needed to get away from the house for a while. She nodded.

"I'll pick you up at seven."

"Okay."

"May I have a smile? Even a small frog one," he said, referring to an old joke of theirs. Soon after Lisa's family started coming here for the summer, she had been furious at her mother at not being allowed to spend the night at a home of a family Meara didn't know. Lisa had angrily run from the house, straight into Kelly, who was then eighteen.

"That's the most awful frog face I've ever seen," he had observed teasingly. Lisa had considered the comment carefully, visualizing the downturned ugly mouth of a frog. She'd had to smile despite herself, but it was a tiny reluctant smile, and he'd grinned. "Well, that's a little better. A sorta frog smile."

Remembering, Lisa couldn't help but smile. He'd always been able to coax a grin from her. It was feeble, she knew, but a smile nonetheless. Even if it was a frog smile.

*   *   *

Kurt sat in the Cloister dining room, alone this evening, as he'd wished. Most of the other attendees at the International Economic Development Advisory Council would not arrive for two more days.

When he made his travel arrangements, he'd said he needed a brief vacation before the meetings.

Two days to arrange a meeting with Meara Evans.

He hadn't decided what he would do yet. He knew she had a daughter. He had seen photos of both of them, and their images were stamped firmly in his mind.

He knew Sanders Evans had been a federal agent, and he had been worried about that. When he heard about the man's death a month prior to the conference, he was exuberant. Fate was with him; nothing could go wrong now. Both Meara and Lisa Evans would be very, very vulnerable at the moment.

The woman was pretty enough from the picture, but the daughter was a true beauty. His eyes had narrowed with appreciation as he'd looked at the long blond hair and prettily molded face. A true Aryan. If he hadn't other plans . . .

The service in the elegant dining room was impeccable for an American restaurant, and the food superb. As he waited for the lamb he had ordered, his gaze moved around the room.

There was a mixture of older couples and what looked like honeymooning couples. The young and the old and few in between. His glance finally settled on a couple in a corner, principally because the girl looked sad while most of the other young couples appeared besotted with each other.

His eyes widened as he recognized her as the one in the photo he'd been memorizing. Another amazing twist of luck. Or fate, he thought again. Or justice.

The meal lost its appeal. He considered several means

of approaching her. There would be no better opportunity than an accidental meeting in one of America's premier resort hotels. What better opening.

The waiter was serving the couple's salads. He had time. He ate slowly and turned his entire attention to the excellent meal in front of him. He did not want anyone to notice undue attention.

His mind worked quickly but practically. He didn't question the coincidence. He had been told there were few fine dining establishments in the area, so it made sense residents would sometimes come here. Now how best to use the advantage?

He couldn't approach them. An accidental meeting? Possibly, but that could easily end as quickly as it began. No, he had to have a reason to visit the Evans home. He smiled to himself as he thought of one. He just needed a bit more luck.

Kurt smiled to himself. He had no false modesty. He was a bachelor, a much sought after one. He knew he was considered handsome by most with his angular face, dark blond hair, and light blue eyes that glittered in a carefully tanned face.

He ate slowly, appreciative of the superb service which was never rushed. He was just starting his dessert when the couple rose and started his way. The two would have to pass his table.

His hand suddenly knocked a knife off the table, and he leaned down just as the woman passed by, and his shoulder went into her, causing her to throw out a hand for balance. Her purse went down to the floor.

Kurt was up in a second, murmuring profuse and elegant apologies. "I'm so sorry, I didn't see you. So careless of me, so unbelievably clumsy. Please allow me to retrieve your purse."

He knelt, his back hiding the movement of his hands

which quickly opened the clasp and spilled out the contents, knocking a compact under the table and out of sight. A waiter was there then, helping, and together they gathered the rest of the items: a wallet, a lipstick, a pen, some matches, a package of cigarettes. After carefully replacing them in the purse, Kurt stood and handed it to her with a courtly bow, noticing the sudden flush in her cheeks at his elaborate courtesy. She was, as he had hoped, distracted enough not to look to see whether she had everything.

"Let me present myself," he said smoothly. "I'm Kurt Weimer. I'm here for the International Economic Conference, not," he added with charming self-mockery, "to crash into lovely young ladies. I hope I'm forgiven."

Lisa blushed. "I wasn't looking where I was going," she said shakily as she looked up into the handsome face.

"But it was my fault completely," Kurt said. He looked over at Kelly. "May I buy you an after-dinner drink in the way of an apology."

Kelly's arm went around Lisa's waist protectively. "I think not," he said. "Miss Evans is not feeling well, and it's really not necessary. Accidents happen."

"Miss Evans?" Kurt said inquisitively.

Kelly had no choice but to respond. For some reason he didn't understand, he was uncomfortable and wary. "This is Lisa Evans and I'm Kellen Tabor," he said abruptly. "I hope you enjoy your visit to our islands."

The response was dismissive and barely polite, but Kurt felt a tiny ball of triumph growing inside. Lisa Evans was regarding him with interest.

He bowed his head slightly in acknowledgment. "A privilege," he said. "And again my apologies." As the man named Tabor moved deliberately forward, Kurt stepped aside, a slight smile on his face. He nodded in polite farewell, and sat down again, watching them leave the dining room but not before Lisa Evans turned her head and looked back. He smiled, and she quickly turned back to her escort.

Kurt leaned down and found the compact and pocketed it. His hand moved along its surface. There was engraving on the metal which meant it must hold importance for her. So much the better. So much greater her gratitude when he returned it tomorrow.

With a pleased smile, he turned back to the English trifle.

Chris leaned against the seat of the rented car. It was a dark, nondescript vehicle, one he had selected himself. He had found a quiet, oak-shaded spot on the edge of a motel parking lot. He could see Meara's cottage three houses down.

He had waited here for two hours now, and though the car was shaded, the sun was making him miserable. He looked at his watch. Noon. Sunday.

There were two cars in the Evans's driveway, a gray Chevrolet and an older blue Buick.

He felt like a Peeping Tom, but he knew no other way of seeing her, of seeing her daughter. His daughter. His stomach was bunched in knots, his arms rigid against the steering post. He had been patient twenty years. He could be patient a few more hours.

Time moved slowly. Impossibly slowly. He saw several people glance at him curiously, and he hastily brought his wrist up and looked angrily at his watch as if waiting for someone. He sure as hell didn't want the police to investigate.

The door opened, and a young woman emerged, a shaggy dog with her. He thought he had seen the dog before, on the beach yesterday with a woman, but he wasn't sure. The tide had been low and the woman walked along its edges, leaving considerable distance between him and the figure.

The woman leaned down and emerged from the porch, the dog on a leash. For a moment she seemed to look right at him, but then she turned, walking in the opposite direction.

She was lovely, young and lovely, with long blond hair swinging across her back. Her face had much of Meara's in it, high finely shaped cheekbones, a wide mouth, stubborn chin. He couldn't see the color of the eyes, but he could make out the long golden lashes framing them.

His daughter was wearing dark blue shorts which revealed long shapely legs and gently curved hips. A light blue blouse was tucked carelessly in the shorts, and she wore sandals on her feet. She was really quite beautiful.

His hands tightened around the steering wheel as if grasping them for life, as if he were to fall into a deep dark chasm. He wanted to go to her, God help him, but he wanted to stride over to her and tell her who he was. He wanted to hold her close, to talk to her, to discover her hopes and dreams. To share her sorrows. And protect. Dear God, he wanted to protect that innocence.

Chris watched as she disappeared down the side of the road. He wanted to follow, to somehow arrange a meeting, but he realized how wrong that would be. He owed Meara more than that. He had already promised himself he would disappear without ever contacting them if he decided Meara and Lisa were not in danger.

Minutes later, he watched Meara emerge from the house, an envelope in her hand. She was as slender as she had been twenty years ago, but her movements were not so obviously spontaneous. There was a deliberateness to them now.

That long glorious golden-red hair had been cut and tamed into a short feathery cut that framed her face becomingly, yet he wished for the old wild streaming curls which had made her appear so utterly free. She wore a blouse and skirt and, like Lisa, a pair of comfortable sandals. Also like Lisa, her face held no hint of a smile or laughter. Neither was it vulnerable as it once had been. Instead, her expression was controlled. That, more than anything, caused him pain. Was it Sanders's recent death that painted the mask there, or had it been there for years? Because of him . . .

He didn't know how long he stayed, unable to act. It was dangerous doing so, he knew. He had been here much too long. Yet he hungered for another look, for more bits and pieces of their lives.

The girl came back first, and she had just gone inside when he saw a Mercedes glide slowly past the house, turn around and turn into the Evans's driveway. He continued to watch as a tall man, not lean but well proportioned, exit the car and confidently stride to the door. The door opened almost immediately, and after a few minutes the man entered the house.

Chris didn't have to guess who he was. He had studied the pictures carefully.

His throat tightened as fear twisted his heart.

Kurt Weimer.

Lisa was absently petting Raggedy Andy when the knock came. She'd neglected him lately, and she expected she'd enjoyed the walk as much as he had. She released a sigh of relief to find her mother gone, although she didn't know exactly why. She didn't really understand why she was so resentful at the moment, but she hadn't been able to push aside those feelings. So many emotions had swept over her since her father's death: rage, loss, grief. It was the first time she had ever lost anyone close to her, and she realized she wasn't dealing with it well. Not like her mother. She resented her mother for doing something she couldn't. At first, she reasoned that it was because she had loved harder, but that wasn't fair. If not passion, there had been a sort of tender understanding between her mother and father, a respect, that she had rarely seen between married couples.

The knock came again, and she unwound her legs from the position in which she was sitting and stood, ambling more than walking. It was probably Kelly, and as much as she liked him she was feeling suffocated right now.

She knew her mother hoped someday she and Kelly might marry, but Kelly had never mentioned it, and marriage was the last thing she wanted now. She wanted to explore the world, test her wings. She wanted to learn. She wanted adventure. She wanted so many things that she believed marriage would stifle.

Her mother had been stifled. Lisa had recognized that. Perhaps that was why her mother closed herself up so much. When Lisa had brought Raggedy Andy home, half-starved and cowering, her mother had not wanted to keep him. When Lisa had demanded why, her mother said she would only get hurt when the dog died or disappeared.

Lisa didn't understand. She had been twelve and wanted a dog more than anything. It was her father who'd gently persuaded her mother to allow her to keep Andy. Perversely, the dog had taken her mother as his special person although he'd received little attention from her in the beginning. Now her mother and the dog seemed to have a special relationship which needed little in words or even contact.

Andy had never been overly demonstrative for a dog, and he'd been definitely wary of strangers, particularly men, yet he stuck with her mother, who hadn't wanted him, like glue.

Andy rose reluctantly and stretched at the knock on the

door. He was, Lisa thought, a total failure as a watch dog. Once Andy retired for the night, an army couldn't wake him, and on seeing a stranger, he usually disappeared to the closest hiding spot. He was approximately ten years old now, and he became more endearingly cowardly by the year.

He waited now, his tail between his legs. Lisa smiled slightly as she reached the door and opened it, discovering the handsome stranger with the intriguing foreign accent.

Her eyes must have shown her surprise because he nodded slightly as she fumbled for words. "Mr. . . . ?"

"Weimer," he said with a slightly sheepish smile that was extremely attractive, possibly because it seemed out of place on a face which radiated self-assurance. "Kurt Weimer. I am sorry to bother you again, but I apparently missed one of the articles from your purse last night. As I was leaving, I found this. I remembered your name and asked the manager, and he gave me your address."

Lisa's gaze roved over his face. He was very attractive in a continental way, his face nearly perfectly sculpted, his eyes admiring as he returned her look.

She took the compact. "Thank you," she said. "I didn't know it was gone until this morning. It was a gift."

"Then I'm delighted to return it," he said.

"Would you like to come in?" she asked. "There's some lemonade." Then she bit her lip. He looked far too sophisticated for lemonade.

"I would be most grateful," he said. "I'm not used to your warm temperatures."

She held the door open, and he entered, seeming not at all out of place. He was medium tall, several inches under Kelly's rangy height, but well-built and impeccably dressed in a casual suit. He spoke excellent English but there was a definite foreign accent.

"You're from . . ."

"Germany," he said. "I'll be here several weeks for an economic conference."

It was, she knew, a modest statement. The papers had been full of reports about the upcoming meeting. Even the president, it was said, might visit briefly. She smiled, and she knew it was the first unforced smile since she'd learned of her father's death. "And you took time to bring me the compact. It's very kind of you."

He grinned. "It was entirely my fault, after all, and it was the least I could do."

Lisa was surprised. He must be very important if he was a member of the conference, although he looked rather young and attractive for an economist. She had only glanced over news of the meeting, and she knew few details. Now she wished she had paid more attention. Yet he seemed very easy to talk to.

"Excuse me," she said. "I'll get the lemonade." She went into the kitchen, her pulse fluttering with unaccustomed awareness. Andy, who had regarded the newcomer with suspicion, followed at her heels.

She hesitated there, resting her palms on the counter. She didn't understand her somewhat shaky reaction to the visitor. She pushed back a strand of her hair and wished she'd put lipstick on this morning, but now it was too late. It would be obvious if she did so now.

Lisa quickly poured two glasses of lemonade, which her mother had made yesterday.

She slowly went back in the other room, and found him looking out of the screened porch from which the ocean was barely visible over the dunes.

He took the lemonade with a smile and tasted it appreciatively. "Excellent," he said. "You'll have to tell me how to make it."

"Lemonade?" He looked as if he would be more comfortable sipping something exotic.

He laughed. "You'll never know how refreshing it would be after days of stuffy meetings."

"Is that what you do?"

"I'm afraid so. I just finished several months of them and now I have weeks more."

"What do you do exactly?" she asked.

"I advise my government on the economic impact of prospective new laws or policies."

"In Germany?"

"In West Germany," he corrected. "But I'm also involved in predicting the impact of government actions of our trading partners. For instance, how the tightening of your money supply will affect the value of our deutsche mark."

Lisa felt well out of her depth, but curiously it wasn't Mr. Weimer who made her feel that way. He talked to her like an equal, and his glance made her feel attractive, even in her old blouse and shorts.

It was as if he understood her uncertainty. "I envy you," he said. "Your lovely seaside home."

He was envying *her*. He had traveled throughout the world, he had probably met with heads of states and made decisions that influenced thousands, maybe millions, of people. Her father would like him. Her father . . .

The pain came rolling back, the emptiness. For a few moments she'd forgotten he would never like anyone again.

Kurt Weimer was watching her. "Forgive me for prying," he said gently, "but you looked unhappy last night, and again, just now. Is there anything I can do?"

His sympathy rocked what little composure she had. "My father . . . died just recently."

He moved to her and tactfully put a hand on her arm. "I know how you must feel," he said in a low voice. "My father died when I was a boy. I still . . . think about him."

"Mr. Weimer . . ."

"Please call me Kurt. Now we have sadness in common."

"I still can't believe it," Lisa whispered. "I expect him to come home and grin at me and call me his sweetheart."

"And the young man with you last night . . ."

"My friend."

"Nothing more?"

Was he? Lisa wasn't exactly sure. She'd always felt safe with Kelly, just as she had with her father. They had fun together and laughed together and liked most of the same things, things like stray dogs and hot chili peppers and roasted marshmallows. She knew him so well. She always knew what to expect from Kelly. There was no pounding excitement or shivers of anticipation.

"No," she said.

"Then perhaps you'd allow me to take you to dinner?"

Lisa stared at him in surprise. She knew she was relatively pretty, though she never thought of herself as anything more. Her mother's coloring was much more vivid, striking, and she'd envied that. *You always want what you can't have.* How many times had her mother told her that? And when you get it, you want something else you can't have. It was one of her mother's favorite warnings.

But while Lisa always had plenty of dates and invitations, had broken hearts and had her heart broken, they'd all, with the exception of Kelly, been boys near her age. Kurt Weimer had to be in his mid-thirties at least, suave and sophisticated and probably accustomed to sleek, confident women.

He smiled disarmingly at her confusion. "I promise to be a gentleman."

"Yes," she said in a surprisingly calm voice despite a thumping heart. "I would like that." She heard the front door open and her mother entered, stopping suddenly as she saw the man in the house.

Her mother looked from her to the visitor, who had risen from the sofa where he was sitting next to Lisa, and then back again.

Lisa stumbled over the introduction, wishing her mother had been gone just a little longer. "Mother, this is Kurt Weimer. He's at the Cloister for the International Economic Conference that's been in the paper. I . . . lost my compact last night, and he was kind enough to bring it by."

Her mother stood stiff and straight, her entire body visibly tensing as she heard the German name.

"Mother?"

Her mother stood there in unwelcoming silence, and Lisa suffered acute embarrassment.

"Mother?" she tried again, a trace of puzzlement in her voice.

Meara smiled bleakly. "Thank you, Mr. Weimer That compact meant a lot to my daughter. Are . . . you going to be here long?"

"Several weeks," he said easily, ignoring her distress. "Your daughter has just made it a much more pleasant trip by agreeing to have dinner with me."

Meara's eyes, sharp and wary, went to Lisa. She had badly wanted something to distract Lisa from her grief. But a German? Recollections of another German painfully returned. Recollections and sharp agonizing memories assaulted her like electrical shocks.

He looked nothing like Michael. Yet there was something in his face, something familiar that pricked at her consciousness. She looked at Lisa's eyes, bright for the first time in days, and at the visitor, who was standing easily and politely in the middle of the room. She saw something flicker in his eyes, something knowing, and she felt odd, frightened. As if evil had entered the room.

No! She chided herself. Imagination. That was all. Imagination heightened by the turmoil and tragedy of the past few weeks. If he was one of the visiting economists, he must be eminently respectable, above any reproach. She had never been prejudiced. Since the war, she had met other Germans and had never reacted like this. Was it because of the way he looked at her daughter?

Whatever it was, she couldn't quiet the sudden fear which ran through her.

"I would think you'd be too busy for that," she finally managed ungraciously.

Lisa stared at her. Her mother was never, ever rude, no matter how provoked. It was one of the things that had always annoyed her, that control that was polite, even warm, but never intimate.

But the cold reply didn't appear to bother Kurt. "It often gets lonely in a new country," he said, "and your daughter has been very kind." He waited expectantly as if the statement had been a question.

Meara didn't know how to respond. She couldn't very well object. Lisa was old enough to make her own decisions, and Meara was afraid any obvious opposition would only serve to make the man more attractive. And he was, she had to admit, attractive enough already with his courtly continental manners and accent. She didn't have to be told how effective European charm could be.

She saw a wary secretivenesss in his eyes. A secretiveness that she remembered from years before. Yet there was also a difference between the two men, between this German and the one she had loved years ago. She wished she knew what it was, for even at the end, even when she discovered that Michael had lied to her and betrayed her, even then she hadn't felt the revulsion she felt now. She probably should have. But while she'd hated, she'd never felt this hard, cold chill.

He won't be here long, she told herself. He'll be busy most of the time. And Kelly's here.

She forced a smile. "I have some work to do."

"And I must be going," Kurt Weimer said. "It's been a pleasure, Mrs. Evans." His smile widened as he turned to Lisa. "Thank you for the lemonade. Should I come for you at eight?"

Lisa hesitated. "I'm not really very good company right now."

"You're perfect company." Kurt assured her. "And I'll bring you home early."

"All right," she replied. "Eight o'clock."

He bowed slightly. "I look forward to it."

Meara watched him leave, before turning to Lisa. "What about Kelly?"

"Kelly's a friend," Lisa said shortly.

Meara sighed. She liked Kelly very much, but again she knew pleading his case would only have the opposite effect. But as she'd told herself seconds earlier, this man would be here only a few weeks.

Once more, a kind of premonition took hold of her. A few weeks. A life could so easily be changed in a few weeks.

Chapter Eighteen

CHRIS WATCHED WEIMER LEAVE.

There was little resemblance to the Weimer he'd known. Hans had been heavier built, his hair darker, and his walk swaggering, except in his role of gardener. There was no swagger in this man, though there was a hint of arrogance.

So he'd been right to be worried. He felt no satisfaction in it. He had hoped he was wrong, that Weimer's visit to the coast had only been coincidence.

There was no longer any doubt.

It had been all he could do to stay in the car and not barge in. But the fact that Weimer had openly parked a very distinctive Mercedes in the driveway, visible to all the neighbors and a large number of walkers and bicyclers, told him that there was no immediate danger to the occupants of the house. Whatever else he was, Weimer was not stupid. But still, it took all Chris's control, and he didn't relax until he saw Weimer leave.

Chris started the car; he had already stayed here too long. He drove back to his rented house and went inside,

284

opening himself a soda. He needed no alcohol to cloud his thoughts.

He could go to the police. Revealing the truth had always been an option. But who would believe him? No one knew what had happened that night except him; no one knew Hans's real identity, only the name of the gardener; and he had no idea how much Sanders Evans had revealed of that night or how much he had protected Meara.

Kurt Weimer was a highly respected German government official. His suspected Odessa connections were only that. Suspected. Rumored. And even those suspicions were circulated only among a very small group of men; certainly they were not known by the German Federal Republic.

If Chris went to the police, he would have to reveal his own identity. The consequence to himself no longer mattered. He would readily go to jail if it would protect Meara and his daughter. What did matter was that the whole story would emerge, including Meara's small role and possibly even Lisa's parentage. He couldn't do that to them, not to either of them.

Now that he knew that Kurt was planning something, he could protect them. He was sure of it. The detective agency he'd used through the years also specialized in protection and security, and he had the money to provide whatever was needed. Yet Meara must know. No one could be protected completely without their cooperation.

Painfully, he knew he had run out of options. He had to tell Meara of the danger, tell her that the nightmare that started twenty-one years ago was continuing, that because of him she and her daughter were in deadly danger. How in the hell was he going to do that? Dear God, how?

Chris knew what to look for now, a slender woman with red hair and a ragged, clownish-looking dog. He watched the beach from his porch all afternoon, knowing somehow that she would be there. He finally saw them that evening as the tide crept up. The time was after seven, when most of the tourists were eating, and the beach was nearly empty.

There was still daylight, but the atmosphere was hazy, the sky gradually turning cinnamon as the sun neared its home beyond the horizon. Everything seemed lazy, almost in slow motion, even the birds that now swooped in slow, long, languid circles for one last meal, even the ocean, which lapped softly against the sand as the water crept higher in fingerlike movements.

A small hint of pink glowed in the west, and a breeze cooled some of the hot summer sun. He looked down at his clothes; slacks and a lightweight cotton shirt, casual enough yet very formal for a beach. Hell, what does a dead man wear when he returns to life? It was a morbidly humorous question, he knew, but he felt morbid, like a man going to his execution, as he left the haven of the porch and started down the beach.

She was walking north toward the campgrounds where the oaks grew close to the beach. Her shoulders were slumped and she looked, even at a distance, defeated. His heart hurt for her, feared for her, ached for her. She had apparently suffered deeply in the past weeks; she would suffer again in the next few hours.

Chris dragged his feet, reluctance and dread weighing him. How would she react? Would she believe him? Why would she? Yet she must. They had passed the last of the houses, and the untouched wildness of this part of the beach brought back the old mood of the island, the one that had been with him during the past years.

The few people on the beach disappeared, and there was no one but him and the two figures, the woman and the dog, moving slowly ahead of him. Relief mingled with apprehension. He needed her alone.

He found a secluded cranny carved out of the dunes by the water, and he went over to it, leaning against one of the sides. He would wait here until she turned back this way and then draw her into its privacy.

With bemusement, Meara watched Andy mosey along. *Mosey* was the only word for it. Andy had to investigate every piece of flotsam that washed up on the beach, every recently deceased denizen of the sea: a partial jellyfish, a piece of seaweed, a partially inhabited shell. No matter how many times he investigated the beach, he always seemed to find it intriguing although he thankfully no longer chased seabirds into the sea, emerging from the ocean wringing wet and spraying water and sand all over her.

It would be nice, she thought absently, to worry about nothing more than the next fascinating item to be sniffed.

No matter how hard she tried, she hadn't been able to dismiss this morning's distinguished-looking German visitor from her mind. New worry clouded the grief and loss she felt, would always feel. That loss seemed even more profound now, for there was no one to turn to, no one who would understand her strong, hostile reaction to the man.

Her senses, she feared, were overactive. Why else would she fear a seemingly pleasant stranger? Certainly, Lisa was lovely enough to attract him; with her soft coloring and ebullient nature, she had always attracted men. Meara had missed that quality in the past few weeks.

Andy was wandering off again, and she started to call him when she saw the man. She would have said he was lounging against a bank except his stance was . . . tense. As if he were waiting for someone.

She couldn't see his face. The last of the sun directly

hit it, and partially blinded her. Yet there was something hauntingly familiar about him.

So many times, she told herself. You've thought you've seen him so many times. Mirages? Wistful thinking? Certainly not that. How could she ever wish to see Fielding again? Especially now that Sanders had been gone such a very short time. Once again, as she often had during their marriage, Meara felt unworthy, disloyal.

She heard a whistle, low pitched and seductive, and she saw Andy turn toward the man and bound toward him. That in itself was unusual. Andy usually stayed away from men.

Meara called, but Andy didn't return. Instead, he had reached the figure, and the man had kneeled, his hand stroking Andy's too large head as a tail wagged in frantic approval. Stunned at the uncharacteristic behavior, Meara looked around the beach. She saw no one else, and she felt a sudden apprehension. Too much had happened lately. Nothing was ordinary anymore, nothing was safe.

The sky resembled a candy rock mountain, layers of enticing pastel colors, pink cotton candy upon cinnamon upon lemon. She looked at the man caught in the flash of sun, and something tugged at her, something unknown and fearful and aching. She suddenly wanted to run.

Instead, she walked toward the two figures in the sand. The man's head was bent, his blond hair glinting in the sun like pieces of gold, like hair she remembered. His head lifted, and she saw his face. She stumbled, and shook her head to clear it. She was going mad.

The man stood, deep blue eyes unfathomable, lines etched deeply around them, the mouth firm and somber, a muscle straining against the tight bronze skin of his cheek. Twenty years peeled away, and she stood on the beach as she once had, bound to a man she didn't know at all.

She reached out a hand as if to see whether it was an apparition, a ghost brought on by recent events. But her hand touched skin, and she jerked it away as if burned, stumbling backward, falling like a lifeless rag clown, until his arms caught her and lowered her gently to the ground. She remembered that touch. She had never been able to forget that irresistible combination of strength and gentleness.

She looked up, back into eyes so deep and blue that they seemed to swallow her.

"Meara," he said, his voice low and musical, as it had been the first time he said her name.

She struggled loose from his hold, his touch. "Who *are* you?" She hated the catch in her voice. She'd never been a physical coward. Whatever else she had been, she hadn't been that.

She felt a warm body huddle next to her, and part of her mind became aware of a shaggy head looking anxiously from her to the man now kneeling next to her. An excuse. An excuse to look away. She petted the dog, thinking that when she looked back there would be just another human being, a stranger, a man who resembled a dead man. A dead spy.

Meara felt emotions raging within her, like an ocean in the midst of a hurricane, deadly violent waves growing with ever increasing fury. They battered at her, hot waves, freezing ones, each intermingling until she felt herself drowning in them, extinguished by them. She heard herself whimper, and once more she felt his hands, and she knew beyond a doubt that it was he. The same fire branded her skin, the same electricity. Mother of God, how could she remember it so well, so easily, as if it were yesterday?

She twisted away from his touch, looking up at him with stark hatred born of desperation. "Don't touch me. Don't ever touch me."

He stepped back as if given a body blow by the words. His eyes fleetingly revealed something like stark agony, but it disappeared quickly into those damned deep depths she'd never really been able to penetrate. His mouth tightened, however, and he ran his fingers through his hair in a gesture that was hauntingly familiar.

She sat there in the sand, her hands on the dog as if frantic to find something to do with them, and stared at him as if he'd ascended from hell. She was curled in a tight knot, protective and hostile and afraid. And bewildered.

She didn't know how long she stayed like that. She felt herself shaking. "You're dead," she finally accused flatly, not looking at him. Empty, for a few blessed seconds, of emotion. Shock had replaced the first violent reactions.

"No." The answer came softly, gently, with a wry, almost apologetic tone.

"I saw—" She stopped, trying to remember what she had seen.

"You saw an explosion. I left the boat before it happened."

The shaking of her body increased and she saw his hand start to reach for her again, and she flinched away from it, just as Andy had cowered at times when he thought a blow might be coming. It never did, not at her house, but she'd known that he'd experienced brutality.

Immediately, the hand retreated.

"Why . . ." She finally managed the word, but it was cracked and high, as if it had come from someone else.

"Why didn't I die?" His voice was raw.

Meara knew she was staring. She felt the mist gather in back of her eyes. From sorrow? From horror? She didn't know. She was numb, disbelieving. Nothing registered as being real. Another dream. Another nightmare.

She tried again. "Why . . . are you here?"

He was on one knee in front of her, inches away. No

ghost. A ghost didn't age. And he had aged. Less than most people, she thought. Lines had deepened in his face, but they had only made a stronger whole. His body was just as lean; but she could see muscles in his shoulders that hadn't been there before. His eyes, if anything, were even bluer, but perhaps it was only time that had clouded their image in her mind. She had tried, dear God, how she had tried to blot them from her memory. He had smiled easily once, but now his lips were grim and his face rigidly set.

She could feel tension radiating from him, even fear, but that didn't make sense.

All of a sudden, all her emotions exploded. In almost an identical gesture as on that night in the power house, her hand went back and she slapped him, as hard and as violently as her body allowed, even harder than her ordinary strength would permit. He took it without trying to stop her, without moving, and she saw the red impact on his cheek and blood trickling from his mouth where her engagement ring had opened it.

She sat back, limp again, shaking again. He was like a statue, inhuman. But his steady gaze never left her; his hand never moved upward. It was as if he had expected it, expected it and accepted.

"Damn you," she whispered.

His eyes closed briefly, and she watched one of his hands tighten in a fist.

When he opened them again, their dark blue depths hid his feelings, just as they had so many times before. "Rest assured," he said slowly, "I've paid. I've paid and paid and paid."

She looked at his casually expensive clothes, his still lean muscled body. "Have you?" she asked bitterly. "Have you?"

"More than you'll ever know," he said, and now his voice was harsh.

"But not enough," she whispered. "Never enough."

"No," he agreed. "Not for the pain I've given you. There isn't, hasn't been, a day I haven't remembered the way your face looked that night."

Her hand clawed into the sand, seeking substance, but there was none. "What do you want now? Who or what do you want me to betray now?"

The control slipped from his face, and Meara saw naked anguish in it. She was glad, even while the feeling sickened her. She had never before enjoyed someone else's pain. She didn't like herself for doing it now.

"You . . . might be in danger," he said carefully.

"Danger?" Meara laughed sarcastically. "You were worried about that? My God . . . Michael . . . or is it Michael? Isn't it late for you to worry about that?"

"I never thought . . ."

She turned away from him, from any explanation. She didn't want to hear it. How many times had she relived that night? How many times had she awakened in that power house, sick from the drug and sick from fear, both for herself and the children lying still? How many times had she heard the other German's voice taunting her, threatening to steal the children, to take the Connors, to take her and use her? How many times had she known the cold terror and despair when he'd told her of Michael's role? How many times had she recoiled when she remembered the gunshot and saw the German sink down, his body covered with red.

And dear God how many times had she relived the explosion, the fire that had destroyed the last embers of her heart as well as the flaming remnants of what she thought was Michael Fielding?

"When did you arrive here?" she asked in a flat, lifeless tone.

"On Jekyll Island? Two days ago."

"And to this country?"

"I never left," he admitted slowly.

"Oh, there were other missions then," she said bitterly. "Were you more successful with those?"

"That night ended the war for me," he said slowly. Soft words. Lying words.

"I don't believe you."

"There's no reason you should," he admitted dryly.

"You lied and lied and lied." The pain glowed through the words, as new now as it had been then. As new and as deep and as hurtful.

"Yes."

"Damn you," she whispered again and turned away from him. It was too agonizing.

"Meara, you must listen." His voice was compelling, but then it always had been.

"Why? Liar. Spy. Enemy. Oh, God, why did you come back?"

"I had to," he said simply.

"Why?"

He hesitated. He didn't think she would believe anything he had to say. Not now. Not yet.

"Why?" The question was stronger now, her gaze filled with anger.

"A man visited you today."

"Still a spy," she observed bitterly. "You must have been keeping in practice. What does a spy do in peacetime? You were so very good at it. You had everyone believing in you."

A muscle twitched in his cheek. "Listen to me, Meara. Please."

"Why?" She thought with sudden, absurd sick humor that she must sound like a broken record. Why? Why? Why? Dear God, why?

"The man who came to your house today," he tried again. "He could be dangerous," he said, ignoring her observation.

"Like you?"

"Worse than me." There was a deep brooding sadness in the words that almost disarmed her. Almost.

"How can that be?"

"I know . . . what you must think . . . feel . . ."

"You know nothing," she spat out. "Nothing."

He stood, and Meara noted absently that he did so stiffly, as if the old injury still bothered him. Not an injury inflicted by Germans but by her own people. He had even used that to gain her confidence.

Andy, next to her, wriggled closer to her, as if he understood her distress, and she held him tight, trying to keep tears from her eyes. She wouldn't give Michael Fielding, or whoever he was, that satisfaction.

Then another thought struck her. He had watched her house. He would have seen Lisa. What if he realized . . . ?

Get away from him, she thought frantically. Run for your life. But how? She couldn't seem to move. Nothing worked, not even her brain.

"Does the government know about you?" she said suddenly.

He looked at her steadily, weighing his answer. Her husband had been with the FBI. One phone call, and he'd probably be sitting in jail, or a federal office someplace, and Meara . . . ? But he was through lying.

"No."

Her eyes glittered for a moment with a malice he'd never thought possible, and then it faded, and she looked defeated. The laughter was gone from her eyes, the laughter he'd loved so much, the spirit, the adventure. They'd all been tamed and now there were only eyes which had seen too much. They were still lovely, the green just as vivid as ever, but now there was compromise and knowledge and despair in them rather than a glorious quest for life. The golden red hair curled in restless tendrils around a face that was still easy to read. But now he hated what he saw there. Fear. Distrust. Even hatred. He shivered under its impact. He'd known this would be difficult; he had not known how difficult. He had not thought she would have changed so much, had hoped that somehow she would have survived more whole than she apparently had.

But then he had not done well himself. Why should he think her any different?

"A phone call," he said softly. "One phone call, and I'll be in jail." He had to discover how strong her hatred was.

Meara remained motionless. "I don't understand . . . why you came back. Where have you been?"

"The northwest. I went to Oregon from here."

"You didn't go back to Germany?" she asked again.

"My mission failed . . . my family was in danger. This way, I died a German hero, and I thought they would be safe."

"Your family?" He'd said there was no one. Another betrayal, another lie.

"A mother and brother," he said softly. "It was because of them I accepted the . . . mission."

"Where are they now?"

"Dead. They died in 1944 during a bombing raid." It was said tonelessly.

"Why should I believe you? Why should I believe anything you say? I heard you say you were calling in the submarine. I heard you agree to taking Tara and Peter."

"Hans enjoyed killing, Meara. I had to make him think I agreed. It was the only way I could buy time, to protect you and the children."

"Hans. Was that his name? What is yours? Is it Fielding? Is it von Steimen?" She had never forgotten one instant of that confrontation, nor the name referred to by her captor.

He hesitated. "It was von Steimen," he acknowledged quietly.

"Was?"

God, she was quick. But then she always had been. "I've changed it."

"Again?"

"Obviously it was necessary." A trace of wry humor was evident in the brief glimmer of an ironic smile.

"Nothing about you is obvious," Meara retorted, the bitterness back in her voice. "I've heard of a man with a thousand faces. You must be the man with a thousand names. Might I ask what it is now?"

Hell, Chris thought. Everything else is gone. "Chris . . . Christopher Chandler."

"A fine American name," she replied stiffly. "Who did you kill to get it?"

"I told you the war ended for me that night," he repeated quietly. He hesitated, wanting to explain, to make her understand just a little. "I was a naval officer, Meara. I had fought honorably for two years until I was . . . wounded. I wasn't a spy by choice. I never wanted any part of what happened but I didn't see any way out, not then. I intended to do what I was told, but something happened to me that had never happened before. I fell in love. And I was trapped."

He stopped. How could he justify the unjustifiable? How could he justify making love to her? How could he justify betraying people who trusted him? But he tried, as much for himself as for her. "But I still had a duty . . . and responsibility . . . to Germany and to my family there. God help me, I was prepared to honor it until I found out that the orders included children."

"Honor?" she retorted fiercely. "Making people trust

you, like you, when you know you're going to destroy their lives. The Connors. Peter and Tara. Sanders. You have a strange concept of honor."

He noticed she didn't include herself. His hand clenched tighter in the pocket of his slacks. What else did he expect? What else could he expect? He stood there silently, waiting for the next volley, the next blow. He had told himself all this a hundred times, but it was even more bitter coming from her.

"If you were so . . . offended about . . . the children," she said, "why didn't you go to Sanders instead of . . . what you did?" She couldn't bring herself to relive the explosion again.

"My mother and brother would have been killed," he said quietly.

"And you would be tried for espionage?" she accused.

"Probably."

"You just had a sudden change of heart," she asked sarcastically. "Or did you just think you might be trapped here on the island?"

"Does it matter?" His voice was weary now but a muscle worked along his jaw, revealing some of the tension he obviously felt.

"No. I wouldn't believe anything you said."

Meara stayed in the sand. She didn't think she could rise if she wanted to. Her whole body was like melted wax. There was no strength, no core. But for some insane reason she had to keep talking. She had to know.

Know what? She already knew everything. She had gone over every minute in her mind a hundred, a thousand, times. He had used her, betrayed her in the worst possible way. But why was he here? Did he know about Lisa? Please don't let him know about Lisa. Meara bartered with God as she never had before.

"How did you find me?" she said finally.

"A private detective. Years ago. I had to know you were all right."

"All right?" She couldn't stop a momentary hysterical giggling. "All right? I fell in love with an enemy spy who used me. I killed a man. I was kidnapped. I thought for a while the children were dead. I'd seen you blown to bits." She choked on those words before continuing. "All right? My God, it was kind of you to worry." She couldn't help it. Her whole body started trembling. "Damn you. Damn you to hell."

Chris stood there, frozen. There was nothing he could say. He had known that first day on the island years ago what was happening. He had known it and allowed it to happen. "I'm sorry," he whispered in a voice hoarse with emotion.

Tears. Tears which had been damned up inside her for years starting falling. She felt Andy squirm next to her and she took him in her arms, burying her head, and the wetness, in his fur. She didn't want *him* to see them. Her whole body was shuddering, shaking, quivering with so much grief that had accumulated. The unshed tears of the past weeks when she had to be strong for Lisa, the tears of lost and betrayed dreams. Tears for Sanders and tears for herself. They poured down, like a river released from a dam.

She felt his hands around her shoulders, so tender, so gentle that she wanted to yield to them, and then she remembered. *You can't trust him.* Once more, she jerked away from his touch.

"Don't," she said in a jagged cry as she tried desperately to retain a shred of dignity.

"Christ," she heard him say in a low agonized voice, and she sensed rather than saw that he was walking away. Against her will, she looked up. He was looking out toward the ocean, his face ravaged, the muscles at his throat working convulsively, and even in the gathering dusk she could see a tear trickling down his cheek.

"Michael." She didn't even know she had said the name until he turned, and she knew she had never seen so much pain in another person's face. She remembered his earlier words. "I've paid and paid and paid." And now for the first moment she believed him.

Something buried inside her reached out to his agony. "Michael," she said again, and then he was beside her, his hand wiping tears from her face with tentative, uncertain fingers, ready to move away if she wished it.

But for this moment, this one hurting instant, she didn't wish it. Together, they rocked in the sand, not with passion, but with a shared hurting anguish, with a need so violent that it eclipsed lifetimes.

"Oh, Michael," Meara cried one last time in both torment and the strangest desire to comfort.

Chapter Nineteen

M EARA DIDN'T FEEL joy in the embrace, only the sense of finally coming home.

His every movement, every touch, was tentative, obviously wanting to succor without invading. There was something oddly touching and comforting about his hesitancy. The arrogance, the self-assurance she had once known were gone.

What are you doing?

The one still reasoning part of her brain punctured the brief insanity. This was the man who had lied to her repeatedly, who had betrayed her, who'd made her believe he was dead when she was carrying his child.

His child. Was that why he was back? Had he somehow learned about Lisa? A private detective, he had said.

With a sob, she tore herself away from him. She managed to focus her eyes on his face. "What do you want from me?"

You. He wanted to say the word. It was true, as true as it had been twenty years ago. The pull was just as strong, if not stronger. The lovely, laughing girl had been replaced by a mature, beautiful woman. He wanted to bring back the laughter to her, the joy. He wondered if it were too late. If he had indelibly altered her. The thought was excruciating.

He controlled himself with tremendous effort. His arms ached to hold her, his hand to reach out to her, but he knew she would reject it despite that one brief moment of contact, of incredible closeness. There was deep suspicion in her eyes, bitterness.

They searched and questioned.

"I didn't want to hurt you again," he finally said. "But I had to warn you."

Meara tried to remember everything that had been said. But thoughts and words were whirling around in her head. Only his presence was real, and she wasn't even sure of that at the moment.

"I . . . don't understand . . ."

Once more, she watched him struggle against emotions she sensed were barely held in check. Why? A spy didn't have emotions or conscience. Or heart. So why had he been watching her these years? Suddenly, she felt anger at the invasion. He had been watching her while she thought him dead. It was a sickening thought. She wanted to strike him again, but her strength was gone, depleted in that spontaneous storm's eye of violent need, a need she hated and despised herself for. She suddenly wanted to hurt him as much as possible and she wanted to punish herself for still feeling anything.

She struck out blindly. "If you've been spying on me, you know I married Sanders."

"Yes," he said evenly, only his eyes showing bleakness.

What else did he know? "Then you know he died recently. Is that why you came, you thought you were safe? Still the coward."

He visibly flinched.

"You thought I would fall at your feet again. Just as I did before. 'So easily,' your friend said. It *was* easy, wasn't it, Michael, so incredibly easy. Did you think it would be as easy again? What do you want this time? Who do you work for now? Who do you want me to betray? Sanders? Sorry about that, but he's dead. The FBI? Well, I'm afraid I've never had a very good track record with them, not after you. I'm not the best security risk in the world, even with Sanders as a husband. It held him back, you know. My susceptibility to the wrong men. Who was to say I wouldn't repeat the mistake. Mistake? My God, catastrophe."

He reeled back with each succeeding blow, and she felt the satisfaction of sensing they hurt more than a physical punch. But he made no effort to defend himself. If he had, she knew, she would have found the strength to hit him again.

She continued, all the pain revealing itself on her face. "After you . . . ran, Sanders and I were left with the pieces. I spent days, weeks, in strangers' offices explaining every sordid detail. How you kissed me. How you made love to me. What you said when you were doing it. The reluctance. The nobility." She spit out the last words. "You really were a master at it, weren't you? Tell me, are you a natural or did you take courses in seduction? A kind word here. A hint of reserve there. Just enough mystery to intrigue. And yes, make sure the moon is shining bright. And tenderness. Don't ever forget tenderness. How much practice do they give you, Michael?"

He leaned against a dune, as still as marble, his blue eyes fathomless as he stared out to sea. She remembered what Sanders had said about him once, that he had never seen a man who seemed so alone. He was that now. A solitary, untouchable figure. She closed her eyes and heart against any feeling except rage, against a sudden urge to reach out to him again.

In self-defense she struck out again. "Tell me, damn it," she demanded. "Tell me."

He turned to her, expression rigidly controlled. "I know you can't believe it, Meara, but I loved you. I fell in love with you that first day on the launch. You're not saying anything to me I haven't lived with every day of my life. I could only hope that . . . Sanders could give you the love I wanted to, but couldn't. I wanted you happy, Meara. I wanted that more than anything in the world." His voice was low, even faltering. So unlike the confidence and strength she remembered.

She wasn't going to succumb. Not this time. Her voice hardened. "Then why did you come back? Why couldn't you leave things alone? Why couldn't you stay buried?"

"You may be in danger," he replied slowly.

"You said that before. Who am I in danger from? And how would you know? Why would you even care? You didn't twenty years ago."

"I wasn't going to let anything happen to you," he said. "If you don't believe anything else, believe that."

"I was there, remember," she said. "I heard everything. I killed your . . . friend. You didn't."

"But you couldn't kill me," he said softly, searchingly. The reminder was a mistake.

"I still couldn't believe it then," she said. "Not Michael. Not the gentle Michael who'd held me so lovingly. My Michael couldn't be a spy. I didn't fully realize then that my Michael was also Germany's Michael."

They were off track again, and Chris knew it. Whenever he started to explain the danger now, the past interfered, interjecting itself into the present. Any moment, she would get up and leave. He felt it. He saw apprehension in her eyes, and he suspected she wondered if he knew about Lisa, that their daughter was why he was here. At least that was one gift he could give her. She would never know that he knew.

"Listen to me, Meara. Please."

She looked at him obstinately, a look he remembered well.

Shock, he thought, was the only way to get through to her. "Your visitor today—he's the son of the man you killed that night."

The words struck through the haze of Meara's mind like a knife. "His son?"

"The man who . . . died that night was Hans Weimer. Kurt Weimer is his son."

Meara stared at him. "I don't believe you."

"Believe me, Meara." There was a convincing evenness in his voice that made her listen.

"But what . . . why . . . ?"

"He's been checking into your life, just as I have," Michael said. Or was it Michael. But he would always be Michael to her. Good or bad. Love and hate. He was Michael. "That's how I knew," he continued. "My detective . . . accidentally discovered someone else had been making inquiries."

Meara looked up at him with confused eyes. "I don't understand. He's with the German government."

He wanted to touch, God, how he wanted to touch her, to wipe the sick bewilderment from her face.

"He's a very distinguished member of the German government," Michael corrected. "But my sources say he's a member of Odessa."

"Odessa?"

"An organization of ex-Nazis, mostly former SS officers, who still believe in the German Reich."

"But he's too young to have been in the war."

"Too young for the SS, but he wasn't too young to fight

in the war or to be thoroughly indoctrinated in Nazi principles. Hans Weimer, his father, was SS."

"You . . . ?" The expression was pure horror.

"No. I told you I was Navy. I was just unlucky enough to be wounded and have Canadian connections—everything they needed. Hans was borrowed from the SS. I was borrowed from the German Navy."

"Why doesn't our government know about . . . this man?"

"Listen to me, Meara. I know I'm throwing a lot at you, but concentrate." The command in his voice struck through her confusion. "No one knew the name of the man sent here with me. American officials only knew he had been hired as a gardener. I doubt there's even a surviving record in Germany. It was a highly secret mission. The man who directed it, Canaris, head of German Intelligence, was later implicated in the Hitler assassination plot and killed. There can't be too many others who know."

"Then how does Kurt Weimer know?"

"I don't know. A letter . . . one of the planning staff. I simply don't know. The only reason I know his real name is that I was introduced to Hans Weimer when he was still a member of the SS, before he assumed his other name."

Disbelief flickered over her face. "How do you know there're no official records?"

"I'm a wealthy man, Meara. I won't explain how and why now, but I have resources. I had the records checked for my name, and Weimer's name. There was nothing. Just by luck, my investigator found Kurt Weimer, and the more he checked, the more I worried. There's damn little negative about him, only very quiet rumors in very discreet groups. But he too has the influence and money to discover what he wants to know.

"Where did your money come from?" Meara mocked.

"Do you really want to know?" His eyes were shadowed, and strain showed at the edges of his mouth.

"Yes," she said flatly.

He was handing her the weapon she needed for revenge. He knew it. But he didn't care anymore. He cared only about convincing her of the danger . . . and accepting his help, no matter how resented it was.

"I didn't steal it," he said tightly, knowing that was what she was implying.

"Then tell me."

He stifled a sigh. "I'm owner and president of Northwest Lumber, one of the largest privately owned lumber firms in the northwest."

He waited for her bitter comment, and it came. "A present from a grateful German government?"

"No. I was a lumberjack for years, then foreman and superintendent. I was able to work my way up."

"Like a cat, you land on your feet."

He shrugged. She would never believe the hell of those years. He was lucky she was listening at all.

"And if I told the authorities?"

"I could go to jail, certainly be deported."

"But there're no records. You just said so."

He stared at her. "A thorough check would show that Christopher Chandler died in Illinois almost fifty years ago. And I wouldn't lie. Not any more."

"Noble of you," she observed astringently.

"No, I'm just damned tired of lies," he admitted wearily.

"If you believe this man is a threat, then why don't you go to the police? Or the FBI? Why come to me? Unless you're worried about your own hide?"

To the heart of the matter. Well, she had always been very good at that.

"Several reasons," he said. "I didn't know how much the FBI knew. I gathered from the newspaper reports that local authorities were kept completely ignorant of the German factor. And there is no evidence that Kurt Weimer is anything but what he seems."

"Perhaps he is exactly what he seems," Meara said hopefully.

"How much do you believe in coincidence? I wasn't sure myself until I saw him at your house. How did that happen?"

"My daughter met him at the Cloister last night where she and her boyfriend went to dinner. She'd dropped her purse, and he came today to return a compact." Meara almost choked on the word "daughter," but if he'd checked on her, he would know she had one. Hopefully, he would believe she was Sanders's.

"She's very pretty," Michael said objectively, and Meara felt a surge of hope. He didn't know. She didn't think she could ever cope with Lisa learning the truth. It would destroy her daughter if she knew that rather than the father she adored, she was fathered by a German spy who duped her mother.

"She loved her father very much. She's still hurting badly."

"And she's emotionally vulnerable at the moment?" But it wasn't really a question.

Meara stared at him, at the strong, handsome face that had stolen her heart. "Like mother, like daughter," she exclaimed bitterly. "Is that what you mean? You think he'll use her to get to me, like you used me to get to the Connors." She felt herself trembling, and she hated herself for it.

"No," he said softly. "After that first meeting with them, I didn't need you. I just damn well couldn't stay away from you. And no, they don't teach things like that in spy school, or I would have been better prepared and left you alone. Perhaps then we might have succeeded. You stopped the kidnapping, you know. You and you alone. I hope Evans understood that. I hope you do."

Meara wanted to believe. But she couldn't. She'd lived twenty-one years believing the worst. Hate had helped her survive in some ways.

Now he was telling her that those events in the spring of 1942 were threatening her daughter.

"She's really in danger?" Meara's voice was shaking.

"I think both of you are."

"But why Lisa? Why not just me?"

"You have to understand the SS mentality," he said, "and their means of exacting punishment. They always took and killed hostages when one of their own was killed. They knew that pain was worse when inflicted on a loved one rather than the person directly responsible." For the first time, his voice was bitter, and she remembered him saying something about a mother and brother. Truth or lie. She no longer knew, and she was too emotionally tired and confused to know the difference.

"You still haven't said why you, or I, can't go to the police if we really are in danger."

"First, I don't know if they'll believe you . . . me . . . us," he said. "And if they did, the whole affair would be reopened. I didn't know if you'd want that."

He allowed her to consider what he'd said, then added quietly. "I'll do whatever you wish. I'll go to the FBI and tell them everything if you want. Or I'll stay here and try to find out what Weimer wants. I have people who can protect you."

The whole affair reopened? Meara's heart stopped. Dear Mother in heaven, Lisa knew nothing of what had happened. Nothing. Not even the fact that her mother was once involved in a kidnapping. Both Meara and Sanders had carefully kept it from her, afraid that one piece of information might lead to another, that Lisa might connect certain dates.

Sanders had once broached the possibility of telling Lisa the truth. But again, what could be told? The whole affair had been labeled top secret and everyone warned never to say anything. And what could she tell Lisa about her real father? Meara stared at him now, seeing pieces of him in Lisa. The blond hair. The blue eyes. Thank God, Lisa's weren't quite as blue, for if they had been, Michael would know in a second that Lisa was his. Even now, there was that danger.

She had no place to turn.

Except to him.

The man who had lied to her, betrayed her. As he might be lying now.

She hadn't known the dead man's name. She didn't know of any connection between him and the seemingly personable German economist she'd met today. Perhaps it was all a lie to ingratiate himself in hers and Lisa's lives.

But Meara remembered the slight chill she had in Kurt Weimer's presence, that fragmentary sense of familiarity. She looked up at Michael's face and saw the worry there, worry and something deeper.

And she knew. She knew he wasn't lying.

In that second, she knew he saw acceptance in her face.

He started to reach for her hand, and she jerked it away as if branded.

"Don't ever touch me again," she said, repeating what she had told him earlier. She knew if she relented, she would be lost. One caress, one touch, and she'd be lost again. She could still feel her soul burning from the contact minutes ago. "I'll accept your help because there's nothing else. But don't touch me. Do, and I'll report you to the FBI and happily see you in prison. Do you understand me?"

His mouth twisted into the self-mocking wry smile she had once loved. "You've always had a way with words, Meara."

"I'm going to walk back alone. I have to think."

He nodded, his eyes hooded.

She started to get up, and fell back, her legs stiff from the awkward position. She saw him start to reach for her, then withdraw his hands, and she felt triumphant . . . and infinitely sad.

On the second try, Meara made it to her feet through sheer determination. "Where can I find you?"

He gave her the address of the cottage and telephone number.

She didn't look at him again. "Come on, Andy," she said to the dog who was ambling to his feet. She walked down the beach, only vaguely aware of the darkness, of the sky now inky blue and decorated by a million stars.

It was no longer romantic. Only menacing. And lonely. Very, very lonely.

Not until she arrived back at the house and found it empty did she remember she hadn't told Michael that Lisa had a dinner date with Kurt Weimer that night.

She went into sudden panic and thought about running back to Michael. He would still be there. She sensed it. Then she stopped. He had thrown too much at her. Her mind wasn't functioning logically in any way. Michael alive. Here. Nazis. Odessa. Revenge. Danger for her daughter. In the comfort of the house, where she could hear the soft sound of the surf, it seemed impossible, crazy. But then the thought of a German raid on Jekyll twenty-one years ago had been just as bizarre.

Meara paced the house. Her existence, grown peaceful over the last few years, had been turned upside down a month ago. Now she felt her life was like a juggler's ball, twirled first one way, then another, always in danger of tumbling.

Where was Lisa? Surely she would be safe since Weimer was escorting her openly and publicly. But what did Weimer have in mind, if he was what Michael said he was? What if Michael wasn't what he said he was?

Christopher, he'd said, Chris Chandler. A respectable northwest lumber baron. She felt her whole body shaking.

Sanders. Help me, Sanders, she cried silently. She remembered the funeral, and Sanders's partner, John Malcomb, saying Sanders had asked him to look out for her. Had Sanders had a premonition? John. John Malcomb. Perhaps she could call him.

Then she remembered Michael's words. The whole affair could be opened. Like Pandora's box. Could the terrible secrets be contained once the lid was lifted, if only a small bit. She was bitterly afraid not.

Could she trust Michael? She had once. How could she even think of doing it again? Should she risk her daughter's life to hide a secret that might be every bit as destructive to her as a bullet?

Meara went into the master bedroom, the room that she'd shared with Sanders. She was barely aware of Andy padding behind her and grateful for his company now, useless as it was. Some guard dog; Andy had been known to tremble at the sight of his own shadow. She looked around the room slowly. She had avoided using the room, sleeping in the guest room instead. Illogically, she had thought she could escape the finality of his death that way.

Now she slowly headed for the closet. Her hands went to a box on a shelf above, and she carefully took it down and opened the top, staring at the small Colt pistol inside. Sanders had insisted that she have one at both houses since she and Lisa were alone so much. He had seen that both of them had lessons in its care and use, taking them to the FBI practice range.

Lisa, who had always wanted a law enforcement career, had been particularly adept, but Meara had still remembered the night when she'd killed a man, and every moment had been torture. But Sanders, who had seen every kind of mayhem, had quietly insisted. Thank God. Again, she wondered if he'd had some kind of foreboding.

Her hand curved around the butt of the pistol. She'd hoped she would never have to touch the weapon, a feeling reinforced by the killing of Sanders. He'd been killed by a bullet. Just like the German. Guns were malignant things, their use usually limited to destruction. Yet she forced herself to handle it, to check to see whether it was loaded. It was.

Meara looked about the room. Sanders was everywhere. In the rocking chair where he frequently read, in the photos of the family on the dressing table, in the painting of the Pennsylvania farm country she had commissioned for his birthday. It was a warm room, and in her loss she suddenly realized how much she had loved him. Quietly, undemonstratively, but undeniably. She hoped he knew that.

Her hands still locked on the gun, she wondered what he would do. What he would wish her to do.

After her questioning by the FBI, he had never again mentioned David Michael Fielding. But she'd been aware, through the fog of grief and anger and hate during those intense sessions, that he had been remarkably charitable to the man who had betrayed him as well as Meara. His questions had, at times, been curious indeed, as if he were puzzled at certain details. But he'd never said exactly why.

Did you sense something I didn't, she asked silently. She wanted to believe in Michael Fielding/Chris Chandler.

But if she believed him, she also had to believe Lisa was in desperate trouble.

She went through the living room to the small study where she and Sanders had shared a desk. She found his address book and flipped through it until she found John Malcomb's number. She would ask him to check on Kurt Weimer.

He answered on the second ring, just as she'd almost decided to hang up, and he sounded pleased to hear from her.

"Could you do be a favor, John?"

"Anything," he answered quickly.

"Have you heard of the Economic Conference being held at Sea Island?"

There was a pause. "No, I don't think so."

"Well, apparently a number of economists and government officials are here for it. One of them, a German economist, has shown interest in Lisa. Could you please check him out?"

There was another slight pause. "Do you have a specific reason why?"

"It's just that, well, he's a great deal older than Lisa and there's something about him that frightens me a little. Perhaps it's just . . . because Sanders isn't here. But would you mind?"

"Of course not. What's his name?"

"Kurt Weimer."

"I'll do it in the morning," he promised. "Anything else I can do?"

She thought about asking him to check on a Christopher Chandler, but dismissed the idea. What if it led them to Michael's true background?

If it did? He deserved prison. One word. That was all it would take, he'd said. But she couldn't.

Just as she hung up, she heard a car pull into the drive. She went to the window and looked out. Kurt Weimer had gotten out of the car and gone around to the other side, opening that door for Lisa. He offered a hand, Lisa accepted it, and stepped lightly from the car. Her movements were easier and lighter than they had been in weeks, and Meara saw her look up at the German and smile. He said something, and Lisa laughed, her hand still entwined with his. They walked slowly to the house, their heads bent toward each other, and Meara froze. Was that the way she had once looked at Michael? The thought was devastating. They were at the door now, and Meara quickly put the pistol in a drawer of the desk and retreated to the kitchen where she started to heat some milk for hot chocolate. She didn't want Lisa to think she was spying on her.

The door opened, and Meara jumped. She didn't know what she would say, how she'd react, if Kurt Weimer came in the house. But he didn't. Lisa appeared alone in the doorway of the kitchen, her face glowing.

"He's wonderful, mother," Lisa said. "He was so kind . . . and . . ."

Meara felt her face stiffen. She remembered that feeling of euphoria. Only too well. Don't say anything, she told herself. Don't chase her away.

"Would you like some chocolate?" she said, forcing the words.

"No, I don't think so. I'm deliciously full. Do you know Kurt's an adviser to the West German chancellor? He's even met President Kennedy."

Be careful, Meara warned herself. "He's probably going to be very busy now."

"Of course, but he asked me to attend a formal dinner next Saturday, and whether I could show him Savannah Sunday."

What little hope Meara had died at the words. "Lisa, don't you think he might be a little . . . old . . . for you."

The light went out of Lisa's eyes and the old resentment

took its place. "No," she said. "Daddy was that much older than you."

So was Michael, and look what happened, Meara thought.

She tried again. "But he's so much more—"

"So much more what?" Lisa was hurt. Meara knew from the tone of her voice. Part challenging, part wounded.

Meara hunted for the safest word. "Experienced," she finally said.

The stubborn look was more and more pronounced on Lisa's face. "You think I'm still a child," she accused.

"Oh, darling, I know you're not a child. But I just don't want to see you hurt."

Lisa's face softened. "I won't. He's very nice."

Meara wanted to forbid her daughter to see the man, but there was no way to do that. She was twenty, already a college graduate who would enter law school next fall. Any command would be ignored, any warning would fall on deaf years.

"Just be very careful, Lisa," she tried anyway. "Please."

"I will, Mother," Lisa said, but her glowing eyes said otherwise. She turned and went to her bedroom.

Meara eyed the scorched milk in disgust, and poured it out.

You have to know the SS . . . they understood the pain was worst when inflicted on a loved one rather than the person directly responsible.

Was her daughter going to pay for her mistakes of twenty years ago?

She turned out the light in the kitchen and then returned to the living room and to Sanders's desk. She took out the pistol and walked slowly down the hall to the master bedroom. She would sleep there tonight.

Meara placed the pistol in the drawer of the bedside table and huddled alone in the large bed.

Chapter Twenty

Lisa wished with all her heart that her father were still alive. She would like to have shared this evening with him.

He would have understood. He always did.

Kurt. Even the name was continental and exotic. She had never met anyone like him, who made her feel like a Cinderella.

He had been warm and fun, and full of charm, asking everything about her, as if he were very interested. He had wanted to know about her life, her ambitions, her family.

He had been sympathetic when tears welled up in her eyes when she told him about her father. She had been embarrassed. She should have more control by now, but she'd always been very emotional, crying at movies, or a sad book, or even news of a distant tragedy. It was a trait she abhorred, and one she knew she would have to discipline if she were to go into any area of law enforcement or even law.

Her father had tried gently to dissuade her from the former, but when she insisted, he was her staunch supporter although her mother was opposed to the idea. She wasn't

316

opposed to a career, she'd said. Any career but law enforcement. But that was what Lisa wanted.

She knew her mother had once wanted a career of her own, that she'd given it up for Lisa and her father. Her father had told her as much once when Lisa thought her mother had been overly strict again. Lisa also knew that he'd had another child and wife, and that both had been killed. Lisa sensed that the loss had made him protective of his own. But she had never quite understood the occasional tension between her parents, the traded glances that seemed to hold secrets. She had fiercely resented those looks, as if she were being left out of something important, and the blame invariably fell to her mother because Lisa could never see anything wrong in her father, who had been the dearest person in her life.

After her outburst several days ago, she'd been immensely ashamed of herself, and she knew her father would have been ashamed for her. Her mother, too, had always been there for her, but not in the same unqualified way as her father. Or so it had seemed to her.

She was so confused, so lost, and she hated herself for it. She was twenty years old, almost twenty-one, old enough to cope with a tragedy that she'd always known was possible. Perhaps that's why Kurt so appealed to her. He made her feel older, more able to cope, while Kelly's warm, sympathetic presence seemed merely to elicit more tears.

Lisa thought of the light touch of Kurt's lips this evening when he brought her home. Almost more of a courtesy than the barely restrained passion she always felt in Kelly. But it had excited her in a new, adventurous way, and her heart had jumped when he'd asked her to dinner and to spend Sunday with him.

She only wished her father could meet him.

*   *   *

Kurt Weimer nursed a drink in his room, a smile of satisfaction on his lips.

He had not known, until he had arrived, exactly what he intended to do. Now he knew. Everything had fallen into his lap, as if certain events were preordained.

The conference would be a nuisance. Ordinarily, he would have sent a subordinate to attend, since it was principally an information-exchange event. But when he had heard its location, pieces started falling together. At long last, he would see where his father died and have the opportunity to pay a long overdue debt.

There was another factor now. The South, in upheaval from the civil rights movement, was a bitter, seething region of hate and violence. School integration, demands for voting rights and political power, restaurant sit-ins, had rocked this usually easy-going conservative part of America, giving rise to numerous white supremacist groups. Those in Odessa had never forgotten the part America paid in Germany's defeat, and they had sworn it would never happen again. Long-range plans to neutralize possible enemies had been formed years ago, and the time was ripe now to plant seeds, and nurture them.

Kurt planned to kill two birds with this one trip: to bring the strongest of the white supremacist groups under the control of Odessa and to even the score with Meara Evans. But Kurt knew he had to be careful. There had been too much time and money invested in him to throw everything away on a personal matter. He had emerged as one of the leaders of Odessa and the neo-Nazi movement, although they were careful not to call it that. Their people would return to leadership, to control, and unite West and East Germany and make it strong again. Just as Adolf Hitler had after World War I.

It was not impossible that he would one day become chancellor. But not if he acted unwisely.

When he had learned of Sanders Evans's death, he knew that fate was with him. Evans had worried him. He had not wanted to tangle with the FBI and all its resources, and that possibility, no, probability, had stayed his hand for years. But it was no longer a factor.

Pretty little Lisa. She was his weapon. Nothing could be traced back to him, other than a temporary affair with a willing young woman.

As her mother had robbed him of a father, he would rob Meara of a daughter. And in the cruelest possible way.

Kurt downed the rest of the glass of schnapps with a sigh of anticipation.

Chris went out to the porch. It was just past sunrise, and he had been up for hours. He was so damnably restless. He longed to take a long walk, but he was afraid to get far from the telephone.

He knew that once Meara had left him on the beach, it was altogether possible she'd reconsidered everything, that she would decide not to believe him. The story was, after all, bizarre: a respected official of a friendly government seeking revenge after so many years.

All night he'd halfway thought there would be a knock at the door, that federal agents would be there.

And then there was Lisa. Chris's stomach coiled in a tight knot as he thought about Weimer with Lisa. Meara's daughter. His daughter.

Lisa wasn't much younger than Meara had been that spring of '42. And probably more impressionable. Meara had been mature for her age; she had worked hard for everything she had, everything she'd had to give up, because of him.

"Damn it," he exploded. He had not meant to hurt Meara, and yet he had, in the most terrible way. He had known exactly how much last night when sobs ripped through her body. If Weimer meant to hurt Lisa, it could be accomplished easily. The man was, from all reports, convincing, personable, charming. And Lisa was too young, too inexperienced, to see through him.

He poured himself another cup of coffee, and waited, using the time to wonder about Lisa, and what she was like. The sight of her had just whetted his appetite for more and more information. He wanted to know everything about her. Everything. But he knew he had to be careful. Meara didn't trust him.

But he wanted to know so much. He wanted to know how Lisa planned to spend her life. His investigators had told him she had graduated from the University of Virginia with top grades. It was something, but not enough. Nothing was enough. He had an enormous hunger to know everything there was to know about her, everything a father should. He had a fierce desire to protect.

Yet he sensed if he said any of that, Meara would see it as a threat. He could well understand it. She had tried to bury the past, and now he'd returned to dig it all up again. But had she buried it completely? For a moment last night when she had cried out his name, the hunger and love was there, just as it had been years ago. When he had held her those precious few moments, he'd experienced that tender oneness he had known only with her. She had felt it too. He knew it. But was it too late?

Call, he demanded silently.

He looked down at his watch. Nine-thirty. He wondered about walking over there, but he knew he couldn't do that. He went to the telephone and hesitated, wondering whether he should call, when the phone rang shrilly. Chris picked it up quickly.

"Chandler," he said automatically.

There was a pause on the line, then her voice. Uncertain. "I don't know if . . . I can get used to that name."

"Meara, thank God. I've been going crazy."

"I had to wait until Lisa left."

"She's gone, then?"

"She has a summer job in Brunswick. With a law firm."

Chris stood there stiffly and waited.

"He . . . Kurt Weimer took Lisa to dinner last night. He wants to see her again this weekend. Why?" The last word was bewildered.

"Can you come over here?"

Again, there was a pause. He could almost feel her hesitancy over the phone wires.

"Or I could come there?" he offered.

"No," she said immediately.

He waited again, not wanting to push.

"I'll be over there in ten minutes," she said finally and hung up the phone.

Chris started a new pot of coffee and found another cup. Just as it finished percolating, he heard the soft knock at the door.

The dog was with her, and Chris grinned suddenly, but there was a hint of uncertainty in her eyes. "Reserves?"

"Hardly," she said, looking at the dog. "A fly makes him flinch. This is Raggedy Andy. I didn't introduce you last night." There was something of the old flash of humor in the words, yet they came too quickly. As if she used them to avoid panic.

"Raggedy Andy?" he queried with the lifting of one of those heavy cocked eyebrows.

"My daughter named him for her favorite doll. They were both misfits. The doll was awkward looking with stuffing falling out everywhere, and Andy, well, Andy didn't look any better. Lisa had dragged him off the middle of a road in Virginia."

So the daughter had the same soft heart as the mother.

A piece of information to treasure, Chris thought. But he confined his words to asking her about coffee.

"Please," she said formally, woodenly, as she looked around the house. It was very neat, unlike that of most men living alone. Or was he? For a single desperate moment she wondered whether he had ever married.

"Are you . . . alone?" she finally asked.

"Yes."

"In—in Seattle?"

He glanced at her with hooded eyes. "Yes."

"You never married?"

"No," he replied slowly. "I'm afraid a fugitive is poor husband material."

"You're not a fugitive. No one knows you're alive."

"Except you. I half expected the police last night."

"I thought about it," she said quietly.

"I imagine you did."

She was silent, and he went to the kitchen, pouring them both a cup of coffee and returning to the living room where she still stood, the dog still at her side.

Chris handed her a cup. "I remember you didn't like anything in it . . . or has that changed?"

She stared at him with amazement. They'd only had coffee once during those two weeks. "You remember that?"

"I remember everything," he said. "What you ate, the dresses you wore, how the rain felt."

His voice was slow, slowly seductive, as he made her see and feel the same warm, confusing, sensual feelings she had felt then. No, she told herself, jerking out of his trance. She wasn't going to let him do this to her again.

She sipped her coffee, and lowered her eyes. She didn't want him to see what perhaps was in them. She had learned to hide her feelings, but not always.

"I called a friend of Sanders's at the FBI," she said suddenly and had the slight satisfaction of watching him tense ever so slightly. "I asked him to check on Kurt Weimer." She paused a fraction of a second. "I didn't say anything about you."

"What excuse did you give?"

"Only an overprotective mother after all that has happened. He understood."

"I doubt whether he finds anything."

"You did."

"I had information they don't."

"Like the name of the man I shot."

"Yes," Chris said simply.

"I've been trying to remember everything that happened that night. I don't think his name was ever mentioned. But you said Hans last night. Hans Weimer. That was his real name?"

"Yes."

She looked down at her coffee. "It always seemed strange, to know you've killed a man and not even know his name." There was a bleakness in her voice.

"You had no choice, Meara. He would have killed all of you. After he found the radio was useless, he knew the mission was ruined. The submarine wouldn't come in without contact. The only way he could have escaped was killing you. Believe me, he wouldn't have had any remorse."

She was silent a moment, thinking back. "Sanders always wondered about that battery. . . ."

"Did he?" Chris said noncommittally. He had thought about telling her everything, but he didn't think she would believe him. It would be, after all, obviously self-serving. He had to earn her trust now, and then perhaps he could tell her exactly what happened that night. But once again, he was grateful to Sanders Evans. He had planted a seed in Meara's mind, a doubt.

Meara's voice suddenly hardened. Questions had been plaguing her all night. "Michael Fielding? Who was he?"

"There was a Michael Fielding, a Canadian on a British destroyer. He was captured."

"What happened to him?"

"I was told he died of wounds," Chris said.

"You believed that?"

"I didn't have any reason not to." But he had. He knew the way German Intelligence operated. No loose ends. He hadn't wanted to think about it, hadn't wanted to believe a prisoner had died because of his resemblance to him.

She closed her eyes. "Did I ever know you?" Bewilderment was in the question.

"I think you knew me far better than anyone ever has."

"That's not at all, is it?" Meara said sadly.

His dark, impenetrable eyes studied her. "Maybe not," he replied finally, enigmatically.

They were talking in even voices, normal tones, like two people who had met after an absence, catching up on each other. But both of Meara's hands had to clasp her cup to keep them from shaking, and Chris was striding back and forth, his fingers flexing at his side. Electricity was palpable; it snaked across the room. Each seemed to be waiting for something as they probed and retreated, parried and retreated.

"What do you think he wants from me?" she said finally, returning to the subject of the meeting.

Chris shrugged. "I don't think he will do anything openly violent. He's worked too hard to get where he is. For whatever reason."

"Then . . . ?"

"He might try to hurt you through your daughter."

"How?"

Chris shrugged. "Can you ask her not to see him?"

Meara stared at him hopelessly. "No, not without explaining everything." Her voice died as she realized she was about to say too much.

He smiled tightly but did not probe any further. "She's stubborn? Like her mother?"

"Yes," Meara said in a barely audible voice. How could she explain her strained relationship with Lisa, how, when she didn't understand it herself?

"Then we'll have to protect her the best we can."

Meara looked at him hopelessly. "How?"

"We have an ace Weimer doesn't know about. Me. He has no idea I'm alive, that someone knows what happened that evening." Chris paused. "Sanders never indicated to anyone that I might have survived?"

"No," she said with certainty. She and Sanders had seen the explosion seconds after seeing Michael leave in the boat. "They searched for a body, but the explosion and fire were so fierce they weren't surprised when . . . nothing was found." Her voice shook a little as she remembered the aftermath, the teams of federal agents searching every part of the island, even the marshes.

"I'm sorry," Chris said softly, seeing the pain on her face. "There was no other way."

"There was always another way," she said in a strangled voice.

"Perhaps, but I couldn't see it then."

One of Meara's hands left the cup and rubbed her eyes, her face, as a long, deep sigh escaped her throat. Let the past go, she told herself. Think about today. About Lisa.

"Why?" she said suddenly.

"Why what?"

"Why are you so . . . concerned now? After all these years?" *Do you know about Lisa? Do you know she's your daughter?* That was what she really wanted to ask, but couldn't.

"Because I feel responsible for everything that happened," he said simply.

"Nothing else?" she asked suspiciously.

"Once this is over," he replied carefully, "I'll leave and never contact you again. If that's what you want." He couldn't help adding the last sentence.

She relaxed slightly, as much as she could when he was in the immediate vicinity. "What do we do now?"

Chris liked the "we." He liked it very much. "I have a very good investigative agency I've used throughout the years. I'll call and have Weimer followed, particularly when he's with your daughter."

"He won't realize . . . ?"

"Not with these people. Especially since he has no idea that we're aware of him."

"I feel so helpless," she said. Everything seemed out of control.

Chris hesitated. "They'll need to know something about Lisa."

Meara looked at him suspiciously. Again, the thought flickered through her mind that this all might be only because he wanted to get close to Lisa, that he knew she was his daughter. She wished John Malcomb would get back to her. She wished she knew whom she could trust and whom she couldn't.

"Meara. Trust me." He was reading her mind, just as he'd always been able to. Damn him.

"I don't know if I can," she said, her heart aching with the truth of the statement. She wanted to trust him. She needed to. But twenty years was too long to harbor hurt and betrayal, not to be left with a deep residue of suspicion.

Frustrated, he looked down at her and felt that peculiar weakness he had always known with her, a crumbling of defenses, an overwhelming need to hold and love and protect. Her eyes were wide and hurt and confused, like a cornered animal, yet he remembered what she'd said last night about touching her. He couldn't risk frightening her, sending her running away.

Meara, whose gaze was locked on his challenging one, was the one to surrender first. She had to trust someone, and her instincts had warned her against Weimer from the moment they'd met.

"All right," she said reluctantly. "What do you want to know?"

Chris released a long breath that had been stuck in his throat. "Any special friends."

"Kelly."

"Kelly?"

"Kellen Tabor, but his friends call him Kelly. He's an attorney who lives next door with his widowed mother. Lisa's working in his firm this year. They've been friends for years. I think he's in love with her."

"And Lisa?"

Meara sighed. "I know she cares for him a lot, but mostly as a friend, I'm afraid. He's just always been there."

"Will Tabor help us?"

"Help us?"

"If we . . . you . . . quietly asked him to help keep an eye on her, on the house, would he? Without asking too many questions?"

"To the first question, yes, to the second, I don't know. He's very bright, very instinctive."

He smiled sightly. "You like him?" he observed.

"Very much. I was hoping that someday . . ."

"Can you arrange for me to meet him?"

"Why?"

Chris knew the question was coming. He recognized her continuing doubts. He understood her fear. And there was not a damn thing he could do about it. Not yet. "I want to meet her. It would be easier to do that through Tabor than try to explain myself as your friend."

"That *would* be hard to do," she said bitterly.

"The more people watching her, both of you, the safer

you'll be," he replied quietly, although his mouth tightened at the sudden caustic jibe.

A lump formed in her throat, as she considered what
he was asking. How would she keep him from knowing,
if he and Lisa met and became friends? And they would.
She knew it. She knew his charm only too well. The lesser
of two evils. She couldn't take chances with Lisa's life. She
finally nodded, but added, "You said when it's over—"

"I'll leave," he finished. "I give you my word."

"Does it mean anything?" She meant the words to hurt,
and she knew instantly that they had.

"You'll have to make that judgment, won't you," he said
evenly.

"I don't have any choice, do I?" The hopelessness in her
voice struck him.

"You told me there're always choices."

"The police, you mean."

He nodded.

She winced. "And risk exposing you and everything that
happened?"

Then it hit her with the force of a bullet. He knew! He
knew about Lisa. He had to know. Otherwise why would
he know she would be so reluctant to have the past revealed? Nothing else was that damning—just the question
of Lisa's father. She had been fooling herself from the very
beginning. If his investigators were as good as he'd said,
of course they'd found the birth date. What a fool she'd
been.

"You know, don't you?" she whispered brokenly.

Chris didn't have to ask what. He clenched his hands
behind him. "Yes."

"Why didn't you say anything?"

The muscles at his throat worked. "You didn't want me
to know."

She stared at him in silence. "What do you intend to do?"

He was suddenly angry. "What do you expect me to do? Run to her and say 'I'm your father,' just after the man she knew and loved as a father died? I know you have no reason to trust me, Meara. But, Christ, what kind of person do you think I am?"

"I don't know what kind a person you are," she replied stiffly. "I didn't know twenty years ago, and I don't know now."

"But you were ready to trust me in this," he said evenly.

"I don't even know that," Meara said. She buried her head in her hands. "I don't know anything, anymore. Everything is upside down. Black is white, and white is black. I can't believe you're here. I can't believe Lisa's in danger. Dear God, I don't know what I believe any more."

Chris ran his fingers through his hair. "I only want to help, Meara. I have no intention of saying anything to anyone. I want you to be happy. I want Lisa happy. And safe."

"Do you know what will happen if she finds out?" she said. "Her father taught her to value honesty. If she knew he and I have been lying to her all these years—" Her voice broke again and she couldn't continue.

"I swear to you, Meara, I'll never say anything." His voice was gruff, full of emotion, and there was anguish in those usually unscrutable eyes.

She believed him. She didn't know why she should, but she did. "If I ask you to leave now?"

Chris hesitated before speaking softly. "I will, but not until certain measures are taken for your safety and Lisa's."

"All right," Meara said defeatedly. "I'll arrange a meeting with Kelly. But I warn you, he'll be curious. And he's very, very bright. We might open something we can't close again."

"But he loves Lisa?"

"Yes."

"And he'd do what's best for her?"

She nodded.

"I'll take my chances then."

"You'll call the detective agency?"

"Immediately. Someone will be here tomorrow."

"I'll try to talk to Kelly tonight and ask him to meet me for lunch tomorrow. You can run into us at the restaurant and take it from there." She hesitated. "I'm sure you can win him over. You're very good at that." The bitterness was back in her voice.

He deserved that. Chris knew it. But the constant reminders of his earlier deception stung far worse than she probably knew.

"Let me know if Weimer calls, or if your FBI friend finds any information."

She nodded.

"More coffee?"

"I have to go."

"Meara." She was up and heading toward the door, but she turned at the sound of her name. She wished it didn't sound so tender on his lips.

"Yes?" she managed coldly.

"Everything will be all right."

"Will it, Michael? Or should I call you Chris now?"

"Chris would be better," he said with a wry smile.

"Chris Chandler," she said. "It sounds strange." She looked down at Andy, who was snoring on the floor. "Andy, let's go."

The dog looked up surprised, wagged his tail, then obediently but lazily followed her to the door.

Meara didn't say good-bye, but neither was her look entirely hostile as she left.

Chris watched her leave. Slowly but surely he was making progress. He went to the phone, and started dialing Ben Markham & Associates.

"I need your services . . .," he started without preamble when Ben answered.

Chapter Twenty-One

THE CALL FROM John Malcomb came that afternoon, and it was as Michael said it would be.

Kurt Weimer was an upstanding, respectable rising star of the West German government.

"A real catch," John said.

"A bit old," Meara observed.

"Hey, I'm his age and I don't feel ancient. Besides, he's due back in Germany in two weeks. I wouldn't worry."

"You're sure there's nothing? Nothing at all."

There was a silence. "Is there something you're not telling me, Meara?"

"No, of course not," Meara said. "It's just that with Sanders . . ."

"I know, love. Let me know if there's anything else I can do."

"I will, John."

"Oh, and Meara, I've been cleaning out Sanders's desk. There're some photos I thought you would want."

"Photos?" she said, almost blankly.

"I'm sorry to be so late in getting these to you, but I had

to finish up the case, and . . . the agent in charge thought
it best I cleared Sanders's desk."

Meara stood absolutely still. Strange how final the conversation sounded. Part of her still believed Sanders would
come back through the door as he had so many times after
a case.

"Meara? Are you all right?"

"Yes," she said finally. "Thank you, John."

"I'll send them today, or should I come myself?" A note
of worry was in his voice.

"No." The answer was so abrupt it was rude.

There was a pause on his end. "Are you sure you're all
right?"

"I'm sorry, John. I still haven't quite . . . gotten used
to . . ."

His voice was soothing. "I know. But please remember,
if there's anything, anything at all."

Meara was tempted, dear God, but she was tempted. Yet
he was a bureau man to his bones. She would have to tell
him everything, and Michael—no, damn it, Chris—would
be arrested, Lisa could quite possibly discover everything.
If, that is, she was even believed and not thought over-
wrought. It seemed every direction she looked, she was
trapped.

"I'll call," she assured John Malcomb, wondering if she
was doing the right thing.

"My wife sends her love."

"Me too," she answered hollowly.

"Will you be staying there?"

"For a while."

"Keep in touch," he said.

"I will, and thank you, John."

After she put the phone down, she thought about his
comment. Perhaps if she moved back to Virginia . . . the
house was there. But again what excuse would she use to

Lisa. If Kurt Weimer was intent on harming her or Lisa, wouldn't he just follow her? He would have a better excuse to be in Washington than here.

If only she could take Lisa and get in the car and escape to where no one would find them. Not Weimer. Not Michael. But Lisa would never go.

She went to the screened porch where she could see the dunes beyond. Her island of dreams had become an island of nightmares. She shivered in the heat as she leaned against a post.

She heard Andy's padding paws behind her, and she stooped, burying her head in the animal's fur. She needed his undemanding, uncomplicated affection.

What so confused her now, she knew, were her reactions to Michael, even though she was still mourning Sanders. What kind of person was she? Was it just that she was so vulnerable, just as Lisa was? Or was it deeper? Had her feelings for Michael really survived that terrible night and the years that followed?

She felt terribly disloyal to Sanders, disloyal and undeserving of him, and the years they had shared. No wonder Lisa disapproved of her, and her control. What Lisa didn't know, couldn't realize, was how much that control had been needed to survive, how it had then become habit, a protective shield that would keep anything like that from happening to her again, to her and to those she loved.

It hadn't worked. She knew that now. She swallowed deeply, trying to dislodge the thick lump in her throat. Should she call Michael and tell him of John's report? It was as he had said it would be. She wanted to talk to him, to hear the low, calm, confident voice. But there was a danger in that too, of depending on him, of being around him. Nothing had really changed in her reaction to him: the electricity that still flashed so surprisingly between them, the accelerated beating of her heart, the response to his barest touch. Nothing had changed. Yet everything had changed.

"I did love you, Sanders," she whispered desperately. "It was a different kind of love, but it was more real."

She could almost feel him near her. I know, he seemed to whisper back. *I've always known.*

Kurt Weimer argued in his cool, precise way. No one in this meeting knew how completely bored he was, how eager he was for the session to be over. Still, he was a master at manipulation, and by the time the conference was through, his standing in the economic community would be stronger than ever.

He was anxious, now that it was started, to get on with his plan for retribution.

Kurt had found his father's grave yesterday, an unmarked pauper's grave in a Brunswick cemetery. The site was located only because of registration in a stark office. He had claimed to be looking for the grave of a man with a name starting with the same last initial as his father's cover. He had pretended confusion when he couldn't find the name he had sought, but his eyes had quickly found another one and the location of the grave.

A pauper's grave. For a German hero. The knowledge had galled him as little else had. How he longed to take the body back and have it buried with honor. But he was denied that. As he had been denied a father because of an interfering woman.

He wondered about the man who was sent with his father. He too had apparently been killed in an attempt to escape. Had the man deserted his father? Kurt had discovered little about him except that von Steimen had been a naval officer and the son of a Nazi general. But Kurt intended to find out exactly what happened that night. He had planned very carefully how to do it.

It would take a little more time than he had thought. Lisa Evans was obviously a virgin, and he'd realized from dinner the other night that her seduction would require more time and effort than he had first envisioned. But he could do it. He knew all the signs—the adoring, fascinated eyes, the eagerness in her voice when he called, the way she responded when he had kissed her the other night.

But she was also intelligent if young, two qualities that usually did not find favor with him. He usually preferred older women, sophisticated in the ways of love and barren of opinion. But he had flattered Lisa's quickness, her unusual knowledge of events, and he had known instantly that he had been correct in doing so.

American women. So independent. He knew how to use that independence and turn it around into dependence.

It would, however, take longer. He had already notified his office that he planned to stay in America a few weeks more than planned. A much delayed vacation, he said. At the same time, there were Odessa matters that could be handled. A few visits to its supporters and beneficiaries in America. A little applied pressure for more money. He wanted to meet and talk to one of the white supremacist leaders who had demonstrated definite promise. He had contempt for most of them, crazies who did more harm than good, but this one had been steadily, quietly, developing a strong organization. Kurt had already steered some money that way.

He knew he had to be very, very careful. Yet he trusted it to no one else. Odessa needed a strong organization in America; that was Hitler's mistake. He had underestimated America, and America's will. It would not be a mistake which was repeated.

Kurt finished his brief presentation and turned his attention to the next speaker. He was careful to keep his eyes alert and an interested smile on his lips.

*   *   *

Lisa typed the brief slowly, her mind on anything but the notes in front of her.

Her thoughts went momentarily to her mother this morning. Her eyes had been red and bloodshot. When Lisa mentioned it, her mother had quickly dismissed the signs as a beginning of a cold. Lisa wondered.

Lisa loved her mother, but she was intimidated by her. Not because her mother did anything cruel, far from it. But it was that control, that perfection that Lisa had never understood. She had tried to emulate it once. I will not cry or yell or say hurtful things, she had once pledged. Not for three whole months. Unfortunately, that intention lasted three days until she saw a sad film and cried buckets. Two days later, she found herself yelling at someone who was teasing Andy.

She could never be like her mother, and a small vein of resentment and rebellion had started then. She knew she was wrong to feel that way. She knew it, but she couldn't help it.

She had once asked her father if her mother ever lost control. He had looked at her intently, and nodded. Her mother had lost someone long ago, he'd said, and it affected her deeply. The facade of calmness, he had said, was her way of protecting her feelings.

Whom did she lose? It was, of course, natural curiosity, but for once her father didn't answer directly. "No one you knew. A boating accident before you were born. Don't say anything about it to her. Promise?"

She did promise, because he had asked it of her, but she had never stopped wondering about it. Lisa also knew her mother had worked hard as she was growing up, even working as a maid for a fine family. She had heard wonderful stories about the way they had lived, both on Long Island and on Jekyll Island in the thirties, and her mother still received Christmas cards from Elizabeth Connor and her two now-grown children. But she had never met them. She had wanted to, but something had always interfered.

Her mother's life affected her own. Lisa had wanted to work summers, but her mother had continually opposed such proposals, saying Lisa should have this time to enjoy herself. Lisa had always thought she would enjoy herself more if she could earn her own money, but in this instance her father had agreed. Be young, he had said.

So this was only the second summer she had worked, and that had been interrupted after only one week by her father's death. Now she was having difficulty concentrating, even on the simple task of typing. Her father's death, her mother's distraction, and Kurt were all recurring themes in her head.

Thank goodness, she was working for Kelly, who understood her so well. He had asked her last summer, knowing she was eager for a job and that she planned to study law. She had quickly adapted, usually enjoying even the most elementary tasks of recording deeds at the courthouse, typing complex briefs, and answering the phone. Law fascinated her. She was constantly intrigued by the way an attorney could make a believable plea out of either side of a case. It was much like a chess game, she thought. A good lawyer had to anticipate the other player's moves and counter them.

Kelly was extremely patient, always answering her questions, giving her time off to watch a particularly interesting case.

She didn't know exactly how she felt about Kelly. Except she'd always felt safe with him. He had been her best friend for a long time. But she'd never felt the excitement she was feeling now with Kurt.

Kurt!

She wished there was someone close she could talk to

about him, but there wasn't. Her mother would never understand. Lisa couldn't imagine her ever having experienced these giddy, excited feelings.

Lisa understood that part of her fascination was awe. She'd never met anyone quite like Kurt Weimer, with his European manners and lovely accent and the way everyone looked at him with respect. That he apparently enjoyed her company was, to her, astounding and flattering.

She had told Kelly about dinner, because she usually told Kelly almost everything, but she had instantly regretted it when she saw his eyes cloud. It had surprised her because Kelly had never been more than a very good friend. Of course, they had kissed occasionally after going out for an evening, and they had been very nice, very satisfactory kisses indeed, but he had never said anything that justified that instant of pain she thought she saw in his face.

Ever since she and her family had started to come here for the summers, Kelly had looked out for her. He had been seven years older, yet he had always treated her as an equal, and their friendship had grown stronger as she grew older. When she was eighteen, he had started taking her to dances and movies, and she had always assumed it convenience more than anything else, since there were few young people on the island.

Now she wondered. His father had been an attorney, and Kelly's family and her own had become close friends. When Kelly's father died, Sanders had been the anchor for Kelly and his mother, and Lisa had assumed that Kelly had been returning the favor.

The door to Kelly's office opened, and he came out, bringing another sheaf of papers for typing, and she took several minutes to look at him anew. He was tall and lanky, his face pleasant but not exactly handsome. It was, instead, the face of someone you wanted as, well, your best friend.

It was sensitive and friendly, with an easy smile and warm brown eyes. His hair was a russet color, thick and slightly curly, and he wore it a little long, more because he didn't take the time to go to the barber than intent, she thought. His clothes were what they had to be, suits on days he appeared in court, and more casual when he knew he would be in the office all day. His collar would be open and his tie loose and the cuffs of his sleeves rolled up. He cared little about appearances when he wasn't in court, only about the quality of his work, and she respected him enormously. He did a lot of pro bono work for indigent clients if he thought they had been treated unjustly, and he hurt when he lost one of their cases.

Perhaps it was because she knew him so well that she didn't feel the thrill with him that she had with Kurt, whose impeccable grooming and clothes made everyone turn and look as they walked in the restaurant, or the way the leather of the Mercedes felt, compared to the slightly torn upholstery in Kelly's often paper-littered car.

She winced at her thoughts, thinking them shallow indeed. Yet she was intrigued by so many other things about Kurt. He was so . . . different, even frightening in some ways.

Lisa felt Kelly's hand on her shoulder. "How are you doing?" The voice was sympathetic.

"Fine," she said as brightly as she could.

"I have a lunch appointment. Can you stay here until I'm back? Dan's out today, and Margaret has already gone to lunch."

Dan was Kelly's partner, and Margaret the legal secretary. Kelly always wanted at least one person in the office at all times during the day.

"Of course," she said, knowing she had already inconvenienced the firm with her recent absences.

He stayed there a second longer, regarding her gravely.

"Would you like to go to a movie tonight?" His voice was a little cooler than usual.

She smiled. "I would love it."

She was rewarded with a quick grin. "Good. I have to work late here, but I'll pick you up at seven-thirty. We'll get a bite to eat afterwards."

She nodded.

Kelly hesitated a moment, then slung his sports coat over his shoulder and strode out. He had ten minutes to reach The Deck, a seafood restaurant that stood at the entrance of St. Simons Island; that was more than enough time for the few miles which separated it from his Brunswick office.

He had been surprised at Meara's call last night. Lisa, she said, was taking Andy for a walk, and she didn't want her daughter to know about the call. She had asked him to meet her for lunch today. Something important. And please don't tell Lisa.

Kelly had to cancel another luncheon engagement, but there had been something in his neighbor's voice that was compelling. A fear that was palpable over the phone. He had readily agreed.

He saw her standing as he entered the restaurant. Kelly had always admired her, the calm but kind demeanor she always had, the ease with which she met people, the way she had helped his mother when his own father had died. She looked fresh and cool, as she usually did, in a light blue blouse and dark blue flared skirt that swirled as she moved gracefully. But as he looked closer, her eyes were haunted, her face tired.

"Meara," he said gently. It always seemed strange using her first name after calling her Mrs. Evans for so many years. But when he took over some of the Evans's legal business, she'd insisted.

"Thank you for meeting me," she said, a kind of tone-lessness in her voice.

"Any time, you know that."

A hostess interrupted and seated them, and they waited to talk until a waiter took their order. Then Kelly looked at her levelly. "What's wrong, Meara?"

"It's Lisa," she said slowly, still wondering what and how much to tell him.

His hands stilled. "What about Lisa?"

Meara tried to construct her words, but it was difficult. How little, how much, should she say without opening the whole can of worms? "Did she tell you about . . . seeing a German delegate to the conference on Sea Island?"

"Yes," he said shortly. "In fact, I was there when they met."

"What did you think of him?"

"Then? I didn't pay too much attention, to tell you the truth. Lisa was unhappy. I was worried about her."

"Think back. You're good at people. Any impression at all?"

"Very smooth. Very charming. I didn't realize how much until this morning when Lisa said she went out with him," he added with some resignation. "Why?"

"I don't like him," Meara said flatly, unable any longer to skirt around the problem. "And I don't trust him."

He looked at her sharply. "Do you have a reason?"

She hesitated. "He's much older, much more sophisticated. As bright as Lisa is, I can't understand why he's attracted to her."

"I can," he said softly. "Lisa is very pretty, and as you said very bright. There's another reason, isn't there?"

Meara felt her heart sink. She knew this wasn't going to be easy. Kelly was only twenty-eight, but she had heard he was already exceptional in court. The only way to be exceptional was understanding people and what motivated them.

"Yes. I can't tell you what or why, but he has reason to dislike me."

Kelly absorbed the information. "You think he might try to get at you by getting to Lisa?"

"Yes."

"How did he contact her?"

"He said he found a compact that belonged to her."

The fall at the Cloister. Could it have been planned? Now he thought about it, the incident had been strange. He remembered the man's intense eyes as he had looked at Lisa, the invitation for a drink.

"You can't say anything to Lisa?"

"No." The word was full of pain.

He leaned forward. "I'm an attorney, Meara. Anything you say to me is privileged. Perhaps I can help."

Meara wanted to tell him everything. Dear Lord, how she wanted to. She'd been living with secrets and guilt for so many years. But she couldn't. What if he let something slip? He was so close to Lisa. Or what if he felt duty bound, as an officer of the court, to reveal Chris Chandler's identity?

Chris. Michael. Even now, she wanted to protect him. Even as she had that night when she couldn't fire on him.

Meara just looked at Kelly miserably, the denial clear in her face.

"Did Sanders know . . . about whatever you're worried about?"

"Yes."

Kelly felt relief. If Sanders knew, whatever secret existed couldn't be too disastrous; it wouldn't be illegal. Yet he had never known Meara Evans to be excitable or an alarmist. "What do you want me to do?" he said simply.

"Keep an eye on her, both at the office and at the house. As much as you can."

"What about the other times?"

"I'm . . . making arrangements."

Frustrated, he settled his elbows on the table and placed his chin on folded hands, looking at Meara intently. "I love her, you know."

"I suspected as much."

"Then don't you think I have a right to know more."

"I wish I could tell you, Kelly. But it's not my secret alone. Other people are affected."

"And all I can do is help watch her?"

"For the time being."

"Damn it, Meara."

Meara saw a tall figure being led toward the back, where she'd suggested he request a table. She saw his eyes search each table, then find her. He said something to the hostess, then turned her way.

When he reached them, he reached out a hand to Meara. "Mrs. Evans. It's been a long time. I heard about Sanders. I'm sorry."

Meara turned to Kelly. "This is Chris Chandler, an . . . acquaintance of my husband's." Turning back to Chris, she continued, "This is Kellen Tabor, our attorney and friend."

Kelly stood and shook hands, but there was no invitation in his brief greeting. He was, Meara suspected, still too preoccupied in what she had been saying. She was grateful for Chris's timing, for she knew Kelly had been preparing more questions in his mind.

"Are you alone, Mr. Chandler?" Meara's question was cool.

"I'm afraid so," he said.

"Why don't you join us then?" she said, feeling Kelly's

frustration across the table. She was effectively blocking any more questions, and he was aware of it.

Chris looked toward Kelly, who had no choice but to echo the invitation.

"Thank you," Chris said. "It gets lonely eating alone."

"Are you from this area?" Kelly asked politely, although he doubted it. There was nothing southern about the clipped accent, the severe business suit, and Kelly knew most of the movers and shakers in the southeast Georgia area. This man definitely fell into that category. There was a hard and businesslike quality about him, an air of success that was difficult to feign.

"No," Chandler said. "I'm here on business."

"What is your business?" Kelly asked out of courtesy more than curiosity.

"Lumber," Chandler replied, but the shortness of the answer was offset with a quick, charming smile that completely changed the austere face and made one want to smile back.

Kelly's gaze moved to Meara. Although she had invited the man, she was keeping her eyes from him. Her face was frozen, and he didn't know whether it was because of the conversation they had been having or the arrival of the newcomer.

"Looking for more lumber?"

"Not exactly. We want to expand. I'm looking for a small to medium size company we can buy on this coast," the newcomer said easily as the smile moved up to strikingly blue eyes.

Kelly would have asked more, but the waiter was back, bringing their food and taking Chandler's order. Instead, Kelly took the opportunity to watch Meara and the tension that had invaded her body since Chandler sat down. Her hands were under the table, and he would wager his next case that they were clutching each other.

As Chandler gave his order for a seafood salad, Kelly studied him closely. Chandler was Sanders's age, late forties or early fifties, he guessed. In many ways, he looked younger except for the lines around his eyes and the slight hint of gray in his hair. Something about the man pricked at him, but he couldn't put a name to it and he wondered why. Chandler had the kind of face you remembered, the type of strong features and vivid eyes you wouldn't easily forget.

"Have you been to the Georgia coast before?" he asked.

Meara felt her blood run cold. It was all she could do to keep from flinching.

"No, I met Sanders and Meara in Washington," Chris said, and Meara thought how easily he lied. But then he was an expert at it. She couldn't, shouldn't, forget that.

"Are you going to be here long?"

"A month possibly. I'm combining vacation with business, and I was told about the island. I was going to stay at the Cloister, but it was filled because of the Economic Conference, and I rented a house on Jekyll."

"Where?" Kelly said with growing interest.

Chris told him, and Kelly looked sharply at Meara, as if guessing there was more to the meeting than chance. Chris also saw it.

"I was hoping to run into Sanders and Meara, but then I heard about Sanders, and, well, I was going to call."

Nicely done, Meara thought bitterly. She resented how well he lied, even in behalf of her daughter.

They talked about small things for a while as if, for Meara's sake, Kelly and Chris were taking the conversation as far as possible away from the subject of her husband's death. By the time they had a cup of coffee, the two men were talking as if they were old friends.

"I might need some legal work if anything works out," Chris said. "Would you be available?"

Kelly nodded. "Why don't you come to a Rotary meeting with me? I can introduce you around. You might hear of something interesting."

"Sounds great. When?"

"Friday."

Chris nodded. "In the meantime, I wonder if you might have a little time, give me some suggestions as to whom I should see."

"Be glad to. I'm tied up today. What about dinner tomorrow night at my house? Mother will be delighted to see a new face."

Chris grinned. "A home-cooked meal is always welcome."

"Good."

Chris insisted on paying the bill despite Kelly's protestations, and the three left together, Chris for his rental car. Kelly escorted Meara to her car. "We need to talk some more."

"I know," Meara replied. "But in the meantime—"

"I'll keep an eye on her. But I have to know more."

"It's more a feeling than anything else."

"I'm taking her to the movies tonight. But tomorrow afternoon, before dinner, I want to talk to you. Down on the beach. Around five."

"There's nothing more to talk about."

"Yes, there is. Please."

Meara saw the anxiety in his eyes and knew he wouldn't stop where she had left off. How much more could she tell him? She didn't know.

"All right," she said.

He opened the door for her, and she stepped inside the steaming car. She sat there until he left, and she saw his car drive away. And she continued to sit there.

He loved Lisa. He had the right to know more. Or did he?

Everything was unraveling around her.

She slowly started the car and drove away.

Chapter Twenty-Two

His insides twisted into knots, Chris paced the living room of his rented house. At this rate, he decided dryly, he would have to replace the carpet at the end of his stay.

But patience had never been his strong point, and his natural instinct to do something, anything but wait, ate at him.

He thought painfully of Meara. Her exuberance, her zest for life, were gone, replaced by a remoteness, an untouchable quality, that hurt him to the quick. He sensed her deep love for her daughter, for *their* daughter, but even that was outwardly restrained as if she were afraid to show too much emotion. He had destroyed the part of her he'd loved most, the openness and laughter, and he would willingly give his life to bring those two qualities back again.

And to hold her one more time.

But she had made quite clear the terms of accepting his help. He knew she still didn't trust him. He had seen the suspicion in her eyes and he understood it, for she had no reason to trust him. None at all. It was likely, in her mind, he knew, that he was somehow after Lisa, that he had

349

planted suspicion on the German so he could worm himself into their lives, Meara's and Lisa's. She had more reason to distrust him than she did to distrust Weimer. Thank God, she had listened at all.

He could expect little else, however, and he knew it.

A knock came at the door and he hurried to answer it, finding, as he expected, a man and a woman, both nondescript-looking, who identified themselves as investigators for Ben Markham and Associates. Kate Ross and Matt Byers.

Chris assessed the woman carefully. He knew and respected Matt, who had done much of the background work on Meara and on several companies he had thought about acquiring. The woman was in her mid-thirties with steady brown eyes that didn't waver under his inspection and a strong handshake that translated confidence and competence. But then Markham had a reputation for the best.

He guided them to a table and invited them to sit before handing them both a copy of a photograph of Kurt Weimer that had been in the Brunswick newspaper. Matt's eyes widened perceptibly, but the woman showed no reaction at all, and Chris's initial satisfaction increased.

"I want you to keep an eye on Weimer," he said, "particularly when and if he is seeing this young lady." He picked up a photo of Lisa, and the woman studied it carefully. Matt didn't have to; he had taken it a year earlier.

"Is there anything in particular we should look for," Matt said cautiously, knowing from past experience that Chris Chandler relayed what he wanted others to know, nothing else. This client, a highly valued one, had not appreciated questions. He didn't know why Chandler had commissioned the investigation of the Evans's family, and the one time he had indicated the slightest curiosity, Chandler had leveled him with a cold stare.

Matt half expected the same thing this time, and he was surprised when Chris answered with an angry intensity that Matt knew he didn't ever want directed at him. "Mrs. Evans is a friend. I have reason to believe that Kurt Weimer means to harm her daughter." He hesitated a moment to allow that statement to impact. Then he continued slowly, emphasizing every word. "When he is with Lisa Evans, I don't want them out of your sight, not for a minute. If they go into his cottage for more than several minutes, make an excuse to interrupt and get her out of there. I don't care how you do it. But do it. Understood?"

They did. They didn't ask why their client didn't call the police. It wasn't their business.

"When he's not with her?" Matt asked.

"Keep him in sight." Chris hesitated. "And I want his room wired."

Matt raised one eyebrow. "That's illegal."

"Only if it's discovered," Chris answered cynically.

"I'll have to check with Ben."

"I'll talk to him again today," Chris said. "In the meantime, keep a close eye on Weimer. He's staying at the Cloister on Sea Island. One of the cottages. He'll probably be in meetings much of the time. I know, however, that he's taking Lisa Evans to a banquet Saturday night and plans to spend the day with her Sunday. Stay with them."

"Yes, sir," the woman said. "We'll do it in relays so he won't spot us."

"He has no reason to expect he's being watched," Chris said. "If you're careful, he won't. I want you to report to me each night, and every few hours when he's with her."

They nodded. "Anything else?"

Chris hesitated. "I want you to meet Mrs. Evans so she'll know who you are." He picked up the phone and dialed the number he had quickly memorized. "Can you come over?" he said without preamble.

There was a hesitancy on the other side of the line. "Why?" The voice was cautious.

"I want you to meet the detectives I've hired."

There was another silence at the other end. "All right," she said finally. "I'll be there in a few moments." There was no good-bye as she hung up.

"Coffee?" he asked the two detectives, and Matt nodded. Chris had barely poured cups from the constantly renewed pot when he heard her at the door.

She stood there stiffly, dressed in a pair of gray shorts which showed still shapely legs to perfection, and a green blouse which emphasized the emerald color of her eyes. She wore no makeup and her hair was tousled, curling around her face in uncombed tendrils. She seemed tired, her eyes dull.

He had to ball his hand in a fist to keep from reaching out to her. She looked so damned vulnerable. Hell, she was vulnerable. He smiled reassuringly. "Come in."

She followed him in and stood hesitantly as the two strangers stood and were introduced. They both exuded a confidence she couldn't seem to find.

"I just wanted you to know who they were in case you saw them," he said gently. "I didn't want you to be worried."

"Worried? Me?" She raised one of her eyebrows, and he caught a fleeting glimpse of humor. But this time it was dry and ironic, nothing like the old bubbling happiness. "Why should I be worried?"

He held back a smile. The spirit was there. The old spirit that had stubbornly loved him, that had made her fight back that last night in the power house. She had been uncommonly brave then. She was the same today. Doing what she had to do to protect those she loved.

He had never loved her as much as he did now. And she had never been further away.

Matt and Kate took their leave. Kate hesitated a moment, and then went over to Meara, offering her hand. "We'll take good care of her," she said.

Meara smiled gratefully, watching as they left and climbed in a Ford as nondescript as they themselves were. "I'd better go," she said. "I . . . was cleaning out some things."

"Don't go," he said, and he disliked the plea in his voice, but it stopped her.

"I can't stay here." Her voice trembled slightly.

"The beach then. Will you go for a walk with me?"

She turned and stared at him. "Why?"

"There's a lot to talk about."

"Is there?" Her voice was cold in self-defense. She knew what happened to her every time he was near. The magic she remembered was even stronger, the pull even greater. It was as if she naturally gravitated to him, as earth to the sun. No matter what she told herself, how often she reminded herself of how he used and manipulated people, the attraction between them was as real and irresistible as it had been on the cruiser that March morning.

She hated herself for it.

She hated him for it.

But she couldn't deny it. She couldn't say no. She tried, but she couldn't. Dear God, she didn't want to leave him. She nodded.

He opened the back door for her, careful not to touch, not to do anything to break the very fragile truce. The beach in front was nearly deserted as was most of the stretch where the houses were located. There was the occasional bicycle rider or shell hunter or couple holding hands.

The sun was hot and the sky clear. A very slight breeze swept off the ocean, ruffling hair and cooling hot skin. The afternoon was lazy, and even the birds had disappeared for rest as the waves lapped softly at the smooth sand.

As they walked north toward the heavily wooded park, Chris saw some children playing in the sand, and he was reminded of the sand castle they'd built that fine spring day, and how carefree Meara had been with bare legs tucked under her and the comical consternation on her face as she had surveyed her ruined castle.

Time seemed to stop, to never have gone beyond that day, that image, the unique pleasure he had felt at being included in the small charmed circle. He stuffed his hands in his pockets and looked away, the sudden pain unbearable.

For lack of anything else to say, he asked about Tara and Peter Connor. It was a mistake.

But then everything was.

He was walking in an emotional minefield, each step triggering another memory, reviving another horror for her. Chris looked at her frozen face, and wanted to kick himself. "I'm sorry," he whispered.

She didn't look at him, but her face gradually relaxed. He suspected it took an effort. "They're fine. Peter's running his father's company and Tara's happily married to a state senator."

"No lasting effects?" He had to ask it.

"Not lasting. There were nightmares for a while," she said quietly. "They kept asking about you. Elizabeth finally told them you had gone to heaven trying to help them."

"How . . . ?"

"Sanders put out the story that he sent you for help since the telephone wires were down, that apparently the boat hit something in the darkness. The FBI wanted no leaks of the . . . Nazi plan. Even the members believed it to be an ordinary kidnapping attempt." She was silent a moment. "The house was a legacy from the Connors, who thought I had saved the children."

"You did," Chris said.

"They wouldn't even have been in danger were it not for you," she said, "and my foolish infatuation." The guilt was heavy in her voice, and he inwardly cringed at it. Did the damage never end?

"That's not true," he said. "I didn't know until that night, but they planned to take the children all along."

"Why didn't you know?"

He shrugged. "I don't think they entirely trusted me. It was one reason Hans was sent. I had been an officer, not . . . one of their hired killers."

"You seemed ready enough to go along with it."

"No," Chris said simply. "But I don't expect you to believe me."

"Good," she retorted, not quite looking at him. She knew she should stop the barbs; it was totally unlike her. But she was afraid if she let go of her anger, if she stopped striking at him, that something else might happen, something she knew she had to prevent at all costs. She couldn't, wouldn't, lose her heart to him again. He was altogether too dangerous, too unpredictable.

"Why did you keep coming back here?" he asked softly. The question had been pounding at him, not only for the past days but for years. He knew there was one answer he wanted to hear, but he doubted it would come.

"I don't know," she said tiredly. "I suppose I could tell you that it was inexpensive. Or that there's a fine peace here. But this island's always been like the serpent's apple. A compulsion I can't resist."

The words hung in the air. She started to stumble as a mist formed in back of her eyes, and she felt his strong hand reach out and steady her, then hesitate before leaving. She didn't want it to leave.

Nothing had changed in twenty-one years, she thought with amazement. Her heart still raced when she was around him, her senses still spun wildly. She had told herself so many times that it had been her youth and inexperience that had responded to him that summer. That and the island and the magic and the war. Not love. Never love. How could she be capable of loving a spy, an enemy, a liar, a user?

But she could not blame anything on youth now. She was forty-three, a widow and a mother, and she still responded in the same tempestuous, all-consuming way. The barest touch of his hand sent rivers of warmth rushing through her body. What was wrong with her?

She knew she kept sniping at him for her own sake, to remind herself of the danger, rather than any attempt to wound him. The fierce desire to hurt ended the first day. The lines in his face, the slowness of the old easy smile, the stark agony in his voice when he'd said he had paid and paid, all had told her he had suffered too. She believed that, anyway. She didn't know what else she believed. Or whether she could ever trust him again.

Meara glanced down at her watch, the watch Sanders had given her. She swallowed and looked away, toward the sea, toward the endless, churning sea that always changed, yet never changed. Perhaps that was why she was so drawn to it. A constant in her life. A wellspring, a source, that always reminded her that there were elements and forces that miniatured human problems and usually put them in perspective. Usually.

"I have to get back," she finally said, wondering at the silence that wasn't awkward, that was even comforting. "Lisa will be home soon."

Chris nodded.

"I'll go back alone," Meara added. "I don't think it wise for her to see us together."

"No," he agreed, but she saw grief flicker across his face, and for the first time she hurt for him too. It couldn't be easy for him, knowing. . . .

"How long have you known about Lisa?" she said abruptly.

It was his turn to look toward the ocean. He couldn't face her now. "Since right after the war. I couldn't stop thinking about you, whether you were all right, what had happened to you. I had read the story about the kidnapping in the newspaper, and I knew that at least that part of it was all right, but . . . I heard you call my name that night. I've heard it nearly every night for twenty years."

His voice was raw with emotion, raw and splintered as if each word was torn from his throat. "I tried to work myself into oblivion during the war—lumberjacking is a demanding and exhausting business—but I still heard it. Dear God, Meara, I never meant to hurt you. If you don't believe anything else, believe that. I just couldn't stay away from you. I knew what I was doing, but I couldn't stay away."

He turned to her, and Meara saw wetness in his eyes, and she didn't know whether she could bear his hurt. She could bear her own; she had discovered that, but she didn't think she could bear his. It was so stark, so stark and bleak and lonely, and he'd had no one while she had been lucky to have Sanders and Lisa.

But while she ached to reach out to him, she couldn't. An old adage kept echoing in her mind, one that Lisa had picked up at school. "Fool me once, shame on you; fool me twice, shame on me."

He continued slowly. "I saved every penny I earned, and after the war I hired a private detective firm to make sure you were . . . all right. It was then I found out about Lisa, and that you'd married Evans." He couldn't tell her how gut-wrenching it had been, how he had taken up wandering half the nights, how he tortured himself with guilt, how he had collected photos of Lisa taken by his detectives and stared at them for hours at a time. He couldn't tell her any of it.

"He saved me, you know," Meara said. "That night and again when I found out about the baby. He was a very good man."

"I know," Chris replied gently. He wanted to ask more, much more, but this was a tenuous start at best, the first step, he hoped, on the road to trust. He wanted that as much as he'd ever wanted anything in his life, that and the safety of his daughter.

"I have to go," she said again, her hand knotting at her side. Go, she screamed to herself. Go. But she didn't move. Her legs were rooted in the sand.

It was as if he recognized her need and understood it, just as Sanders had understood so much. His face unfathomable, Chris turned back, in the opposite direction, and moved away. Meara stood there watching, surprised, as he continued walking down the beach. He still limped slightly, but his body was straight and his shoulders squared, the gold hair blowing slightly in the breeze. She felt her stomach turn to lead, her heart beat frantically. He was giving her time, giving her space, as her daughter would say.

She was grateful. Or was she?

Meara watched him until he disappeared around a slight bend, and then she turned. And walked slowly home.

Walking away had been damned difficult. But staying would have been worse.

Chris had known the instant he could have touched her again, could have taken her in his arms. But it wasn't time yet. Later, she would have hated herself. And him.

He had pierced part of the armor around her. But only

part, and he was bitterly afraid that once away from him she would rebuild. As she had the sand castle once.

But he had learned patience in the past years, had learned to live with the fact that another man lived with the woman he loved, would always love, and had raised the child that should have been his.

Perhaps there was a chance now. Only a chance. But a chance was enough.

Lisa didn't eat much at dinner. "Kelly's taking me to the movies tonight."

Meara tried not to show her sudden delight. "What are you going to see?"

"The Great Escape," Lisa said.

Meara felt a twinge of apprehension. She had read about the film, a War World II prison camp escape with Steve McQueen. The ironies never stopped. The reminders never stopped.

"Mother?"

When Meara looked up, Lisa was looking at her curiously. Meara forced a smile. "It's supposed to be a good movie. I'm glad you're going."

Lisa nodded and slipped Andy a piece of meatloaf. A tail thumped gratefully.

Meara pretended not to see. Feeding Andy at the table had always been frowned upon, but Andy was the ultimate optimist. Meara asked about Lisa's day.

"It was a waste, I'm afraid. I can't seem to concentrate."

Because of Sanders. Or was it because of the German economist?

"I know," Meara answered. "I've been trying to work on an article, but nothing wants to come."

Lisa lowered her gaze. Her mother's eyes had been red-rimmed for days, and she regretted everything she had said several days ago. "I'm sorry, Mom," she said. "I'm really sorry about the other day."

Meara realized it had been a long time since Lisa had called her "Mom." When had it stopped? How long ago? And why? Meara rose from her chair and went over to where Lisa sat, placing her hand on her shoulder. "I love you, Lisa. I haven't said it enough. I know. And I didn't tell your father enough. But it's always been there. Always."

Lisa's fork, which had been merely moving food from place to place, stilled. "I know," she said in a low voice. "He loved you so much." Her voice choked.

"I'm always here for you."

"I know. I've always known that."

Andy whined under the table, sensing the emotion which filled the room.

"If you ever need to talk . . ."

Lisa looked up at her mother, at the evident love in her face, and she wondered if she had been wrong in more ways than one. Why had she never noticed it before? But habits were hard to break, confidences difficult to share. She had only done so with her father.

"I have to get ready," she finally said awkwardly, not knowing what else to say at the moment.

"Okay," Meara said. She took the dishes out, helped by Lisa, then brushed Lisa away. "You go get ready. I'll finish."

Lisa hesitated. There was something different about her mother, something very vulnerable. "Are you sure I should go tonight?"

"Yes," Meara said strongly. God knew she wanted nothing more than to cement the relationship between Kelly and Lisa. "I'm going to work tonight."

"One of these days, you'll write that novel."

"Maybe," Meara replied noncommittally.

An hour later, she watched Lisa leave with Kelly, thinking how good they looked together, seemed together. But how can you tell someone whom they ought to love?

She cherished that brief moment of intimacy she'd had with her daughter, and Lisa's emotional response. Why hadn't she made the gesture earlier? Had she become so brittle, so detached, that she had not realized how she had retreated from showing real feelings?

Meara remembered how hurt she had been years ago when Michael had distanced himself from her emotionally. Had she done the same thing to her family all these years? Had she learned all the wrong things from him?

She was desperately afraid she had, and hadn't realized how much until she saw him on the beach a few days ago and everything had ripped out, feelings not only for him but for Sanders, for her daughter, for herself. She had been bottling them up for years.

Was it too late? She knew the agony of keeping secrets. Now they were greater than ever before. As were the lies. They were building, each lie upon the other, and she knew the weakness of that kind of foundation.

They had wreaked havoc twenty years ago. What would they do now? What could they do to Lisa?

Chapter Twenty-Three

THE SUN WAS dipping in the west when Kurt approached his father's grave. It was the second time, and he knew the trip was both stupid and dangerous.

When I get back, Kurt, you'll meet the Führer. This family will be recognized, you'll see. We are the new Germany, you and I.

His father had seemed so tall, so powerful, and his voice was compelling as he stooped down to clasp Kurt's arms. He was wearing his uniform with the death head, and Kurt had trembled with the glory of it.

Always honor the Führer. He is bringing greatness back to us. He is Germany's hope. And our hope. Fight for him. He is our honor.

How many times had he recalled those words, had tried to live up to them. And he had. He was helping to build a new Reich, a new society of which his father would be proud.

He hated the collective guilt of his people, the way they now denied the existence of something great, would still be great were it not for the traitors, those members of the military who spent their energies plotting against their leader and country rather than their country's enemies.

They had been the shame, not National Socialism, not the goals to purify Europe and make it the strongest, most powerful nation in the world. Both Russia and America were countries of mongrels, and only Germany's internal enemies had led it to a momentary defeat.

Kurt stared down at his father's grave. Only a marker with a number. But I haven't forgotten, he said silently. I haven't forgotten anything you told me.

He slowly looked at the other markers. Strangers. Not only strangers, but enemies. "Somehow," he whispered, "I'll get you back, and I'll find out what happened that night. I'll avenge you. I swear it by Germany."

He looked around the cemetery. There was only one other person, a woman whose face was shielded by a wide-brimmed hat and who was kneeling in front of a grave. Kurt turned around slowly and headed back to the car, his stomach twisting. He had been surprised earlier when he had called Lisa Evans, and, after the shortest of pauses, she had turned down the offer of dinner tonight, saying she had other plans.

The rejection, he knew, stung more than it should have. He had, after all, told her earlier, very reluctantly of course, that he would be unavailable until Saturday. But he was unused to rejection, and it had surprised him. Along with the knowledge that everything was taking longer than he expected. He'd thought the girl would be easy. Most of his conquests were. But after dinner with her, he had detected a strength he hadn't really expected.

His plan would take longer, that was all. Once he had arrived and met Lisa and Meara Evans, he'd known exactly what he was going to do: seduce the girl and sleep with her. He'd then tell the mother what he had done, what she had done to his father, and then he would also take her. He planned to kill them both, but not until the woman told him everything that happened twenty-one years ago, not until she had paid in full.

In a way, the girl was a shame. She was a perfect Aryan, and her naive intelligence and admiration amused him. Seducing her should be both interesting and pleasurable. But he needed to keep his mind on the principal objective.

Kurt thought about bedding the girl. Soon. Perhaps even Saturday. His footsteps suddenly lighter, he reached the car and climbed inside.

The moment Meara had dreaded came even faster than she had anticipated.

She had heard Lisa come home with Kelly the previous evening, but Meara forced herself to lie still. She didn't want Lisa thinking she was checking on her. Yet she had a terrible urge to get up and go to her daughter, to make sure she was all right, to warn her. To warn her to be careful, to warn her not to trust easily, to be wary of insidious charm.

But how could she do that without telling Lisa why?

If she felt this way when Lisa was with Kelly, how could she possibly allow her daughter to go out with Kurt Weimer? No matter how much protection she had.

When she finally rose after a sleepless night, Lisa was in the kitchen, eating a bowl of cornflakes and drinking a glass of juice. Meara started a pot of coffee for herself. Lisa had never cared for it.

"How was the movie?"

"Exciting," Lisa said. She hesitated a moment. "What do you remember about the war?"

Meara froze. Lisa had never shown much interest in the war before. Was this new awareness because of the movie? Or Weimer? Or both?

"Not much," Meara said finally. "A lot of rationing.

There wasn't much gasoline, and we walked everyplace. There were food shortages, clothing styles changed because cloth was needed for uniforms and silk for parachutes."

"I don't mean that," Lisa said impatiently. "It had to be, well, rather exciting."

Meara nearly dropped the cup she was holding. "I remember the woman next door receiving a telegram, informing her that the second of her two sons had died. I remember stars in her window, and so many other stars in so many other windows. Each one represented terrible grief, Lisa. There's nothing exciting about death, and that's all war is." Meara knew her voice was full of emotion, but she couldn't stop it.

Lisa was silent for a moment. "I can't picture Kurt as an enemy, as doing some of the things they showed in the film."

Careful, Meara told herself. Be very, very careful. "War changes people," she said slowly. "You can't always control events. Sometimes they control you. No country has a monopoly on good or bad, remember that, and loyalties can make you do things you might otherwise never do." She stopped, realizing she was saying the words for herself more than Lisa.

"As for Kurt Weimer . . . I hope you will be very careful. You don't know him. You don't know anything about him, and . . . I . . ."

"What?"

Meara had been ready to say she didn't trust him. Or like him. But she had said enough already.

"I don't want you hurt, darling. He'll be leaving shortly."

And what difference had that made to you? she asked herself. It had only accelerated her feelings, made everything more desperately important. She closed her eyes against the feelings of déjà vu that were swamping her. Or was it exactly the same thing? Had Michael Fielding ever been any better than the evil he now attributed to Weimer. Had he ever been more than a spy, a traitor to her, a ruthless brigand who ended up deserting his country too? Had he ever been any of those things she had once thought she saw in him?

Would she never stop wondering about something she would never know?

"Mom?"

Meara shook her head to clear it and looked at her daughter. How she loved Lisa, had always loved Lisa. She had been so innocent, so untouched by evil and violence and betrayal. Meara had always wanted her daughter's life to stay that way, had always wanted to protect her, to make her strong, stronger than she had been.

It was happening all over again. Another German was coming into their lives, threatening everything dear to her. And there was no one she could trust, not with the truth, not with the secrets that could destroy her daughter.

No one, no one but the person who had set events into motion twenty-one years ago. And she couldn't even trust him. Not completely.

"I won't get hurt," Lisa was saying through the haze of memories. "He's very, very nice." With the complete confidence of the young, Lisa smiled and changed the subject. "Kelly has invited us over to dinner tonight. He said a friend of yours and Daddy's is coming."

It was another in a series of jolts. She had known a meeting between Lisa and her blood father was imminent. But this soon?

Yet she herself had helped arrange the meeting between Kelly and Michael. No, Chris, damn it. But he would always be Michael to her. Always. She closed her eyes. Concentrating. Chris. She couldn't make a mistake now, not in front of Lisa or Kelly.

Damn! It was too soon. She should have expected Chris would take full advantage of the situation. He always had. That . . . persuasiveness of his had probably been the reason he was sent here as a spy. A spy. She couldn't forget that. She could never forget that. He was a man of different faces.

Lisa was continuing. "I told him I would ask you." She hesitated. "Kelly thinks you need to get out more."

Meara wanted to say no. Perhaps if she did, Lisa wouldn't go.

"Who is he, Mom?"

"Just someone your father met in business."

"FBI?" Lisa asked with increased interest.

"No." Even Meara knew the answer carried more emphasis than it should have. She softened her voice. "Chris Chandler is a lumberman. From the northwest."

"How did Dad meet him?"

"One of . . . his cases, I suppose."

"But Kelly said he knew you too."

"He visited . . . us once . . . a long time ago."

"What's he like?"

What was he like? Meara wished she knew. She also wished she could say no to dinner. But it was useless. She was as drawn to him now as she had been as a girl. All she could hope for, pray for, was that this business be finished quickly and that Chris or Michael or whoever he was disappear from her life forever. She shrugged, hoping the gesture indicated an indifference she wished she felt.

Lisa looked at her intently, as if she detected something unusual.

"I don't know him well. He's about your father's age." What else was there to say? That he was charming, intriguing, dangerous. That he still made her senses swim giddily, that he could reach inside and know her every thought while she never knew what he was thinking. She looked down at her watch. "You're going to be late, young lady, if you don't get started."

Lisa gulped down the juice. "You're right, and Kelly's been tolerant enough. What should I tell him about tonight?"

Meara's heart thumped. It was a miracle Lisa didn't seem to hear it. Say no. "Yes."

"Good," she said. "Oh, Kurt called yesterday and wanted me to go to dinner, but I already had a date with Kelly."

"Did he say anything else?" Meara asked cautiously.

"He asked about you. I think he liked you a lot."

"I think he's probably just amusing himself," Meara said stiffly, and immediately regretted the statement when she saw Lisa's face. It had looked hurt, then resentful.

"I didn't mean it the way it sounded," she tried to recoup. "It's just that he's only here for a short time. A week or two, and I'm sure it's nice for him to have some pleasant company."

A *week or two*. It had taken Meara less than two days to fall in love. A week or two was a lifetime.

But Lisa's strained expression didn't relax, and Meara knew they had lost those few minutes of closeness, of real communication, and she wanted to kick herself.

"I'll see you later," Lisa said shortly and grabbed her purse as she whirled out the door, and Meara felt she had taken one step forward and two back. She listened as the screen door banged several times in closing.

The day did not improve. A thick, padded package arrived with the mail, and Meara saw John Malcomb's name on it. She opened it and found a framed photo of herself and Lisa, and another of the three of them. She held them for a long time, feeling the warmth of the connection, a renewal of the sharp grief she felt at its loss.

She fingered them for several moments. For some reason, she didn't want to let them go. She didn't understand how she could feel the things she still felt for Michael so soon after Sanders's death. She felt faithless and unworthy. She had asked Michael what kind of person he was. What kind of person was she that he still aroused such strong emotions in her?

Meara only knew she couldn't deal with any more grief, any more guilt at the moment. She took the photos upstairs and placed them next to the jewelry box on the dressing table. It didn't contain much, for she had never cared a great deal for jewelry. There was a string of pearls Sanders had given her on their tenth anniversary, some gaudy but infinitely dear brooches a young Lisa had proudly presented to her at birthdays or Christmases, a watch that no longer worked.

Small things with big memories. Like the photos he had treasured.

She rested her hand on the frame for a moment, then left the room and closed the door behind her. If only she could close the door to her thoughts.

I'll get some work done, she told herself. She went down to the office and sat at the typewriter. She could send some query letters to various magazines on several story ideas. But she only stared at the blank page in the typewriter. An hour later, the blank page still blank, she reached for the telephone and tried Michael's number. It was busy.

Twenty minutes later, she was still trying. Restless beyond endurance, she decided to walk down to the beach. Perhaps she would go by the house he was renting. But then she reined herself in. She couldn't let it happen again. Not again.

She argued with herself. It was only that she needed to prepare him, and herself, for this evening.

Liar, she scolded. If nothing else, you've tried to be honest with yourself.

Suddenly impatient with herself, she called Andy and headed straight for the beach, proud of herself when she turned in the opposite direction from Chris's house. She would take a long, exhausting walk, and then she would call him about tonight. There was safety that way.

Safety? Was there any such thing any longer?

Chris cradled the phone against his shoulder, and his fingers tapped a nearby table impatiently.

"I can't come back now."

He heard the bafflement in the voice of his vice president, Allen Crandal. "They won't make a deal unless they talk to you personally."

"Damn it, I'll call."

"That's not good enough. They're demanding certain assurances about their employees and forest lands they control."

"Tell them we'll put it in the contract."

"Our attorneys say no. It can create a host of problems. But the Hatches will accept your word, I think, if only you can sit down and talk to them. A day. Only a day."

"I can't," Chris said.

There was a long pause on the telephone. "You've been trying to get that company for five years. This may be the only opportunity."

"Then I'll lose it," Chris said flatly. "Do the best you can."

"Chris . . ."

"No, Allen." His tone was sharper, more impatient than he intended.

There was another pause. "Is there anything I can do? Anything I can help with?"

Chris's fingers stopped tapping. Allen had been with him more than six years, and they had never had a drink together that wasn't business, never visited each other's homes, never inquired into the other's life. It was the way Chris had wanted it, the way he had learned to live. The way a fugitive lives, a person who has no past. There were too many dangers in friendships, in attachments. One slip and the house of cards could come tumbling down.

Yet he was touched by the concern in Allen's voice, concern which seemed to go beyond business.

"No," Chris said in a more moderated voice. "But you're going to have to handle this on your own."

"When will you be back?"

"I don't know."

"Some papers need your signature."

"I'll send you my power of attorney," Chris said. "You should have it day after tomorrow. Do whatever you think best."

There was another silence. Since Chris had taken control of Northwest Lumber, he had held it tightly. He hired the best and he usually took their advice, but he always knew exactly what was going on and no major decision was ever made without his knowledge and approval. "I'll do my best," Allen said finally.

"Thank you," Chris said, knowing that too was out of character. He paid top dollar and he expected results. He knew he was often delinquent on the niceties. That was part of the barrier he had established between himself and other people. No lowered drawbridges. No unexpected attacks.

"If you need anything—"

"I'll call," Chris said. He gently laid the phone back down. He hadn't wanted to tie it up that long. He wanted to be available for the detectives, for Meara.

It was strange. He had been trying to get George Hatch's company for years, and now it meant nothing, less than nothing. He couldn't, at the moment, care less about the company into which he'd poured all his life and energy for the past twenty years. He had worked twelve- to fifteen-hour days because there wasn't anything else, because it helped him survive.

Now he didn't care about anything but Meara and Lisa. His daughter.

He thought about killing Kurt Weimer himself. It was one solution. But, he realized quickly enough, not a very good one. A subsequent investigation, his photo in every paper in the country. Just one identification, just one, and everything Meara had tried to build would be gone. Someone from those two weeks long ago would remember. Someone always remembered.

The best, the least hurtful solution for everyone was to catch Weimer in illegal activities, to expose his Nazi connections. Weimer was obviously unaware of Chris's existence; otherwise, he too would have been targeted by now. Kurt Weimer must feel very, very safe.

Chris knew, however, what hell it must be for Meara. Remembering. Fearing. Unable to do anything but wait. All on top of her husband's death. And his own devastating return.

He felt terribly weary, weighed down by the havoc he had instigated years ago. So many debts to pay. He could never completely atone for them. Some things he probably couldn't have avoided. But Meara? His inability to stay away from her when he knew, damn it. When he knew what kind of damage could result. But even then, his mind could never have imagined this. Never! He would have to live with that burden every day of his life. He stood and went to the drawer where he had put his gun. Until he had purchased a gun a month ago, he hadn't held a pistol since the war, although he had used a rifle.

His company's best client owned a hunting lodge, and Chris was required occasionally to put in a command performance. Many of his clients were, in fact, hunters, an activity that held no attraction for Chris. He had seen enough of death during the early years of the war, and when he was forced to join the hunting parties he made damned sure his shots went wide of any game.

If it weren't for the exposure to Meara and Lisa, he would be tempted to stalk Weimer now. The actual fact of prison couldn't be worse than the hell he lived now.

The phone rang again, and he picked it up slowly. "Chandler."

He knew from the hesitant soft breathing on the other end who it was. "Meara?"

"I . . . wanted to warn you that Kelly has invited Lisa and me over to dinner tonight. I knew of course you were coming, but . . . I hadn't thought he would also invite us."

There was obvious panic in her voice, and it hurt. God how it hurt. She dreaded him meeting her daughter, their daughter. He understood it. But that understanding didn't stop the flash of pain ripping through him.

"I'll be careful," he said stiffly.

"She . . . she's still hurting . . . "

"So are you," he said, vicious self-contempt in his voice. "Because of me."

"No," she said slowly. She had been thinking all day, remembering. She had gone after him that spring with one-minded determination. During the walk this morning, she had remembered how many times he had warned her, how he had tried to keep his distance. Why hadn't she remembered that before? Because she hadn't wanted to. It was easier to blame him. "I wanted you too."

"You wanted what you thought I was," he said in a fiercely objective way.

"I don't know." Her voice too was tired. "But none of that matters any more," she said lifelessly. "The only thing that does matter is Lisa."

"And you."

"No," she said simply.

"Meara . . ."

"I just wanted to prepare you," Meara said quietly. "That's all. Kelly told her you were a friend of Sanders."

"What else . . . was said?"

"She asked me about you. I said you lived in the northwest, that you were involved in one of Sanders's cases and we'd met once when you came to Washington. That's all."

"All right," he said mildly. "Thank you for calling." There was a silence on the other end, then he heard the connection severed. He slowly let the telephone slip from his own hand and leaned back against the sofa.

He had spent his life in rigidly disciplined lines, had subdued and conquered emotions, had learned to control his every expression, his every word. Except for two weeks in the spring of 1942. Except for then, and the consequences of that weakness had been devastating.

And now, tonight, he would meet one of the results of that fallout. His daughter. His chest tightened until he thought he couldn't breathe, and for a moment he wondered if he were having a heart attack. The physical pain was all consuming, spreading over him in aching waves. Slowly it receded, but time had passed. He didn't know how long. Some of the pain receded, but not all.

His daughter. He had thought about her, dreamed about her, wondered about her. He had treasured the few photos he had of her, and pictured others in his mind: her first party dress, her first date, her graduation from high school. Each had been an aching, agonizing reminder of what he had surrendered. His hands pressed together until they were white.

He knew he was often called the iron man at the company.

Tonight, he would have to prove it.

Chapter Twenty-Four

CHRIS STUDIED HIMSELF in the mirror. He had been doing that for a very long time this evening.

But there was no vanity in the examination. He had looked at himself in the mirror for years, searching the face of a man he despised. He had seen himself grow older, had seen the shell grow harder, the eyes grow more empty each succeeding year.

No, there was nothing to admire in the face that looked back at him.

But there was another reason to look now.

How much did his daughter resemble him? Would there be a certain acknowledgment between them? He had spent so much time this afternoon looking at her pictures, and recalling the morning he first saw her here.

Her hair was gold, a slightly darker shade than his, but that was not unusual. Meara's red hair was also touched by gold, and Sanders, he recalled, had light brown hair. No giveaway there.

Eyes? Her eyes were blue. He hadn't seen them a week ago, but he knew from the information sent to him that they were blue. Bright blue. Not the dark inky blue of his own. There was nothing else, he thought, to link them. Lisa had Meara's bone structure, the same wide, stubborn mouth. Perhaps Lisa had some of Chris's height, but then Sanders had also been tall.

He had made a promise to Meara, one he meant to keep, no matter the cost to him. Lisa would never know from him that he was her father. He would stay out of her life, hers and Meara's, once he had insured their safety.

It was the only gift he had.

He looked down at his watch. Ten minutes. He didn't want to be early. He didn't want to seem eager.

Chris looked down at his clothes. He had dressed with care in a light blue summer suit he had found in Brunswick earlier. He wore an even paler blue shirt, and a dark blue tie, dark blue socks and black shoes. He looked imminently respectable, he thought with a twisted smile. He wondered what his hosts would think if they knew what he really was: a fraud, a name on a cemetery stone. That, and more.

His hand shook as he picked up his wallet and placed it in a pocket, and ran a comb once more through the unruly hair which curled in the damp coastal air. He glanced at his watch again. Five more minutes. He thought about a drink, and how much he wanted one, needed one, and then how much he couldn't afford it. He needed every ounce of discipline he could master.

Time. It was time to go. Time to meet his daughter. Time to see Meara again.

None of them, not Eric von Steimen or Michael Fielding or Chris Chandler, had ever known fear like this. Fear—deep, sickening fear.

Yet there was something else too. Elation.

Chris straightened his tie one last time.

*   *   *

Would Lisa suspect anything?

Meara glanced desperately around the room, again wanting to run and hide and take Lisa with her.

She had been ready for thirty minutes. As if to deny that anything unusual was happening, she wore casual clothes, a brightly colored but cotton skirt, an emerald green blouse and a pair of sandals. She had used only the barest touch of lipstick on her lips.

She poured herself a gin and tonic, knowing it was probably a mistake. There would be drinks at Kelly's. Her hands shook as she held the bottle of gin, and more splashed in the glass than she intended. She usually used only the slightest trace. But now she gulped the drink like a person stranded in the desert for days without water.

Where had the hard-won peace gone?

She had worked so hard to achieve it, had even been able to lock many memories away. Not those of Michael, nor the force of the brooding blue eyes. But she had been able to put aside the violence of that last night. And now it was all coming back, each detail magnified.

No one here knew anything about that night. No one had ever connected Meara Evans with the twenty-one-year-old kidnapping and death of the supposed kidnapper. Lisa knew nothing about it. Neither did Kelly. Kelly's family had come to the island years after the club closed, and none of the old members of the Jekyll Island Club returned after the state took ownership. And while Meara had personally maintained loose ties with the Connors, she had always managed to arrange roadblocks to keep them from meeting Lisa. She did not want an unintentional word to rip her fabric of lies.

Lisa emerged from her room, wearing a blouse and slacks, her long blond hair pulled back carelessly in a ponytail.

So young. I want you to be young forever. But Meara held her tongue and merely smiled. "Ready?"

"You're sure you want to go?" Lisa said, worry etched on her face as she saw her mother's tense expression.

No. I don't. "Of course," Meara said instead. "It'll be good for both of us."

Lisa smiled, some of the old brightness in it.

"We'll wow them," she said.

"You already wow Kelly."

Lisa tipped her head. "You think so?"

"I know so, young lady. Let's go. We're already late."

Chris arrived at the Tabor home exactly on time, and immediately knew he had dressed too formally. Kelly Tabor was dressed in slacks and a polo shirt, his mouth stretched in a wide welcoming grin. "I should have told you we do things rather informally down here."

Chris was, if anything, resilient. With an easy grin of his own, he slipped off his jacket and tie, and rolled up his sleeves.

"Much better," Kelly said. "Come meet my mother. Meara and Lisa haven't arrived yet."

Chris hesitated. "Before they do, I would like to make an appointment with you. Tomorrow morning, if possible. I have to convey a temporary power of attorney."

"No problem," Kelly said. "I have a court date in the morning, but my legal secretary can handle the power of attorney easily. I'll talk to her first thing, and you can come in any time after nine."

"Thanks."

"For business? Hell, I have to thank Meara. How long do you plan to be here?"

"Two to three weeks, possibly longer."

Kelly nodded. "If you need anything else—" Just then a woman, tall, slender and of an age comparable to Chris's, entered the room. Her auburn hair was tinged with gray, and she had the warm brown eyes of her son. "Mr. Chandler?"

Kelly's mouth twitched. "If you wait a moment, Mother, I'll introduce you properly. Chris Chandler, my mother, Evelyn Tabor. Mother, this is Chris Chandler."

Evelyn smiled at him warmly and held out her hand. "I understand you're a friend of Sanders's and Meara's."

Feeling the fraud he was, Chris nodded. "I was sorry to hear of Sanders's death. He was a good man."

"That he was," Evelyn said. "We miss him, too."

"Can I get you a drink?" Kelly interjected.

"Scotch and water if you have it."

Kelly nodded.

"Light on the Scotch," Chris added.

Kelly disappeared into the other room.

Chris turned all his attention to Evelyn. "It was kind of you and Kelly to invite me. I travel a lot, and it's very nice to get a home-cooked meal."

"I don't know how home-cooked it is. Kelly's cooking some steaks outside. He thought you might enjoy that more."

"Sounds perfect," Chris said, glancing casually around the house, trying to stifle the desire to look at the door, toward the windows. "You have a lovely home here."

"Thank you. My husband built it, along with several other homes on the island."

"A builder?"

"No, a lawyer, but he was interested in many things. Too many. He died two years ago of a heart attack. He could never slow down."

"I'm sorry," Chris said.

"Don't be," Evelyn said with a smile. "He lived exactly the way he wanted to."

"And is your son like that?" Don't pry, Chris told himself. But, damn it, he wanted to know everything about Kellen Tabor. He wanted to know if he was an ally. And if he kept talking, perhaps he wouldn't be quite as nervous as he was. Christ, he was a bundle of nerves.

"No. Kelly's a good attorney, and he often works long hours but he also can enjoy a sunset. My husband never could."

The doorbell rang just as Kelly returned to the room, holding two glasses. Chris took one, and Kelly held the other while Evelyn answered the door.

They were both beautiful. His daughter. And . . . Meara. He allowed himself only a moment to study them both: Meara's stiff expression, Lisa's curious one as she looked his way.

Kelly quickly made the introductions to Lisa, who looked up at Chris with two of the widest blue eyes he had ever seen. Chris took her hand for the briefest of seconds, just long enough for politeness, before he did the same with Meara, but it was Meara who snatched her hand away, and Chris wondered if she'd felt the same impact as he had. His hand felt like fire.

"It's good to see you again, Meara," he said, and his smile broadened at the almost wistful look she gave him. But her mouth smiled. A little. Mechanically. And he knew that whatever he was feeling, she was probably even more uncertain, more apprehensive.

It was Lisa who broke the sudden silence. "Kelly said you knew my father."

My father.

"Only slightly," Michael said. "But I liked him." True enough. Liked. Admired. Envied.

She gave him a smile, slow and sad and incredibly sweet, that slid straight into his heart, and he knew he had already started storing memories. Just as he had with Meara. Memories that would have to be like snapshots, indelibly etched in his mind, for he would have nothing else. In a few weeks he would be gone, out of her life once more, and it was better that way. For her. For Meara.

But hell for him. Just this brief taste of what could have been.

"I want to know all about how you knew him," Lisa said, her face serious and intense.

"Later," Kelly said. "Right now, I require an assistant cook."

Lisa grinned suddenly, making her face startlingly beautiful. "To keep you from burning everything."

"An infamy," Kelly decried with twinkling eyes that admitted the accuracy of her charge.

"But true," Lisa said with the insistence of a long time friend. But she gave Chris an apologetic smile and left the room with Kelly.

"Gin and tonic, Meara?" Evelyn asked.

"Yes, thank you."

"I'll be back in a minute."

Don't go. Meara nodded.

After she left, Meara turned to face Chris. She had to remember. His name was Chris, not Michael. His smile had come so easily with Lisa, but then it always had. He could turn charm on and off as abruptly as a water faucet. There was no sign of the same tension, the same heartbreaking apprehension as there was in her. It seemed as if he had met a complete stranger. The dark side of her felt resentment. Then reason took hold. What, for Heaven's sake, had she wanted him to do? Grab Lisa and declare everything? She bit her lip, trying to make sense of something that had no sense.

"Meara?"

His voice was low, pleading, as if he understood.

She turned slowly.

His face was as it had been, seemingly relaxed, but the

side of his mouth twitched with something like anxiety, and his hand raked his hair in a way she recognized. He only did so in times of great stress. That she did know.

But while she admired his control, she hated it too. Had always hated it. It had covered so much duplicity.

"Yes?" she managed coolly.

"She's . . . lovely."

"And young . . . too young for all this—" Meara's voice broke. "Too young to know . . . terror."

"So were you, Meara." For a second the control was gone, his voice reaching out to her, his eyes beseeching in a pleading way she had never seen before.

"I couldn't bear it if anything happened to her."

"Nothing will." There was so much pained emotion in his assurance, yet confidence too. It gave her confidence. She looked at him and wondered how seconds ago she could have believed he was taking the meeting lightly. He was hurting. As much as she ever had.

She knew that. And she knew something else in that instant. *She still loved him.* No thought she'd ever had was more frightening, more cataclysmic. But now as she saw the raw pain and defeat and loneliness in his eyes and felt its impact, she knew she had never stopped loving him. And never would.

He must never know. For her daughter's sake. For her own sake. For no matter how much she loved him, she would never entirely trust him again. He was a chameleon, able to blend in anywhere with an ease that astounded her.

How easily he had mingled with members of the Jekyll Island Club, with the Connor family, even with Sanders, who had been trained to ferret out such impostors. And now president of a successful company. A spy. A German spy now a respectable and obviously wealthy American businessman. All through subterfuge, through lies. How could she ever believe him?

But she did. She had believed his warning about Kurt Weimer. Part of that, she justified, had been her own instinct, her immediate aversion to the German, and it was not wholly because of her own experience with a German years ago. Despite what the man now with her had done, she had never sensed evil around him, had never felt the chill of cold ruthlessness as she had with Weimer.

Now Chris Chandler seemed very alone and exposed, standing awkwardly with hand partially outstretched as if in entreaty, unable to claim his daughter, unable to say what he so obviously seemed compelled to say. She swallowed against sympathy, against the welling warmth within her.

She heard Evelyn's footsteps before seeing her, just in time to turn away, to compose her face, for Michael to compose his face.

"Mr. Chandler, can I get you anything else?" Evelyn said.

"Chris," Meara heard him say in that damnably seductive voice of his. Chris. Of course, Chris. Not Michael. Michael was gone. The chameleon.

"All right, Chris then," she heard Evelyn say, and Meara's eyes went to the other woman, seeing the light in her eyes as she looked at her guest. Meara felt jealousy, wild and fierce, jolt through her. Evelyn was an attractive woman, intelligent and active, and she had obviously already succumbed to her guest's easy charm.

This dinner was going to be a nightmare.

But it wasn't, and one reason was Chris. He was the perfect guest, keeping the conversation going, asking impersonal questions which somehow turned personal until he knew the particular interests of everyone at the table. He even made Lisa laugh, something much too rare since Sanders's death, when he described his feelings the first time he topped a tree as a lumberjack, how scared he had been as the earth got farther and farther away.

Except no one at the table believed he'd been scared. There was a self-assurance about Christopher Chandler that proclaimed he could, and did, handle anything that might confront him.

Despite the banter, though, Meara detected a certain tension. She suspected she was the only one to see it, and then only because she knew his expressions so well, remembered the way his mouth had firmed when his injured leg had hurt. She wondered now how he had climbed those trees with it—probably only through that enormous willpower and determination she had come to know so well years ago when he'd continued to walk even though she knew he was in agony. It was the one thing she had never stopped admiring about him.

Lisa, however, was obviously fascinated with the man who had been a lumberjack and was now president of a business. She was "into" the environment now, and she wanted to know whether the lumber industry wasn't destroying the forests.

"Some do," he admitted. "Our company tries to do as little damage as possible, replanting trees when we're finished. We know it takes hundreds of years to replace these trees. But you live in houses made of wood, and you read books whose pages come from forests. It's a trade-off."

"But I've seen pictures of whole forests laid bare," she said.

Chris's eyes warmed. He liked her concern, the passion which reminded him of Meara. "It happens," he said slowly. "I've backed legislation that would require lumber companies to reseed and replant, but many of the industry leaders don't agree, and they have powerful influence."

"It seems we're destroying everything," she said sadly.

"Sometimes you have to destroy to build," Chris said.

Lisa looked at him quizzically. "That's a cryptic remark."

Chris grinned. "I guess it is. You're a very bright young lady."

Lisa was obviously delighted with the conversation, with the challenge of dueling with someone like Chandler, who treated her as an equal.

"That was a cop-out," she observed dryly.

They all laughed at that, even Meara, who felt a peculiar sense of rightness about how well Chris and her daughter appeared to get along. There was even a brightness in his eyes she'd never seen before.

"You would make a good lawyer," he remarked.

She laughed. "You knew."

"That you wanted to be a lawyer. I think someone mentioned it, but then I could have guessed."

"Eventually, I want to join the FBI, if they ever open it to women." It was a challenge of sorts, to see whether he would laugh or condescend, as so many others did.

"Like your father," he said quietly, and Lisa knew immediately he understood.

"Yes," she said softly.

"I think," he said, "you can do anything you want to." *Like your mother if I hadn't interfered. But then there wouldn't be a Lisa.* For the first time in years some of the bitter guilt dissipated.

"You're right," Kelly said. "But I'm trying to get her to join my firm when she's through. Tabor and Evans. Has a nice ring to it."

"Evans and Tabor," Lisa complained, and they laughed again at the teasing complaint in her voice.

Meara sat back in her chair, her knife and fork doing little but moving food around. She was terribly restless, her shoulders cramping with tension she couldn't release. She had no reason to fear; he was perfect with her daughter, revealing nothing other than ordinary interest in and appreciation of a charming young girl. He displayed just as much interest in Kelly and Evelyn. And in her when his eyes turned to her direction and regarded her levelly, all his thoughts and emotions concealed behind that shield she knew so well.

"Tell me how you knew my father," Lisa said suddenly, and Meara thought the silence stretched out over years instead of the few seconds it actually did.

Chris hesitated, but he had prepared himself for the question since Meara's call. "We met years ago when he was on a case."

"What case?"

"I never knew exactly," Chris answered. "Or how it turned out. I don't think he could talk about it."

"But you became friends?"

"Yes," Chris said. "I think we did."

It was as fine a combination of nonanswers as Meara had ever heard, a tiny kernel of truth in each one. But Lisa didn't question them. Her father seldom talked about his cases, and never about ones involving U.S. security.

It was Meara who changed the subject, her first contribution to the conversation all night. "How do you find our coast compared to the Pacific?"

Chris's eyes fastened on her, grateful for the switch in topics. How to answer? He came to life on this island, not because of the coast but because of her. The difference between day and night, light and darkness.

"It's . . . gentler," he said cautiously. "More peaceful."

"Not always," she returned quickly, unable to keep the challenge from her voice, and Lisa looked at her strangely. "We get," she continued more carefully, "some really bad storms, even hurricanes."

The slightest movement of a muscle in his cheek was the

only indication he knew that wasn't what she meant at all, that she was remembering that night of violence.

There was a sudden silence at the table, as if all five were aware of a sudden mistral gusting through the room.

Kelly felt it too, the uncomfortable feeling that something was happening he didn't understand. Meara's usually composed face looked uncertain, anxious, but then it had been only little more than a month since her husband's death, and he knew it had affected her much more than she'd let others realize. He had seen it in the despairing way her shoulders had slumped when she walked the beaches, the emptiness in her eyes. Lisa, he suspected, hadn't seen it, or helped share it, because she had been too involved in her own grief.

Quite gently, he broke the uncomfortable silence by offering more wine, an offer readily accepted by everyone but Chandler, who had nearly a full glass remaining.

Kelly then turned the conversation to the elections the following year. President Kennedy, whose popularity had plummeted, was already campaigning hard. Kelly admitted wryly to being one of the few Republicans in the state, but said he would probably vote for Kennedy this time though not happily. Lisa was a committed Democrat, so the conversation was spirited with good-natured teasing while Meara and Chris listened, a slight smile on the latter's lips as he enjoyed Lisa's defense of Kennedy.

"He makes us feel good about ourselves," she argued. "He cares about people."

"But he's ineffectual," Kelly contended with a smile.

"Only because of stuffy conservative Republicans," she retorted.

Kelly lowered an eyebrow accusingly. "Stuffy?"

"Stuffy," she confirmed.

Evelyn Tabor laughed. "My son's been accused of a lot of things, but I don't think stuffy is one of them."

"Well, his politics are," Lisa said defensively.

Kelly looked over to Chris. "Help!"

"I can't," he said with amusement. "I'm on her side."

"Outnumbered," Kelly grumbled. "Meara?"

"Don't look to me for help," she said, a smile finally playing on her mouth.

"I guess I know when I'm surrounded," he said. "What about the Yankees . . ."

The tension faded away as the bickering switched to baseball. Meara didn't even wonder at Chris's extensive knowledge of baseball as he and Kelly debated the merits of various west and east coast teams. Nothing, she decided, surprised her any more. She looked up and saw his eyes on her. Then he looked away and she felt suddenly deprived, cold, empty. The feeling lasted as the evening wore on until she was finally, thankfully, able to leave graciously.

Chris took her hand in parting, just as he did Evelyn's, and she hated herself for the warmth that started there and flowed throughout her body.

"It's been delightful," he told his hosts. "I hope I can reciprocate by taking you out to dinner. All of you," he corrected turning to Meara and Lisa.

Evelyn nodded, as did Kelly.

"I—I'll have to see," Meara hesitated.

"I'll call," Chris promised. "May I walk you both to the house?"

"It's just next door," Meara said, wanting desperately to get away from his spell.

"Then it's no trouble." He didn't give her a chance to say more, but took her arm, politely but firmly. He waited until Meara unlocked the door, then turned away. When Meara got inside, she started to close the blinds and saw him standing in front, his eyes on the house. When he saw Meara in the window, he gave her a rueful grin before turning away.

"I liked him," Lisa said behind her.

Had she seen him standing there? She doubted it. She hoped not.

"Did you know him well?" Lisa probed again.

"I barely knew him at all . . . and it was years ago," Meara said honestly. She *hadn't* known him at all. She only thought she had.

"Well I liked him a lot. He reminded me a little of Daddy." It was the highest compliment Lisa could give.

Meara felt queasy. Of course, Lisa liked him. Charm was his stock and trade.

Damn his soul, it was working again. Even knowing everything she did, it was working again.

Chris stuffed his hands in the pockets of his trousers. He hoped like hell Meara didn't realize how difficult it had been to take his hand from her elbow.

Or how difficult it was to take his hands from her at all.

He was so damned afraid she would run like hell if he hadn't.

But he'd had twenty-one years of learning to control his emotions, of regretting the two weeks when he had not. He would not make that mistake again. He couldn't bear hurting her again.

Chris walked past his rented house. He didn't go in. It was empty. Empty and lonely. His suit coat over his shoulder, he continued to walk to the dunes, down to the ocean. Since the evening when he'd confronted her on the beach, he had not come here again at night. He hadn't wanted to.

It had not been far from here, the first time he had made love to Meara. He felt a smile come to his lips as he remembered how sweet it had been, how sweet and desperate and all-consuming. He had never thought of the sexual act as sweet before that time. She had taught him. The incredible sweetness of honey mixed with tempestuous passion. Nothing had been so fine before, or since, nothing so exquisitely painful. Then she had tried so hard not to ask anything of him, but in not doing so, she had asked much more.

He had been unable to give it to her, to give anything to her.

Except Lisa.

He sat on one of the rocks that now constituted a sea wall, protection of the dunes against the encroaching sea. So much was the same that he almost expected Meara to appear, just as she had the other dark night, the night he had returned from contacting the U-boat. It all seemed so long ago, so unlikely. A bad play with a melodramatic ending.

Since he had been here, he had read several short histories of the island, seeking to find confirmation that it had all indeed happened. There were references to a rumor that the Jekyll Island Club had been closed by order of the government, even supposition that General George Patton himself had arrived to make sure the club was closed for fear of German raids. Another account, however, described the rumors as nonsense. The club merely closed because of the war, the shortages.

Americans. He was one now. Of sorts. Unless he was discovered, his real identity revealed. What would he be then? A man without a country. He had betrayed Germany, despite the reasons or intentions behind it. He had spied on America.

He remembered when Meara had once asked him whether he had a home. What had he answered then? He didn't remember exactly, but he knew then as he did now that he belonged nowhere, that he never had. Seattle had been merely a stopping place, a temporary shelter from the storm. It had never been home. Home was where people you loved were.

Home had been here, for two weeks, two bright weeks one spring. Meara's island of dreams. It had been his, too.

He closed his eyes. Perhaps when he opened them, she would be here as she once had been, walking toward him with those bright eyes, that wistful smile.

But when he opened them, he was still alone. He shivered, but not with cold. The surf seemed to mock his thoughts. Alone. Alone. Alone . . .

Meara made herself a cup of hot chocolate and went out on the porch. She had tried to sleep, but couldn't. She stared out at the dunes beyond.

He was out there. She knew it.

He was out there waiting.

Dear Heaven, how did she know that?

A short walk, and his arms would enfold her, comfort her, love her. She knew that too.

One of her nails dug into the palm of her hand, and she felt the warm trickle of blood.

She wouldn't. She couldn't. Not again. Never again would she expose herself and her daughter to the kind of pain she had once experienced. Never again.

Sanders, she screamed silently. You've always been there. Why aren't you here now?

The silence was deafening. She had to depend on herself. She had to make herself stronger than Michael, than the call that reached out to her. Chameleon, she told herself again. A darting, elusive, cunning creature. Sometimes even beautiful when its colors caught the sun, but then the colors turned drab as they melded into those of the earth.

Changing. Always changing, the brilliance swift and temporary and treacherous.

With a groan that rose from deep in her soul, she turned back toward her room, feet dragging. It would be a long night. A very, very long, lonely night.

Chapter Twenty-Five

"**H**OW DO I LOOK?"

Lisa's voice was clear and happy as she swept into the den where Meara was working, trying to work, on an article.

Meara looked up at her daughter and breath caught in her throat. Lisa was wearing a cocktail dress, a dark blue that made her eyes darker, almost like Michael's. There were two thin straps holding up the bodice, and a flared skirt that swung gracefully around Lisa's long, lovely legs.

She looked young and fresh and innocent. So innocent that Meara thought her heart would break. How could she allow Lisa to go out this night with Kurt Weimer? How could she allow evil to touch her?

Meara had asked Michael that earlier in a panicked phone call.

Patiently, Michael—Chris—had reviewed her options. She could tie her daughter up, lock her in a room, plead with her to break the date, tell her daughter everything, or . . . trust him. Nothing, he assured her, would happen

393

to Lisa. He had all the bases covered. All of them. Lisa would never be out of sight of the detectives he had hired.

Two additional men had joined the original couple. One had even hired on to help with the banquet tonight. Another had purchased one of the coveted invitations to the dinner and bribed the staff to place his name card next to Weimer's. They were the best, Michael said. The very best.

A bugging device had been planted in Weimer's cottage, and technicians were listening in a truck sent to repair a water leak in an adjoining cottage. Michael did not explain the opportune leak.

But still, Meara could barely tolerate the thought of the man with Lisa, even under a hundred watchful eyes.

She had tried to write all afternoon: a proposal to a history publication that had previously published several of her articles. She had established a solid reputation in that field, and had even sold an article on Georgia's coastal islands to *National Geographic.* That had been her prize piece. But now the words wouldn't come, nor the thoughts organize in any logical way. All she had been able to do was wonder whether she was wrong in keeping the past secret, whether she was endangering her daughter by protecting herself. If only she thought the knowledge wouldn't destroy her daughter, destroy her faith and pride and love in both Sanders and herself.

Perhaps Lisa was stronger than she thought. But was anyone strong at twenty, and twenty-two? She hadn't been. She had thought she was. She had thought herself strong and indestructible and even wise. And she had been so wrong.

Meara had wanted to die those weeks and even months after Easter. Only the baby and Sanders had kept her alive. But she had lost all confidence in herself, and it had stayed lost for a long time.

She couldn't let that happen to Lisa. She couldn't destroy Lisa's world. She couldn't let Lisa know she had been lied to all these years by both herself and the father she'd loved so completely.

Lies. How easily they took over a life until they almost became truth.

"You look lovely, darling," she said at last.

Lisa looked nervous. "There's going to be so many important people there—diplomats, economists. . . ."

"They'll think you're enchanting," Meara said softly, meeting Lisa's surprised and grateful look. Had she been so stingy on compliments, in talking to Lisa?

"You don't think this dress makes me look too young?"

"No," Meara said. "I think you look perfect."

"I don't know what time I'll be home," Lisa said a little awkwardly, and Meara knew she was being asked not to question Kurt Weimer about that topic.

"Lisa," Meara said suddenly. "You will be careful, won't you. He's . . . different from the men you know."

Lisa's eyes shone in a way that Meara didn't like at all.

"I know, but he's been a perfect gentleman. And he's exciting. Imagine someone like that being . . . interested in me."

That, Meara was afraid, was part of the attraction. She had wondered the same thing with Michael Fielding. How could someone so attractive and experienced be interested in her? Well, she had found out. He'd needed her, needed her contacts. Just as Kurt Weimer needed Lisa for some reason of his own.

"Just make sure he continues to be the perfect gentlemen," Meara warned.

"I will. I have no intention of getting involved with anyone. Not until I finish school. But he *is* fascinating."

Just then the bell rang, and Meara slowly went to the

door, wondering how she could keep the aversion and dislike from her eyes.

Kurt Weimer was breathtakingly handsome in formal
clothes. He bowed slightly in a European manner, or what
Meara thought was a European manner.

"Mrs. Evans," he said smoothly with a smile. "Is Lisa
ready?"

Meara nodded, turning away before he could see the
cold hostility in her eyes. She went over to Lisa, touching
her lightly. She wanted to grab Lisa, to hold her away from
this . . . intruder. But she merely said "Good night."

Then they were gone, and she felt herself crumpling into
a ball on the sofa. How could she? Dear God, how could
she let Lisa leave with the man? Cold chills ran through
her until she shook.

She couldn't do it. She started for the door, opening
it, ready to go after them. As she opened it, Michael was
standing there, tall and strong, his eyes serious and concerned, his mouth grim.

"She'll be all right," he promised. "I swear she'll be all
right."

He'd known. He'd known exactly how she felt. She
looked up at him, knowing her heart was in her eyes, and
he opened his arms and pulled her against him. "She'll be
all right," he said again, and, God help her, she believed
him.

He stayed for several hours, talking. After the initial embrace, he very carefully kept his distance, sitting in a chair
away from hers. He was there, she knew, to keep her from
going crazy, from doing something that might ruin everything.

He talked about Seattle, his business. About everything
but their common past.

He made them some coffee, several pots, and they drank
them all, the act of bringing a cup to lips a distraction

against what they both feared, a defense against moving together.

Chris sprawled in his chair, his mind every bit as frantic as he knew Meara's must be. He had nearly gone crazy earlier in the afternoon. He had slowly walked up and down the street at the time he expected Weimer, and had watched the man come and leave . . . with Lisa. With his daughter. He had to restrain himself from charging the man, from killing him then and there.

He had been a bundle of erupting violence when he bounded up to Meara's door. Her white face, her shaking body, had stunned him to the point he could only open his arms to her. She had felt so good in them. For a few moments until she had jerked back, wariness still in her eyes. But she hadn't asked him to leave. She needed him. As much as he needed her.

He had to fight himself. Every minute he had to fight himself. He wanted to touch her, to hold her, to comfort her, to comfort himself. But he had taken advantage of her before, and he wouldn't do it again. He might be no wiser now in wanting something he couldn't have, no less susceptible to her, but he had learned control. Dear God, how he had learned control.

So he soothed with neutral words, with neutral actions, although every part of his mind and soul ached for more.

They talked, almost as friends, but not quite. There was always the sharp sword there between them, a reminder of past hurts and past betrayal, and past pain.

He often found her gaze on him, steady and searching, trying, he guessed, to decide whether or not to trust him. And every time she did so, he felt emotion slamming through him, his body tensing with almost unbearable need.

She was so pretty. So soft and pretty, with the red gold hair feathering around her face and the green eyes so vul-

nerable and her lips red and swollen from where she had
bit them. She had curled her legs under her body, and she
looked like a girl, like the girl who once sat that way on
the beach happy and carefree. How he wanted to give those
two things back to her.

Searching almost desperately to break the leaden, taut
silence, Meara asked the question she had been asking herself for years. "What's your real name?"

"Eric." There was a rough uncertain edge in his voice.
He didn't want the reminder. But he owed it to her. He
owed that and much more. "Eric von Steimen."

"Eric," she tried, lifting her eyes to meet his directly. "It
suits you." It did. He had once seemed a blond God to
her, and the Viking image fit him well. Sailor. Raider. Warrior.

"I haven't heard it for a long time," he said, almost
wonderingly.

"Your family . . . ?"

"My father died in the early days of the war," he said,
his voice suddenly harsh. "My mother and younger
brother died in the bombing. They thought I had died
here. A German hero." The last comment was bitter and
self-mocking. "She was Canadian—that's one reason I was
selected, that and the fact I spoke English perfectly because
of her. She was trapped in Germany, and they used her
as a weapon against me. And there wasn't a damn thing
I could do about it."

Meara stared at him, hearing the frustrated helplessness
in his voice.

"Why . . . Christopher Chandler?"

He smiled, a tight, grim smile without humor. "A tomb-
stone. Now that *was* something I learned in Admiral Canaris's little spy school . . . how to obtain a new identity.
Find the grave of a child. There's usually a birth certificate
available, and then you can get any kind of identification

you require." Self-loathing was evident in his voice as he recited the procedure as if by rote.

Meara absorbed each piece of information, weighing the cold words against the swift emotions moving across his face. She was amazed that they were there; they had seldom been there in the past.

"How did you get away that night?"

He didn't want to answer. He didn't want her to know he had planned everything. But he was through lying.

"There was a fishing boat I'd found earlier. When I was in St. Simons with Sanders, I purchased a small motor. After the . . . explosion, I swam to the other end of the island and reached it."

Meara closed her eyes, remembering the fiery explosion. "I . . . thought . . ."

He flinched against the sound of her voice. Grief was still in it. Grief for him, even after she'd learned about him.

"I . . . wanted to die too," she continued in a small voice.

Spasms shook him. He looked down and his hand was shaking, but he couldn't stop it. He fought for breath that was caught somewhere in his throat. Revulsion at what he had done to her, the memories he had made her live with, swamped him. He wanted to hold out his hand to her, but he couldn't. Even if he did, she'd have every right and reason to knock it away.

Saying he was sorry wasn't enough. Nothing would ever be enough. But perhaps by helping her now, by helping Lisa, he could mitigate some of the terrible injury he had done her.

He looked at her levelly. "Do you want me to go?"

"Yes . . . no . . . I don't know," Meara said. And she didn't. He offered strength and power at the moment, strength she badly needed, yet he still sent her senses spiraling in storm-tossed confusion. She would always look at him and, under that stoic handsome facade, see something else, something she didn't know if she could ever accept.

"I think I do," he said softly as he rose. "Call me if you need anything."

"Do you really think she'll be all right?" Meara said. "The thought of him touching her—"

"The agency I hired specializes in protection," he replied softly. "We'll get him. I don't know exactly how yet, but we will. And Lisa is bright and sensible."

"I thought I was too," Meara said wistfully and without malice.

The words were like a razor to him, shredding skin away piece by piece, as he realized she was comparing him with Weimer.

Well, she had no reason not to.

"Good night," he said carefully, not wanting to show how much her words, intended or not, had wounded. "I'll call you if I hear anything."

She nodded, not rising from the sofa, sitting there blankly as she heard the door close behind him. Don't go, she said silently. Please don't go.

But it was too late.

Lisa felt like Cinderella. It had been an exciting, stimulating, thrilling evening, and Kurt Weimer was her prince.

She had never felt quite as pretty as when he leaned over and whispered compliments in her ear, his soft breath intimate as it brushed her skin. She was the loveliest woman in the room, he'd said.

She couldn't help it, but she was swept up by the power here. Economists and diplomats from around the world stopped at their table, their greetings respectful when directed at Kurt and flattering when addressed to her. Kurt translated, and it was quite obvious that he spoke several languages fluently.

This was one of the few formal occasions of the conference, he had told her, and was hosted by the U.S. State Department. Most of the other women there were wives of American hosts and delegates.

There were formal toasts and the food was exquisite, each course served with a different wine. Baked Alaska climaxed the elaborate meal. Entertainment included a Broadway star who sang a selection of Rodgers and Hammerstein songs, and finally an orchestra for dancing.

When Kurt first asked her to dance, she felt a flurry of fear that she might embarrass him, but he was a superb dancer, graceful and powerful, and she found herself more comfortable than she had ever been on the dance floor. He was incredibly easy to follow. When she looked up at him, his eyes were warm and admiring, his mouth smiling.

"Happy?" he asked as he led them back to the table after one dance.

"Hummmm," she murmured, her mind still whirling like a dervish.

He held the chair out for her as she sat, and excused himself for a moment. "There's someone I must see a moment," he said, his eyes lingering on her face a moment before leaving.

Lisa glanced around the table. She was the only woman among the eight. The others included five economists and an executive from the *Wall Street Journal*, and he had interested her more than the others although Kurt had claimed most of her attention. The newsman was heavyset with alert eyes and a lively sense of humor.

"A delightful picture," he observed. "You look like you'd been dancing together all your lives."

Lisa blushed. "He's a very good dancer."

"Ah, but he can't do it alone."

"No," Lisa admitted with a gleam of humor as she considered Kurt dancing by himself in the middle of the room.

"Perhaps you would honor me with a dance?" he said, "although I have to warn you that my feet are not nearly as light as Mr. Weimer's."

"I think I'll risk it," she said, unable to refuse his good-natured invitation.

He was much lighter than he looked, and a much better dancer than his words, and Lisa found herself enjoying his thoroughly disrespectful monologue as he discussed the recent toasts. "International cooperation, indeed," he chuckled. "Given a chance they would all cut each other's throats for a deutsche mark or a pound or a franc. They're here to discover how to outwit each other."

"You're a cynic, Mr. Taylor."

"Ah yes, a necessity of my trade, lovely lady. And how did Mr. Weimer happen to find you?"

"I live here."

"Ah, he has a fine eye for opportunity."

Lisa leaned back. "I don't know if I exactly like . . . that choice of words."

"Then pardon me. I'm only jealous I didn't see you first." He was flirtingly insincere, and she knew it, but he did it with such an impish look in his eye, she had to laugh.

"I think you're a rake, Mr. Taylor."

"And I think you're much too observant, Miss Evans. But our Mr. Weimer. Is he not a rake too?"

"I don't know," she said, suddenly serious as she considered the question.

One of his hands tightened slightly around her waist. "I know his reputation, lovely lady. Be cautious."

Lisa stumbled. There was something very serious in the warning, in his voice, but suddenly his hand relaxed and the devil was back in his eye. Imagination, she thought. Only imagination.

The music stopped, and she had no more time to wonder. She was being led back to the table, and Kurt was there, his smile strained. She caught a glimpse of cold, hard anger, as if he were furious that she had danced with the newspaperman. But like Mr. Taylor's enigmatic warning, the look fled quickly, and he was thanking the other man for keeping her occupied.

But something in that momentary look bothered her. It had been calculating, the warmth gone. Some of the pleasure of the evening disappeared.

When they started to leave, he asked her to his cottage for a nightcap, his hand running down her arm in slow, sensual movements, and Lisa felt a stab of apprehension, that she was, in some way, beyond her depth.

"Not tonight," she demurred softly. "I'm really very tired."

His hand tightened momentarily, then relaxed. "Very well," he said with a fleeting smile. "I want you to be fresh and relaxed tomorrow," he said. "For our outing."

Suddenly, she didn't want to go, but she didn't know why. Surely, it wasn't Mr. Taylor's remark. It had only been in jest, she was sure of it.

Lisa was quiet on the ride home. At her door, he leaned down and brushed her lips, and then deepened the kiss as if he couldn't restrain himself. "Lisa," he whispered, and Lisa responded slowly to his searching mouth, wondering why she didn't feel more than she did. She had expected fireworks, but while the kiss was pleasant, she felt a curious lack of warmth.

Perhaps she was tired. Perhaps she hadn't gotten over the numbness caused by her father's death.

When he finally released her mouth, he put his hand up and took her chin in his fingers. "Tomorrow, Lisa," he said.

"Thank you," she returned. "Thank you for a perfectly lovely night."

"I'll pick you up at ten tomorrow," he whispered. "Until then, happy dreams." His hand lingered a moment longer, and then he turned around and strode to the Mercedes he had rented.

She watched him drive away, surprised at the sudden relief she felt.

Chapter Twenty-Six

KURT REACHED HIS cottage well after midnight. Another hour and he would call Stefan Kranz, his mentor and now colleague in Odessa.

He had collected some newspapers, and he read them carefully. Civil rights demonstrations were continuing in Atlanta and throughout the southeast. Sit-ins and marches were more and more common. Martin Luther King, Jr., was planning a march on Washington, and violence was rife all over the South, spurring the rapid growth of white supremacist groups. Another black church had been burned in Alabama; a civil rights worker had been shot in Mississippi.

One of the white supremacist groups had announced a rally to counteract the proposed civil rights march on Washington. The group, the White Citizens Brotherhood, was holding the rally in Atlanta in two days. Kurt knew the group well. He and others had already directed money into the Brotherhood and to other white supremacist groups believed to be viable. Now was the time to capitalize on them, to guide them, to build a force in this country. Now—when southern anger was at its peak.

The leader of the Brotherhood was a charismatic young white man who was seeking to bring the various groups— Ku Klux Klan and other white supremacist organizations—together. It might be well worth his time to make a trip up to Atlanta and watch the man in action, and determine exactly how much, if any, additional support should be given him.

He would, he knew, have to be very, very careful. He could not be recognized, but that was easy enough: a pair of wire-rimmed glasses, a different part in his hair, a hat, and some workers' clothes. He had helped enough fugitives escape Germany that he knew every trick.

Kurt looked at his watch and then thought about the evening. It had been mostly successful, he thought. Lisa Evans had appeared delighted and impressed with the evening, and had looked at him with a tinge of awe when they had danced. He'd been disappointed when she had refused his invitation to his cottage, but he was not entirely surprised. The plan would simply require a little longer than he'd thought to break through that middle-class morality. The end would be all the more sweeter for her reticence. He had no doubt he would succeed.

At exactly one o'clock, he called Stefan, and the phone on the other end was picked up almost immediately.

"Is the line safe?" Stefan asked almost immediately.

"*Ja,*" Kurt answered. There was no reason to believe it wasn't.

"We're having some problems in Argentina," Stefan said in German. "One of our . . . assets believes he's been discovered by the Israelis. We've got to get him out and provide him with a new identity."

"Who?" There was a number of former SS officers in

Argentina, most of whom were wanted by Israel for their part in the so-called Final Solution.

"The Bull."

There was a pause. The Bull was the nickname they had given one of the top officers at Auschwitz. "Give the job to Dieter. We have an account in Rio. Do whatever is necessary to get him out, or if it's too late, neutralize him. He knows too much about us."

"That was the opinion here," Stefan replied. "We are agreed then. When will you return?"

"A week later than expected."

There was a silence. "The personal business?"

"Yes. It will take longer than I thought."

"Don't jeopardize everything, Kurt."

"I know what I'm doing," Kurt replied tersely. "There will be nothing to trace. Nothing at all. I'm going to visit one of the American groups tomorrow night. The White Citizens Brotherhood. It should prove interesting."

"I don't know if that's wise right now. There's a lot of interest—too much interest—in our small organization."

"We need support in other countries to achieve what we must," Kurt said. "You know that."

"We can't afford to lose you. Not now."

"Have faith, Stefan. Nothing worthwhile is accomplished without risks, you know that."

"But you take too many."

"*Nein,*" Kurt replied. "There is no suspicion. I am an honored, respected guest of the American government."

"Try to keep it that way," Stefan said. "In two weeks then."

The conversation completed, Kurt replaced the phone gently. He went over it word by word. Damn it, but Stefan continued to try to control him, just as he had when he was a boy. But it didn't work anymore. Kurt had as much, if not more, power than his one-time mentor. The fact that

Stefan needed his approval in the Argentina matter indicated as much.

Kurt knew no one could stop him now. He was well on his way to more power, and he was building support outside of Odessa, a necessary precaution. It was one reason he wanted to view Robert Cannon, the commander of the White Citizens Brotherhood, personally. Then he would set up a very private meeting.

But first things first. The picnic tomorrow. Time to further disarm and charm Lisa Evans. He might even start hinting at marriage. That usually accelerated matters, he thought quite coldly. He had used the technique before in seduction.

It could be quite enjoyable. Miss Evans had very kissable lips and very sensuous eyes. Once awakened, she could, he thought, be a very passionate bed partner. But he had also, in the past, enjoyed fear, the sense of power that rape gave him. If Lisa did not cooperate in one way, she would in another, he thought with a thin smile.

Kurt Weimer poured himself a glass of schnapps, sipping it slowly and with appreciation.

Lisa was ready when Kurt stopped by the following day. Even in his casual clothes, he looked elegant and sophisticated and again she felt a quick, flattered thrill that he was interested in her.

She had dismissed the brief stab of apprehension she'd felt last night and was determined to enjoy the day despite her mother's lack of enthusiasm.

"I wish you wouldn't go," her mother had said over breakfast.

"Why?" Lisa queried frankly. She really wanted to understand.

Her mother's face was tense, unusually so, and her eyes were tired as if she hadn't slept. Her hands fidgeted nervously on the table, something Lisa had never seen before. "There's just something about . . . him."

"It's because he's German," Lisa guessed. "It does make him a little more formal. But it's sorta nice, too. He's such a complete gentleman it frightens me a little. I'm not used to being treated so elegantly."

Elegantly. Was that what it had been with Michael? The mystery? The attraction of difference? The newness? Or the intensity of the man? Did Kurt Weimer have that same intensity?

"You . . . aren't really interested in him?" Meara finally asked.

Lisa thought for a moment. How did she feel? She was flattered. She was attracted to him. She even occasionally felt a thrill when he touched her. But she didn't feel any deep warmth, nor did she feel altogether comfortable with him, not like she did with Kelly. But for some reason she didn't want to admit that to her mother. Her mother would have been comfortable with him; she was comfortable with everyone.

"He's terribly attractive," she said instead, "but I know he'll be gone soon."

Meara shivered slightly. It was no answer at all. She knew that time, or lack of it, could often be more of a catalyst than less of one. She changed the subject. "Kelly called last night."

Lisa glanced up, relieved that the subject was changed. She didn't want to talk about Kurt Weimer, not when she didn't understand herself how she felt. "What did he want?"

"I think several of his friends were having an impromptu oyster roast on the beach."

"Damn," Lisa said, before looking up guiltily at the unusual profanity, but for some reason she felt unreasonably disappointed. It was ridiculous. After all, she had been the center of attention at an affair most girls only dream of. But oyster roasts were one of her most favorite things. And she didn't want to disappoint Kelly. She thought of him momentarily: the lanky build, the thick but very straight brown hair, and his eyes, most of all his eyes, twinkling light brown, always open and honest.

Unlike Kurt's, which sometimes seemed cold, and even angry.

Now why did she suddenly think that?

"I'll see him in the morning," she said. "Oh," she said as she heard a car drive up. "That must be Kurt. I'll see you later."

"Lisa . . . ?"

Lisa turned and saw panic in her mother's eyes, and then it was gone.

"Be careful," her mother whispered. "Don't be back too late."

"Aw, nothing ever happens around here." Lisa grinned comfortingly. "Nothing at all."

"Nothing," Meara echoed in a bleak voice as the door closed behind her daughter. "Nothing at all."

"We picked up something," Matt told Chris over the telephone. "But the conversation's in German, and I'm damned if I can understand any of it."

"Is he gone?"

"Yes, Kate and another operative are following in different vehicles."

"I'll be over there shortly, then."

"You speak German?"

"I can understand a little of it."

"I'll expect you shortly."

"Thirty minutes." Chris replaced the phone in its cradle. He didn't want to go. Not now. Meara might need him.

But he had to find a way to stop Weimer, and there might be a hint in the conversation. It was just as likely there was not. It could have been an ordinary call to his office. Hell, it could be anything. But he was desperate, and growing more so by the hour although he had tried not to let Meara see it.

He didn't like his helplessness. He wasn't used to waiting and allowing others to fight his battles. Not in the past twenty years, damn it.

Chris let the door slam behind him as he went to his car and drove straight out, glancing only briefly at the Evans's house. He was afraid if he did, he would stop.

He drove over to Sea Island and found Kurt's cottage, and the one next to it with the plumbers' truck parked alongside. He wondered briefly how Matt was arranging such a long time to repair a plumbing leak, but then that was Matt's problem. He parked in some trees and quickly strolled over to the van, knocking lightly on the door.

"Chandler," he announced.

The door opened, and Matt ushered him inside. Another man sat at a table crowded with electronic equipment.

Matt introduced the two men, then turned to the seated man at the desk. "Play the tape."

Chris listened carefully; his mouth was grim but his eyes gleamed with sudden triumph. Kurt Weimer was making his first mistake, and it was a bad one. Like his father, he was too self-confident. When the tape was finished, Matt looked at him expectantly, but Chris didn't explain the contents. "Make me two copies," he said.

He listened again as the technician reran the tape twice, making a copy each time as he did so. Kurt Weimer was as much a fool as his father had been, a fanatical fool searching for a dark kind of power. Although the tape wouldn't constitute any kind of proof, its existence gave Chris a weapon, a very lethal weapon.

And, he knew, it would give the United States government a weapon. The exposure of a top member of the West German government could be devastating to the current leadership. Although the conversation had been careful, the implications were very, very clear and very obvious.

"Keep listening," he told Matt.

Matt shrugged. "It's your money."

"I want to know every move he makes today, every step. I take it your people will call in periodically."

"Every two hours, unless there's something unusual."

"Then call me every time there's a contact."

"Where are you taking that?" Matt's eyes went down to the tape. This was as illegal as hell.

Chris smiled wryly. "Don't worry. It will never be traced back to you." He paused a moment. "There's something else."

Matt raised an eyebrow.

"He's apparently going to Atlanta tomorrow. To a meeting. I want two of your people with him all the time he's there. Two new people. I don't want him to get suspicious. And I want all the pictures you can get."

"Do you know where he's going?"

"I have a damned good idea," Chris said. "Just stay with him. He might try to disguise himself."

"He won't get away from us," Matt said.

Chris's mouth was grim. "He'd better not. Keep me posted. Every two hours."

"Righto."

"And Matt?"

"Yeah?"

"Thanks."

Matt tried to hide his surprise. He had done work before for Chandler, and he had seldom before seen the man perturbed or worried. Now Chandler was both, and he showed it.

"Anytime."

Chris looked around the van. "How long can you stay here?"

Matt grinned. "We just, by accident, discovered the whole pipe system's rotting away in this cottage. We're doing them a real favor working this weekend. Might even take a few days beyond that. Have to cut through walls, then get carpenters to repair the damage. Damn shame. They just don't build things like they used to."

Chris chuckled. "How much is it costing them?"

"Oh, they'll be getting a bargain when we get through," Matt said. "Markham's already made arrangements with the owner for extensive renovation. But it's going to cost you a bundle."

Chris smiled dryly, but merely inquired: "Is there anything Markham can't do?"

"Ain't found it yet if there is," Matt said. "He's got more damned contacts in the strangest places."

Chris nodded. He'd heard the rumors. The owner of the P.I. agency he used was a former federal agent of some kind. That knowledge ordinarily would have scared Chris away. But Ben Markham had a reputation for intense loyalty to his clients, and Chris had never been disappointed.

Without more words, he left.

Would the day never end? Meara reached for the phone a dozen times, but always dropped it midway through dialing. She wouldn't become dependent on him. She wouldn't. He had said he would call if there was any news.

At noon, she tried to eat. Lisa had said she planned to show Kurt Weimer some of the sights, including Savannah, seventy or so miles to the north where they would probably have lunch at one of the city's noted restaurants. How could Chris's detectives possibly watch them all that time? Yet Chris had said several times that Kurt would do nothing openly. He simply couldn't afford it.

What did he want with her daughter?

Just after twelve-thirty, the phone rang. "My people just called," Chris said. "She's fine."

Meara clutched the phone. She needed him. She needed him beside her. She needed his confidence. She needed his strength. "Thank you," she said stiffly.

"Why don't you come over here and wait," he said, an almost pleading note in his voice.

It was exactly what she wanted to do. "No," she said. "I don't think it's wise."

"No," he said softly. "Perhaps it isn't. But I have something for you, something you should have."

"What," she said suspiciously.

"A tape."

"What kind of tape."

"One very damaging to our Mr. Weimer if it fell into the wrong hands," Chris replied.

"Oh," Meara said, considering the answer.

"He's made his first mistake, Meara," Chris continued. "There will be others. He's very sure of himself, which is all to our advantage."

"How?"

"He believes he has time. He thinks no one suspects anything."

"Which means he might take greater risks."

Chris knew she'd pinpointed the problem. Kurt Weimer obviously believed he was immune to detection. Otherwise he wouldn't be fool enough to go where Chris believed he planned to go tomorrow. His silence frightened her.

"Do you think . . . ?"

"I think she's perfectly safe, or else I wouldn't be sitting here," he interrupted with fierce possessiveness. "I would kill him myself if I didn't think there was another way that wouldn't hurt either one of you."

The bitter intensity of his voice startled her. She could almost feel the violence underlining each word. In this one thing, at least, they had a common goal, common pain. She didn't doubt it now.

"I'll come over," she conceded.

There was another silence. "You don't have to."

"I know. I'll be there in a few moments." She hung up before he could answer.

She despised herself. She was doing it again, just as she had years ago. She was running when he crooked his finger. Damn it. Why did she keep doing it?

For Lisa. For Lisa, she told herself again. But that was only part of it. She knew it. Only a part. She could no more stay away from him now than before.

But he would be gone before long. And the recurring nightmare would be over.

Or would it?

His return had awakened all the memories of that spring, the new, fresh stirrings, the deep longing, the glorious passion that had sent her to the stars and back. Could she ever return them to the box where she'd stored them in her mind.

Almost hopelessly, she left the house.

Kurt Weimer ran his hand down the curve of Lisa's throat, feeling it throb under his touch.

Finally, they were alone. It had taken most of the day, a day of ridiculous sightseeing. Americans were enamored with a past only a few centuries old. A mere few pages of history when compared to Europe. Yet he had tried to appear interested when she showed him where a Spanish settlement was once located, and where the British met the Spanish in a bloody clash.

Savannah had its charm, but even that city was an infant compared to the cities he knew and admired—except for Berlin, which the Americans and Russians had destroyed.

But they had finally come to Christ Church on St. Simons Island, and they were alone in a small attractive graveyard framed by great oak trees.

"You're enchanting, you know," he said softly, hiding his impatience.

She looked up at him. He was very close, and his light blue eyes were darker than usual and intense. His hand moved from her throat to the back of her neck, sending little flashes of sensation cascading down her back.

During the day, Kurt had been everything she'd ever thought she might want in a man. Gallant. Attentive. Amusing. Even gentle at times as his hand touched hers. Heads turned every place they went with his blond attractiveness. Yet now some of the gentleness was gone, replaced by a certain aggressiveness and impatience.

But she wanted him to kiss her. She wanted to know whether she'd just been tired last night when his kiss left her strangely unmoved. He was so handsome, and sophisticated, and at lunch he had even hinted that she was the kind of wife he wanted. The words had sent pictures flying through her mind, blinding her for a few fleeting seconds as she imagined herself meeting heads of state and moving in the highest of circles. It was an exhilerating thought. Then she thought of the previous night. She had enjoyed it, enjoyed the novelty of pomp and ceremony, but then she also considered how disappointed she was this morning at knowing she'd missed an oyster roast, one of her favorite things. With a little hidden amusement, she doubted there would be oyster roasts in Berlin.

Yet there was still something fascinating, and even dangerous, perhaps forbidden, about her companion and that sent anticipatory shivers down her back. Or maybe it was the way his fingers caressed the pulse in her throat and then moved to the back of her neck. The touch was provocative, increasing the tempo of her heartbeat.

When his lips came down, she was ready, and lifted her face to meet his. She felt his lips touch hers softly at first, and then possessively, his tongue seeking entrance into her mouth.

His arms tightened around her, and she felt a momentary panic she didn't understand. She had wanted this, but the kiss was suddenly invasive, not tender.

Lisa was twenty, and she had certainly been kissed before, even deep, passionate kisses that aroused something warm inside, but she had never gone further than that. Her father, without preaching, had once told her that love, real love, was warmth and gentleness, a gift without price, and never to give it lightly, that she would know it when it came.

Now she felt unaccountably trapped, knowing that Kurt's kiss was different from others, that he was demanding not only this kiss but a conclusion to the passion she had aroused in him. But despite the trembling caused by his touch on her neck, his kiss invoked no fireworks, no flashing lights, only a desperate need to have it end. She knew she wasn't responding as he wished, and that seemed to make him more aggressive as his tongue forced its way into her mouth. As she struggled to free herself, she felt more and more entrapped as his tongue started to ravage the interior of her mouth.

"Excuse me." The voice seemed sent from heaven as Kurt's arms loosened, his mouth reluctantly pulling from hers.

Lisa stumbled back, almost desperate in her relief. Kurt looked angry, his blue eyes cold as they stared at the intruder, and she suddenly knew she had not mistaken that same look last night. Confused, she looked at the woman who had interrupted them. Dressed in shorts and a blouse with medium-length hair held back by two barrettes, she looked flush, embarrassed at her interruption and very much the tourist.

"Excuse me," she said again, "but I'm hopelessly lost, you see, and my husband is going to be so very, very angry if I'm not back at the hotel when he returns from fishing. It seems I've been going around in circles for hours."

"Where are you going?" Lisa asked, terribly grateful for the interruption.

"The Cloister," the woman said. "Are you staying there too?" Her eyes went from Lisa to Kurt, lighting with appreciation as she did so. "In fact, I think I've seen you there. Are you with the conference?"

Kurt's eyes swept her coldly, but he kept his voice blank and polite. "Yes."

"That's thrilling," the woman trilled on. "And you are . . . ?"

"German," he said impatiently.

"German, how wonderful. I have some friends who are German . . . maybe you . . . but of course not. They've been here since the war." She shifted her feet as if afraid she'd said something she shouldn't have, then looked back to Lisa. "If you could just give me some directions . . ."

Lisa smiled. "We can do better than that. Why don't you just follow us." She looked at Kurt. "That's all right, isn't it?"

His lips tightened, but she had left him little choice. He nodded curtly, his back stiff. He moved away from her, realizing his opportunity was gone. Damn the interfering tourist.

Almost by rote, he forced a smile and courteously followed Lisa to the car, opening the door for her, and then walking swiftly to the driver's side as the woman sauntered slowly to her own car.

Cursing silently, Kurt slid into the driver's seat and started the car.

Chapter Twenty-Seven

Meara's face was even paler than he remembered. Her eyes were huge in her face, huge and sad and so damned lost looking.

But he knew her feeling of helplessness. He was experiencing it himself; the frustration was grinding and crunching him down.

"Come in," he said softly as she hesitated at the door.

He put his hand on her shoulder, not intimately but as correctly as he could make it.

She stood in the center of the room for a moment, then went to the window facing the sea.

"It looks so peaceful," she whispered.

Chris went and stood next to her, but was silent.

"I . . . told her to be careful and she said nothing ever happened on Jekyll Island." She turned around, her voice cracking. "Why? Why did you pretend to love me?"

"Whatever other lies I lived, that was not one of them," he said softly. "It was war, and I was a soldier, and I followed orders." A hollow excuse, and he knew it: a discredited justification after the Nuremberg trials. "I'll not apologize for that. I can't. But I'll always live with guilt for hurting you. That was the real crime, and it had nothing to do with the other. I loved you, Meara. If you never believe anything else, believe that."

"You told me that once," she whispered. "And I believed you."

"But not now?"

"No." The one word was so absolute, so final, that Chris flinched.

He turned away, his hands clenched in fists, the denial echoing in his head. What had he expected?

The phone rang, and he answered it, speaking in monosyllables. When he was through, he looked toward her face, strained and expectant. "Everything is fine. My people are still with them," he said.

He reached down and picked up a package from the table. "This is the tape I mentioned. If anything happens to me, send it to your FBI friend."

Her chin jerked up. "What do you mean, if anything happens to you?"

He shrugged. "Nothing. It's just wise to have several copies."

Meara's eyes narrowed, her chin elevating even higher, and her eyes flashing in a way he remembered. "What are you thinking about?" The question was accusatory.

"Nothing," he said flatly.

"Michael—"

"There is no Michael Fielding anymore."

"Isn't there?" Once more, the voice was accusing. "So many secrets. I always thought there were so many secrets in your eyes, but I never realized how deadly they were." She moved away. "They're still there, Michael. I still don't know you. I don't know what you want. I don't know why you're here. Why . . . after all these years?"

Chris stared at her levelly, and reached into his pocket,

extracting his wallet and carefully taking out the picture, faded and crumbled with use. He handed it to her, and she stared at the obviously much handled picture of her and Lisa; the knowledge that he had kept it all these years pierced some of her defenses.

"She's my daughter, Meara. My daughter," his voice was ravaged, more emotional than she had ever heard it.

"My daughter," she corrected, trying frantically to rebuild her crumbling resentment.

"Which makes her that much more precious."

"You have no right—"

"No," he agreed, hating the sudden look of fear that had come over her face. "I have no right. I know that. But I will protect her."

"Michael . . ."

His fists clenched and released, then clenched again. "I want to kill that bastard," he said suddenly, his eyes hard and cold, and Meara knew he was capable of it. "I'm tired of doing nothing."

"You're not doing nothing," she replied desperately, fearing the violence in his voice, in his face. "You're doing everything you can."

"Everything that money can," he amended caustically.

"No," she said in sudden fear. "You can just make everything worse."

"How can it be worse? It's destroying you. He's destroying you."

"And you think a killing, you on trial, will help Lisa? Do you think murder will solve anything?" she added desperately. More questions, she thought. More and more questions. Just like before. Days and days of intrusive questioning. She wouldn't allow Lisa to go through it as she once had.

"I don't know," Chris said. "I just know you can't go on this way."

"I can do anything I have to," Meara said.

His face gentled, some of the harsh lines fading. His hand went up and touched her left cheek for the barest of seconds. "I know."

Meara felt her body tingle down to her toes. She fought against it, against moving closer to him. "What's on the tape?" she asked finally. "Is it anything that might keep him away from us?"

"I don't think so, not by itself," Chris said. "I hope to get more evidence tomorrow night. Together, they might make him decide to return to Germany." But then, he thought, you . . . we . . . will have to live with the threat the rest of our lives. But she had enough fear in her eyes that he didn't have to voice that insidious thought.

"What evidence?"

"I think he's going to a meeting he shouldn't. Our detectives will be there."

Ours. In a way the word sounded so natural to Meara. But it wasn't natural.

"You won't do anything reckless?"

"No," he promised.

There was a sudden softness, uncertainty, in her face that he couldn't resist. He bent over, his lips touching hers very, very softly.

Meara's lips parted. She couldn't prevent it. His mouth was searching, so hesitant, so achingly desperate, that all the feelings she had tried to bury emerged in response, as intense and fiery and raw as they had ever been.

Her arms went around him, as his tentatively clasped her. Her fingers buried themselves in the crisp golden hair as her body started to tremble under the immensity of what she was feeling. The wounds were still terribly open and raw, but the naked need remained, striking like lightning through all the protection she had thrown up.

The almost fragile quality of the kiss deepened, and both

Meara and Chris knew that the magic which had always existed between them had only intensified with separation.

Yet the fragility remained, the uncertainty between them alive and singeing as they realized that events and history, past and present, had changed them indelibly from the two people who once loved so passionately. The passion was still there, stronger than ever, but the trust wasn't. Meara didn't understand how she could have one without the other, but she did. God help her. She did.

Chris was afraid to hold her tight, afraid that she would break away. Her momentary surrender was a brittle thing, her presence here only because she had little or no choice. Yet she felt so good, so right, and all the yearning of all the years fed on itself until he was ready to explode with the power of it.

Yet it was Chris who forced himself to let go. She was vulnerable now and he knew he could probably take her to bed. But she would hate him for it. Hate him even more than she already did.

Damn it to hell!

She stood back from him, her eyes slightly glazed from the intensity of the moment. "It's happening again," she said stunned.

Chris stood silently, expressionlessly. Her statement was an accusation more than anything else.

"How could I?" she asked with self-disgust so excruciating that it bit right through him.

"You're frightened," he said finally, tonelessly. "It's only natural you turn to someone." He closed his eyes against the condemnation he thought he would see in her face and the pain he knew was naked in his own. There had been moments in the past few days when he had hoped . . .

But he had been a fool. The damage had been too great.

"Chris?" Her voice was suddenly soft, even apologetic, and he turned slowly back to her.

She stood so damned straight, so damned brave despite the puzzled uncertainty in her eyes. Her mouth trembled slightly as she said, "I'm sorry."

"For telling the truth? You have every reason to hate me."

"I don't hate you," she said in a trembling voice. "I'm afraid of you . . . the effect you have on me."

"And you hate that effect," he said, unable to keep a cutting bitterness from his voice.

"I don't . . . understand it."

"No," he said. "I don't either." But it was a lie. He did know. It was love. It had always been love. At least on his part. It was still love.

"I'd better go." There was a hesitant note in her voice as if she wished he would dissuade her.

"Yes," Chris agreed. "I'll call you if there's any news."

She started for the door.

"Don't forget the package," he said.

She stopped and went to the table, her fingers clasping the package, clutching it tightly. It had been a mistake coming here. It was always a mistake.

"Good-bye," she said.

He nodded, his eyes fathomless.

There was nothing more to say.

Chris stared at the door, and then the empty room. Her scent remained, a light flowery essence. He couldn't forget her tortured eyes.

He had to end this before they destroyed each other. Tomorrow night! He had to make sure his detectives got the pictures they needed. Weimer would be slippery. He always had been, judging by the length of time he had so ably hid his Odessa connections. Chris was amazed even now that he would do something as risky as attend a public meeting. He would have to disguise himself in some way.

Chris had memorized the pictures he had of Kurt

Weimer. He knew he would recognize the man under any circumstances. The more he thought about it, the more he decided he should attend the meeting the next night with Weimer. As backup.

And perhaps something else!

The fury that had grown in his mind since the last phone call solidified into hard, cold hatred. The mention on the tape of "personal business" had killed any hopes he had that he might be wrong about Weimer's intentions.

Murder and scandal would scar Lisa's life. But an anonymous death in Atlanta? If anything happened to Chris himself, there would also be anonymity. There were no fingerprints on file, no way to trace his true identity.

Your promise. A promise not to be reckless. And he wouldn't be. No, he wouldn't be that.

Kurt Weimer didn't know him. He didn't even know that Eric von Steimen still existed. He had never seen Chris Chandler. A moment. A moment alone. That was all he would need. He would discover what Weimer wanted. And kill him, if necessary.

Chris went to his bureau and took out his gun, checking it carefully. Cradling the weapon, he went to the chair next to the telephone and waited for the next report.

Kurt Weimer looked at his dinner companion and knew he had failed. Temporarily anyway, and only in his initial plan. He had a backup one. He always did.

Lisa Evans had been distant since those few moments in the church graveyard. Distant and unresponsive although she responded politely enough to his questions. Something had happened in the graveyard. He didn't know what, but he knew he had lost any chance to seduce her.

Those foolish middle-class values, he told himself. But it was more than that, and he knew it.

He could do nothing now. He had too openly escorted her. Nor could he do anything tomorrow. He had already booked a flight early in the morning from Brunswick to Atlanta. But when he returned . . .

A house fire. A tragedy but an accident. A cigarette in bed, perhaps. He had noticed cigarettes in Lisa's purse, although she had not smoked with him. And the lighter. Her father's gift. How very appropriate. No one could ever connect a distinguished foreign dignitary to such an event.

He watched her, trying to keep his eyes warm and interested. He had a double score to settle now. He was not accustomed to rejection, not from a woman, and he didn't like the feeling. The obsession he had with punishing the mother had magnified in the past days, every time he saw her. So prim. So comfortable. Every time he saw her, he wanted to rip her world apart. She had taken his father away, had denied Hans Weimer the recognition he deserved, had stupidly, unknowingly, dealt a strong blow to Germany. A woman. That had been the worst of it. A mere woman.

Kurt didn't worry about being caught. He'd been fooling people all his life, including the self-righteous hypocrites in the West German government who tried to deny the greatest years in Germany's history.

He had originally planned to leave America Friday, then had extended his visit. Now he would go back to his original plan and pay a little visit to the Evanses in the early morning hours before he left.

It wouldn't be difficult, he knew. He had killed easily during the last days of the war and even once since then to ensure silence about Odessa. Killing had never pricked his conscience. Only failure.

"Kurt?"

He turned his attention back to Lisa and gave her his

warmest smile. "It's been a charming day," he said. "But I think it's probably time to get you home."

"You seemed preoccupied."

His hand covered hers intimately. "I was just thinking how much I will miss you."

"Thank you for everything," she said shyly, but relieved that the day was coming to an end.

"I'm going to Atlanta tomorrow—an economist at Georgia State University I've been wanting to meet. We've been corresponding for some time. I'll call you when I get back."

She tipped her head. There was a strained note in his voice she only partially recognized. She didn't know exactly what it meant, but she knew he was distracted, that he mouthed words he really didn't mean. Perhaps it was the occasional coldness in his eyes, the swift irritation on his face, both qualities she hadn't really seen until today.

Lisa sighed, partially with relief. Today had become an effort she hadn't really expected, and she was glad it was almost over. "We really should be going. I have to get back to work tomorrow," she said, realizing how pleased she would be to do exactly that. She looked forward to seeing Kelly's teasing, open grin.

"The attorney's office," he remembered with the barest of interest.

"Yes."

"Do you enjoy it?"

Lisa realized that they hadn't talked about her much at all. He had asked about her family, particularly about her mother, but he had never really asked about her own ambitions, her own dreams. He had dazzled her with anecdotes and stories of his own life and career, but he had never asked her about her own. Strange that she had not realized it until now.

"Yes," she said. "Very much." She did. She liked Kelly

most of all. She had not seen him outside the office since they'd had dinner with Mr. Chandler, and she realized how much she missed him.

Kurt watched as she smiled, but her eyes were far away and he sensed she was thinking of someone else, possibly her escort the other evening who was, he now knew, also her boss. He felt the anger growing inside, but he stifled it with the briefest of smiles. "I too have some business tonight," he said. "But I must thank you for making the last few days so very pleasant."

"For me too," Lisa said politely. They had ended the day with dinner at the Cloister, and she felt faintly guilty that he had taken her to lunch, then dinner, and he was getting little in return. Yet she wanted to go home. She wanted it very badly.

The drive back was uncomfortable. Kurt was unusually silent, preoccupied, as they drove across the causeway. It was near dark, the setting sun casting great streamers of gold over the marsh waters. Her favorite time of day. She looked at him to see whether he also appreciated the almost ethereal beauty of the evening.

But he was stiff, his lips tight, and both his hands busy on the steering wheel. He had changed completely from the amusing, attentive escort of this morning.

When they reached the house, he took her to the door, kissed her lightly, even indifferently, and promised to call her Tuesday.

"Have a good trip," she said, in lieu of anything more personal.

He smiled for the first time since dinner. "I will. Thank you for a fine day."

Lisa watched him turn and walk back to the Mercedes, and wondered why she didn't feel disappointment or regret. She knew he wouldn't call again, and she was glad. The car disappeared down the road before she opened the door. Her mother was inside, reading, and she looked up quickly with a smile too bright.

"Did you have a good time?"

Lisa hesitated. For some reason, she still didn't feel comfortable confiding in her mother. Yet it was only the two of them now, and she sensed her mother needed her as much as she needed her mother. In the past few weeks, her mother had seemed more approachable, more vulnerable, less certain perhaps and more human.

"No," she said quite honestly and knew a certain satisfaction when her mother's eyebrows went up in surprise.

"Why?" Meara said with sudden worry. Had Kurt Weimer . . . ?

But Lisa just shrugged. "I don't know. It was interesting, but I think I missed Kelly."

Nothing her daughter could have said would have delighted Meara more. "I was wondering when you would recognize that," she said with a slight grin.

Lisa looked at her quizzically. "What do you mean?"

"Nothing, love," Meara said. "Just that Kelly is a very nice person."

"He is, isn't he?" Lisa said with just a little grin of her own, a sharing grin that warmed Meara's heart. "I kept thinking how I would rather eat oysters than baked Alaska. Do you think there's something wrong with me?"

"I don't think so. I like oysters better myself."

Lisa smiled at her mother, who smiled back, a bit of a choking sensation in her throat.

Chapter Twenty-Eight

THE HALL WAS filling rapidly, and the level of noise was making it hard to concentrate.

Chris had arrived early and stationed himself close to the main doors. Several other men, all with watchful eyes, were doing the same. He recognized the same look that Sanders Evans had, and he had little doubt they were FBI or some other police agency.

He had flown to Atlanta in his private plane. Upon arrival, he had sought out a used-clothing store and purchased a workman's uniform of cheap blue trousers, dark shirt, and cotton jacket. As an afterthought, he stopped at another store and purchased an Atlanta Crackers baseball cap, pulling it over his hair. Kurt, he imagined, would wear similar clothes.

The pants and jacket were baggy enough to hide his gun in a tightly fitted belt holster, although he suspected, given the occasion, there would be many other weapons there tonight. He also had a miniature camera given him by Matt.

Matt had not liked the idea of his client attending the

meeting. He and his associates could handle it without interference from an amateur. He had not expressed his feelings in those exact words, but the implication was there.

Chris was tired of sitting and waiting—allowing Kurt Weimer to make all the moves. He remembered everything from his German Intelligence training years ago, a past of which Matt and Ben Markham were totally ignorant. He knew he could handle himself in nearly any situation, and after working on a freighter and as a lumberjack, he also had no doubt that he could fit right into the mostly blue-collar crowd at the White Citizens Brotherhood tonight.

As the audience streamed inside in larger numbers than he'd expected, he took stock of them while pretending to glance at a tabloid publication whose masthead sported a symbol resembling a swastika. Its front page featured a twisted body hanging from a branch, an old photo of a Jewish businessman accused and lynched years earlier of killing a young girl employee.

The whole scene was all too familiar to him. Those attending, with the exception of obvious media representatives and law enforcement officers, could have been brownshirts, the violent arm of the Nazi party, twenty-five years earlier in Germany. Mostly burly men with disgruntled expressions, they were, on the whole, largely people who had failed in honest competition and were now looking for scapegoats to blame—blacks or Jews or Asians. It didn't matter. Anyone who was different was an enemy. Chris could smell the violence, the hostility, the pent-up anger, and he shivered with the feeling of déjà vu.

He had tried these many years to block out those memories, to forget that he had ever been a part of it, that he had in a small way defended a society built on hate. Kurt Weimer was trying to bring it back.

Almost on cue, he spied the man. Only the arrogant walk betrayed him. Had not Chris spent the night before studying a photograph of Weimer and guessing possible ways the man might try to disguise himself, he might not have spotted him. Weimer too was dressed in old clothes, but he had also donned some thick glasses through which the eyes were almost completely eclipsed, and his hair was slicked back under a trucker's cap.

Weimer entered amidst a large compact group and artfully turned his face to say something as he passed a gauntlet of federal agents. Chris brought up the cigarette lighter which hid the camera and snapped several photos as he looked for some of Matt's agents. He didn't recognize anyone, and he wondered whether Weimer had given them the slip after all.

Chris followed Weimer and took a seat several rows behind and at an angle where he could take more pictures. Once more he curiously studied the other people in the audience. There were some women and children, most of whom also wore looks of perennial dissatisfaction and discontent. There were even a few Ku Klux Klan robes. What was really surprising to him, and dismaying, was that the hall was fuller than he expected.

The meeting opened with a prayer, an ironic twist, he thought, when followed by a speaker who launched into a litany of hate, blaming every conceivable injustice or wrong on minorities.

"We have to protect our wives and daughters," the speaker said with a roar of rage and approval from the audience.

Chris listened in disbelief as nonsense after nonsense drew huge hands and shouts of agreement. Weimer's head was tipped upward in a pose of complete absorption.

The one sign of hope in the sea of radiating hatred was the skeptical, even amused looks of the media who were scribbling in notebooks. Germany thirty years ago had no such spotlight, and when Hitler assumed control of the newspapers, there was no one to expose the mania taking root and growing so rapidly, spreading like some terrible epidemic.

No matter what Weimer planned, it would never succeed, not now, not today, not here. But that was small comfort at the moment.

When Robert Cannon, a young man whose energy vibrated with every step, strode confidently on stage, Chris saw Weimer's body tense, and he knew instinctively that this man was why Weimer had come, and he turned his full attention to the featured speaker.

Unlike the others, Cannon spoke in reasoned terms and a soft voice, his appeal aimed at patriotism rather than the outright hatred espoused by earlier speakers. It was a masterpiece in staging, the crowd already primed and excited while this man took what, for this group, was the high road: protection of American values, of families, of community. Once more, Chris felt he was reliving a horror as he watched the almost glazed expressions of fanaticism. This man could be dangerous, given respectability and money. He felt sick as he realized that this was exactly why Kurt Weimer had taken such chances tonight, and no longer were Meara and Lisa the only important issues.

Chris waited until Weimer left the auditorium. He followed at a distance, watching as another man, a better-dressed man, joined him briefly. Chris took another photo and saw the two disappear out a side door.

Should he go after him? He still didn't recognize any of Matt's people, but then he didn't know them all. But he was afraid to risk the film if he continued to follow Weimer. His hand went to the small of his back where his pistol was holstered. He might not have another chance, not like this one.

Then he saw two more men move purposefully out the same side door and debated whether they were Matt's people, bodyguards for the leader of the Brotherhood, or even federal agents, although he doubted the last. But they had the feral look of hunters, of predators. In any event, he doubted whether he could accomplish anything now. There were simply too many people around. Cursing silently to himself, he nonetheless used the side door and saw Weimer and the men he'd left with enter a nondescript car.

Chris stood there and lit a cigarette, and then with heavy steps he turned away. There had to be another time, another opportunity. In the meantime, he had the photos. There would be some people very, very interested in them.

He hailed a taxi and asked about a late night restaurant and was delivered to a place called the Varsity. He then called Matt, who was supervising his case. There was a long pause when he identified himself.

"We lost him," Matt said.

"I didn't," Chris replied matter-of-factly.

There was another pause. Chris could almost hear the silent chagrin over the phone. But it didn't matter. Nothing mattered now but the film he had.

"He did go to the Brotherhood meeting then?" Matt said finally, knowing his boss was going to have his head for this. An amateur succeeding where his own men had failed. It made him wonder even more about his mysterious client. "After our two people realized he had somehow left the hotel, they went to the rally but couldn't find him." Or you, Matt wanted to add.

"His own mother wouldn't have recognized him," Chris said comfortingly.

"Then how did you—?"

"It doesn't matter," Chris said, his voice suddenly curt. "But I do have some film I want developed tonight."

"Where are you?"

Chris had already obtained the address. He read it off.

"Someone will be there in less than an hour."

"I want it by midmorning."

"You'll have it," Matt said. And any other damn thing you want, he almost added. He'd probably be back doing divorce cases after this. "Delivered to your door."

Chris hung up, ordered a hamburger, and wandered through the various rooms of the large drive-in restaurant. Each room had a television set tuned to a different station, and patrons sat before them in school-like desks. He noticed the news coming on one channel, and he settled his long rangy form in one of the awkward seats. He listened carefully to the news. Two black students had been admitted to the University of Georgia for the first time, and there were widespread protests and threats. Then there was a brief report on the White Citizens Brotherhood rally.

The cameras had not been allowed inside, but they had panned people going in, and the reporter had been admitted. In a few terse sentences, he estimated the size of the crowd at approximately seven hundred and repeated several of the most memorable quotes. To someone who had not seen the rapt faces inside, they sounded ludicrous and melodramatic. But taken in context with the next report, a new outbreak of violence in Mississippi, it was all too familiar and ominous to Chris.

After the news went off, he slumped back in the chair. He would probably get a hotel room tonight and leave at sunrise. He was tired and uncertain. He had the ammunition he needed now to confront Weimer, but could be withhold it from American authorities? Or would he be betraying both his native and adopted countries by allowing Weimer to continue?

And Meara? He should have called, but he knew she would try to stop him, and he had reached the point where he had to do something. Anything. He couldn't sit back and wait any longer. It was fortunate that he had, considering the fact that Matt's team had failed.

Chris also knew he had to get accustomed to the fact that he would be leaving soon, not to return again. She didn't want him, didn't want anything to do with him, and he couldn't blame her. He had hurt her badly before. Not just badly. He had almost destroyed her. If it hadn't been for Sanders . . .

But Christ, it would be hard to leave her. As she had years ago, Meara had made him feel whole again. The mere sight of her filled him with warmth and craving and even justification for a life that was hollow and meaningless. She needed him now, and he had cherished that momentary trust. But that was all it was, momentary and out of pure, desperate necessity. When the threat was gone, she would want him gone too. The knowledge was like burning acid.

He doubted whether she even knew he was gone today. He had told her that Weimer would be away, and she knew Lisa was safe.

And Lisa? Pretty Lisa, who was just discovering the world. He would never see her again except perhaps in photos. He had promised that, and he would never break faith with Meara again. But perhaps she would send him pictures. It was a damned lonely prospect, but the best he could expect. He leaned back, unaware that a slight groan had escaped his lips.

He had closed his eyes when he heard a soft voice, "Mr. Chandler."

He opened his eyes and found a young man standing nervously next to him. The room was almost empty, and although he didn't recognize the man, he did recognize the look. Chris arched an eyebrow. "Yes."

The man took out his billfold and showed his identification as a private investigator with the agency Chris had hired.

Chris saw he was discomfited and guessed he was one of those who'd lost Weimer. Well, maybe he'd learned something tonight. Chris took the film from his pocket and handed it to the detective who took it slowly, curiosity written all over his face.

"We'll have it for you tomorrow, sir," he said.

Chris nodded and ambled up out of the chair. "Can you drop me off at a hotel?"

His contact nodded warily, and the two of them left the room where *Casablanca* was now showing.

Meara had dialed Chris's number for hours Monday. She had even taken Raggedy Andy for a walk past his house. Several walks, if the exact truth be told.

Chris had frightened her the previous day. There had been something cold and unforgiving and determined in him. It had reminded her of the night in the powerhouse, when he had talked to the other German. She'd felt icy, just as she did then, and despite his promise she knew he intended something dangerous.

It scared her to know how much that frightened her, how much she cared about him. She had hated him for so long; how could she feel so much concern about him now? It didn't make sense, but then nothing about him ever did.

The one relief she had was Lisa's confidences last night. Not only was it a breakthrough in their relationship, but she had been delighted that Lisa was starting, at least, to recognize her feelings for Kelly. They had always been there, Meara suspected, but hidden in familiarity.

But if Kurt Weimer didn't win one way, would he try another?

Meara didn't think so. A man in his position? She wasn't important enough. Lisa wasn't important enough. Yet she knew Chris thought differently, and she was growing desperately afraid that he might do something rash, something dangerous both to himself and to Lisa.

Meara had started calling Chris after Lisa left. She had wanted to tell him that they probably didn't have to worry about Lisa any longer, and she had not been surprised when he wasn't there. Thinking he was probably on the beach, she had pulled on a bathing suit and gone down herself, expecting any moment to see him.

The day was hot. Heat radiated off the sand, and the sun tipped the edges of the waves. She had walked through the water, and even that seemed lukewarm at the moment, but she thought about it only absently. Her main concentration was on the few people on this section of the beach.

Andy had no such fixation. He chased birds, plunging after them in and out of waves with unrestrained glee. After shaking himself, throwing water and sand all over her, he took off down the beach after another dog, trembling with friendly ardor.

Meara watched him with bemusement, wondering whether Andy ever became frustrated in chasing birds, in his constant quest for the impossible, the elusive. Or whether it was the impossible that was so damned attractive. Did one always want what he could not have?

She walked and walked, but without success. She finally turned around and returned, and some of the sparkle was gone from the water, from the sand.

Where was he?

When she returned, she read the paper and then turned to her typewriter and the final draft of her proposal, determined to concentrate, all the time willing the phone to ring. At four, she had finished, and she started dinner. Lisa would be back around five-thirty.

She tried his phone again, and damned him and herself for caring as it rang and rang.

*   *   *

Kurt Weimer was ushered into a hotel room. He had been led up a back way and assured that no one had followed them. Even if they had, he thought with satisfaction, no one would recognize him. He'd made quite certain earlier that no one had seen his transformation from Kurt Weimer.

When he had arrived at the Dinkler Hotel in downtown Atlanta upon his arrival from Brunswick, he had asked for a room close to the stairs. After resting several hours and making some phone calls, he had changed clothes, looked out at the empty hall, and taken the stairs to the second floor. He had then used a freight elevator to the basement and exited through the service entrance.

It was not that he suspected he was being followed but mostly habit and precaution.

He'd even used a pay phone to reach Robert Cannon, giving a name he sometimes used for Odessa business. Almost immediately Cannon was on the phone.

"I'm in Atlanta tonight. I thought I would come to the rally. Perhaps we can get together afterward."

There was a hesitancy, then quick assent. The speaker, who Cannon knew as Hans Kaiser, had already poured money into the Brotherhood. "I'll have someone meet you afterward and bring you up to a hotel room rented by an anonymous friend. What will you be wearing?"

Kurt quickly told him, and Cannon in return told him who to look for at the rally.

Now as Kurt entered the room, Robert Cannon rose from a sofa to greet him, his hand outstretched and a broad smile on his face. "It's good to meet one of our best supporters," he said. "What did you think of the rally?"

"I'd hoped for more people," Kurt observed. He had been impressed, but he didn't want to admit it. Not yet.

"We're building. Slowly but surely. The problem has been too many splinter groups, and no common goal. I think we're beginning to correct that, but it takes time. And money."

"If I provide more funds, how would you use them?"

"More literature, more communication with other groups, more rallies. I have to show the other groups we can do something they can't. Their leaders don't want to surrender what power they have."

"How do you explain the funds?"

"From anonymous donors who can't afford to be allied openly with us. At least not yet. We can't let our members know any of it came from Germany. Some of our members are veterans."

"Yet we have a common cause."

Cannon looked at him steadily. "Right now, most of our members are worried mainly about their jobs, that and the way the society they have always known is being changed. Change produces fear. We have to feed those particular fears to grow."

Kurt nodded. "What do *you* want?"

Cannon smiled, and the smile was suddenly feral. "I want to build the Brotherhood into a major party, a major power in this country. We've already elected some town and city officials, and we are recruiting more. The media laughs at us. They don't know what kind of membership we already have. One day, they'll wake up and find we're too strong to break. But we have to keep your support silent."

The answers were everything Kurt Weimer had wanted to hear. Cannon was a shrewd and patient manipulator who could, if properly controlled, become a real asset in this country. "Let me know what you need," he said. "Use the regular channels."

Cannon recognized acceptance and also dismissal. "It

will be used to good advantage," he said, walking Kurt to the door. "It's been a privilege meeting you."

"We'll be in touch," Kurt replied, and slipped out the door where the man who had accompanied him there was waiting.

Chapter Twenty-Nine

THE PHONE WAS ringing when Chris walked into his rented house. Unable to sleep the night before, he was tired and irritable, and faced with several very undesirable choices.

His voice was short as he picked up the phone and barked into it, "Chandler."

"Michael . . . Chris . . . thank God you're all right." Meara's voice was so heartfelt that unexpected elation soared through him.

"I'm fine," he said in a gentle voice.

"I've been . . . worried about you."

He felt warmth curl inside. He didn't know the last time anyone had worried about him. Probably never, he thought wryly. But then she was concerned about Lisa. Don't put too much value on it, he warned himself.

Chris made an instant decision then. "I think we have everything we need now to get rid of Mr. Weimer." Chris knew he would sell his soul to take the worry from her voice, and that, he thought, was exactly what he was going to do.

"Can you tell me about it?"

"Not yet. I'm waiting for some pictures to be developed. How's Lisa?"

"Disenchanted with Mr. Weimer." There was a note of supreme satisfaction in her voice.

"Why?"

"I don't know exactly. But that's good news, isn't it?"

"Of course," Chris said, but secretly he wondered. Kurt Weimer, he suspected, was much like his father. He wouldn't give up easily, and being blocked in one plan he might well turn to something else. Chris knew he had to checkmate the man as quickly as possible. "Is Lisa at work now?"

"Yes, she's with Kelly, and I've asked him to keep an eye on her."

"No questions?"

"Lots of questions but he hasn't voiced them. Not yet."

"Just as long as he stays with her now."

"You think Weimer might try—"

"I don't know," Chris replied. "But if he's rebuffed, he might try something else. The conference is almost over and he's running out of time. I would just feel better if someone were with her all the time, especially the next several days."

"Your detectives?"

"They will be there too, but I don't want to take any chances." He couldn't tell her that they lost Weimer in Atlanta, and Ben Markham's agency was one of the best in the country. Weimer was one hell of a lot smarter than he'd originally given him credit for. But he should have known. Anyone tied to Odessa for so long, and still a respected government member, had to be damned clever.

"Meara?"

He heard her breath catch. "Yes?"

"It will be over soon."

"Thank you," she said in a whisper quiet voice.

"I'll call you later in the day."

"Be careful."

"Good-bye, Meara." Unconsciously, his voice caressed her name, and he sensed her hesitation on the other end of the line. He laid down the phone carefully, his hand resting on it a moment, telling himself he was the bloodiest fool in the world.

The photos arrived several hours later, brought by Matt himself.

"Weimer?" Chris asked.

"Got back this morning," Matt said curtly. "Heads are rolling on this one."

"As long as you don't lose him again."

"We won't," Matt said with harsh conviction. He held out an envelope. "Your photos."

"Have you looked at them?"

Matt grinned self-consciously. "Yes. I could say I looked to see whether we did well on the quality, but I was curious. Have you ever thought about another line of work? How in the hell did you recognize him?"

"I knew what to expect."

"Mind elaborating?"

"Yes," Chris said good-naturally as he took out the pictures and reviewed them with satisfaction. "How many prints did you make?"

"Two of each."

"I want a third copy. As soon as possible."

"And then what?"

"I'm going to pay a little visit to our Mr. Weimer."

"Need some assistance?"

"No," Chris said abruptly.

"These . . . pictures, and the tape, could be of some use to our government," Matt said carefully.

"The government isn't paying you," Chris replied sharply.

Matt absorbed the rebuke with trained equanimity. "No, sir," he admitted.

Chris led him to the door. "Have the extra set of prints sent to Mrs. Evans personally."

Matt nodded.

"I'm going to see Weimer after the conference meetings today. I want a report on everything he does afterward—around midnight."

"Yes, sir," Matt added.

"It's going to be more difficult. He's going to know he's under surveillance and that his line has been tapped."

"We won't lose him again," Matt repeated grimly.

"Make sure you don't."

Chris had several hours to kill. He walked down to the beach. The day was not quite as hot as it had been, and the breeze felt good against his skin.

There were more people than usual, the cooler air driving them from the aid-conditioned motels. The water was calm, the silver-gray glinting in the sun as the tide started to ease its way up the beach, one wave at a time. There was a family not far away, the children building a sand castle.

Haunting memories returned as he remembered the shining day when Meara had looked up at him with laughter and trust and liking. He could recall Tara's small hopeful face, and Peter's open admiration. There had been so much innocence then, so much youthful hope. God, he wished he could roll time back again.

But would he have really changed things, given the circumstances? Could he have? It was a question, he knew, that would plague him the rest of his life.

He didn't know how long he sat there, long enough for

the castle-building family to leave and for the ocean to sweep over the fragile structure, erasing the dream as if it had never been, erasing the footsteps in the sand. He rose, brushing the sand from his clothes. Finally it was time to play his hand.

Kurt Weimer carefully stepped inside the cottage. The door had been unlocked and he would have sworn he had locked it. It could be a maid, of course, but this was rather late in the day for that possibility.

"Come in," said a disembodied voice, and when Kurt hesitated, he heard the cock of a pistol. He looked around cautiously and finally saw a man leaning against a wall, his form partially hidden in shadows. A gun was in his hand.

"Who are you?" he said with contempt. "I have little money here."

"I don't want your money."

"Come out where I can see you."

The intruder leisurely moved forward, and Kurt felt his contempt change slowly to fear. Despite the lazy movements, the man had the coldest, most menacing eyes he had ever seen. They were not the eyes of a thief. They were the eyes instead of a professional hunter. He had hired enough to know.

"What do you want?"

"Just a little conversation."

"Who are you?" Kurt said as he slowly moved toward a bureau.

"I already found the gun," his uninvited guest commented with an amused smile. "And got rid of it."

Kurt hated the fear, the failure circling around inside him.

"Do you know who I am?" he blustered.

"I know exactly who . . . and what . . . you are," the visitor said coldly. "The question is who else will know."

"You speak in riddles."

"I'll try to be more exact."

The tone sliced through Kurt, and he knew what was coming. Somehow he knew from the knowing eyes staring at him. He knew. But still he bluffed. "I'll have you arrested—"

"For breaking and entering? What about treason? I wonder how your government would consider membership in an organization of people who, shall we say, are dedicated to protecting criminals wanted by the German government."

"You're insane."

"Oh, am I? I wonder whether this government, and your own, will think the same when they hear certain tapes and see some very excellent photographs of a top government official at a somewhat questionable meeting."

"There are no laws against curiosity. . . ."

"No, but there is one about—what is the term?—neutralizing an Argentine resident. Interesting term for murder. The Bull, I think his name is. I wonder what he would think about the order. I understand the Israelis know who and where he is. And your friend in Germany. Stefan? I wonder if German Intelligence has a file on him. Or you."

The color drained from Kurt's face. "What do you want?" It was little more than a croaked whisper, and he despised himself and hated the man across from him for causing it.

"Right now? A simple walk on the beach."

"Why?"

The man laughed. "After what I just told you, you ask? You disappoint me."

Kurt understood immediately. The room had been bugged, of course. His mind ran over the past couple days. He must have been followed too, otherwise how would they know of the rally? And Cannon? Did they also know about that? How much had he said on the phone to Stefan?

But it was also interesting that the intruder apparently didn't want their conversation overheard. Otherwise why leave the room? Why? Nothing made sense.

He shrugged, as casually as he could, his eyes on the gun. "Won't you be a bit conspicuous on the beach?"

"Oh, it will be in my pocket. But in case you decide to get foolish, please realize that copies of the tape and photos I mentioned are in very safe places. If anything happens to me, they go immediately to the FBI and German Intelligence."

Kurt balled his fist in a tight knot, wanting to strike out, but he couldn't. Not in this room. Not with listeners apparently nearby. He cursed out loud as he realized how completely he was trapped. He nodded and stepped out of sliding glass doors to the beach, feeling the ominous presence of the man behind him. He took the few seconds to analyze. Who was his opponent? What did he want? If the man were a federal agent, Kurt knew he would probably be headed for a small office someplace, answering some very embarrassing questions and trying to keep from being deported back to Germany. The tape could involve him in conspiracy to murder. There wouldn't be enough evidence to convict, not an illegal tape recording, but he would be publicly and politically destroyed.

Bastard. He wanted to kill the man behind him.

"That's far enough," the man said, and Kurt saw a bench on a dune overlooking the beach.

"Sit down, Weimer."

There was something tantalizing about the man's voice, something he knew he should recognize but didn't. It nagged and worried at him. A hint of Germany, perhaps, but no. There was no accent, none at all, and perhaps that was what struck him.

"What do you want?" Kurt asked again, keeping his tone calm and emotionless.

"I want certain assurances from you."

Kurt glared at him with hatred. "What kind of assurances?"

"That you will stay away from the Evans family."

Of all answers he expected, this was the least of them. Money. Power. Those two he expected.

"I don't know what you mean," he blustered.

"I'll make it very clear then. I'm a friend of her late husband's. I look out for them. Both of them. Do you understand me?"

"You *are* a lunatic. I've merely taken Lisa out several times."

"I don't like the way you part your hair, my friend. I don't want you around her again. Am I clear?"

"You have no right."

"I have every right now," the man said. "I have the pictures and tapes, remember."

Still partially disbelieving, Kurt stared at the man opposite him. It was difficult to tell his age. Late forties possibly, but his body was still superbly fit, muscles evident in the arms and shoulders. His eyes were dark blue, menacing and unblinking. If there was gray mixed in the corn silk blond of his hair, he couldn't find it. The only indication of age at all were the deep lines around the man's eyes and mouth.

"What is it you want exactly?" Kurt finally managed.

"I have three copies of both the photographs and the tape of your conversation to Herr Kranz. One set is on its way to an attorney in New York, another to a German solicitor. If they hear of anything happening to either Meara or Lisa Evans, both have been instructed to send copies to the Central Intelligence Agency, German Intelligence, and the *New York Times.*"

"What do you mean, anything?"

"Oh, anything from an auto accident to . . . a natural death. Anything at all."

"I don't believe you," Kurt said. "You haven't had time."

"You can do anything if you have enough money. Surely, you know that, Herr Weimer."

"You aren't serious."

"I'm very serious. One accident and everyone will know that the respected Kurt Weimer is a leader in Odessa and trying to seed violence in the United States."

Kurt felt himself trembling. Nearly twenty years wasted. "You can never prove it."

"I don't have to," the man said. "I have enough to start others digging. Enough to ruin you."

"Why?"

"I told you. I owe Sanders Evans a debt. I'm paying it now. I take my obligations very seriously."

"I can't be held responsible for anything that might happen to them."

"Then *make* it your responsibility. Oh, and there is something else. You will be cutting your trip short. Sudden problems in your office."

"I want copies of everything. I want to know they exist."

"Take my word for it, although I must admit those glasses and that hat last night didn't improve your image."

"And if I do as you say?"

"Your image will remain untarnished," the man said with cold humor.

"How do I know that?"

"Simple, you trust me." There was a glint of humor in the man's eyes for the first time.

Kurt cursed fluently in German.

"Sorry. I don't understand German."

"Then how . . . ?"

"Did I translate the tape? I didn't. An associate of mine did."

"But you said—"

"The man is in my employ. Completely trustworthy."

"Damn you."

"Perhaps, but in the meantime I would like an answer."

Kurt couldn't stop the question on his lips. "What do you know about Meara Evans?"

"That she's a very nice lady, and when you showed an unusual interest in her daughter, she worried. She had good instincts."

"Are you a federal agent?"

"No, otherwise I would be duty bound to turn this information over, wouldn't I? As it is, we will make a simple bargain. No notoriety or harm for her daughter, none for you."

Kurt looked into a bland expression. The man knew far more than he was saying, but Kurt realized he would learn no more. He had made several crucial mistakes.

But then so had the arrogant bastard in front of him.

"I'll do as you say," he said.

"Good. I believe there's a flight out tomorrow morning for Atlanta. And then New York."

"Who *are* you?"

Chris smiled. "As you have your secrets, I have mine. Let's leave it that way. Now start walking back to your cottage and don't look back."

When Kurt reached the door of the cottage, he couldn't help but look back. But no one was there.

Kurt Weimer made several calls, aware now that all were being taped. He cursed himself thoroughly for not checking, but he'd had no reason to suspect anything. As as he went over every minute of his stay here, he started to remember small things, like the woman at Christ Church who somehow seemed familiar. Now, as he thought about it, there was a resemblance in build to the woman he had also seen in the Brunswick cemetery where his father was buried.

Which meant his visitor probably knew a great deal more than he'd said.

He would have sworn that no one was following him in Atlanta. But it didn't matter now. Nothing mattered but escape.

He didn't believe his visitor. Not for a moment did he believe the information the man had taken so many pains in gathering would stay confidential. At any rate, he couldn't risk it. Any extensive investigation by the West German government would show certain financial manipulations and irregularities. Huge accounts could possibly be traced back to him. At the least, he would go to prison.

A planner by nature and training, Kurt seldom left anything to chance. He had always known exposure was possible, and he had established several other identities, all with access to numbered bank accounts in Caribbean banks. After years in Odessa, he knew every trick there was, every government that could be bought, every banker who knew how to be discreet. And he could continue his role in Odessa in an even more active way.

But the Evans bitch would pay for this. Both she and her daughter. Now it really didn't matter if he was careful. Kurt Weimer, in any event, would disappear.

The first step was to rid himself of his watchdogs. They were obviously very, very capable. But they had underestimated both his resolve and his resources.

Chris drove slowly back to Jekyll Island. He had done one of two things: frightened Weimer off or brought him out into the open. Instinct told him it was the latter.

If Weimer returned to Germany, Chris would do as he

had promised. Temporarily. But he would eventually have to find a way to destroy or kill him; otherwise Meara and Lisa would never be safe. But it would have to be away from here. Far away, where nothing could touch the Evans family.

He knew he had taken a risk in showing himself to Weimer. But he had done it purposely. He had shown Weimer that he too had power, enough power that he wasn't afraid to show himself, to confront Weimer directly. The mystery, the puzzle, would be more intimidating than a man hiding in the shadows.

Now he had to wait. The next few days were crucial, and he knew he could not leave Meara or Lisa alone. Not for a moment. Not until he knew Weimer was in Germany.

And if Weimer did indeed arrive in Bonn, Chris knew he would have to make more permanent arrangements.

Chapter Thirty

"No," Meara said. "I won't go."

"You will," Chris said, his eyes boring into hers as the sun set just beyond them.

"I've been running away nearly all my life. I won't do it anymore."

Chris wanted to shake her. "You've never run away from anything. You have more guts than any woman I've ever met."

"No," Meara said slowly, as if she were realizing it for the first time. "I've been running away from life since that night, from real commitment, from involvement. Sanders knew it. Lisa sensed it. I'm not going to do it anymore. This is my problem as much as yours. I'm the one who killed his father."

"Only to save the children," Chris said.

"Now I have to save myself," Meara said.

"And Lisa?"

"I'll send her away."

"How?"

"I don't know. I'll have to enlist Kelly's help. She doesn't like being manipulated."

For the first time that evening, Chris grinned. "Like her mother." But then the smile disappeared. "I'd still prefer that you leave."

"If he does come back, won't he check to see whether I'm here before trying anything?"

Meara had immediately placed her finger on the one problem in his plan. He had intended to move into her house, and wait. But Weimer was no one's fool, despite his anger.

Perhaps, he thought, he wouldn't come at all. But Chris didn't really believe that. He had seen the man's glacial eyes, the hate that circled within them, the kind of hate that became senseless. He had seen it before in Germany, a fanaticism that fed on itself until reason was entirely gone.

He might well have pushed Weimer over the edge. But it was either that or allow Meara and Lisa to live in Weimer's shadow all their lives.

After the meeting with Weimer, he had briefly told Matt selected portions of what had happened and saw the quiet disapproval of the man's face. Matt didn't like the idea of letting Weimer off the hook, but then he didn't know the stakes. Chris had warned Matt to keep his people on Weimer until the man boarded a plane for Germany, and to be damned sure that it was Weimer who boarded.

Frankly unhappy, Matt agreed, and Chris had driven back to Jekyll and called Meara, asking her to meet him on the beach.

"When will we know?" Meara asked.

"I told him to take the first flight tomorrow. He knows now he's being watched so I doubt if he'll try anything now. He'll wait until he believes we think we're safe.

"I would like Lisa . . . and you . . . gone tomorrow."

"No," she said simply. "Lisa yes. But I won't leave."

His dark blue eyes studied hers, and his voice was very grave and quiet when he spoke. "I intend to move into your house."

That statement stopped her momentarily. How could she possibly survive several days—and nights—with him? He had never been in her home, and yet in the past few days he was already everywhere, including the bedroom. Twenty years had not dimmed the exquisite, glorious pleasure of being with him. Perhaps those years had even magnified those memories until they no longer had basis in reality. She only knew whenever she was with him, she felt the old magic which she'd once thought she would never find again, that she wanted to reach out and touch him, to draw the etched pain from the lines around his eyes, and feel the treasured wonder of being held so gently against that strong, hard body. All of which spelled disaster with capital letters. He was still the same man, ever so competent with lies and deceit. And she would have to live with the fear that someday Lisa might learn who he really was.

Yet the prospect was irresistible. She felt strong and brave and invincible with him. She realized now that she always had, even that night in the powerhouse. She had, somehow, known she was safe. She remembered the knife he accidentally dropped, the way he had distracted Weimer, the curious remarks Sanders had made. "He could have killed me," he'd said.

"Why didn't you kill Sanders?" she asked suddenly, the unexpectedness of the question piercing the armor Chris had constructed around the incident.

"The truth?"

"Yes."

"Will you believe it?" It was asked with a note of hopelessness, as if he himself was convinced she wouldn't.

"Yes," she said again. Softly.

He turned to look at the sea, the red glow spreading like blood across its calm surface. The sky itself was crimson, violent shades of crimson, not the golden glow that usually spread peacefully across the water. It was angry, like that night had been angry. There would be a storm tomorrow, he thought absently, trying to put his thoughts, his words, in some kind of order.

When he turned back, his eyes were bleak, wary, his expression wry. "I knew he would take care of you," Chris said simply.

The simplicity of the statement said so much more. Longing and despair echoed quietly in the air.

"And that mattered?" Her question was a cry of pain. For years, she had felt merely used by him, used and discarded as a convenient thing. It had destroyed her sense of self-worth, of confidence. Or had it? She had rebuilt in another way, and she'd had Lisa. And Sanders. She'd really had a great deal, and he had, in different ways, given it all to her. She looked at him, the aloneness she had noticed years ago so much more pronounced, his eyes dark and haunted and desolate. He *had* paid a much higher price than she.

She swallowed against the emotions welling up inside, against the need to reach up and kiss away the slight ironic grimace on his lips as he watched her. He was ready to accept her disbelief, just as he had accepted all her accusations and bitterness.

She wanted to say something. She wanted to say so much, yet they were feeling their way so gingerly. Years couldn't be dismissed easily. Change couldn't. She had thought she knew him once, and she hadn't. Despite all the warm, curling feelings she was experiencing now, she didn't want to make that mistake again.

Instead, she said with a small, uncertain smile. "You'd be welcome in my house."

He stood stiffly, his expression a little like a prisoner winning a reprieve, uncertain as if not quite believing his sudden change in fortune. He raked his hand through his hair in that gesture that was so darned endearing to Meara.

"Are you sure?" he said finally.

"Yes," she said, her eyes clear, and she knew he was asking more than whether he would merely be there to protect her. *Welcome* meant more than *allow*.

He nodded, as if uncapable of saying more, and Meara felt ridiculously light-headed and trembly and warm inside. And safe. Despite his fears about Kurt Weimer, she knew she would be safe with Chris Chandler, just as she knew now she had been with Michael Fielding.

"What about Lisa?" he said, trying to concentrate on anything but the sudden light in her eyes. It was fear, fear and need and even, maybe, a little gratitude. Nothing else.

"I'll talk to Kelly," she said, suddenly tense as she wondered how much she would have to explain.

"Would you like me to do it?" he said gently.

"What . . . could you say . . . explain why we don't go to the police?"

"Trust me, Meara," he said.

Surprisingly, she knew she did.

The rented house was lonelier than ever when he returned. But he hadn't wanted to push Meara. He could scarcely allow himself to believe they had come this far. Hope had flared briefly in him, but he knew in the depth of his soul that he and Meara had no future. The past was still too raw and painful, and though she trusted him now, in this matter, he could never hope that she would trust him completely.

He read over some contracts Allen had sent, and then called him. Seattle time was three hours earlier, which made it seven o'clock there. Allen was still in the office.

They discussed the contracts briefly, Chris grateful for the distraction, but he knew he surprised Allen when he again told his vice president to "do what you think best."

"When will you be back?"

"Within a week," Chris said crisply. It would all be over then. One way or another, it would all be over. Meara would get on with her life. He would return to his. The thought was excruciating. Three months ago, the contracts he held would have absorbed all his attention, all his interest. Now they were merely pieces of paper. His life. As flimsy and inconsequential and austere as those damn pieces of paper.

Matt's call came two restless hours later. There was a certain admiration in his voice. "I don't know what you said to him, but it sure as hell worked. He's cancelled the rest of his sessions here and booked a flight tomorrow morning with connections to New York. He also made reservations for a flight Thursday to Germany."

"I want people with him every step," Chris said. "When he gets off the planes. When he gets back on."

"You think he might try to come back."

"I think it's a possibility."

There was a pause. "What else do you want us to do?"

"Just make sure he's in Germany. Then your job is done."

"And the ladies?"

Chris thought rapidly. Perhaps it wouldn't hurt to have one watch remain. If Weimer did somehow escape through his net, another safeguard might be wise. "Keep a twenty-four-hour watch until I call you off."

"Yes, sir."

"Keep me posted."

After Matt hung up, Chris looked at his watch. It was too late to call Kelly. He would do it in the morning and try to make an appointment for lunch. It would be a very ticklish conversation, but he was much better at prevarication than Meara, God help him.

Lunch was at The Deck. The urgency in Chris's voice had prompted Kelly to cancel another appointment. He was filled with curiosity when he met Chris Chandler.

Despite his often misleading relaxed, good-natured disposition, Kelly had always been very sensitive and intuitive about people. He disguised it well, but he knew when to bore in and when to extract gently. He had almost immediately sensed the currents between Chris Chandler and Meara Evans at lunch and then dinner at his home, and they had been much more than those usually between old acquaintances. The way they had avoided each other's eyes had spoken volumes to him, although he doubted anyone else had noticed.

Now as they were seated, he waited. He didn't have to wait long.

"Can you get Lisa out of town?" Chris said directly, without preamble.

"Can I ask why?"

"She might be in danger."

"Might be?"

"Yes," Chris said without elaboration.

"Meara mentioned something like that," Kelly said cautiously. "The German. That he might have some grudge?" It was a question.

Chris nodded.

"What's your interest in this?"

"I told you. I was a friend of Evans."

Kelly's face showed open disbelief. "I don't understand why you don't go to the police."

"Because," Chris said slowly, watching Kelly's face very carefully, "there's some history involved that could hurt Lisa if she knew. And nothing might come of it. It probably won't. This is only a precaution."

"Something about the kidnapping years ago?"

Chris's eyes snapped up. "How did you—"

"After I talked to Meara a week ago, I started thinking. I go over a lot of old documents and even newspapers in my work. I started wondering about Meara, and I suddenly remembered another Meara, a Meara O'Hara, who was something of a heroine years ago. Yet she has never talked about it, and I know Lisa doesn't know. There had to be a reason."

Chris was silent, reevaluating Kelly Tabor.

"What about Meara?" Kelly said finally. "Why doesn't she take Lisa someplace?"

"She wants to stay."

"Is she in danger?"

"I don't know. Possibly, but I think I can handle that. If Lisa's out of the way."

"This sounds like a bad detective novel."

A muscle worked in Chris's cheek, giving away the first emotion Kelly had seen. "Meara believes . . . you will help."

Kelly hesitated. "I'll have to call Meara," he said, wanting Chris to know he wasn't entirely trusted.

Chris nodded. It was certainly a precaution he himself would have taken.

"How long do you want her gone?"

"Four days."

"When?"

"Today if possible, no later than tomorrow morning."

"You don't want much, do you?" Kelly's voice was more hostile now as he felt total frustration. He was an officer of the court, sworn to protect the laws, and he had the sick feeling that he was getting involved in something very dangerous. And yet he knew from Chandler's face he wasn't going to learn much more. He had to take this man and Meara on faith or possibly risk Lisa.

"All right," he said. "Lisa's been wanting something more challenging, and I have a case involving a young man originally from Chicago. I need some more background information on him. I'll send her there, make sure she's tied up for several days."

"Can you go with her?"

"No. I have a case in court right now. In fact I'm due back in an hour, and I have a lot to do between now and then if we're to get Lisa out of the way."

"Thank you," Chris said.

"I'm next door to Meara if you need anything."

Chris nodded.

"Are you sure you know what you're doing?"

"No. But there's no other way," Chris said.

Kelly stood reluctantly, wondering if he'd made a wise decision.

"Before you go," Chris said, "I have something for you." He held out a packet. "If anything happens to me, mail these envelopes."

Kelly had even more misgivings than before, but he slowly accepted the package. "Damn it—" he started to say.

"You should get back to your office," Chris interrupted. "I'll take care of the check." His expression left no room for disagreement. It was hard and determined, and dangerous.

Kelly wished he knew more about the man. He had no doubt that he was a lumberman; he'd prepared the power of attorney himself and sent it, but Chris Chandler was more than that. Much more. He realized Meara was probably in good hands. It was his job to make sure Lisa was safe.

But still he hesitated. "I care about Meara," he said, and there was a warning in his voice.

"Doesn't everyone?" Chandler asked evenly, but the note of sad regret struck Kelly.

"Apparently *almost* everyone," Kelly amended.

Something flickered in Chandler's eyes, but Kelly didn't know quite what it was. Pain. Or something like it.

Meara looked up as the door flew open. Lisa's face was brighter and more excited than she'd seen it since Sanders's death.

"I'm going to Chicago," she said almost defiantly.

"What? Why?"

"For Kelly. He has a client, a young man charged with murder. He thinks there might be some extenuating circumstances in Chicago. Apparently the boy was terribly abused as a child. He wants me to go through records, interview neighbors, the family. It's what I've been really wanting to do. In fact, he has a friend there, a man he went to law school with, who's now married. He's going to help and I'm going to stay with them."

He did it! Chris did it. And Kelly. God bless him.

"That's wonderful, Lisa," she said, truly meaning it.

Lisa stared at her a moment. "I thought you might object."

"Why?" Meara asked. "I think you're old enough to make your own decisions."

Lisa practically glittered with excitement. "You know that's what I want to do . . . like Dad. Be an investigator."

"I know." Meara smiled. "And I know you will be wonderful at it. Now, when do you leave?"

"Kelly's already booked a flight for me first thing in the morning."

"I'll take you to the airport."

"All right. Kelly has to be in court, and I don't want to leave the car out there." Lisa's car, a present from Sanders and herself on their daughter's eighteenth birthday, was her most prized possession.

"Do you need any help packing?"

"I think it's time I start doing my own," Lisa said with a half grin and a camaraderie they'd never had before.

"Can I at least watch? If I bring some lemonade?"

Lisa looked at her with a little surprise but a quick smile that had been too rare lately. "Sounds wonderful."

Chris received a phone call that night, Wednesday night. Kurt Weimer was in New York. He was staying in a hotel that evening and was scheduled to leave on Lufthansa in the morning. "Call me when the plane leaves, with Weimer on it."

"Right," Matt said.

He then received a second call from Kelly Tabor. "Lisa will be in Chicago with friends of mine for the next few days."

"Thanks."

There was a long pause. "Could you come over tonight for a drink?"

For information, Chris thought dryly. "I'm expecting some calls."

"Then I'll come over there." He wasn't going to give up, and he meant to let Chandler know it.

Chris sighed. "All right."

When Kelly arrived, his face was set. "I went to the library after court today, and found clippings of that kidnapping attempt. There were two curious aspects . . ."

Chris furrowed his eyebrows together. "And . . ."

"How could Weimer possibly be connected? The kidnapper was a former American soldier."

Chris shrugged.

"There have been rumors for years that the Jekyll Island Club was closed because of German submarines . . . the possibility of a raid . . ."

"I wouldn't know," Chris said levelly.

"There was a second curious factor."

"What would that be?"

"There were damned few details, damned few facts for a major kidnapping. It was almost as if the paper had been . . . censored."

"I didn't think that happened in America," Chris said lazily. "Would you like a beer or Scotch? It's all I have."

"What I want is to know exactly what's happening." Kelly's voice was angry. "In addition to Meara and Lisa, my mother is next door."

"A Scotch, then," Chris said as if he hadn't heard anything.

"Damn you, Chandler, who in the hell are you?"

Chris poured several ounces in both glasses. Neither of them needed to lose their full reason. Chris knew Kelly wouldn't stop now. He was like a bulldog with a bone.

"How much do you care about Lisa?" he asked finally.

"I love her."

"And Meara?"

"She saved my mother's sanity when Dad died."

"Then don't ask any more questions. I will tell you that part of what you're thinking is correct. That's how Sanders and Meara met, and Sanders pulled her through a very rough time. She doesn't need reminders."

"How do you come into it? Were you in the FBI then?" It made sense to Kelly. Chris Chandler was no ordinary businessman. There was something elusive about him.

"It's Meara's story," Chris said finally, slowly. "You will have to ask her."

"But I can't, can I?" Kelly said bitterly. He remembered the vulnerability in her eyes at lunch that day.

"Just know I mean her no harm, nor Lisa. They are both very important to me."

"That's all I'm going to get?"

"That's all," Chris said.

Kelly stared at him, the blue eyes that revealed so little. Blue eyes like Lisa's. He suddenly sat up straight in the chair. Lisa's blond hair. What was it about genetics? Sanders's eyes had been brown, and his hair also brown. And Meara? Green eyes and red hair.

Good God.

He knew his face, which could always be so inscrutable in court, reflected his thought, and he watched Chris Chandler tense.

Kellen Tabor wished like hell that particular moment that he had never demanded to come over. He swallowed his drink. He didn't know whether his sudden realization was correct, but he did fully grasp that if true, this fact would indeed hurt Lisa Evans. She had always adored her father.

He had asked the question earlier at lunch. Now he asked it again. "Are you sure you know what you're doing?"

"Yes."

"Then what can I do?"

Kurt Weimer left his hotel at dawn for the New York airport. Now that he knew he was being followed, he readily spotted the tails. He would make them work to his benefit this time.

He'd made several phone calls to Odessa contacts in public phone booths. All the arrangements had been made. He hadn't contacted Stefan yet, however. He wasn't ready for the confrontation, even by phone. He'd made some very bad mistakes, and he knew it. But more than one person was going to pay for them.

He paid the taxi driver and tipped him, generously and slowly, until the car following him drew up. It was, in a way, an amusing game to play. But he played it better than the others.

After checking one of his bags at the counter, he took a small satchel and sauntered to the international gates, waiting until a particularly large group deplaned from an international flight and headed for the restroom. He mixed in with them.

His eyes ran around the room until they found a man who was amazingly similar in build and coloring as his own. Kurt went into one of the stalls and started stripping his clothes off. When a satchel matching his own was nudged under the separating wall, he placed his own clothes in his, and exchanged the two. The satchel contained a pilot's uniform with a captain's cap and a pair of sunglasses.

Kurt heard the other stall door open and he waited, looking at his watch frequently. Five minutes. Ten. It should be safe enough now. He opened the door and found the restroom almost clear now. He didn't recognize any faces. He put the glasses on, pulled the cap down, and strode purposely out the door toward the exit. In another twenty minutes he had rented a car under one of his aliases, and was pulling out of the airport.

Jekyll Island was about twenty hours away.

Chapter Thirty-One

Meara dropped Lisa off at the airport and returned to the island. For the first time in several years, she drove around to the old Millionaire's Village as the Jekyll Island Club was now called by the tourists.

She had avoided the area for a long time, both because of sad memories and because of regret over the dilapidated state of the clubhouse and cottages.

All of them were vacant. Peeling paint, broken windows, an empty, broken swimming pool, were sad echoes of a unique time and place in American history.

For her that time had been enchantment. A chapter from a fairy tale, complete with its own Prince Charming. She had made her prince into a black villain for many years, but now she was discovering he was not that.

As a child and young adult, she knew she had always seen things in terms of black and white, good and bad, with little in between. She had never accepted that where there was black and white, there must also be gray. Little in the world is absolute. She had, however, stubbornly clung to that belief because it had been easier for her to judge Michael harshly, to condemn him totally because it somehow made her own sins seem less. To believe he had purposely planned to use and seduce her had made the seduction somehow not her fault. It made him black and she white, the helpless victim. But the fault had been no less hers. She had avoided that knowledge, the guilt, all these years. She had wanted him so desperately that she had tossed aside all her upbringing, all her values.

She had remembered everything in the past few days, even those moments she had stuffed in the back of her mind: the times he had tried to pull away, the veiled warnings, the sadness and regret in his eyes, the loneliness in the often squared shoulders that seemed to defy the world. And in the end? If Sanders's enigmatic comments led to a logical conclusion, Michael had betrayed his country for her and the Connors' children.

Why hadn't she considered that before? Because the other emotion, hatred, had been easier to bear. Because she couldn't accept gray, either in him or in herself. Absolutes.

She turned off the ignition of her parked car and walked around the grounds. Memories. Memories of a spring day when a sky had been so blue she wanted to cry and the air smelled of newly bloomed flowers and the birds sang with the pure joy of being alive. Memories. Memories of a tall man, limping impatiently across a lawn with a wry smile at the corner of his lips. Memories. Memories of a walk, of falling down on the rich earth among the fragrant pine needles and feeling the first thrill of love, the touch of tender lips, the initial tingling of nerves that hinted of emotions and feelings yet undiscovered.

Memories. Memories of another man, a gentle man, who had given her a good, rich life.

It had been good. For both of them. She knew it now. Perhaps she hadn't been able to give Sanders the furious, splendid passion she'd shared with Michael, but they'd had something else, something really fine: a rare friendship, a warmth, an understanding, a deeply shared love of their daughter. She swallowed, her body and soul a rushing river of emotion and need and sadness and even happiness.

Grays. Not extreme joy or extreme sadness, but mingling colors and shades that gave a portrait depth and richness and character. Until now she had locked her life in black and white, and her picture of him that same way. She had tried to do the same to Lisa in order to protect her, never giving her enough room to test her own wings, because she believed she had made such a mess of her own. But she hadn't.

She'd had bits and pieces, and perhaps even the heart, of a very complex man who'd sacrificed his identity and country for reasons she didn't entirely understand yet. She had Lisa, who was a part of both of them, and she'd had Sanders, with whom she'd shared so much. Now she was being given a second chance at a dream. No, not a dream. Not a white fantasy. A chance for something very, very real.

Only Kurt Weimer and her own fears could kill that chance. Meara knew deep down in her bones that Chris Chandler would see to Kurt Weimer. She knew she was safe with him, had always been safe with him. Chris Chandler. She smiled slowly. Chris Chandler. A portrait of deep intricacy and hidden facets. A man who had to be studied a very long time to discover all the nuances.

It was a warm thought.

She walked toward the dock. It was partly gone, only remnants left. She closed her eyes and remembered that night, Rain. Thunder. She could still hear running footsteps, see Sanders kneeling to shoot. There was an explosion and the water itself was in flames, the world a fireball, and she heard herself scream.

Meara opened her eyes. The bright sun blinded her, and she blinked. The day was clear and the water calm, as if it had never seen violence.

He had tried to free her that night. Perhaps part of her had always realized it, just as Sanders had. Maybe that's why she kept coming back to the island, back to the healing she'd always found here despite the violence. She'd once told Michael Fielding it was her island of dreams. And it had been. She had found two loves here. She had found great happiness, contentment, and tragedy.

And always dreams. Dreams of the future. Dreams of the present, dreams of the past.

Now it was time again for the future.

She returned to her car and drove slowly over to Beachview Drive. The road was cluttered with cars and bicycles carrying tourists, and she thought briefly, regretfully, of the crushed-shell road and the few vehicles that once traveled the island, of the ancient but elegant little cars called red bugs.

But then the island was too lovely to reserve for a few. Let it give others dreams. Dreams and laughter and love.

Meara saw Chris's rented car in front of his house. She felt nervous and scared and excited. As she had years before. That was one feeling that had never changed. She and Chris were like match and tender together.

He must have heard her drive up, for he had the door open when she reached it.

"Meara?" he said, his voice low and tight and questioning. "Is anything wrong?" Then he flinched at his own words and despite the seriousness of everything, she couldn't help but smile. It *was* a ridiculous question, given the circumstances.

"I just wanted to tell you Lisa left this morning—she's safe."

He stood aside for her to enter, but Meara could feel the tension radiating from him. She turned to face him. "What is it?"

"Weimer boarded a plane for Bonn today."

"Then it's over. You've won."

He hesitated, his eyes dark and clouded. "It would seem so."

"Seem?"

"I just have a feeling he wouldn't give up this easily. There's so damn much about him that reminds me of his father. He would have gone to hell himself before giving up."

Meara looked up at him, her heart pounding. If the danger was gone, perhaps he would leave too. "Then what . . ."

"I know I promised to leave when it was over, but I think I should stay—" His voice broke off, and his eyes were dark and shuttered, his mouth tight.

She hesitated. He had said nothing about a future, only obligation. "Whatever you think is best."

He smiled then, a slow almost painful smile. "A few days more until he's seen in Bonn."

"The detectives?"

"I have one near your house, but I would still like to stay there the next few nights." The statement was more a question, hesitantly put.

She tipped her head slowly, looking up at him. "Why?"

"Weimer outsmarted my people before." He shrugged. "It's probably just paranoia." *Or maybe it's just an overpowering need to be with you for a few more hours.*

"Michael . . . ?"

His gaze was steady but neutral.

"Thank you," she said awkwardly, wanting to say more but not quite sure how.

His eyes warmed but he didn't move. "Don't thank me yet. I don't know whether it's over."

"What do you think he intended?"

He hesitated. "I can only guess."

"Then guess."

"I think he was trying to find a way to hurt you most."

"And how."

"If he really has returned to Germany, and turns up active in the Bonn government, it means he trusts us to keep quiet. I made it very clear that even an accident would send what we have to the West German government. It's not enough to convict him, but it is enough to plant doubts, to ruin him." Chris didn't continue. He didn't say that eventually something more would have to be done.

"And if he doesn't go back?"

"Then he feels that we will, one way or another, find a way to spread the information anyway, and he'll go into hiding."

"How long before we know?"

"A few days."

A few days. She had a few more days with him. Then how could she let him go again? What if he wanted to go?

"I'm sorry," he said finally.

She walked over to the picture window that looked over the dunes and the water in the distance. "I went over to the Jekyll Island Club today. It's sad."

"I know," he said in a low voice. "I drove by there."

"I could almost see everyone the day of the picnic." It was the first time he had kissed her.

He remembered that kiss.

"And hear the children laugh," she continued in a choked voice.

His hand went to her shoulder. He remembered how she had laughed. She shuddered under his touch but she didn't try to pull away. "Do you remember what I told you?"

"No," she whispered. But she did. She remembered everything, every word. She remembered that he had never told her he loved her. She thought he had with his hands, with his mouth, but he had never actually said the words. Not until he'd returned more than a week ago.

"That I cared. That I always would."

"Yes." *But there were so many other things you didn't say.*

"I'll always be there for you, Meara. Any time you need anything."

I need you. But she merely nodded.

Chris stood silently, helplessly. He wanted to kiss her, to take her in his arms, but he felt her tremble and once more was afraid of frightening her away. He forced himself to move, to put a distance between them.

"You're probably going to have some questions from Kelly," he said, trying to make his voice normal again.

"How much did you tell him?"

"As little as possible, but he already guessed some of it. He knew about the kidnapping years ago."

She stiffened.

"He won't say anything to Lisa, but I thought you should know."

A sob tore from her throat. "Where is it going to end? One lie leads to another."

Anguish crossed his face. No one knew the price of lies as well as he did. He only wished that he alone could pay the price. "You'd better go home," he said softly. "I'll be over later."

"When?"

"After dark. Someone is already watching the house. Just don't go for any walks alone, all right?"

She tried to smile back at him. It was a wan attempt at best, but still there was courage in it, courage in her will to stay here, to fight back, to protect Lisa. She had so much of it, then, and now.

"You're a valiant lady, Mrs. Evans," Chris said.

"No," she denied. "I feel so helpless, sitting and waiting for something to happen."

"That's the most difficult kind of courage."

"Chris . . ."

He grinned. "That's the second time you've used the name."

"I think I'm getting used to it."

"It's taken me a long time."

"I think I like Chris Chandler," she said softly.

"The name or the man?"

"Both. It's just a little . . . difficult to get used to."

"So is Mrs. Evans."

Their gazes locked, and electricity streaked between them, as alive and vital as ever. She finally pulled away first. "I'll get some dinner for us, tonight."

"All right."

She forced her feet to move before she made a total fool of herself. There was, after all, tonight.

Kurt Weimer made good time, better even than he'd hoped. He stopped only for gas, pulling a hat down over his eyes as he paid the bill in cash. At this rate, he should reach Jekyll Island around two or three o'clock in the morning. The island would be asleep by then, except for the toll taker, whose little house straddled the road onto the island. But his rental car couldn't be traced to him, and he would make sure no fingerprints remained anywhere. He had been very, very careful.

He had already planned everything very methodically in his mind. There was a motel near the Evanses' house. He would park there and wander through the backs of the houses as if he were drunk. Just in case. But from what he had seen, the whole island closed down early, including the regular residents. There were no night spots or late-night dining. The island attracted a sedate, early-to-bed, early-to-rise crowd. He very much doubted many were awake in the early morning hours.

He had brought a gun, a German Luger, but he didn't intend to use it. Too noisy. A fire would be best. But not before he made sure that everyone inside was unconscious. Then he would place his cigarette lighter near a bed and make sure the flames had taken hold . . .

The mother first. From his visits to the house, he had a good idea of where the bedrooms were. He would tie the mother, and then the daughter, and use Lisa to make Meara Evans talk. Kurt wanted to know exactly what happened that night twenty-one years ago. He had to know.

Once he was sure they were both dead, he would drive down to Miami and board a flight for South America. It would be worth losing everything to avenge his father, and he had the ready financial resources in Argentina to create a new identity.

He leaned back in the seat, trying to relax his stiff back. His fingers pressed compulsively against the wheel of the car as he passed the sign welcoming him to South Carolina.

When Chris arrived at Meara's house at eight, Kelly was there.

Kelly flashed a quick conspiratorial smile, and Chris knew instantly that Kelly's presence was his way of helping Meara avoid gossip on the small island as well as a protective gesture. Everyone knew of the close connection between the two families. Kelly's face was pleasant and devoid of curiosity, and Chris liked him more than ever. It was obvious that the young attorney was not going to press

Meara, but merely let it be known that he was available
if needed.

He stayed for a while after Chris arrived, then looked
from one to the other. Assured that Meara was in safe
hands, he said, "If you need anything . . . ?"

When Kelly left, the atmosphere once more became electric. "Would you like a drink before dinner?" Meara asked
nervously as she looked at Chris. He was wearing a pair
of charcoal-colored slacks and a light blue shirt, the long
sleeves rolled up to his elbows as usual. He had carried a
dark blue sports coat when he arrived, and it now hung
over a chair. He looked handsome and strong and very
confident. She wished she felt that way.

"Anything nonalcoholic," he said.

She darted into the kitchen and stood there a moment
before taking him a Coke. It seemed so strange, cooking
a meal for him, being domestic for him. Strange and pleasant. She had a roast in the oven along with some potatoes,
some sliced tomatoes, and green beans. She had even
baked a pie this afternoon, pleased at the diversion, at having something to do other than think.

They ate together awkwardly. At least at Kelly's dinner,
there were others to initiate and carry the conversation,
but now there was no one, and each hesitated to probe
into private territory, to probe something hurtful to the
other or to themselves.

"Tell me about Lisa," Chris said finally.

"What about Lisa?"

"Everything. What she looked like when she was born.
When did she walk? and talk? What're her favorite foods?
Anything. Everything." There was a longing in his eyes,
a raw, naked hunger that struck to the core of her. He had
showed her the picture of Lisa, the faded, much handled
picture, but still she hadn't realized the depth of his need.
She still couldn't, and she knew with sudden clarity she

probably never could. But she did understand the courage it had taken to stay away, and now to return, knowing he would leave once more with little more than he'd had before.

She started talking slowly, about Lisa's difficult birth which made her unable to have other children. He hadn't known about that, although he had wondered why there weren't more children. She told him about Lisa's first steps when she was ten months old, and how she'd found a way several months later to climb out of the playpen and crawl into a cabinet one day. A kidnapping had been feared, and several of Sanders's FBI friends had been called when Lisa happily popped out of a floor cupboard, rubbing her eyes which were half closed with sleep.

She told him about the day in grammar school Lisa had decided to be a musician. The only available school instrument was a cello, which she accepted happily. She determinedly and proudly lugged the thing home daily, although it was as big as she, until she discovered an abysmal lack of talent. With tears, she'd sadly returned it, and turned her enthusiasm to the piano, which met with equally unsatisfactory results.

"Unfortunately," Meara concluded with a glint of the old amusement Chris remembered so well, "she has my deaf ear and none of Sanders's talent. He had a beautiful voice." Then she heard what she was saying and looked up to see the pain in his eyes, and she winced at her own slip. Yet over all these years, she had often come to think of Lisa as Sanders's own child.

She bit her lip, another old habit Chris remembered. "It's all right," he said gently. "I imagine Sanders was a wonderful father. I'll always be grateful for that, to him and to you."

"He was," she said. "He and Lisa were so close. I was

the disciplinarian, I'm afraid. She has so much determination, so much enthusiasm, I was afraid—"

Chris stopped her, and he couldn't bear to hear the words, her self-blame for what had happened in the past. "She's lovely, and bright, and now she's finding her way."

"I wanted so badly to protect her." Meara's voice was almost a cry of pure desperation.

"I know," he said. Protect her against men like him.

Against men like him. She could almost read his thought as she regarded him grimly. But Kurt Weimer wasn't like him. No matter how much she had tried to hate Michael Fielding, she had never been able to forget his tenderness, his gentleness, his almost magical way with children. You couldn't pretend those things.

After dinner, she made them a pot of coffee, Chris declining anything alcoholic. His very refusal was ominous.

"Do you really think he'll try something?"

"No," he said. "But I'm not taking any chances."

She cleared and washed the dishes, and he dried them. He looked ridiculously out of place with a dish towel in his hands, very carefully wiping every corner with the same systematic efficiency he seemed to do everything.

It was nearly midnight when they finished. They had talked a long time over dinner, and now the tension was back. It had been there hovering all evening, magnifying as they accidentally touched several times while doing the dishes. Now it was alive and vibrant between them.

He leaned against a table in the kitchen, watching her with veiled, intense eyes so deep she wanted to crawl inside them. She went to him and put a hand on his arm. It was an invitation, and they both knew it, a bridge over the years and the pain.

Chris leaned down and kissed her, his lips gentle and searching and hesitant. They found response and, even more than that, acceptance, trust, and he felt hope, lost hope, seeding inside him.

His finger traced the contours of her face, worshiping each feature with such tender touches that love radiated poignantly between them, burning away bad memories and fanning the fine ones. Her arms went up, around his neck, drawing him close until his hand dropped from her face, and he grabbed her, holding her with a turbulent possessiveness. There was a quiet, fierce communion of need, of healing, of understanding, and he knew he had never loved her as much as he did this moment.

Now, perhaps, there was time. He had to believe that, and his heart pounded with the possibilities, with an optimism he'd never known. His fingers shook slightly as they moved along her back, and she looked up directly into his face, her eyes soft and trusting as he'd never thought they would be again.

He hurt. God, how he hurt inside. But it was a splendid, disbelieving kind of hurt. An aching of gladness, of happiness so strong that it strained against his heart, pounded against his ribs. His lips left her mouth and moved upward, caressing her cheeks, raining soft, tender kisses in sparkling trails across her face. He saw a dampness gather in her eyes and felt her trembling in his arms.

Chris felt an intense burning in his loins, and he knew he had to stop this before he could no longer control himself. He had made that mistake before. He wouldn't do it again. Not now. Not until he knew she was safe. He moved back, his voice slightly unsteady.

"I think you'd better go to bed . . ."

"And you?" Her voice was shaky.

"In the living room," he said, utilizing every bit of control he had. He knew he could share her bed tonight, and he wanted to, so goddamn much.

"I . . . need you."

"I know," he said softly. "And God knows I want you, but I don't think it's a good idea tonight. When . . . this is finished . . . when we know it's finished . . . then we'll talk."

"Talk?" she questioned with the impish grin he remembered and hadn't seen in the past twelve days.

He grinned, feeling suddenly very young. "To begin with," he corrected, his smile turning into a self-conscious, attempted leer which didn't quite succeed but which was incredibly endearing, nonetheless. She was so unused to his uncertainty that it crawled right into her heart the few times he allowed it to show.

She reached up and touched the corner of his mouth, the lines of his face, the strong, uncompromising lines that seldom broke for a smile. He took her hand, holding it tight.

"If you don't leave now, I won't be responsible for what happens," he said, his voice almost a groan.

She didn't want to go. But she knew he was right. A few more minutes, and they would both be lost. A truck could drive into the house, and they wouldn't know it.

"Good night," she forced herself to say.

"Good night, Meara," he replied slowly, his voice caressing her name in a way she remembered only too well.

Almost stumbling, she headed to the bedroom and changed into a nightgown. Knowing she wouldn't be able to sleep, not with him in the next room, she grabbed a book, a current historical novel, and tried desperately to read. Distracted, she found herself reading the same sentence over and over and over again. Finally with disgust, she turned out the light. It was nearly one o'clock, and there was all day tomorrow to explore her feelings. And his.

The thought was comforting. The thought of him in the same house was comforting. Her eyes finally closed.

Chapter Thirty-Two

KURT MOVED SWIFTLY but cautiously toward the house, his eyes always moving. Excitement coursed through him despite the weariness. The feeling resembled the thrill, the stimulation, that he'd discovered during the last days of the war. His blood had rushed then too. Danger. Killing. They had been like aphrodisiacs to him.

Even now he felt his manhood swell under the dark trousers he wore. He thought of Lisa. He would take her tonight, in front of her mother. Before he killed them. It was just retribution for Meara Evans's killing of his father.

A hundred yards from the house, he stopped, swallowed, he knew, by the shadows of the night. There was only a piece of the moon tonight, and a few scattered lights from the residences, mostly porch lights or outside gas lights.

He took one last look around. He had already decided which window to try. Kurt had discarded the idea of trying the door because it faced the main road, and though the traffic was light, one could never predict whether an alert driver might notice something.

483

Kurt had previously watched Lisa go into one of the rooms, and so he suspected which was hers. He had also seen a light on in another room when he had brought Lisa home, and he discounted that one. He wanted the unused room, where the sound of his entry wouldn't be heard.

He was about ready to step from the shadows when he saw a sudden brightness not far from where he stood. The flash of a match, and then the almost invisible glow of a cigarette. So the man with the threats hadn't entirely believed him, just as he hadn't believed his adversary.

Kurt took a knife from a sheath on his belt. He crept soundlessly toward the almost invisible figure standing in the shadow of a tree. From that position, the watcher could see both the front door and the windows in back. Kurt's foot crunched on something, and the man started to turn, but he was too late. Kurt's knife found the man's throat, cutting it before he could utter a word.

Kurt pushed the body away, under the bushes, where the ground would soak up the blood. He moved quickly now toward one of the back windows. Most windows in the area were open to catch the night breeze, but this one was locked. Once more he cursed. That bastard who'd threatened him was probably responsible. Once more, Kurt wondered who in the hell he was.

The curtain was slightly open, and through the light of the open doorway he saw the room was empty. He would have to take a chance of breaking the window. It was multipaned, and he would have to break only one small pane to reach the lock.

He wrapped the handle of his knife in a handkerchief and tapped it gently against the window. The window cracked and he pushed against one piece, hearing it fall inside with a soft tinkling sound. His gloved fingers quickly pulled out several more pieces of the glass until he reached the lock and quickly turned it. He then lifted the window easily and crawled inside.

The room was dark, and the house was completely still. He obviously hadn't been heard. Not yet. His shoes had rubber soles and he had learned to move silently. He had thought about a mask and then discarded the idea. No one would be left alive to identify him.

There was a small light in the hallway, and he quickly found the door to the room he was seeking, the one he'd identified as Meara's. He took a quick look in the other direction toward the living area. It was dark and quiet. His knife held tightly in his fist, he moved to the door and opened it, sliding inside toward the figure lying there.

Chris had been far more tired than he'd thought. He'd had little sleep in the past days, and it was catching up on him. Meara had offered him one of the bedrooms, but he decided to use the couch. Its very discomfort would keep him on the edge of sleep.

He had made sure his coat, with the pistol in it, was nearby, before he took off his shoes and lay down. But despite that nagging worry in the pit of his gut, he thought it unlikely Kurt Weimer would try anything tonight, particularly here. He had wondered briefly if part of his concern wasn't simply a need, an excuse, to be close to Meara again. Weimer was, according to Matt, back in Bonn. There was a detective outside, one trained in protection.

He thought about the evening, and how much he had enjoyed it, enjoyed the homey task of wiping dishes, of sitting with her, of listening to the stories of Lisa, of hearing that lilt in her voice as she told them. They had been pearls of moments, each so rich in texture and beauty.

Perhaps they needn't end. She had responded to him tonight with a trust he'd never thought he could have again. And if he hadn't been feeling noble . . .

Maybe there were second chances. He allowed himself the momentary pleasure of thinking about it, of how it might be to live with Meara, to become a friend if not father to Lisa, and his heart worked madly and irrationally. Then he reminded himself that it was danger, deadly danger, that had brought them back together and created an artificial situation which cast him in the role of protector. Once the danger was gone, her doubts would return, her distrust. How could it be otherwise?

Don't expect anything? It doesn't hurt as much if you don't expect anything, he told himself. But it did. It would.

Exhausted and troubled, he finally drifted off into a deeper sleep than he had expected or intended. He didn't know what woke him, but after several seconds he forced his mind to function again. He heard the soft sound of a door opening and almost felt eyes on him. But his body, he knew, was hidden from the doorway by the back of the sofa. He didn't move. His gun was nearby, but to reach for it would risk being seen, and he didn't know if the intruder had a gun already primed for use.

Where was the damned guard?

A second passed, then another, and he heard a creak down the hall. He moved swiftly, one hand reaching for the gun and then his feet hitting the floor. He headed for the bedroom, his heart pounding so loud he was afraid Weimer would hear it. That the intruder was Weimer, he had no doubt.

All three bedroom doors were closed, but he heard a startled gasp from one and moved toward it, hesitating outside. He was afraid to bust in, to startle Weimer into something precipitous. The man had obviously decided revenge was more important than anything else. Chris cursed himself. He should have known. He should have done more.

A piece of him died as he realized Meara was facing the son just as she had the father twenty years ago. The one comfort he had was that she had handled it well then. He could only hope she would do the same now.

He strained to hear, but Kurt was speaking in a low voice. He caught the word "daughter" and a soft, menacing laughter, and hate, raw, livid red hate enveloped him. Meara would be terrified, wondering what had happened to him. Damn those moments of sleep. He heard some scuffling, a slight cry, and then a muffled noise. Then there was a bark, a thud and a slight whimper.

He heard a slight moan and the sound came close to the door. Damn the carpets on the floor. He stepped back in the shadows as the door swung open and Meara was thrust awkwardly out the door, a gag in her mouth and her hands tied in front of her. Her eyes, visible in the small nightlight, were terrified as they glanced desperately around until they caught his. Suddenly she lurched forward, twisting and falling away from her captor, who was not yet far enough out the door to see Chris. With a muttered curse, he leaned over to grab Meara, a knife bright in his hand, his attention fully on Meara so he didn't see the lightning fast movement of the man to his left.

Chris crashed into Weimer before he could grab Meara again, the impact sending Chris's pistol to the floor. He had known instantly that Weimer was crazy enough at the moment to kill her now, regardless of the consequences. The threat of a gun wouldn't stop him. Not now. Weimer's eyes were wild, wild with frustration and fury and hate.

Chris's hands clutched Weimer's fist which enclosed the handle of the knife, and the two of them rolled against a hall table and down the wall, both fighting with all their strength for control of the weapon.

Weimer had the advantage of youth, but Chris had the muscles developed from years in the logging industry. Even during the last office-bound years, he had occasionally surprised crews by joining them, enjoying the hard physical labor that brought relief to emotional wounds. It had another practical effect, strengthening the loyalty of loggers to the company. He was one of them, not merely a bean counter. Now it paid off.

With one quick movement of his other hand, he slammed Weimer's fist so hard against the wall, the fingers released the knife, which skittered down the hall. Just then, he heard a gunshot echoing through the house, and he realized that Meara, even bound as she was, had somehow reached the gun and managed to fire it, alerting the neighbors.

Weimer also realized at the same moment what had happened. Again everything was lost because of one interfering woman. He had lost, but he would take her with him. He used the momentary distraction of the gunshot to reach for the Luger he had strapped to his leg. His opponent saw the movement and reached for it just as Weimer was extracting it from the holster. The hands of both men closed on it. Weimer pressed the trigger the same second Chris forced the gun down and away from him. Weimer heard the loud report and felt fire envelop the lower half of his torso. His hand went slack and he knew the gun was sliding from it, but it didn't matter now. The fire was stronger, excruciating in its fury and heat, and yet another part of him felt cold, very, very cold. He tried to move, but nothing obeyed, nothing worked. He looked up at the man over him. "Who are you?" he whispered.

There was a pounding at the door, but the noise grew dimmer as he asked again, "Who are you?" He knew his voice was weaker, and he was getting colder. Fire and ice. His body was fire and ice. He was dying. He knew it. He had to know who had killed him. It was important. He didn't know why, but it was.

But his killer just sat there, his dark eyes cold and expressionless. Out of the corner of his eye, Kurt saw that Meara had risen and was trying to get around him to the door. He wanted to reach out, but he couldn't, and then even the man so close to him was fading away. He struggled a moment longer to keep his eyes open, to live, but the ice and fire were consuming him. "I'm sorry, Father," he whispered to the ghostlike figure above him. "I tried . . ." He closed his eyes for a moment. Only for a moment.

Chris leaned over and felt the pulse at his neck. It was still. Just then a window shattered, and he heard voices.

"Meara," one called. "Are you all right?" But she couldn't answer, Chris realized. The gag was still in her mouth.

"This is Chandler," he yelled. "She's all right. Call the police." He rose and untied the gag and then her wrists, his fingers uncustomarily clumsy. She turned to him, desperately needing his strength, his warmth. His arms clasped her to him tightly as they heard sirens outside and more shouts.

After several seconds, he released her. "We'd better let them in."

"Andy . . . ," she said pleadingly. "He . . . woke up and tried to help . . . Weimer kicked him."

Chris went into the bedroom. Andy was trying to stand. Chris ran his hands over him, hearing a brief whimper where there was a soreness, but other than that, the dog seemed fine. Andy finally got to his feet and staggered toward Meara, who knelt to reach him. The dog planted an apologetic swipe of a tongue on her face as Meara buried her hand in his fur. "Poor, brave Andy," she whispered.

Chris reached down a hand to her, and together, his arm around her, supporting her, they walked to the front door. Kelly was there, a hunting rifle in his hand along with several other neighbors, carrying everything from brooms to baseball bats. Looking past them, he could see the flashing lights of a police car.

"What in the hell happened?" Kelly said.

Chris nodded inside. "Weimer. He's dead." The corners of his mouth turned upward, but it wasn't a smile. "I might need your services."

Kelly went in and stooped beside the body. The bullet had ripped a hole through Weimer's stomach, hitting some vital artery, and blood was pooling around him. He nodded for Chris to come over to him; the other neighbors were crowded around Meara.

"What happened?"

"He apparently got in through a window. He got to Meara before I could stop him. She's the one who saved everything; she jerked away from him when she saw me."

They heard car doors slamming.

"The police," Kelly said. "I called them when I heard the gunshot. Quick. Is there anything I should know?"

Chris looked at him steadily. "He's a rejected suitor. Nothing more."

Kelly's gaze was level, penetrating. "All right," he said finally. "But tell me one thing. Might Lisa be in any more danger?"

"No."

"When this is over then, I'll call her," Kelly said. "Meara might need her. You'll be busy with questioning for a while, but I'll stay with you."

"Thank you," Chris said, grateful beyond words for Kelly's silent and unquestioning support.

Kelly grinned a bit weakly. "Let's go face them."

When they reached the living room, Meara turned again to him, and he saw the shock in it, the unfocused eyes which still held horror. Her hands were trembling as they reached for him.

He looked around, at the curious faces of the neighbors, the hard ones of the police, the body on the floor. Twice in her life, Meara had gone through something no one should experience. Terror and violent death. Because of him. Twice because of him. He swallowed against the sickness rising in him.

Chris held her shoulders as the police went over to the body and checked it once more for life. One officer went to the telephone to make some phone calls and another came over to Meara, his hard face softening. He knew Meara, knew her husband had been a federal agent who had recently been killed. There was a bond there, a bond that stretched between all police at all levels.

"What happened, Mrs. Evans?"

Meara turned to Chris. His hand tightened on her shoulder as he spoke slowly. "This man is Kurt Weimer. He'd been dating Mrs. Evans's daughter and she'd evidently spurned him. He'd made some threats." The lies came easily. Too easily. He was so damned tired of lies.

"And you, sir."

Kelly stepped up. "He's an old friend of Sanders Evans who's been staying on the island. He and I have been taking turns looking after Mrs. Evans." In those few words, he lay gossip and suspicion to rest.

"Why didn't you call us?" the older police officer said.

"He's a German government official. We just didn't really think he would carry out the threat. Mrs. Evans didn't want an international incident and scandal for no reason."

The policeman nodded his head. It made sense.

Chris stiffened suddenly. "I also hired a detective agency to keep a watch on the house. There should have been someone outside."

The older policeman, a sergeant by his stripes, nodded to another man. "Take a look."

Meara started shaking, her body shivering with the aftermath. She wanted Chris. Dear Mother in heaven, how much she wanted him now. But his hands had fallen from her shoulders, and he had moved slightly away. His eyes were wary and secretive, just as before while he waited tensely for the policeman to return.

Kelly's mother, who had also arrived, moved over to Meara, guiding her over to a sofa and urging her to sit.

In just seconds, the police officer returned. "There's a dead man out there. His throat cut."

"Christ." Chris groaned. Death followed him around like a shadow.

"I found this on him," the officer said, handing a wallet and identification to the sergeant.

"George Somers," the man read, and Chris felt a brief moment of relief that it wasn't Matt, whom he had come to know and like. Then the sickness settled back down. No matter who it was, he was responsible.

Another wail of a siren came, and an ambulance arrived. The police sergeant ushered everyone out except his officers, Meara, Chris, and Kelly and his mother.

Evelyn Tabor looked at the sergeant. "Can I take her over to our house for some rest."

The sergeant agreed. "But I need Mr. . . . ."

"Chandler. Chris Chandler," Kelly said.

"I need Mr. Chandler for a while."

Panic rose in Meara's face. "I want to stay too."

Chris shook his head. "You go. Please."

"No," she said stubbornly, terrified that they might find out who Chris was, that they might charge him with murder. She couldn't bear the thought of him in prison.

"Mrs. Evans, I'll have to talk to him alone anyway."

"No," she repeated again.

"Then can you tell us what happened?"

Meara hesitated. "I woke up and *he* was there . . . in the room. He had a knife. He wanted Lisa." Shudders ran through her body. "He said he was going to tie us both up and set fire to the house."

Even the officer's face went white at the words, and

Chris felt a choking sensation in his throat. Kelly wished the man wasn't dead so he could kill him himself. Evelyn's hands clutched Meara's even tighter.

"Where is your daughter?" the sergeant said softly.

"In Chicago," Kelly said. "With some friends of mine."

"Another precaution?" the sergeant said dryly.

Kelly nodded, his eyes meeting the sergeant's. They had known each other for years, known and liked and respected.

The ambulance arrived then, and the four of them watched silently as the body was taken, leaving a huge river of fresh blood. Meara blanched and went into the bathroom, emerging several minutes later, her face pale and strained.

"Everything is exactly as it was when the shooting occurred?" the sergeant said.

Chris nodded.

"The state police are sending over some lab people, and I think Mrs. Evans needs to get away from here. Obviously she won't go without you. I want your word you won't leave the island until we talk further. You both can go for now. Where are you staying?"

Chris gave his address.

"And Mrs. Evans?"

"She'll stay with us," Evelyn replied quickly.

"All right. I'll see you in the morning. It seems simple enough. Self-defense."

"The man outside . . ."

The sergeant shook his head. "We've never had a murder on the island before, leastways not as long as I've been here. Heard there was a kidnapping years back—"

"If there's nothing else?" Chris said quickly.

"No," the sergeant said slowly.

Chris walked over to the Tabor house. Evelyn had her arm around Meara, and as much as he wanted to touch her, to hold her, to comfort her, he couldn't do it. He felt dirty, unclean. He had never been anything but misery to her.

At the door, he said good night, ignoring the pleading look Meara gave him.

"We'll take good care of her," Kelly said, looking from one to the other, but keeping his own counsel.

Chris walked the short distance to his rented house. The first golden light of dawn was breaking through the darkness, but it held no glow for him, no hope. He went into the bathroom and looked at himself in the mirror. He was covered with blood. He buried his head in his hands and thought how just hours ago he thought he could have a life with Meara.

How could that be possible when he was a constant reminder of death and terror? He had done enough to her.

He would see the police tomorrow. Then he would leave the moment he was given permission. He would not see Meara again. Zombielike, he took his clothes off and got in the shower. But he knew he could never wash away the smell of death.

Meara woke slowly. Her head felt heavy from the strong sedative she had taken the night before. Evelyn and Kelly had insisted on calling a doctor, and she had been too tired and spiritless to resist.

Now as her brain started to function, she remembered everything, every horrible detail: how the knife had felt against her throat, how she was afraid Kurt Weimer had killed Chris. And then she had seen him as she was pushed out the room, and she'd known everything would be all right. She had known.

Until she had seen his eyes when they reached the Tabor home. They were dead. Dead and hopeless. She had reached for him but he was gone.

Tears started down her face when the door opened and she saw Lisa, her face creased with concern as she ran over to her. Kelly was right behind her.

"Oh, Mother," Lisa said, burying her head against Meara's chest as Meara started to sit up. "I'm so sorry. It's all my fault."

Meara felt her heart contract. She didn't want Lisa to feel the guilt she had all these many years. "No, darling, nothing was your fault. No one could possibly have known."

"Are you all right?"

"Now that you're here," Meara said, holding her daughter tightly. Andy, who had been lying beside the bed, thumped his tail, reminding them of his presence.

"You should be proud of Andy," Meara said with a smile. "He tried so hard to be brave."

Tears glistened in Lisa's eyes. "Kelly said *you* were so brave, and Mr. Chandler—he was a hero. Why didn't you tell me what was happening?"

"Because I didn't know for sure . . . there were just some . . . strange phone calls."

Lisa stared at her mother as if she had never seen her before. Kelly had told her how her mother had kept her nerve, had jerked away from Kurt just at the right moment, how she had fired a gunshot with her hands tied. Admiration and love flooded her. She clutched Meara's hand tightly. "Don't ever do that again," she said. "Don't ever shut me out. We have to look out for each other now, you know."

"I know," Meara whispered, her voice choked. "I know."

Lisa wouldn't let her out of her sight until Meara asked to see Kelly. When he arrived, Meara turned to Lisa. "Can you get me something to drink," and Lisa agreed readily.

As soon as Lisa left, she turned to Kelly, who had known she needed to talk to him. "Chris?"

"He spent the morning at police headquarters. They allowed him to leave at noon. Justifiable homicide."

"Where is he now?"

Kelly looked uncomfortable. "I went over there a few minutes ago. He was packing." Kelly put a hand in his pocket and brought out an envelope. "He left this for you."

Kelly handed it to her and turned toward the door. "I'll be outside if you need anything. I'll keep Lisa distracted."

Meara slowly opened the envelope. The handwriting was in a large bold scrawl.

Meara:

It seems I never bring you anything but unhappiness. I promised I would leave when this was over, and I'm keeping that promise.

But I want you to know the words I could never say. I love you. I've always loved you. Ever since that day in spring when the ribbon from your hair blew away, and I heard your laughter.

It will always be my greatest regret that I stilled that laughter.

If you or Lisa ever need anything, I will always be there for you.

Chris

If you ever need anything . . .

"Kelly," she shouted as she got out of bed. She was wearing one of Evelyn's nightgowns.

He was back, and Lisa with him.

"I need something to wear."

Lisa stared at her, but Kelly grinned. "I'll get something of Mother's."

As he left, Lisa turned toward her mother, a question in her eyes.

Meara held out her hand to Lisa. "There's something I have to do, someone I have to thank."

"Mr. Chandler?"

"Yes. He's leaving."

"I'll go with you. I want to thank him too."

Meara hesitated. "Perhaps later. This is something I have to do alone."

Lisa nodded. At the moment, she would have agreed to anything her mother wanted. Every time she thought how close her mother had come to death . . .

"Please tell him how grateful I am too," she said quietly.

Meara nodded as Kelly returned quickly with a pair of slacks and a blouse. He then disappeared again quickly toward the phone.

Meara took all of ten seconds to dress. She was buttoning the blouse when she came out, and Kelly was hanging up the phone. "No one answers, but he couldn't have been gone long. I know he has a plane at the Brunswick airport. I'll take you."

It was a wild ride, Kelly sensing her urgency. He'd liked Chris Chandler. He didn't know exactly what had happened between Chandler and Meara, but he was good at judging people and he sensed that these two were meant to be together. Like he and Lisa. He had been overjoyed the way Lisa had run into his arms this morning, the way she had held onto his hand, the way she had depended on him. And especially the way she had looked at him. As if she were seeing for the first time.

They pulled up to the section of the airport where private planes were located. It would have taken Chandler a while to file his flight plan, Kelly had explained comfortingly several times.

Meara was out the door and running. She knew exactly

where to go. Sanders had arrived here several times in private government planes. Her gaze darted around the field where planes were tied to the ground. She turned and saw a tall man stride toward one of the planes, a slight limp in his walk, his blond hair shining in the sun. He was carrying a suitcase.

She ran. For her life, she ran, and he turned, sensing more than hearing since her sandals made no sound on the grass that ran along the runway.

He stopped, and turned toward her, his eyebrows furrowed quizzically, his eyes wary and his mouth tight.

"Is this good-bye?" he said in low, tight voice. "You didn't have to."

"You made me a promise," she said solemnly, watching his shoulders tense as if he were to take some kind of punishment.

"I know," he said. "I'm keeping it. Didn't you get my note?"

"You made a later promise," she continued, trying to keep her hands to herself when she needed to touch him so badly.

He cocked his head in question.

"You said if I ever needed anything . . ."

He swallowed. "What . . ."

"You, Christopher Chandler. I need you."

Hope flared briefly in his eyes, but it died quickly. "I've never brought you anything but grief."

"No," she said gently. "That's why I kept coming back here. I finally discovered why these past few days. Because I first found love here . . . I had you for a while. Such a little while, but it was such a fine piece of time. Even when I tried to hate you, it never quite worked. You gave me a part of yourself then, and I think we both always knew it. Now I want more."

Chris straightened, his eyes searching for doubts, for reservations. "Are you sure, Meara?"

"Yes," she said slowly. "No more dreams. No more waiting. I want all the days of forever with you."

He went totally still, his breath caught deep in his throat as he looked at her earnest upturned face, full of faith. In him. His words, when they came, were slow and measured. "Don't ever lose your dreams, love. You're making me believe in them too." He wanted to say more. He wanted to tell her how much he needed her, how tired he was of being an island himself, but not one of dreams, one of isolation and loneliness.

But he didn't have to. Looking at her face, he knew he didn't have to. He dropped the suitcase and opened his arms.

Author's Note

Jekyll Island exists off the coast of Georgia. So did the Jekyll Island Club and its membership, which allegedly represented one-sixth of the world's wealth.

The club did close in 1942. Rumors circulated for years that the U.S. President ordered its closing because of the submarine threat and sent General George S. Patton to evacuate the island. Patton's name even appears under the date of April 3, 1942, as the next to the last entry in the club register, but questions have been raised as to whether it really is his signature.

Island historians say the rumored evacuation is only a myth, that the club closed because of fuel and labor shortages.

Jekyll Island today is owned by the state of Georgia. The old ruins of the Jekyll Island Club have been restored, and the old Clubhouse is now a public hotel. Its beauty is intact.

Patricia Potter attended the University of Alabama and received a degree in journalism and American history. She is a former *Atlanta Journal* reporter and previously edited a major suburban weekly. She now resides in Atlanta, Georgia, as a full-time writer.